LIVING IN THE

Also by Judith Barrow

Pattern of Shadows
Changing Patterns

LIVING IN THE SHADOWS

by

Judith Barrow

HONNO MODERN FICTION

First published by Honno in 2015
'Ailsa Craig', Heol y Cawl, Dinas Powys, Wales, CF64 4AH

1 2 3 4 5 6 7 8 9 10

© Judith Barrow, 2015

ISBN 978-1-909983-29-8

Published with the financial support of the Welsh Books Council.

Cover images: © Mary Evans Picture Library
Cover design: Jenks Design
Text design: Elaine Sharples
Printed by Gomer Press

For David

Acknowledgements

I would like to express my gratitude to those who helped in the publishing of *Living in the Shadows*.

My thanks to all the staff at Honno for their expertise, to Helena Earnshaw for her advice and help, and to Caroline Oakley for her supportive and thoughtful editing.

And again, a special thanks to my dear friend and fellow author, Sharon Tregenza, for her constructive criticism and support.

Lastly, as ever, to David: for keeping the faith and encouraging me to continue with my writing. Oh, and for taking on the weekly grocery shopping.

1969

Chapter 1: Linda Booth

Ashford, morning: Tuesday, September 16th

She'd always been afraid of the dark. The shadows along the corridors of the hospital, the blackness of corners, the sounds, source unseen, on the maternity ward were the stuff her nightmares were made of.

She kept herself busy by checking on the sleeping mothers in each bed and by visiting the nursery, where the babies snuffled and whimpered. She told herself she was nothing if not professional, even as she picked up and cuddled a crying infant, something forbidden by the ward sister.

Now, standing in one of the small private side wards, Linda Booth watched with relief as the sky lightened with shades of pastel blue and gold above the buildings on the opposite side of the hospital grounds.

Behind her the woman in the bed shifted and moaned. Linda moved to her side. 'How do you feel, Mrs Worth?'

Harriet Worth moved her head on the pillow and pushed herself up in the bed, a small action that made her grimace. Linda felt a wave of sympathy. It had been a difficult and protracted labour and, at forty-four, the woman was too old to be having another baby; her records showed that her last child was now a teenager.

'My mouth is dry.' The woman spoke in an apologetic tone.

Linda poured her a glass of water. 'Here, drink this.' She waited, studying her; she was very pale. And so small and frail it was hard to believe she had given birth to a robust baby boy the day before. 'Let me just check everything's okay?' Harriet Worth nodded. Linda moved the covers and examined her. The woman was still bleeding quite a lot; she'd tell the day-staff to keep a close eye on her. But, after changing the sanitary-pad, she smiled at Harriet as she washed her hands in the small basin in the corner of the room. 'Everything seems to be all right. Let me check your blood pressure.' It was low. Linda scribbled on the chart. 'Try to get some sleep. It's only five o'clock. Ring your bell if you need me.'

For the rest of her shift Linda was glad to be kept busy writing up reports. Except for answering an occasional bell rung by a restless mother she didn't move until she heard the sounds of the day shift arriving.

Thank goodness for that, she thought; she was ready for her bed.

Before she left Linda decided to check on Harriet Worth one last time. She peeped into the side-ward. 'Morning again,' she whispered. 'You okay?'

'Thank you, yes.'

'Good,' Linda said. 'Try to rest today.'

The main ward came alive with the sounds of trolleys and wailing babies. The door crashed open and a nurse pushed past Linda. 'This little chap wants a feed, Mother, want to try again? Didn't have much luck last night did we?' She spoke conspiratorially at Linda. 'Always the same with mothers with small nipples.' She unwrapped the whimpering baby from the blanket and held him out. 'Still, we'll give it a go. Yes?'

'I'll try.' Harriet Worth squinted against the brightness of the abruptly-lit corridor and slowly sat up, taking the child in her arms.

The nurse turned to Linda. 'I know it's the end of your shift, Nurse Booth, but if you could just help mother? We're rushed off our feet out there.' Without giving Linda a chance to say anything, she left.

'I'm sorry.' Harriet spoke apologetically. 'You should be going home.'

'It's no trouble.' Linda smiled, unfastened her cape and draped it over the chair near the bed. However tired she was she could see

2

the distress in the woman. 'Right, let's see what we can do, shall we, Mrs Worth?' She washed her hands. 'Sometimes, it's difficult to get them to start feeding.' She glanced over her shoulder, as the baby's whimper grew more insistent, and smiled again. 'He's hungry, so that will help.' She pulled out one of the paper towels from the container. 'Nothing to worry about, I'm—' Her next words were cut off by the door opening so forcefully it crashed against the wall.

The man who filled the doorway was short but stocky, his thinning curly hair a mixture of grey and ginger. Wearing slacks and an open-necked shirt to show off a heavy gold sovereign and chain around his neck, he had an astrakhan coat slung over his shoulders. He was what Linda's dad, in his old-fashioned way, would call a bit of a spiv.

'I'm sorry, no visitors at this time of the day.' Linda dried her hands and dropped the used towel in the bin under the basin.

'I've paid for a private room, she's my wife, and I'll visit when I want.' He didn't look at Linda; his eyes fixed on the woman in the bed who was ineffectually jiggling the now screaming baby.

Linda flushed at the abrupt rudeness. 'I'm sorry, but no. Your wife needs some privacy and anyway the rules are the same for everyone. Visiting time is—'

'When I say it is.' Still he didn't turn towards her, but his ruddy cheeks reddened even more.

It was the anxiety on Harriet Worth's face that made Linda step between the man and the bed. She was the same height as him and met his glare. But there was something about him that caused her throat to tighten. She stared at the scar on his cheek, shaped like a half-moon, at his nose, crooked from an old break, and she sucked in a shocked breath, suddenly aware that she was on her own in a room with a man that, for some unknown reason, she was afraid of.

'You're in my way.' Narrowing his eyes, he gripped her arm, his fingers pinching.

3

'George, please…' Harriet's voice shook as she raised her voice above the crying. 'I'm sorry, Nurse. Just this once?'

Linda took another jagged breath, held it, let it go, forced herself to sound calm. 'Okay. But that baby needs feeding. I'll be back in five minutes.' The man released his grasp when she stepped to one side.

Holding on to the bedrail he bent towards his wife. The baby quietened as though listening. 'Don't apologise for me, do you hear? Never apologise for me.'

'I'm sorry, George.'

'Think on, then.'

The threat stopped Linda at the door. She looked back at Harriet, who fixed her gaze on her and gave a small shake of her head. Walking stiffly from the room, Linda willed her legs not to give way under her. Sweat prickled her hairline; she thought she would vomit at any moment. She mustn't be seen in this state; there was no way she wanted to, or even could, explain the unwelcome and strange terrors that seeing the man bullying his wife had dredged up. Diving into a nearby linen-room she slid down against the closed door to the floor. Pulling up her knees, she rested her head on them and closed her eyes, willing herself to calm down. When she opened them it was pitch black inside the cramped room. With a small cry she struggled to her feet and fumbled for the switch. The light was momentarily blinding, but relief coursed through her. She'd always been afraid of the dark.

Chapter 2: Linda Booth

Ashford, evening: Tuesday, September 16th

The bus station was crammed with people making their way to work in Manchester but there wasn't a queue for the Ashford

4

bus. When it arrived, Linda sank gratefully onto a seat by the door, thinking back to the last few minutes in the ward.

Harriet Worth's husband had gone by the time Linda went back into the side ward. Neither woman spoke about what had happened but it seemed the fractious baby had sensed the tension and steadfastly refused the breast. In the end Linda had made up a bottle of milk and given it to Harriet, glad to get away, aware that, to her own mind, she'd failed the woman, both professionally and personally.

The glass was cool on Linda's forehead as she leaned on the bus window, reliving the incident with George Worth, unable to rid herself of the instinctive dislike and fear. When the bus squealed to a halt on Shaw Street, she was glad to be almost home.

The streets were quiet. Even so, as she turned the corner onto Henshaw Street she collided with her neighbours, the two elderly Crowley sisters.

'Well, we *have* had a night, haven't we Agnes?' Tall and thin, the eldest, Ethel, drew herself to full height. She sniffed. As usual, whatever the weather she had a drip balancing on the tip of her nose.

The other woman nodded. 'The police were at your—'

'house. Bringing your mother home. She was a—'

'disgrace. Shouting—'

Shorter than her sister and plump, Agnes Crowley shuffled excitedly from one foot to the other and bobbed her head, almost dislodging the blue turban-hat that covered small pink hair rollers.

'and screaming at the top of her—'

'voice.' Each hitched their baskets further along their arms.

'Not that we were watching—'

'We just heard all the noise and looked—'

'out to see what was happening—'

'Right under our window.'

'Right under our window.'

They stopped. More from lack of breath, Linda thought, than

running out of gossip. No doubt it would be all over the neighbourhood before lunchtime. 'You're out early, ladies,' she said.

'Shopping.' Ethel flushed and sniffed again. 'We have a lot of shopping to do.'

'Of course you have.' And a lot of rumours to spread, Linda thought. She felt that whatever energy she had left was being drained from her body by the malice in these two women. 'Well, I've just finished work, so I'm ready for my bed.' She moved to get past them.

'I do hope everything's all right at home so you can sleep.' Ethel tutted, recognisably miffed that Linda had shown no reaction.

'Sure it will be.' Linda waited until they moved to one side. 'But if not, I'll let you know. Wouldn't want you to miss out on anything, would we?'

The two women looked at one another. 'Well ...' Ethel said. 'Well ...'

Linda didn't look back.

Inside number 27, Ted Booth was sitting on one of the tall stools by the breakfast counter, his head in his hands.

'What's happened, Dad? Where's Mum?'

He tilted his head upwards. 'Sleeping it off.'

Linda pursed her lips. 'This is the third time this month Mum's drunk herself into a stupor. It's always same; why do you let it happen?'

'She went through a lot when she was younger, love. We have to be patient.'

'I'm sick of being patient, always tiptoeing around. Why do you think our William spends so much time away from here?'

'Because he goes to see that woman of his.' Ted looked shocked, as though the idea of his son being absent from home so often had anything to do with his wife. 'Doesn't he?'

'S'pose.' Linda sighed. 'I'm sorry, Dad.' She put her hand on his shoulder. 'So, what was it this time?'

'Same as last year. Same as every year since your grandma died. I'd forgotten yesterday was the date, but she insisted on taking flowers to the grave. Goodness only knows why she puts herself through it. They hated one another.'

Linda could remember her grandmother: sitting by the fire, always wearing black, with an expression to match and a whinging voice that penetrated every corner of the house. She hadn't liked the old woman and the old woman hadn't liked her.

'Why *does* Mum always go to the grave? Have you asked her? When she's not drunk, I mean?'

'It only upsets her.' Ted Booth covered her hand with his. 'It brings back too many memories.'

'Of what, Dad?'

'Nothing for you to worry about.'

'Just to put up with, then?'

'Don't be so hard, Linda.'

They lapsed into silence. She understood she'd hurt him and regretted it. 'You look worn out.' She unpinned her cap and took off her cape. 'I bet you haven't been to bed, have you? Do you want a brew before you go up?'

'I should be at the shop.'

There was a thud overhead and then the sound of vomiting.

Linda sucked on her lower lip. For heaven's sake. 'She didn't make it to the bathroom,' she said, flatly.

'I'll sort it.' Ted put his hands flat on the table and levered himself up.

'Not on your own.' She took off her navy cardigan and flung it over the bannister at the bottom of the open-plan Parana pine stairs. She glanced around the kitchen. Every surface of the bright orange units was covered in dirty crockery and left-over food. Saucepans were stacked untidily on the gas cooker, and wet clothes, piled up on the new twin-tub since yesterday, had dripped water on to the carpet. No doubt it would all be still waiting for her when she got up later. 'Come on then, Dad, let's get it over with.'

7

Chapter 3: Victoria Schormann

Llamroth, evening: Tuesday, September 16th

Llamroth was deserted. True to form, Victoria Schormann thought: there wasn't a soul around the village. Eleven o'clock at night and everybody had gone into hibernation. She sighed with impatience. She'd been looking out for Seth's camper van from her bedroom for the last two hours.

Just when she thought she couldn't stand the waiting any longer she saw it glide silently down the lane behind the church.

The moon lit up the trees as she clambered over the low hedge in the back garden. Through the shadows Victoria could see the Volkswagen camper parked under the trees behind the church, exactly where she'd told Seth was the best place.

She was disappointed to find he'd brought another boy and two girls with him. She felt a pang of jealousy. It must have shown on her face because he laughed.

'Chill out, sweetheart, you didn't think I'd come all the way to this cruddy place on my lonesome, did you? It's taken us ten hours to get here.'

'No, not really.' Victoria felt the warmth of embarrassment rise from her throat.

Like a Rolling Stone, boomed out from two transistors inside the van. She clicked her fingers to look casual but couldn't resist saying, 'Think you need to turn that down; someone might come to see what's happening.'

'Oh, man.' Seth rolled his eyes. 'Zen?'

The other boy switched one of the radios off. 'Better?' He looked at Victoria.

She nodded, feeling stupid.

'Remember me? Amber?' one of the girls put her arm around Victoria's waist. 'We met at the festival?'

'Oh, yes, of course.' Victoria managed a smile.

'Don't worry, we'll make ourselves scarce,' Amber murmured.

The boy called Zen winked and grabbed hold of other girl's hand. 'C'mon, Jasmine. Let's find ourselves a cosy corner.'

'The church is always open,' Victoria said.

'Ooer, let's go and find God.'

The three of them walked away, laughing.

Seth took hold of her hand. His skin was warm and dry. He came closer. She closed her eyes and swallowed. 'Open them,' he muttered, his lips against hers. It was a command. He was kissing her all over her face, licking her neck, her ears, pausing every now and then as though watching her reaction. She pulled her jumper over her head. She wasn't wearing a bra and she leaned back savouring the sensation as he sucked her nipple.

The heat spread inside her and she felt for the buckle of his belt. 'Undo it,' he said. Her legs trembled as she pulled at the belt on his jeans, unzipped them. His skin was warm there too, warm and hard. He pressed against her.

Then she was lying across one of the seats in the back of the camper, vaguely aware of the coldness of the leather as he eased her jeans, her panties, along her legs, kissing her waist, her stomach, her thighs. She opened her legs to him and he gently moved his fingers in her, gradually increasing the pressure until she was rising each time to meet the rhythm. And then there was a sudden, sharp pain and she gasped. He was inside her. But the pain subsided and suddenly she was driving herself against him, pulling him in. In that moment the decision was made for her; she *would* go with him, wherever he wanted her to go.

When she got back to the cottage it was in darkness.

Back in her bed, she touched the places Seth had been and smiled.

Chapter 4 : Victoria Schormann

Llamroth: Wednesday, September 17th

It would be the perfect time for her to leave. As soon as her parents had left with her brother for the train station she'd run upstairs, drag her duffle-bag from under her bed and pack her things.

She read the note through once again, before folding it and pushing it back into the envelope. She thought it said everything she wanted her parents to know. To make them leave her alone. For now. To make sure, she underlined a couple of the lines. *I need to get away, to find where I truly belong. To find myself. My spirit is crushed in this place. My spirit needs to fly. I'll write. Please don't look for me.*

She'd see them sometime in the future – when *she* wanted to. But for now she needed to be free. Free from being a twin. Free to be…to do what she wanted. Just like last night. The tingle in the pit of her stomach returned as she thought about Seth making love to her. Finally…

Victoria shivered at the thought that she might never have known Seth. If she hadn't gone to the pop festival at the beginning of the summer she would never have met him.

She wasn't meant to be there, but her parents had been with Richard at an open-day event at one of the hospitals in Manchester and she'd refused to go with them. She was sick to death of always hearing them going on about how brainy their precious son was. And it had been bad enough having to trail around to all the relatives the day before. Even worse, having to stay at Auntie Jean's with grumpy Uncle Patrick because they had the most room.

'Look Mum, I don't want to come with you. I'll be bored and you'll only get mad at me. And I don't want to stay here on my own. Please, just let me go into Manchester and look around the shops there. I almost never get the chance to shop in a city. Please. Dad, tell her, tell Mum to let me.'

'I don't know…' Mary looked to Peter for help.

'Perhaps if we find out the times of the bus we can make sure she is safely on it and then we can meet her after we have finished at the hospital.'

'I know the number of the bus to catch, Dad. I found a timetable in Auntie Jean's kitchen. Come on, trust me, I'll be okay. Honest. And I'll probably be back before you, anyway.'

She didn't mention the poster she'd seen on a lamp-post advertising the festival.

When she jumped off the platform of the bus she could already hear the music. A group was playing 'A Groovy Kind of Love' and she hummed along with it, studying the long queue at the entrance. Looking around she saw a gap in the fence further along the road and sauntered towards it. She stood, waiting for a couple to pass her, then quickly ducked through.

'Got you.' A strong hand held her shoulder. She looked up at whoever had caught her. He didn't look official; he had a flowered full-sleeved shirt on and feathers stuck in a cotton band around his head.

She took a chance. 'Get off me.' Twisting away from him.

'Whoa.' He held up his hands in a gesture of submission. 'I surrender myself to the hip Welsh chick in the red dress.'

He'd obviously picked up on her accent. Victoria couldn't help giggling. 'You're not a steward or whatever, are you? You're not anybody in charge.'

'Only of myself.' He grinned. He gestured towards the hedge. 'Actually that's the way we got in.'

'We?'

'Some friends and me.' He looked around in a vague manner. 'They're here somewhere. Some of them wanted to see Herman's Hermits. Not my thing but one of them insisted. You like that group?'

11

Without wavering, Victoria said, 'Oh no.' She thought quickly. 'Joan Baez is more my thing.'

He beamed. 'And mine too. I knew we were fated to meet.' He held out his hand, wiggled his fingers. 'Want to look for my friends with me?'

Victoria took hold of his hand. This was going to be even more exciting than she'd thought.

The opening notes of 'I'm Into Something Good' wafted towards them. 'See? They've started already.' He began to run, pulling her with him and dodging through the scattered groups of people on the edge of the field.

'I thought you didn't like this group?'

'I don't, but I want you to meet my f…my friends.'

She thought he'd almost said his family. Perhaps they were there as well? It didn't matter; for once she was free to do just what she wanted and free to meet who she wanted. She laughed. 'I don't even know your name,' she shouted, trying to keep up.

'Seth.' He spun around taking her in a wide circle around him. 'You?'

'Victoria. Vicky,' she said, breathless. 'Stop, I'm dizzy.'

'Not a Welsh name then?'

'*Nage*…No. My parents are…' she hesitated, 'English. From around here, actually.'

He ignored her voluntary explanation. 'Boring name. I shall think of a better one for you.'

'Oh, will you, indeed?'

'I will.' He untied the band from his head, fastened it around hers and, picking up the fallen feathers, stuck them in it. 'There. Awesome!' He bent to kiss her.

She turned her cheek to him, suddenly shy. 'We should find your friends.'

He scanned the field. Victoria did the same, even though she hadn't a clue who she was looking for. It had filled up a lot since she'd arrived and now seemed to be a kaleidoscope of colour, girls

12

in kaftans, shawls and large-brimmed hats. A group of boys pushed past them, dressed almost identically in flares and multi-coloured waistcoats, their bare arms painted with flowers. Victoria recognised the sweet smell of cannabis that they left in their wake from a party at college. She remembered she'd been too scared to try it. She watched the boys move through the crowds, bending to kiss some of the girls, touching the outstretched arms of others swaying to the music.

She felt drab and boring in her red mini-dress.

'You're cool,' Seth said, almost as though he could read her mind.

She smiled. *He* was *gorgeous*.

The last notes of the song floated towards them on the light breeze, almost lost in the piercing screams of girls. The stage was at the far end of the field. The group looked small, insignificant against the large wooden structure. But Victoria lost sight of that, too, as the crowds stood up to cheer.

'Think we might as well stay here.' Seth sat down cross-legged on the grass and patted the ground at the side of him. 'Unless there's a group you really do want to listen to?'

She could tell from the dismissive tone that he was expecting her to say no. And, to be honest, she would much rather stay with him. But she pretended to deliberate before shaking her head and kneeling down. His body was warm through the thin cotton of his shirt as he casually put his arm around her waist and drew her to him. His lips were warm and firm. She felt the slight touch of stubble against her cheek for the first time; the boys she'd kissed in the past had skin as smooth as hers and she liked the roughness of Seth's. And then his tongue was pressing on her lips, gently opening them, entering her mouth. It was the first time she'd been kissed in that way. And, as the minutes passed and she felt his hand on her breast, the first time a thrill had surged through her body and along her thighs.

Seth drew back, laughing softly, searching her face. 'So…?' he murmured.

13

Mortified, Victoria wouldn't meet his gaze. She moved from her knees to a sitting position a little way from him and affected to concentrate on a girl who was weaving her way through the crowds, towards them. She was singing and turning from side to side, waving a bubble-wand over the heads of everyone. Victoria watched the bubbles as they drifted around, iridescent in the sunlight. One floated in front of her and then landed on Seth's nose where it burst. He sneezed and Victoria giggled.

He grabbed her. 'I'll teach you to laugh at me?' Rolling around on the grass he tickled her until she begged him to stop. He fell back, taking her with him and they lay, gasping for breath and gazing up at the sky. Another group began playing, the thrum of a bass guitar vying with the drummer. The awkward moment was gone.

They lay for a while, pointing out the various shapes of the clouds to one another, breathing in the ubiquitous scent of hash. Dozing.

The sound of arguing startled Victoria. She sat up, leaning back on her arms and watching a couple exchanging heated words before the girl flounced off. Another girl came and sat beside the boy and started necking with him. The casualness excited Victoria. It's a freedom thing, she thought, just doing what you want to.

She glanced down at Seth over her shoulder. 'Your friends will be wondering where you are.'

He waved a lazy arm. 'They'll find me.'

'Oh.' She shivered; the day was beginning to cool down. She rubbed her arms briskly. There were grass stains on her knees; she'd have to get rid of those before she went home. She checked her watch and took in a quick breath. 'I'll have to go,' she said, 'I promised to be back before...' She realised she hadn't said anything else about her family to Seth. In fact they'd hardly talked about anything at all.

Seth sat up. 'So soon? I was hoping we could make a night of it.'

The implication was obvious and she blushed. And then laughed; she could just imagine her parents' faces if they'd seen her this afternoon. It was the most exciting day she'd had. Ever.

'No, I'm sorry, I really must go.' She stood, brushing the grass off her dress, smoothing down the skirt. She'd taken her shoes off and now balanced on one foot after the other to put them back on.

'Wait. Here come the others. I want you to meet them.' Seth jumped to his feet and waved towards a knot of people coming towards them. They were laughing. Victoria's eyes were drawn to the centre of the group where two girls, dressed in ordinary mini-dresses like her, were clinging to one another, heads close. They were whispering together. But then they joined in with the cheers and shouts of greetings as they neared Seth and Victoria.

He took her hand and pulled her upright. As they stood together she was aware of a sense that, somehow, she was important and that, for the first time in her life, she belonged.

Victoria propped the note against the kettle; she knew it would be the first thing her mother would go to as soon as she came through the door. Her parents were so predictable. They didn't realise things were different these days. That was why they didn't understand her: why there were so many rows. They'd never lived in a time that was changing so much, that was so electrifying … so dangerous in a way. Oh, she knew about the war; hadn't she been taunted about Dad often enough by some of the kids in school repeating what their parents said: 'Dirty Hun', 'filthy Jerry's kid'. Not that it'd bothered her; they were the ones sorry for themselves in the end.

And all that war stuff was in the past.

She heaved a long sigh, the queasy exhilaration in her stomach making her restless. But, until Seth came for her in the morning, she had to wait. She'd wanted to go in the night, to get right away before her parents woke but he'd said no; he wasn't spending another ten hours on the road without a *sleep* (he'd leered, grinning, as he said the word and she'd blushed, hoping the others hadn't noticed). But she supposed he was right; it was a long way, especially in the dark.

So she'd tried to persuade him to let her go to him as soon as her parents left the cottage, to meet him at the camper van but he'd told her not to; he was adamant they would come for her. She didn't understand why she had to wait. But she'd agreed in the end.

Gelert, their Alsation, nuzzled her hand and followed her when she went through to the living-room and over to the window. The road was empty. Beyond the trees across the road the grey sea shifted slowly, the waves sluggish on the shoreline.

She sighed, turned and sat on the window-sill, lifted her arms and let them drop again. She liked the jangling of the bangles as they fell so she repeated the action twice more. She glanced at the bookshelves. After packing the new clothes she'd been secretly buying over the last few months – the frayed bell-bottomed jeans, two tie-dyed shirts and, best of all the purple, flowing chiffon kaftan – on top of her art stuff, she'd hesitated over one or two of her books. But Seth had told her last night to travel light. Still, she'd slipped in one of her records. She was sure he'd approve of Joan Baez and 'We Shall Overcome'.

Absently stroking the dog leaning against her, his front paws on the windowsill, she studied the family photographs on the wall. There were loads of her and Richard. Always together; she couldn't remember ever having had her photo taken on her own. All at once it was vital she looked for one. She pushed the dog away, went over to the cupboard that the music centre was on, riffled through the boxes of photographs, invoices and receipts and miscellaneous papers. Not one photo on her own; always with Richard. *Byth yn blydi teg*, she thought: never bloody fair. She felt justified in her resentment: looking back it was always him who was the important one, she'd always been in his shadow. She banged the cupboard door closed, remembered there were more photos in the old roll-top desk on the landing.

Gelert followed close on her heels when she ran upstairs, just as he had for the last hour.

Unlike the rest of the house there was always a jumble of things in the desk. Opening the lid, she went through the top drawer: old papers fastened together with a bulldog-clip, lists, an old wallet. Why Mum hadn't thrown half of this stuff away she'd never know. She pushed a glasses-case, with the arm of a broken pair poking out, to the back of the drawer and slammed it shut.

Tilting her head she listened for the sound of an engine. But all she could hear was the pounding of the pulse in her ears and the low breathy whine of the dog. She pulled the second drawer right out, tipped the contents onto the desk-top and scattered them. A pile of small photographs spilled out of an envelope. Most looked quite old. And then she found one: a picture of her on her own. She looked about three years old. One arm was held out to her side. Holding it closer to her face she could see a small hand holding hers. Must have been Richard but somehow whoever was taking it hadn't got it right.

A tiny photograph fluttered off the desk-top. Victoria picked it up and studied it; it looked quite old and was a picture of a woman, plump with curly hair and a wide smile on her face. She turned it over and read the words on the back; 'Gwyneth, Llamroth, 1950'. She shoved the two pictures into her skirt-pocket, pushed the drawer back into its rightful place and cleared the desktop with one sweep of her arm but then hesitated. Nobody would miss a few pictures. And, despite the rows, she still loved her mum and dad. So it would be good to have a few family memories with her while she was away. She took the envelope.

Moving swiftly to the landing window she checked her watch. 'Come on, Seth, it's nearly half nine. You said half nine.'

'Make sure the "oldies" are out of the way in the morning,' was what he'd said. She wished he wouldn't call them that. But he was

17

right; they were old … and old fashioned. Not like him and the group. Her group, he'd said in the last letter. She pulled it out of the pocket in her long skirt and skimmed through the words … 'your group now, your new family … we can't wait for you to join us … a whole new life, an exciting new world will be yours… All my love, Seth.'

All my love, Seth. His love. The quiver in the depths of her stomach returned. He'd proved his love for her last night. She put the paper to her mouth and kissed his name, carefully sliding it back into its envelope before pushing it into her skirt-pocket again.

In her bedroom she checked herself in the mirror. She thought he would approve of how she was dressed. She adjusted the beaded band around her forehead, pulled the peasant blouse further down her arms to show more of the red flower design she'd painted on her shoulder and flicked her blonde hair back, turning one way and then the other to admire the effect. Her long cotton skirt made a soft swishing sound as it flowed around her legs.

The grandfather clock chimed a slow deep note. Half past nine. Richard would be on the train now. In a way she wished she'd been able to confide in him, tell him what she planned to do, despite her jealousy. There weren't many secrets she kept from him, but Seth was one of them.

Mum and Dad would be on their way back.

Anxious, she hurried downstairs, almost tripping over the dog. 'Out of the way, Gelert,' she yelled, then bent down and hugged him quickly.

As she pushed the photographs into her rucksack and drew the ties together a horn sounded, then there were lots of shouts. Gelert barked. He ran to the window and stood again with his front paws on the sill, looking out and growling. Seth was standing on the frame of the door of the yellow Volkswagen camper, the sides and roof festooned with painted flowers. He was banging the flat of his hand on the horn and laughing. The others

18

were standing alongside, smiling and beckoning her. She laughed, waved back and slipped her feet into her sandals.

Balancing the duffle-bag on the back of the settee, she loosened the tie and peered inside: a last check that she'd got everything.

Gelert whined. Victoria hesitated, suddenly stilled by the enormity of what she was doing. A panicky feeling rose in her throat; what the hell *was* she doing? She dropped her duffle-bag and held on to the back of the settee. The dog took hold of one of the straps and some of her things were strewn onto the floor. 'Leave it, Gelert.' Her voice choked in her throat. She tussled with him to get it back, tears falling onto his head, and went into the kitchen. There she took one of his biscuits out of the tin in the cupboard and knelt alongside him, giving him the biscuit and a hug. 'Sorry, boy,' she whispered, 'need to go.'

She stood up and, looking into the kitchen mirror, blew her nose and wiped the smudged mascara from under her eyes. Idiot, she thought. This was what she wanted. She slung her bag on her shoulder and shook her skirt to make sure it flowed around her legs as she moved.

Without a second glance, she slammed the cottage door behind her.

The envelope holding the letter from Seth fluttered in the draught and slid under the settee.

Chapter 5: William Howarth

Ashford, evening: Wednesday, September 17th

'There's one more to look at before you knock off.' Patrick Howarth threw a set of keys across to his nephew, who was drying his hands on a piece of towelling. 'Mini on the forecourt. Wouldn't start. Jack's just towed it in.'

Bloody Jack – shouldn't even be in the garage, William Booth thought. His cousin was on leave, for God's sake why hadn't he just stayed away, met up with his Army pals, stopped at home? Anything but bugger about in the garage, bloody messing everything up.

'I've finished for the day,' he protested, pulling at the front of his overall until the press-studs popped open. 'I told you this morning. I said I had to get done early; I'm meeting our Richard off the train.'

'You're done when I say so.'

'I've finished all the jobs that were on the list.' William felt the stirrings of anger. He pushed the legs of his overalls down with his feet and stepped out of them. He knew what Patrick was playing at; he didn't like Uncle Peter just because he was German. But William didn't understand why Patrick had carried that dislike forward to his nephew and niece.

'Won't do him any harm to wait a few minutes.' Patrick scowled, then grinned. 'Don't think you'll grumble when you see the driver. Tasty bit of stuff.'

William hated the way his uncle eyed-up all the women customers – as though they'd fancy him, with his belly hanging over his trousers and his careful comb-over. 'I'll have a look at the car. But if it's a big job it'll have to wait 'til morning.'

'It bloody won't.'

It bloody will, William thought. He turned away from Patrick. In all the five years he'd worked at his uncle's garage he'd kept his temper. But one of these days the man would be sorry. Jobs were two-a-penny and garages were crying out for good mechanics. And William knew that he was good at his job. 'I said I'll have a look.'

His uncle was right, though. The girl standing by the red Mini with the Union Jack roof was really pretty. Not as lovely as his Susan, but pretty. Her black hair streamed over a white short-sleeved crocheted top. A pink jacket, casually wrapped around her shoulders, matched the shortest skirt William had ever seen. How the hell does she get in and out of that car without showing all she's got, he thought.

'Hi,' he said. 'What happened, then?' He dipped his head towards the car.

'It just sort of stuttered and then stopped. I'm sorry,' she added, 'I heard you say you were finishing. But I'm desperate. I promised my ... my stepfather I wouldn't be late tonight. My mother's in hospital ... she's ... in hospital,' she repeated. 'I'm supposed to be visiting her.'

'No problem. Let's have a look.' He sat in the driver's seat with one leg out of the car and turned the key. Seconds later he was cursing Jack. No petrol. The dozy bugger must have known what was wrong with the blasted vehicle. He was evidently out to make a bit of extra cash before he went off to Northern Ireland. William felt a twinge of guilt for the irritation. He and Jack had never got on but according to what was in the news it was a bad situation he was being sent into.

The self-reproach rapidly disappeared; Jack was all for going over there. Apparently it was what he'd signed up for – to 'sort out the bastards', he'd heard Jack say on more than one occasion. 'Wilson has the right idea, sending in the Army.'

There was no point in arguing with him. He'd always been arrogant. Just like his dad.

And it wasn't this girl's fault that William felt so aggravated. Taking a deep breath, he said, 'You've run out of petrol.'

'Oh.' The girl blushed. 'I'm sorry. I haven't been driving long and my ... stepfather usually takes it to the garage for me.' She moved from one foot to the other, wobbling on her knee-high silver boots.

'Don't worry, we'll soon have you back on the road.' He took the handbrake off and, pushing the car nearer the pumps, unscrewed the petrol cap.

Even though he was watching the gauge he could sense the girl's tension. 'It's full now,' he said, putting the nozzle back into place. 'That's three pounds ten.'

'Keep the change.' She pushed four one-pound notes in his hand.

'No, I didn't do anything.' He jerked his head towards the garage. 'I suppose they've already charged you for towing in?'

'Yes. But it was my own fault. Please, take it.' She moved quickly, folding herself into the car and closing the door. 'Thanks again.'

William sucked on his lower lip, watching her pull out too fast into the traffic. He frowned, then shrugged.

Putting the money in the till in the corner of the garage he took out a ten-shilling note. He'd earned it. And it was better in his pocket than his greedy uncle's.

'I've gone.' He tossed the words over his shoulder towards Patrick, shoving his arms into his leather jacket and then jamming his crash helmet on.

Jack was standing astride the Triumph Trophy.

'Get off,' William snapped.

'Make me.' Jack grinned.

'You wouldn't want me to do that.' William folded his arms. 'Now get off my fucking bike.'

Slowly, still sniggering, his cousin swung his leg over the seat of the bike, deliberately kicking it.

Gritting his teeth, William caught hold of the handlebars to stop it falling. He lifted the stand with his foot and rocked the bike on its wheels before opening the throttle and kick starting the engine.

With a bit of luck he might just get to the station before the train arrived.

Chapter 6: Richard Schormann

Bradlow, evening: Wednesday, September 17th

Richard Schormann swung the door of the carriage open and stepped down onto the platform at Bradlow. The damp air held the acrid taste of diesel. The draught, scattering dropped tickets and litter, snaked around his ankles. He shivered and glanced around. No sign of his cousin.

He went into the waiting-room, put his suitcase onto one of the seats and felt in his pocket for his hearing-aids. He'd been glad to take them out as soon as he lost sight of his parents, standing arm-in-arm and frantically waving, on the bridge over the railway at Pont-y-Haven. Settling down in his seat and pulling the hood of his parka as far as possible over his face he'd slept, woke, watched passing coastline, fields, the backs of dreary houses and, from under his hood, the ever-moving silent mouths of his fellow passengers.

Now he fitted the aids around each ear and sounds came rushing back: shouts, the thud of feet as the last few passengers left the platform, the hoot of the whistle and the rumble of the train as it ground slowly along the rails and out of the station.

Unzipping his coat, Richard checked his reflection in the window. He adjusted the neck of his black polo-neck jumper and, bending his knees slightly to get a better look, combed his fringe over his forehead.

The door opened, letting in more noise, and Richard fastened his parka, pulling the hood over his head. Not William. A woman, carrying shopping-bags in one hand and a sleeping child in her other arm, sat down with a sigh.

'Waiting for my husband,' she smiled, as though an explanation was expected.

Richard nodded and returned the smile. 'Waiting for my cousin,' he said. There was an uncomfortable moment. 'Think I should go and look out for him.' He pushed his way through the door

It closed with a click behind him. The platform was empty now. Across the rails, lines of waiting passengers stared across with indifferent, blank faces. In contrast to Llamroth, the place seemed unfriendly and, for the first time, the excitement of an interview in a big city hospital waned. He was almost guaranteed a place at Pont-y-Haven where his mother had worked and where his father was so well known. Was it worth all this anxiety? To go somewhere new?

Even as he asked himself the question he knew the answer. However much he loved his parents, their over-protectiveness had stifled him all his life. His father's hang-ups about being German were way over the top; his position in the village as the GP had always shielded him against resentment as far as Richard could tell.

And his father's nationality hadn't caused any problems for Richard. Unlike Vicky, he'd never had any trouble making friends, even though, or perhaps because, he couldn't hear properly. Maybe kids like Stephen, his best friend then, had liked being his mouthpiece.

Leaving the station he looked up and down the road. Nothing. The other passengers had gone. He felt the reverberation of another train arriving. When he turned back to the platform an old freight-engine clanked slowly through the station, a long line of empty trucks behind it. There was no one else around except, at the far end, a porter pushing a trolley and chatting to the station-master who walked alongside him.

His cousin had forgotten about him, there could be no other reason William wasn't there. Hitching his rucksack onto his shoulder Richard dithered. It was only September but already the nights were drawing in and the weather didn't help; the sinking sun could only be glimpsed now and then through layers of grey cloud in the steadily darkening sky.

He remembered from past visits to the north of England that there was a bus-stop along the road from the station and decided to take his chance. There had to be a bus that went to Ashford eventually and, once there, he was sure he'd remember the way to Henshaw Street. The sky had blackened even more and he glanced upwards; hopefully the rain would hold off until one came.

But then a sudden streak of lightning silhouetted the hills in the direction of Ashford, followed, after a few seconds by a low growl of thunder.

He heard the muffled rumble before they came into view. At first he thought it was more thunder. But then, out of the shadows of the houses just beyond the railway station came a group of motorbikes. He peered round the fur of his hood. About fifteen of them. All the riders in black leather. Rockers. They'd see him as fair game: a Mod on his own.

His skin tingled. He felt a sudden trickle of sweat run down the back of his neck. He'd been persuaded by some friends to go to Penarth in November two years ago. They'd said it would be a laugh but he'd never been so scared. They were almost caught up in the riots. Gangs of other Mods fighting with Rockers on the beach. Kicking hell out of each other. He'd not forgotten the fear.

Things had quietened down since but they were still enemies. His heart thudded as he slowly turned his back to the road. The Rockers were now behind him. As the last bike passed him a light came on in the upstairs window of one of the houses, throwing his shadow against the wall. There was a shout. He held his breath, his stomach roller-coasting. The motorbikes slowed, revving grew louder. They were coming back. Idling a few feet away from him.

'Hey, you little Mod!'

Richard ran, his rucksack bouncing against his back. He swerved down the alleyway behind the houses, pulling over the dustbins at the back gates as he went. He heard a crash as the leading bike ran into one of them. A lid skidded alongside him, rolling unsteadily. He jumped over it. They couldn't follow him.

At the end of the alley he hesitated, crossed a road. There was another long rumble of thunder, followed almost immediately by a flashing sheet of lightning and more thunder. He stopped, grinned, the reprieve a surge of triumph. He'd lost them. He dived down a dark side street and then another, sweating under the weight of his parka. But then there they were again. Following slowly. Shouting and whooping. Taunting him. The beams of the headlights wavering around him.

The outline of a cat darted in front of him, disappeared into the darkness. There was a yowl, then another.

It started to rain: heavy slow drops at first and then faster, plastering his hair to his scalp. His rucksack slipped heavily down his arm. He let it drag along the ground, fingers clenched around one strap.

Turning another corner he looked left, then right. At the end of the street he saw a main road: neon signs over shops, advertising boards illuminated by streetlights, people walking, crouched under umbrellas. He lengthened his stride. His throat and chest burned with the extra effort of taking in air.

At first Richard didn't see the red and white plastic barrier through the rain. But then he did. The street was fenced off. Roadworks. He was trapped.

He faltered, choking on the iron taste that had risen in his throat. When he started to run again he couldn't feel his legs. He willed himself forward, focussing on the barrier.

At the same time he heard the Rockers open the throttle of their bikes, revving the engines as they closed in, yelling and shouting. The front wheel of the nearest caught the strap of Richard's rucksack that trailed along the ground and momentarily threw him off balance. He staggered, wrenched at his bag but had to let it go. Now there were two motorbikes on either side of him. He could feel the heat of the engines even through his parka. They were cornering him. He felt a thump between his shoulders.

And then he leapt over the barrier towards the main road, arms and legs flailing.

Winded, Richard lay still, his eyes closed. He hurt.

'Get in! Get in!'

The voice was muffled. Instinctively he checked his hearing-aids. One was dislodged. He pushed it back into place.

'Hey, you. Get in.'

He opened his eyes. It was a car, stopped in the road: a Mini, with the passenger door wide open. People walked around him, muttering disapproval. He rolled onto his side on the pavement. And then, with a start, he heard yelling. 'Get the Mod. Don't let the bastard escape! Come on, get 'im!'

Scurrying on hands and knees, he scrambled into the car.

An arm reached across him, slamming the door shut at the same time as the Mini set off, driving erratically into the traffic.

'I saw you were in trouble way back. I thought I'd never find you in time.'

Richard willed himself to stop shaking. He twisted his head to look at the girl. She was bent over the wheel, gripping it tightly and staring straight ahead. Her jawline was taut with concentration.

'Thanks.' He could hear the wobble in his voice. He cleared his throat. 'Thanks,' he said again, louder.

'I've seen that lot before.' Still she didn't look at him but she raised her voice. 'They would have half-killed you if they'd caught you. Mind you, you can really move when you run … er…?'

'Richard.' He'd heard the admiration in her voice. 'It's called being shit-scared,' he said.

She laughed, glancing across at him for the first time. 'My name's Karen.'

'Hi… Karen.' He inclined his head in a mock bow. 'My saviour, isn't it.' He realised he was shaking. 'I mean it. You did save me. Thanks. How did you know what was happening, though?'

'I told you. I saw you being chased down Argus Street by that lot of clowns. I sounded my horn but you disappeared. I figured this was only main road you could be heading for. I had a line of cars behind me, I was driving so slowly. I just kept looking down every side-street.' She laughed again. 'But I certainly didn't expect you to come leaping out like you did.'

'I hadn't a clue where I was going. I was lucky you found me.' Very lucky, he thought, swallowing. His eyes stung and he blinked, staring out of the side window.

After a couple of minutes Karen switched the windscreen wipers to go faster as the rain increased – and then indicated. 'Do you mind if I pull in here?'

Richard didn't catch what she said. He leaned forward to look at her. 'Sorry?'

'I've not been driving long and I don't like this weather. I'm going to pull in here.'

'*Iawn.*'

'What?'

'Sorry. Sure. You're the driver.' Richard didn't speak again until she'd parked the Mini in a car park at the back of a pub. 'It's really coming down now.'

'Yes.' She drummed her fingers on the steering wheel. 'What did you say before?'

'*Iawn?*'

'That was it.'

'It's Welsh. I come from Wales.'

'Oh. Couldn't make out the accent; I'm hopeless at that sort of thing,' she said.

'Just good at rescuing people.' Richard grinned.

'Been to Wales once for a holiday. Can't remember where; I was only little. Gorgeous beaches.'

'Yeah.'

28

With the engine off the only sound was the rain pelting down on the roof. The lights from the pub reflected in the puddles on the ground, shimmering through the streaming windscreen.

'Fancy a drink?'

'No. No, thanks.'

She turned to face him. Even in the shadows Richard could see she was pretty. Very pretty.

'You're wet through.' She reached over to the back seat. 'I've got a towel here. It'll be a bit damp, I went swimming this morning and forgot to take the bag into the house.'

'Thanks.' Richard took it off her and scrubbed at his hair. 'I'm sorry – I'm dripping all over the seat.'

She waved her hand, dismissing his words.

'Mind if I take my coat off? I'll put it on the floor.'

'That's fine!' She smiled at him.

Heck, she was gorgeous. He became aware how small the car was, how close they were. He leaned self-consciously against his door, running the towel over his face and around the neck of his polo-neck jumper. He'd need to change it, but not here. He stopped. 'I've lost my rucksack,' he said. 'I dropped it back there. It had all my things in it.' His spare clothes, his best suit for the interview, his shoes.

'We can't go back,' she said. 'Anyway, they've probably trashed it by now.'

Richard picked up his parka and rummaged in the inside pocket. 'Still got my wallet.'

They lapsed into silence. Yet it didn't feel awkward. Richard couldn't remember the last time he felt so comfortable in someone's company. And, despite the odd circumstances they were in, she must have felt the same, because she leant her head on the back of her seat and closed her eyes.

When she spoke she kept them closed. 'You were coming from the station?'

'Yeah.'

'Where were you going?'

'Staying with relatives in Ashford for a few days,' Richard said. 'I'm hoping to get a place in the university hospital in Manchester that specialises in training medical students. I've got an interview next Monday.'

'Oh, really? You must be brainy!'

'Not really.' Richard laughed. 'But I do want to be a doctor, if I'm good enough. How about you?'

'I'm in college, training as a hairdresser. And eventually I want my own salon...' She stopped.

Richard raised his eyebrows: why did she sound so defensive?

'My mother thinks I should do what I want... My stepfather ... he keeps pushing me to drop the course and work in his office.'

'Ah. What is it?' Richard shifted around so he could see her mouth better. 'The business?'

'Painting and decorating. Mainly commercial property, now.' She grimaced. 'It used to be my dad's business. He liked doing up people's houses, but after he died Mum married George. He went for shops and offices. He says there's more money in it. And you don't have to "kowtow" to what he calls "jumped-up nobodies".' Richard was stunned when she said, 'I hate him.'

'Oh.' He couldn't think of anything to say.

'He's a pig ... and a bully.' She turned to look out of the side window.

He could see her long eyelashes moving furiously. He touched her hand. She didn't pull away but clasped his fingers tightly for a few seconds. They didn't speak.

Finally the heavy rain stuttered and stopped. Karen leant forward and switched off the wipers. She studied the car park for a few seconds. 'I think that's it for now.' She tucked her hair behind her ears and peered upwards at the sky. 'Where can I drop you off?'

Richard started; he'd been admiring her profile. 'Nearest bus stop, if you don't mind?'

'Rubbish, I'll drive you to Ashford. It's only twenty minutes.'

'Haven't you somewhere else you need to be?'

'No.' Karen paused. 'I was on my way to visit my mum in hospital.' She pushed the sleeve of her jacket up to look at her watch. 'I've missed visiting-time now, though.'

'I'm sorry.' He felt it was his fault. 'Your mother's ill?'

'No.' She settled in her seat and turned the ignition key. The engine hummed into life. 'No, she's not ill.' She shook her head. Richard waited.

'I can go and see her tomorrow.' Karen put the Mini into gear and took the handbrake off. 'She won't mind. She's not ill or anything like that. She … she's just had a baby.' She stopped at the entrance of the car park, waiting for a break in the line of traffic.

'Oh.' There wasn't much else he could say, except, 'That's nice … isn't it?'

'Depends.' Karen clamped her teeth over her lower lip. 'Right – whereabouts in Ashford?'

Chapter 7: Richard Schormann

Ashford, evening: Wednesday, September 17th

'Richard, lad, thank the lord you're here.' Ted Booth flung his arm around Richard's shoulders and ushered him into the house. 'We were that worried. William's gone out to look for you again. He feels that bad he was a bit late meeting the train and then he couldn't find you. We decided you must be making your own way here – but that's hours ago. Where've you been, lad?' In the light of the hall he studied Richard. 'And what the heck happened to you? You look like you've been dragged through a hedge backwards.'

'Been in a spot of bother, Uncle.' Richard tried a smile but his mouth felt stiff, immovable. Now it was over, now he was on familiar ground, he was angry with himself for being so scared.

For running. Even if common sense told him it was the only thing he could have done if he didn't want a beating.

'Looks like it an' all. Come on, come into the living-room, I'll put the fire on. Let's get your coat off, you can tell me all about it.'

'Uncle, this is Karen.' Richard held his hand out to the girl who was hovering on the doorstep. 'She helped me.'

'Oh? Well, any friend of Richard … an' all that.' Ted glanced uncertainly at Karen. 'Come in.'

Ted helped him with his parka. In the bright light they could see it was ripped and dirty. 'You're in a right mess. You hurt? We could do with our Linda here to see to you but you've just missed her – she's on nights.'

'I'm okay – I'm not hurt, Uncle. But I lost my rucksack.'

'Never mind that. So long as you're okay, we can sort that out later.' Ted fiddled with the switch on the gas-fire until flames flared. 'New fire,' he said, with a proud smile, 'called a *Flavel Debonair*. Had it put in last month, ready for the winter. Your Auntie Ellen wanted it.' He cleared his throat, looking embarrassed. 'She's in bed … bit of a headache today. Sorry, rabbiting on a bit. I'll make a brew.' In the kitchen he raised his voice above the sound of the water gushing into the kettle. 'She'll probably stay there tonight, but she's looking forward to seeing you and getting all the news from Wales. Now then…' Ted came to stand by the door. 'What happened?'

'He was attacked by a gang of louts. Rockers.' Karen spoke for the first time. 'I saw them chasing him in Bradlow and picked him up.'

'She saved me from a hammering.' For a moment Richard recalled the rush of gratitude when he'd tumbled into the car.

'So, you didn't know one another before?'

'No.'

'Well, that was really good of you, Karen, some folk wouldn't have stopped.'

'Oh, I don't know.' She was blushing.

32

Duw, makes her look even prettier, Richard thought.

'Well, I do,' Ted said. The kettle switched off with a loud click. 'There's some rough parts in Bradlow. And some rough folk. You were lucky, our Richard.' He went back into the kitchen. 'I'll make that brew.'

'I know how lucky I was.' Richard grinned at Karen. 'In more ways than one.'

Colour rose from her throat to her cheeks. 'Actually…' she felt in her jacket pocket, brought out her car-keys. 'I'd better be off.'

Richard felt a twinge of disappointment; she'd obviously done her bit for a fool who'd got himself into trouble and now couldn't wait to go. Just his luck – he really fancied her.

She must have seen the fleeting disappointment in his eyes. 'Like I said … my stepfather … he'll be wondering where I am. Remember?' she touched his arm. 'I should have been meeting him at the hospital to go and visit Mum?'

'Oh yeah. Will he be all right about it?' Richard remembered what she'd said about her stepfather being a bully. It troubled him. 'Tell him what happened. What you did. How you helped me.'

'No.' A short silence. And then: 'No, he wouldn't understand.' She half-smiled, just one corner of her lips lifting. 'You know? Picking up a stranger. He'd be bound to have a go at me for that.' She tossed her hair back. 'Not that it's anything to do with him.' Her words didn't hide her nervousness.

'But you'll be okay? I could come with you to tell him what happened?'

'No.' She spoke sharply. Then her voice softened. 'No, I'll be fine. Honest.' The way she jangled the keys in her hand showed her impatience to leave.

'Right. Well, thanks again, then. See you around?'

'I'd like that,' she said. 'Look, I know you're only here for an interview … that you don't live here. But I would like to see you again. I'm free Friday night?'

'Yeah?'

33

'Yes.'

'Oh.' Richard grinned. He didn't think he'd ever smiled this much. '*Gwych* … great. And you never know, if I *do* get a place I'll be up here all the time. Well, in Manchester, anyway. I didn't ask you where you lived.'

'Not far. Just outside Bradlow. Little village called Mossbridge.'

'Okay.'

'Have you a pen?'

Richard looked around. 'I don't…'

'There's one there, by the newspaper. And a pencil.' She wrote on the top margin of the crossword. 'This is the number you can get me on. Give me a ring.'

'I will.'

'Between four and five in the afternoon's best. I'll be home from college then.'

'Okay.' He walked with her to the front door. 'Still raining,' he said, 'so be careful driving home.'

'I'll be fine.' Karen stood on tiptoes and kissed his cheek. Even in her high-heeled boots she was still smaller than him. 'Ring me.'

'Yeah. *Noso da.*'

'Welsh again?'

'Yeah. Means good night.'

'Oh. *Nos da,* then?' Her pronunciation made him laugh. He was relieved when she joined in.

Richard watched her drive off and turn onto Shaw Street before closing the door. He touched his cheek. His fingers brushed against his hearing-aid. She hadn't mentioned it. And she couldn't have missed it. He smiled to himself.

Ted came out of kitchen, two mugs in his hands. 'She gone? I thought…'

'She had to. But I think she'll be back sometime, Uncle, if that's okay.'

'Aye, fine. Now…' Ted handed one of the mugs to Richard. 'We must ring your mum and dad. Let them know you're here.'

Chapter 8: Mary & Peter Schormann

Llamroth, evening: Wednesday, September 17th

'Perhaps I shouldn't have told Richard about Victoria?' Mary Schormann replaced the telephone receiver but left her hand resting on it.

'What did he say?' Her husband touched the head of the large Alsatian dog that leaned against him, whining. 'Quiet, Gelert.'

'Not a lot – only for us not to worry, she'll be back.' Her forehead crinkled. 'He said it had been a long day. It sounded as though he'd had a difficult journey.' Always reluctant to speak on the telephone because of his hearing, her son had sounded even more strained than usual. 'I hope he's all right; it's only a few weeks since his last operation.'

'A small operation, Mary. And as you say, it is the last. And the university would not wait much longer; his interview has been deferred already. He is lucky they understood.'

'Well, quite right they did!'

A thought came to her, something she didn't want to acknowledge but knew she must; the twins had always been close. 'You don't think he knows … knew what she was going to do, do you, Peter?' Would he have deceived them as well?

'*Nein.* No. I am sure not.' Her husband shook his head. 'Richard is sensible, Mary—'

'Unlike Victoria?' She couldn't stop the bitterness spilling out.

'Victoria has always been the unpredictable one. We know that, *meine Liebe.*'

'She's hard work.' Mary frowned, having a sudden memory of her daughter's stubborn face that morning, her expression rebellious yet somehow nervous. 'At least now we know why she wouldn't come with us to see Richard off.' She looked down at the note in her hand. The message was short, written in her daughter's large, careless handwriting. 'What does she mean?

35

"Need to find myself"? And this, "My spirit is crushed in this place"? "My spirit needs to fly"?' Her anxiety once again merged with irritation. 'All this claptrap!'

Peter Schormann took the paper and re-read it. 'I do not know.' An old frustrated fear churned inside him. All the years he'd protected his family as best he could, and now this. This was totally out of his control. He breathed slowly against the sudden rapid beat of his heart, forcing himself to stand still, stay strong in front of Mary. 'I will go to the police,' he decided. 'They will have to do something, she is under age. I will make sure we will find her. I promise you.'

But Mary heard the bewilderment under his words and it frightened her. Throughout the years they'd been married he'd been the strong one. At first, against the contempt and hatred of people who didn't know them, and later in his determination to regain his status and be respected for the doctor he was. Now it seemed he was as frightened as she was for their daughter.

She moved restlessly around the room, folding the flowered curtains back into tidy pleats before refastening the tasselled tieback, lifting the cushions into place on the new brown leather settee, touching the spines of the books on the shelves. She stopped to study the photographs on the wall above the bookcase.

One of them showed Richard standing at the entrance to St David's Cathedral. What you couldn't see, unless you knew where to look, was Victoria, in a green cardigan, hiding behind one of doors. She was sulking because she couldn't have an ice-cream. Earlier she'd chosen to have sweets. It had been that or an ice-cream. Typical of her daughter, Mary thought resentfully, she'd wanted both in the end. So, when they were leaving, she'd refused to have her picture taken.

Her eyes shifted to the next photo. It showed the twins with her sister, Ellen, and her husband, Ted, and their children. Ellen was holding Victoria's hand. Mary closed her eyes, an upsurge of distress making her light-headed. She'd always known her daughter took after her sister. Both strong-willed; both determined to do just what they wanted. Now Victoria had proved how right she'd been. She held her finger and thumb over her eyes. The dog plodded across to her and pushed his head against her. Absently, she stroked him.

She was grateful when Peter reached for her hand, his warm fingers wrapped around hers, his thumb stroking her palm. But even that small gesture failed, for once, to comfort her. As though he understood it, her husband pulled her gently to him, held her close.

He smelled differently these days since he'd given up smoking his pipe, but his arms around her were still strong, the curve between jawline and throat still the familiar place for her to burrow her face.

Her tears were hot on his neck.

'Why has she done this? It makes no sense.' She wept. 'Where has she gone, Peter?'

'It will be fine, *Liebling*. We will find her.'

She pulled back from him, searched his face. 'But will it, Peter? Will we?' Mary shivered; it felt as if ice was running through her veins. 'She must have planned to go; she waited until this morning, until we were out. Did she catch a bus? Was she somewhere on the station when we were?' Her voice broke. 'Did we miss her? Has she gone off with someone? Oh, Peter, who knows where she is right now?'

Chapter 9: Victoria Schormann

Evening: Wednesday, September 17th

Victoria woke with a start. The air inside the camper van was heavy with an oily, pungent herbal scent mixed with the smell of exhaust fumes. She was crushed between the two other girls, who were deep in sleep, each resting their heads on her shoulder.

'I feel a bit sick,' she said.

'Hold it together, babe, we're nearly there.' Seth spun the vehicle round the corner of a wide street and then wound the driver's window down. 'That better?'

'Thanks.' She took deep breaths hoping to ward off the nausea but there was no fresh air coming in, only muggy damp air. 'How much further?'

'Don't you recognise anywhere, Summer?'

'Summer?' Victoria looked up.

'That's what I've decided you should be called from now on. Don't you like it, babe?' His hazel eyes locked on hers through the rear view mirror.

Did he look … sound annoyed?

Victoria didn't know what to say. 'Fab,' she managed in the end, forcing an enthusiastic tone into her words. She was almost reassured when he laughed but then realised how artificial it sounded.

'So … know where you are?' This time his eyes smiled. But it was as though he was laughing at a joke only he understood.

The scenery had changed from when she was last awake. The winding roads – that followed the lines of hills covered in a sea of yellow gorse and purple heather that bordered rolling fields, were now angular streets of stone, terraced houses and thin sentinels of lampposts. As she gazed through the windscreen the lights flickered on, one by one, orange and red flashes through the steady drizzle. The tarmac and pavements glistened dark with rain. The colours of the doors of the houses were dull as if drained away, she thought. And as yet there were only a few windows lit to show the family life carrying on inside. Most of the houses were dark shadows.

She managed to keep the shock concealed. They were in Ashford. Why were they in Ashford?

'Remember that time we met up here, the week after the fest? We walked along the canal and I asked you what those buildings were. You told me about the place, said it was empty … don't you remember?'

'I'd forgotten. But it's derelict.' It had been a ruin for as long as she'd been coming to Ashford with Mum and Dad. 'I don't understand. How did you…? You didn't tell me you'd moved,' she said, in the end.

'Well, after you'd said it was empty it seemed the obvious choice, given we got kicked out of that dump in Manchester.' He slowed the camper van down to negotiate some potholes.

Was he laughing at her? He knew she had family here. She wouldn't be able to go into Ashford on her own.

'Problem?' he asked, his eyes narrowing.

'I was just thinking I'd have to be careful going into town, in case I see someone I know.' Where was the freedom? *Ashford* she thought, incredulous. She'd thought she'd be escaping from the lot of them.

He didn't answer for a moment and then he glanced at her again. 'Guy from the council came round after we'd got in. Made noises at first about getting us out but nothing's happened so guess they don't care. The girls have made it a home from home,' he said. 'Didn't take long after we all pitched in. You'll be surprised.'

She would … horrible place. She caught a glimpse of the iron gates that led to the park she'd been to with Linda a few times in the past.

She remembered her cousin once saying she hated this time of day, just before it was properly dark. She'd said it frightened her. And, for the first time, Victoria understood; dusk here was depressing. Or was it just that she was unexpectedly depressed?

The sadness took her by surprise. She wondered how her parents were, how hurt they would be by what she had done. The return of the guilt was unexpected.

And yet, for the first time in years, it was Nain Gwyneth she suddenly missed. Not really their grandmother but as good as, with her lovely warm brown eyes that always seemed to twinkle in a special way just for Victoria. She wished she was still alive. It was impossible, of course; she was already ancient when she and Richard were small kids. Her eyes prickled with tears. She knew the old woman would have managed to talk her out of this, just as she had talked her out of many an escapade when she was younger.

She closed her eyes against the burn of tears. She didn't want Seth to see the doubt she was feeling. The fear.

The two girls shifted against her as they swung around another corner. Amber flopped forward and Victoria caught her before she fell against Seth's seat, dislodging Jasmine. They both stretched, leaning away from her and yawning.

She wondered if they had families, parents. Grandparents. If they had ever felt as isolated, as lonely, as she did right now.

Except for Nain Gwyneth, there'd been no other grandparents. None on Dad's side; she presumed they'd died in the war. And she'd never known Mum's mum. There was a small, old, funny coloured photograph of Grandma Howarth with Uncle Tom, Mum's brother, tucked into the corner of the frame of the family one on the back wall of the living room at home. They were standing arm-in-arm in the garden, in wellingtons and overcoats.

Both dead long before she was born.

Thinking about it, none of her cousins had grandparents. Not Jacqueline, not Linda and William. Well, perhaps Linda, she corrected herself; Linda had that woman she called a grandma; Grandma Nelly. Nelly Shuttleworth – not a relative at all as far as she could tell but they'd often been made to visit her because she was supposedly Mum's friend as well. She wrinkled her nose. The house smelled and was crammed with really old scruffy furniture. And a stinky lavatory in a back yard.

She was better off having no grandma than one like Nelly Shuttleworth, she thought, as Seth swung the camper van off the road towards the two large gates and switched off the engine.

Chapter 10: Victoria Schormann

Ashford, evening: Wednesday, September 17th

'Enjoy supper?' Seth leaned back in an old armchair in the corner of the small room.

Victoria nodded. She hadn't; the thick green soup had tasted odd and the doughy brown bread was lying like a lump in her stomach.

'Great. I'll just run things past you so you'll know the ropes and then you'll show me what you've brought with you?'

Although his words ended as a question, she had the feeling it wasn't a choice. Perched on the edge of the wooden chair by the door, she clutched the rucksack closer to her.

If he noticed, he said nothing. 'It's late, so you'll want to get to bed.'

'Whenever you do,' she said. It was exciting to know that they would be sleeping together just like a proper couple. His next words shocked her.

'You'll be in the dorm with all the other single girls—'

'What? I thought—'

He carried on as though she hadn't spoken. 'There's only a few things to remember, Summer. They're not rules ... just stuff to show we care for one another.'

A tremor of anxiety ran through Victoria. 'I thought you said there were no rules.'

'I've just said, Summer, they're not rules.' He laughed but it sounded a bit forced to Victoria. 'If there weren't some guidelines there'd be bloody chaos. No, it's easier if we all stick to what we've agreed.'

'Who's "we", Seth?' Victoria didn't like the sound of anything he'd said so far. He hadn't told her she'd be sleeping in a room with any other girls. Or that there'd be any rules – however he dressed it up. Guidelines – how stupid is that, she thought.

He passed his hand over his forehead, shielding his eyes. When he spoke his voice was weary. 'Me. The members of the group, Summer… They agreed I should lead long ago.' He looked at her. 'It's cool if you're having second thoughts about being with us. If it's not your bag—'

'No…' Victoria swallowed against the tension in her throat. She was being daft. It would be great once she settled. 'No, of course not.' It was all strange, she thought; she had to give her new life a chance. 'I think you're right, I am tired.'

'Sure you are.' His smile was such a relief to Victoria. When he stood up and walked across the room to her she held up her hand and let him tug her to her feet. 'Let's go find your bed.' He took her rucksack from her. 'Leave this here for now.'

He made love to her gently. Afterwards, when she felt him move off the bed she protested, softly.

'Sshh, I've got things to do,' he murmured. 'You get some kip. Okay? I'll be back.'

She was almost asleep when she heard a rustling at the side of her bed. 'Seth?'

'No, it's Amber.' She was a tall, slender shadow in the gloom of the dorm. She'd changed from jeans and top into a long flowing dress. 'I've unpacked your things. And here's your nightwear.' The annoyance was quick in Victoria; what bloody cheek, going through her stuff. Before she could say anything, Amber had gone.

Victoria turned on her back and opened her eyes wide, trying to see her surroundings. There was only the one wide doorway at the far end of the room. No door. The ceiling was a long way above her head. The window behind her was a long, un-curtained rectangle divided into two panes of grimy glass. A half-moon slipped in and out from behind thin streaks of pale grey clouds.

When she heard the chatter of girls coming up the stairs to the dorm she closed her eyes, pretending to be asleep, even when three of them came to her bedside.

42

'New girl.'

The voice was soft. Scottish?

'Looks nice.'

No accent as far as she could make out.

'Pretty.'

Victoria almost giggled. Almost. She changed it into a quiet snore.

'Leave her alone and come to bed.'

That sounded like the older woman, Chrystal. Victoria didn't know how she felt about the air of authority held in the tone of her voice.

In the end, despite the unusual sounds around her and the shadows of the clouds playing on the wall opposite her bed, Victoria slept.

It wasn't until a couple of days later that she discovered her family photos were missing.

Chapter 11: Nelly Shuttleworth

Ashford, morning: Thursday, September 18th

Nelly Shuttleworth yawned and dragged the bed-covers further over her shoulders, reluctant to wake, unwilling to let go of the image that was so often in her dreams these days. The memory of when she was Nelly Bentley. Hair thick, Greta Garbo-style. Nothing like the thin wire wool that covered her scalp these days. Marlene Dietrich eyes. Slender figure, not the mounds of flesh she sometimes didn't recognise as hers. Young. So young. Making the most of life after that first World War.

'Throwing herself at all and sundry,' her mother had called it. And what a time she'd had. Nelly chuckled, which turned into a prolonged phlegmy cough. She pushed herself up off the pillow and thumped her chest. Eventually lying down again she smirked, not chancing another laugh.

Nobody could take that away from her. Prettiest girl on the street, she was known as, before that old bugger forced himself on her and got her pregnant. Then her mother couldn't wait to get her out of the house and married. Nelly refused to give her husband the dignity of his name, even in her thoughts; she hadn't spoken it since the day he'd walked out on her and their sons. Her sons. One dead and one gone God knows where for almost twenty years. One thing for sure, *she* didn't want to know where.

She yawned, pushing her face into the pillow. Downstairs the letterbox clanged as the postman pushed at it. Bet it's only more bloody bills, she thought, scratching the vast expanse of her stomach. It was no use; she couldn't chase after sleep all day. And the sun was so bright through the thin curtains they might as well not be there. She turned onto her back and opened one eye. There was a long strand of a silver cobweb swaying from the light shade to the far corner of the room that hadn't been there yesterday. Or had it? She pursed her lips. So what? Nobody came into her bedroom, only her. Except for young Linda, of course. But she didn't judge her old gran. It gave Nelly a lovely warm feeling when she thought of Linda. Best thing that had happened in her life, finding out all those years ago, that she had a granddaughter. The one and only thing her elder son had produced in his life that was worth anything.

Nelly pulled the covers under her chin and determinedly closed her eyes. She'd just have five more minutes.

Chapter 12: Linda Booth

Ashford, morning: Thursday, September 18th

Linda could hear the snores as soon as she closed the front door on the noise of the street outside. She smiled, picked a brown envelope off the floor, and made her way to the kitchen. She covered the tripe she'd bought for Nelly's tea with a plate and put it on the cold slab in the pantry. Filling the kettle, she switched it on and went to open the back door, at the same time pushing her little finger under the flap of the envelope. Another reminder for the electricity – red this time. And for an amount that it must almost have cost them to send the bills. Bit of an exaggeration, she knew, but it was for a piffling little amount.

She folded it up and shoved it into her pocket before taking off the short blue-checked box jacket of her suit and hanging it on the back of one of the kitchen chairs. She'd call into the Electricity Showroom on her way home and pay the damn thing.

The kettle boiled. She poured her own tea before waiting five minutes to let it brew for Nelly who hated what she called 'piss-shacks': weak tea. Linda watched the sun creep into the yard. Only the old lavvy, now used to store coal, was in the shade. She shivered; the place had always given her the creeps and, for years, she'd wriggled and held onto herself before admitting she needed to wee. Mum sometimes had carried her kicking and screaming, promising to keep the door open. Of course, by then, she'd wet herself anyway.

Carefully holding the tea well away from her white blouse, Linda climbed the narrow dark stairs and went into Nelly's bedroom. Her gran was still asleep, her lips loosely quivering with each snore.

'Gran?' she whispered. Then, louder, 'Gran.'

Nelly squinted. 'Linda, pet.' Her eyes moved to the mug of tea. 'Ah, a welcome sight, that.' She heaved herself up on the pillows and, reaching over, grabbed her teeth off the bedside table and crammed them into her mouth, working them around until they felt settled on her gums. 'That's better.' She took the tea. 'I were up late, last night, watching the telly,' she said, as a way of explaining why she was still in bed. 'I fell asleep watching that daft woman Fanny Craddock bossing her poor husband around and wearing a ball-gown, of all things, while she cooked. Why they call it a dinner party when it's at night, lord only knows.'

45

Linda smiled; her gran had a strong dislike for the television cookery presenter and a soft spot for Johnny, the bullied husband.

Nelly blew noisily on the surface of the tea. 'Now,' she said, 'what's what?'

'Richard's arrived.'

'He's here?' Nelly slurped her tea, winced as it scalded her mouth.

'Yes, last night. Bit of a mix up at the station. William was late meeting him and Richard decided to catch the bus to Ashford. He got in a bit of bother with some bikers. He's okay, though,' Linda added, seeing Nelly's eyes widen in concern. 'I checked him out when I got home from work this morning.

'Poor bairn, as though he hasn't had enough to put up with these last few months.'

'He's fine. Apparently they just chased him and he was helped by some girl who brought him to our house.'

'Your mum didn't tell your Auntie Mary, did she?'

'No. Dad rang them to say Richard had arrived here but I don't think he mentioned anything about him being late. Anyway, Mum wasn't too good, so she didn't speak to Auntie Mary.' Linda felt her face grow hot with embarrassment. She could tell from Nelly's face that she understood what not being 'too good' really meant, and was grateful when she didn't comment.

'Better not to tell Mary.' Nelly nodded her approval. 'You know how she is about those two.'

'She's always worried about them, Gran.'

'Only because of Peter. Some folks never let the past stay where it should ... in the past.'

'I know.' Linda couldn't help thinking about her Uncle Patrick and his nasty jibes. She often wondered how Jackie was such a lovely person with him as a father. 'Anyway *Richard's* okay.'

Nelly didn't miss the emphasis. Her fingers clenched the handle of the cup. 'What's that mean, love? *Richard's* okay? What else is wrong? Mary—?'

'Is fine.' Linda knew her gran thought the world of her aunt.

In the same way that, without anything being said, she'd always understood that Nelly had no time for her own mother. 'It's Victoria.'

Nelly heaved a sigh that shook the whole of her unfettered bosom. 'Much as I love both Mary's kids, that girl will be the death of us all. What's she done this time?'

'Run away.'

'My God. Where to?' Nelly's mouth dropped open, her teeth shifted on her gums. She pushed them back with her thumb.

'They don't know. Auntie Mary told Dad and Richard on the phone last night.'

Nelly plucked at the eiderdown, her fingers trembling. 'Her mother must be going mad with worry. Oh, poor Mary!'

'Don't upset yourself, Gran.' Linda put her drink down and, kneeling by the side of the bed, folded the old woman's hand in hers. 'They found a note yesterday morning, after they'd seen Richard off on the train. Anyway, she – *they* are eighteen now. And I'm sure Victoria is more than capable of looking after herself.'

'But where will she have gone?'

'She didn't say. With friends perhaps.' Linda saw the way Nelly's breathing quickened, heard the mucus rattling in her chest. There was a tinge of blue around her lips. 'But I'm sure she'll be fine, Gran. There's nothing we can do anyway. And I bet she'll be back as soon as she runs out of money, knowing Victoria.' She forced a smile, patted Nelly's hand. 'Lie still for a bit. I'll go and see if the pot's still warm.'

Downstairs, she found Nelly's angina tablets and quickly poured another cup of tea before hurrying back upstairs. 'Here we are.'

'I don't fancy another drink now, love. Sorry.'

'That's fine. I'll just put it here until I go down.' She sat next to the bed again. The colour in her grandmother's face had returned to normal and she relaxed.

'And I don't need those, either. Bloody tablets.' Nelly settled back on her pillow. She clasped her hands over her stomach, rolling her thumbs around one another. 'I've 'ad a thought. I know why Victoria's done this. Same old thing; she's thinking Richard's getting all the attention.' She's pulled some stunt every time he's had one of his operations. Now what with this last one in July and him going for this special university, she'll be jealous.'

'You could be right.' Linda wouldn't put it past her cousin. It wouldn't be the first time she'd pulled a stunt to get noticed. Although not one as drastic as this.

Clearly determined to prove she was calm, Nelly said, 'So, you'll let me know when she turns up?'

'I will.' Linda kept up the pretence.

'Right. Where's me glasses?' Nelly half-rolled onto her side and fumbled around until she found them and squinted at the clock on the table at the side of her bed. 'Gawd, quarter to twelve and me still in me pit. I must shift meself. Have you been to bed at all?'

'No. I didn't want to waste a nice day like this. I can catch up with my sleep tonight. I'm off until tomorrow night, now.'

'What're you going to do with the rest of your day then, pet?'

'Nothing much. I was going to go into Manchester with Martin but I can't face it.'

'Why?'

'I think Martin wants to get engaged.'

Nelly gave a mock shiver. 'I were married with two kids at your age.' The tone of her words spoke for themselves. 'Biggest mistake of my life,' she said. 'Don't do the same thing, pet.'

'I shan't.'

'You think on; live your life first before you saddle yerself with a bloke. They're worse than any kids yer can 'ave. Well, 'appen. Depends on the kids I s'pose.'

Linda saw the sadness flicker in Nelly's eye. 'You okay, Gran?'

'What?' Nelly stared blankly at her. 'Oh, yes, love.' She gave Linda a smile that didn't quite reach her eyes. 'Just old ghosts.'

Chapter 13: Jacqueline Howarth & Linda Booth

Bradlow: Thursday, September 18th

'Hey, Lin.' Waiting until a bus passed, Jackie Howarth quickly crossed Shaw Street to give her cousin a hug. 'It's been ages…'

'I know. Sorry. Had a load of overtime this month.'

'You look tired out.' Jackie lifted her chin. Questioning.

'Lack of sleep. I've been on nights. Always throws me.'

'Tell me about it. Who'd be a policewoman? We've been run off our feet lately – a spate of burglaries. Been twice this last week on a twenty-four hour look-out shift.'

They smiled in sympathy with one another.

'Anyway, I'm off today. It's great we've got a bit of sun.' Linda hitched her white Naugahyde bag further on to her shoulder and looked up at the sky. The light breeze wasn't enough to move the few hazy clouds scattered against the blue. 'I've been to see Gran. And it's such a nice day I thought I'd walk home.'

'She okay?'

'Same as always.'

'You sound worried?'

'No… Well, yes. I suppose I am. She has a chesty cough. And at her age… I worry.'

'She'll be fine; she's as strong as an ox. And you're a born worrier.' Jackie gave Linda's arm an affectionate shake. 'I love Nelly; she's brilliant for her age. Last time I called in to see her I had trouble stopping her putting brandy in my tea.'

It made Linda smile. 'She does love her drop of brandy.'

'You can say that again.' Jackie kept hold of her cousin's arm. 'Listen, fancy a coffee?' Linda was obviously mithered to death about something and it wasn't just about Nelly. Auntie Ellen? Jackie wouldn't put it past her aunt to be the cause of her cousin's worry. Linda was bottling something up, just as she'd always done. But one way or the other Jackie would get it out

49

of her, would try to help. Wasn't that what they'd always done for one another?

She glanced along the row of shops and cafes on Shaw Street. 'There's that new place, the Cottage, just down the road? Next to the Spar?'

'"So near, so Spar," as Gran always says.'

Jackie groaned. 'That old chestnut.' She linked arms with her cousin and looked her up and down. 'Nice suit by the way. Blue always suits you – shows your eyes up. Off out somewhere?' She tugged at Linda and they began to walk slowly along the street.

'Was,' Linda said, 'I was going to Manchester to meet Martin but I've changed my mind. I really should go home. Things are a bit difficult there. Mum—'

'I know. I've just been to Henshaw Street to check on things.'

Linda grimaced.

'Sorry, Lin, it's my job. My sergeant told me to call in and have another word with your mum.' Jackie was careful not to say 'warning' which was what her sergeant had said. And she resisted the temptation to say how embarrassing it was to find her aunt in custody again. 'She's fine; anyway, she'd just got up. Your dad was going into the shop for a couple of hours. Richard's keeping an eye on her until he gets back. It was good to see him again.' Jacqueline had a fondness for her young cousin. Unlike his sister, Richard was always easy to chat to. 'I hope he gets into the Manchester uni, it'll be great to have him around.'

They stopped to look into the window of Madam Barbara's Boutique. 'That style went out in the fifties.' Linda pointed at a blue polka-dot flared dress with a large bow-tie collar.

'Watch it, she's hovering behind that coat,' Jackie mumbled, her head down. 'Bet she can lip read.'

'We'll have to get our Richard to check.' Linda smiled, then frowned. 'Did he tell you about those idiots chasing him, yesterday? When he got off the train?'

'Eventually. I mean, your dad told me first. Took me a while

50

to get the details out of Richard and he won't let me report it. Mind you…' Jackie tightened her lips, 'I do have an idea who they might be. Might pass on a few names.'

'As long as Richard doesn't find out – you know how he hates bother.'

'He won't,' Jackie said. She hadn't been a policewoman for the last six years without knowing how to make discreet enquiries.

They moved away from the clothes shop.

'He told you about Victoria running away from home as well?'

'He did.' Jackie flipped a dismissive hand. 'She's always been a drama queen. It'll be because he's been getting attention, first that operation in summer and then coming for his interview in that university in Manchester.'

'Gran said that as well.' Linda hesitated. 'Auntie Jean doesn't know about it yet.'

'No doubt she'll have something to say about it when she does find out. My mother will blame Auntie Mary; she's always said she's too soft on the twins.'

'And my mother says yours has always been too strict … with you, anyway.'

So, that'll be both me and Victoria turned out wrong, according to Mother's opinion, Jackie thought.

'Anyway…' Linda paused again for effect. 'Did he tell you he'd met a girl?' She grinned, pleased she could pass on a bit of nice family gossip.

'What, in Wales?'

'No, here. In Bradlow. Yesterday. Apparently she rescued him. Picked him up in her Mini when she saw what was going on and took him to our house. Dad says she's really something and Richard's told him they're going to see one another again.'

'Fast worker, our little cousin, eh?' Jackie gently punched Linda's arm.

'And here's us, always thinking he's so shy.'

They shared the laugh. It's as though we've always presumed

he would never have a girlfriend just because he has to wear those horrible hearing-aids, Linda thought. But what do we know? He's a good-looking lad; he might have had loads of girls chasing him in Wales.

'He did tell me he lost his stuff when he was being chased, though.' Jackie scowled. 'And he said Uncle Ted's lent him money to get a new suit and what-have-you for his interview. You're so lucky; you do know that, don't you? Your dad's a lovely man.'

Unlike yours, Linda thought. 'I know. But I really should get back, if Richard wants to go shopping.'

'No.' Jackie settled her arm further into Linda's and walked faster, taking her cousin with her. 'I mean, like I said, your dad was only going to the bakery for a bit. He'll be back by now, so no need to rush home. And you're not going to Manchester, so time for a coffee, I think. One of my mates from work says it's a decent cup at that place, and there's a jukebox. Should check it out, huh?' She watched Linda struggling to make a decision as they stopped opposite the Spar shop. 'Twenty more minutes won't hurt,' she cajoled.

'Okay then. Might grab a butty as well, it's past dinner time.'

'Great.' Jackie grinned; if Linda was eating it gave her an excuse to eat. She was always hungry. 'Might force something down as well, then.'

'Force?' Linda laughed. 'When have you ever had to force food down? You've got the appetite of a horse.'

'Cheeky!' Jackie pulled in her stomach. 'I might have you know these jeans are a size twelve.' She sniffed. 'Mind you, they are getting a bit tight. And I have had trouble fastening the buttons on the jacket of my uniform lately.'

'Oh, stop worrying. You're looking great. And I'm sure Nicki loves you, whatever size you are.'

'She does.' Jackie smirked. 'She says more to get hold—'

'Enough!' Linda put her hand over Jackie's mouth for a moment. Jackie laughed through Linda's fingers.

'Okay.' Linda said, 'Come on.' They waited for a lorry to pass before running across the road. 'But remind me to call in at the Electricity Showroom afterwards, will you? I need to pay Gran's bill before she gets cut off. At least that'll be one worry out of the way.'

One worry? Jackie thought. She pushed open the orange door of the café.

Jackie wove her way across the café, carrying two mugs of coffee and a menu, to the table by the window where Linda was sitting. 'I've put a couple of records on.' She jerked her head backwards towards the jukebox. She unzipped her short leather jacket and sat down. 'I need this.' She touched the mug with her finger. 'I thought I might as well go to see Mother now I'm in the area. Duty visit.'

'Everything all right?'

Jackie pulled a face. 'Jack saw me and Nicki in Yates' Wine Lodge a couple of days ago. I think it's time I bit the bullet and told Mother about us before he does. That's if he hasn't already.'

'Would he?'

'Jack? You must be joking, Lin.' Jackie clenched her fists on the table. 'I mean, he's the biggest shit-stirrer in the world. If he hasn't, I bet he's enjoying dropping hints about it all over the place so it gets back to them eventually.'

The first few notes of 'The Carnival Is Over' were almost inaudible below the buzz of chatter from the other customers until the vocals started.

'You and Judith Durham,' Linda laughed.

'Love her.' Jackie grinned, running her fingers through her short curly hair. 'Who couldn't?'

'So that's my news, such as it is,' she said, settling back in her chair. 'What about you? What's mithering you?'

Linda blew at the froth on the surface of her coffee. 'It's Martin. I've put off going to meet him today because I think he's going to push for us to get engaged, again.'

'And you don't want to.' It was as much a statement as a question. They'd discussed this often enough.

'I'm not ready.' Would she ever be? The thought took Linda by surprise.

'And anyway you've realised he's a tight-arse?'

'Jackie!'

'Sorry.' Jackie tipped the chair back on two legs and rocked slightly. 'I mean, he's your choice and he *is* a nice bloke, Linda, but you have to admit he is a bit tight with his money…'

'Suppose. But it's not that. I just don't want to get married. Not yet anyway. I want to see how far I can get with my job … have a career.'

'So tell him.' The chair landed with a thump on the floor as Jackie leant forward, grabbing hold of Linda's hands.

'How can I, Jackie?' Her voice came out husky and she cleared her throat. 'We've been going out for four years. I've been sleeping with him for the last three. He expects us to get married and I don't want to hurt his feelings.' Sudden guilty tears stung her eyes.

Jackie gave her a few moments. She blew her cheeks out, making a popping noise with her lips. 'Can I ask you something?'

'Okay.'

'Are you saying you don't want to go out with him any more?'

'No.' Linda looked up, her eyes wide with shock that her supressed thought was being voiced. 'I don't know… I still love him.' She stared at Jackie. Who was she trying to persuade? What a mess everything was.

Chapter 14: Jacqueline Howarth

Ashford, afternoon: Thursday, September 18th

Jackie stopped, the wooden gate smooth under her hand, and stared up at the house she'd been brought up in. As usual the green paintwork on the downstairs bay window-frames and door was immaculate. The brass letterbox glinted in the sun. A jittery feeling rose in her throat; she felt breathless. She reached over and clicked open the latch.

She hoped Jack wasn't at home. There was no doubt he'd seen her and Nicki in the Wine Lodge. Well, hopefully she'd be able to beat him at his own game; she'd tell her mother first. With a bit of luck her father would be out as usual.

No such luck, she thought when she walked into the living room; Jack and he were on the settee in front of the television. Her mother was in her chair, knitting.

'Hi,' Jackie said.

'Shut up.' Jack glared round at her before turning his attention back to the screen.

Her father didn't speak.

Her mother nodded warningly towards the television and mouthed, 'Ireland.'

Jackie waited a moment and then went through the dining-room to the kitchen and, finding a glass, filled it with water, listening to the voice of the newscaster as she drank.

'The August riots were the most sustained violence that Northern Ireland has seen since the early nineteen-twenties. Both Catholic and Protestant families were forced to flee their homes and The Royal Regiment of Wales is still in the Falls/Shankill area in a limited operation to restore law and order...'

Jackie sat at the dining room table watching her family through the door. Her father slumped, his belly straining the buttons of his shirt, his arm across Jack's shoulder, still staring at the television. Her mother had dropped her knitting needles onto her lap, her hand to her throat.

'So that's it then,' she said, turning to look at Jackie. 'You know what this means?'

'Shut up.' Patrick and Jack spoke simultaneously. Patrick glowered at his wife.

55

'The Prime Minister of the Irish Republic, Jack Lynch, has called for Anglo-Irish talks on the future of Northern Ireland. But this is deemed unnecessary by the Northern Ireland Prime Minister, James Chichester-Clark, who has stated in the House of Commons that the riots are not the agitation of a minority seeking by lawful means the assertion of political rights. He believes it is the conspiracy of forces seeking to overthrow a government democratically elected by a large majority.

'Further troops will be deployed there in the next week.'

'I knew it,' her mother said, 'I knew it.'

'That's it, then.' Jack stood up, rubbing his hands together. 'That's us, at long last. I'll give my mate, Charlie Pearson, a call to see when he's going back to barracks.'

'You sound as though you want to go,' Jackie said, putting the glass down and going to stand by the living room door.

'Course I do … I'll sort those bastards out—'

'There are a lot of decent people over there.'

'Well, Charlie says if they're not bloody terrorists they're bloody weird. And he should know, he's been over there twice.'

'And he's an expert? A psychiatrist? Sounds to me like he's the weirdo.'

'Yeah, well, you should know.' He smirked. 'Shouldn't you, sis?'

'What's that supposed to mean?' Anger boiled up inside Jackie and she felt like slapping him.

'You know…'

'No I don't.'

'Now, now, you two, don't start. Don't start.' Her mother pushed herself out of the chair with a groan. 'My knees are killing me today.' She hobbled towards the door. 'I'll put a brew on.' As she passed Jackie she said, 'Our Jack's going to that godforsaken place, so don't start one of your arguments at a time like this.'

'I'm starting nothing; I just want to know what he means.' It was now or never – she had to tell her parents about Nicki, it wasn't as though she was ashamed. Even so, she was relieved when her father spoke.

'I've had enough of this.' He swept his hair over his head with his fingers, went into the hall and took his overcoat and trilby off the stand. 'I'm going for a pint. Coming, son?'

'Yeah, the air in here suddenly feels all *queer*.' Jack sniggered as he followed his father.

'You little shit,' Jackie hissed. That was it; she knew he wouldn't be able to resist telling her parents. She would have to do it now. At least there was only her mother to face first.

She went into the kitchen. 'You go and sit down, Mum, I'll finish making the tea.' Anything to make this easier, Jackie thought.

Jackie slowly stirred two sugars into her mother's tea and put the spoon into the sink, thinking about how to approach the subject of her and Nicki. She picked up the spoon and rinsed it under the tap, dried it, put it into the cutlery drawer. Everything had its place in the kitchen. Except for a tray of scones covered by a tea towel, there was nothing on the worktops, no clutter anywhere. Her mother had always been house-proud; Jackie couldn't remember her without either a duster or a dishcloth in her hand or her apron pocket. She even had a saying about it: something about 'work in the morning, play in the afternoon.' Not that Jackie could remember much playing here, only at Linda's house.

She stared out of the window; the sun was still quite high, the trees at the end of the garden barely shifted in the wind. Yellow and orange marigolds edged the flowerbeds at either side of the path; behind them white and soft orange dahlias were staked and fastened upright. Jackie sighed; even the bloody flowers had to measure up to her mother's idea of order and neatness. 'Everything in its place and a place for everything'; the words were suddenly there in her mind, another of her mother's sayings. Where would she fit in after this? With her mother's narrow outlook on life how the hell would she ever accept the way she and Nicki were living?

Jackie knew she was putting off going back into the living room. Coward, she thought, bloody coward. Standing upright she pulled her shoulders back and picked up the tea. The cups rattled in their saucers.

Jean had taken up her knitting again. 'Thanks,' she said when Jackie pulled out one of the nest of tables and put both teas on it. 'I made some scones, if you want one?'

'No, I'm okay, thanks, Mum.' Jackie knelt on the floor by her mother's chair.

'Not like you to turn down a scone, Jacqueline.' Jean put her knitting down. 'Not like you, at all. Aren't you feeling well?'

'I'm fine.' Where to start? Jackie took the cup of the saucer and held it to her lips. Her hand was shaking.

'Something on your mind, then? I can always tell. Come on, what is it? What is it?'

For a moment Jackie thought of telling her mother about Victoria running away. The predictions of the trouble that her cousin would get herself into would occupy her mother for days.

Coward, she berated herself. Coward. 'It's about me and Nicki—'

'Nice girl,' Jean interrupted and took up her knitting again. 'Do you know, love, I think I'll have a scone, if you don't mind buttering one for me?'

Jackie clenched her jaw. 'Just the one?'

'Oh, yes, got to watch my waistline.' Jean patted her ample midriff.

In the kitchen Jackie took one of the scones off the baking tray and quickly cut and buttered it. Usually she couldn't resist the smell of fresh baking but today it turned her stomach.

'Here.' She handed the plate to her mother. Taking in a deep breath, she started again. 'It's about me and Nicki—'

'You haven't fallen out, have you?' The words were muffled as

Jean chewed on the scone. 'She's been such a good friend to you. I hope you haven't fallen out?'

'That's just it, Mum,' Jackie blurted, 'she is a good friend... In fact, she's more than a friend ... she's my girlfriend.' She watched as her mother slowly stopped chewing.

Jean swallowed, her face reddening. Then she coughed, spluttered out crumbs. Dabbing her mouth with her handkerchief she reached for her cup and gulped at the tea. 'What exactly do you mean?' she asked, when she could speak.

Jackie moved to the settee opposite her mother and clasped her hands. This was going to be as bad as she thought it would be. She noticed her knuckles were white and loosened her fingers. 'I mean,' she gave each word emphasis, 'Nicki and me ... we're not just friends ... we're lovers.'

There was a long dragging pause. Then: 'No.' Jean clashed the cup into the saucer, pushed herself from her chair. She fluttered her hands, rejecting Jackie's words. 'No. Don't tell me. I don't want to know. What you're saying ... what you're saying ... it's disgusting. Disgusting.' She left the room, bumping into the door-frame as she went.

Jackie waited, wondering what to do. Unable to keep still, she stood up, massaging the back of one hand, listening for any sound from the kitchen. Eventually, hearing nothing she followed her mother.

Jean was watching the next-door neighbour taking in her washing. 'That woman has never spoken to me, you know,' she said. 'Not once. She doesn't even acknowledge I'm on the other side of the fence when I'm in the garden.' Her tone was bitter. 'I asked your father years ago to put a higher one up but he never did. Too much like hard work, I suppose. Too much like hard work.'

'Mum.' Jackie touched her back.

'No.' Jean moved away into the dining room. 'No.' She stood in front of the mirror over the sideboard and tugged at a curl by her temple. 'See? More grey hairs? I need a visit to the hairdressers, I think.'

'Mum—'

'No.' Jean swung around, faced Jackie. 'I don't want to hear any more of that talk. Ever.'

Jackie kept steady eye-contact with her mother. 'I think it's a bit late for that. Jack knows.'

'Your brother knows? How can he?' Jean's mouth opened, closed and opened again. 'How?' Holding on to the table and the backs of the chairs as though she would otherwise fall, she walked towards Jackie.

'Half-brother.' Jackie couldn't stop herself. 'Jack is only my half-brother and he's always resented me.' Even though, as a child, she'd adored him. 'You know that.' The way Jean idolised Jack, she sometimes thought her mother didn't remember that he wasn't her natural son: that she'd been forced to take on the child of one of her husband's many affairs. 'He knows because he saw me and Nicki together.'

She waited but Jean ignored Jackie's last words. 'He wouldn't think anything of that.' Jean pushed her lips out. 'He knows … thinks you're just flatmates.'

'We were holding hands.' They'd actually been kissing, believing they wouldn't be seen in the small booth concealed from the bar, celebrating Nicki's promotion to legal administrator at the solicitors' firm where she worked.

Jean flinched and closed her eyes. 'You mustn't tell your father. He must never know anything about … what you've just said.'

'That I'm a lesbian, Mother?'

'Don't use such disgusting words.' Jean slapped Jackie, hard, across the face. Breathing heavily she said, 'He mustn't ever find out… he must never find out what you are.' Her lip curled. 'It's been bad enough with you going into the police force. You haven't a clue what I've had to put up with from him about that. But this…'

Jackie held her cheek. 'I'm a lesbian, Mother. Jack knows. And, before long, so will Dad. Jack won't be able to resist telling him. And there's nothing you – or I – can do about it.'

Chapter 15: Mary & Peter Schormann

Llamroth, morning: Friday, September 19th

'There has to be something to tell us where she's gone.' Mary pulled open the last drawer of Victoria's desk and emptied it on the bed. 'Something. A letter, a photo of somewhere, someone. Something….' She ended on a wail, sweeping the pile of papers, files, drawings onto the floor.

Downstairs, Gelert barked.

'Mary.' Peter stopped her, pulled her into his embrace. 'Look at this room. See what you have done. And yet we have found nothing. Victoria has made sure we do not know where she has gone.'

'Why? Why?' She leaned back to gaze into his face, searching for an answer. 'Have we been such dreadful parents…? So awful she's had to escape from us?'

'No, *meine Liebe*. But she has always been the strongest, the most determined.'

'Spoiled, you mean.' Mary flung herself out of his arms and sat on the bed, scattering the remains of the papers.

'*Nein*. No. You don't mean that, Mary.' Peter sat down alongside her, holding her hand. 'Victoria has her own mind.'

'We have to find out… We have to know she is safe.' Mary's face was blotched and puffy; she began to shake, the ashy taste of fear in her mouth. 'We have to find her.'

'She doesn't want us to find her, *Liebling*.'

'I don't care,' Mary said. 'She's too young to be out there on her own. Anything could happen to her.' She pulled away from him, her eyes flitting over the rest of the room, frantic to find something, anything, that would tell her where her daughter had gone. 'There must be something.' A thought crossed her mind. She jumped up, excited, pleased that she knew what to do. 'We can go to her college, find out who she's friends with there. See if they know anything.'

'And then what? What can we do?'

'We can bring her home.' She didn't understand his reticence. What was wrong with him?

Peter shook his head. 'No. She is not a child, Mary.'

'She is. She's our child.'

Peter voiced his oldest fear. 'Perhaps that is the problem, *Liebling*. Perhaps that has always been the problem.'

So that was it. 'No, I won't have you saying that.' Mary held him to her; she'd always known the fear he held for his children, for her, just because of his nationality. But she couldn't stand the thought of him mithering. That heart attack two years ago might only have been a slight one, but it was a warning, and she'd tried so hard since then to be the barrier between him and the worries. 'You have been – you *are* – a good father.'

'Still … it has not been easy for them.'

The minutes ticked by in the silence that followed.

In the end Peter sighed. 'We can only wait, *Liebling*. Perhaps, soon, she will let us know where she is.'

Chapter 16: Richard Schormann & Karen Worth

Ashford, evening: Friday, September 19th

Richard was furious with Victoria for driving Mum and Dad mad. She always caused trouble when things weren't going her way, kicking against everything, taking anyone and everyone on just for the fun of it: at home, in school. *Mae hi'n dwp*. Stupid. Always jealous of him. And she didn't need to be, she was welcome to all the attention – leave him out of it.

Folding down his shirt collar and knotting the new narrow blue tie, Richard grimaced at himself in the wardrobe mirror.

The last few weeks had been no different. She'd been impossible to live with; if she wasn't sulking, she'd been trying to pick a fight with him. It was one reason he'd come up to Ashford so many days before his interview.

But not the only reason. And he felt guilty. He couldn't stand the tension, the unspoken questions, the inability of his father to understand why he didn't want to go to Pont-y-Haven. Dad didn't realise that he wanted – needed to train at a proper university hospital; the one in Manchester was new, the first of its kind and he had to go there. If they'd have him. What he'd do afterwards, he hadn't decided. And he knew his father wouldn't understand why he didn't want to join the Llamroth practice when he did qualify. If asked, he doubted that he could have answered the questions anyway. Except that he needed to make his own way in life. He didn't want to hide behind his father: to be safe, secure in the knowledge that there'd always be a job for him. He had to prove his deafness wouldn't hold him back in whatever he wanted to do.

Still, all the justifications didn't make him feel better right at this moment. Any more than transferring his anger from himself to Victoria helped.

Where the hell was she? Richard shrugged on his jacket and looked around the bedroom, checked he had his wallet.

'Next on Radio Luxembourg, a track from the brand new album, 'Play On' from Fleetwood Mac, released only today. But first a word from Horace Batchelor ...'

He peered through the net curtains. No sign of Karen yet. He should really have gone back home; he could have checked with all Vicky's mates. Mum and Dad wouldn't know everybody she mixed with in college.

'That's K- E –Y- N- S –H-A- M, Keynsham, Bristol. I'll spell that again ...'

'T-H-A-T,' Richard muttered, grinning as he switched the radio off and picked up his boots. 'Stupid bloody ad.' Frowning again, he remembered his mum's last words when he'd spoken to her earlier. And how distraught she'd sounded.

Calling Richard downstairs, Uncle Ted had shaken his head and patted him on the shoulder. 'She sounds a bit worked up,' he'd mouthed. And he wasn't joking.

63

'Nobody has seen her anywhere, Richard. Your father and I are beginning to think she's not around here any-more.' His mother's voice was shrill. 'I wondered if she'd met someone. You don't know if she'd met anybody, do you?' she repeated. 'Somebody from away?'

'No, Mum, I don't. I would have told you by now, isn't it.'

There was a muffled crackling on the phone, some hushed whispers. Richard strove to hear. The next voice he heard was his father's.

'Sorry, Richard, I asked that your mother would not telephone you before your interview but she is very worried…'

'I know, Dad. But like I said to Mum, I would have told you if I'd known anything.'

'I know.'

There was a pause. Richard concentrated on listening.

'Good luck for Monday.' His father said, eventually.

'Thanks.' It didn't help the guilt he felt to hear the earnestness in the words.

Richard heard the toot of a horn. Karen. He closed the bedroom door and dashed down the stairs.

His aunt and uncle were in the living-room, listening to the calm tones of a presenter on the radio. At least Uncle Ted was.

Even so, he glanced at Richard. 'You all right, after your mum's call?'

'Yeah, thanks.' No point in saying anything else.

'Your dad?'

'Yeah, he sounded A1.'

Ellen shifted restlessly in her chair and twisted around to face Richard.

'We're going to watch that new programme on the telly. What's it called again, Ted?'

'I've got to go. Karen's here.' Richard tapped his new parka coat pocket. 'I've got my key.'

'What's it called, Ted?'

His aunt was tetchy again. Richard felt sorry for his uncle. She needed help for her drinking but, like his mum said, she wouldn't admit she had a problem. Was it selfish to hope she didn't kick off the night before his interview? He'd feel obliged to help Linda and her dad.

'Right, lad.' Ted nodded. He gave a small sigh and rustled through the *Radio Times,* which was resting on his knees. 'Um, *Randall and Hopkirk Deceased,* it says here. Something about 'em being private detectives but one of 'em is dead. Rum title. Even more rum idea, if you ask me.'

'I didn't.' Ellen looked irritated. 'How long is this on for?'

'*Dwi'n mynd nawr.* Going now.' Richard hovered in the doorway. 'Bye then.'

Only Ted answered. 'Bye, son.' He lifted his chin at Richard and smiled before peering over his reading-glasses at his wife. 'It's nearly finished. I told you I wanted to listen to this. It's an interview with John Spencer. He's the World Snooker Champion—'

'I want the telly on, I…'

Their voices were muted as Richard quietly closed the living room door. He was fond of both of them but his aunt sometimes drove him round the bend.

'Pictures?' he asked Karen, folding himself into the passenger seat. 'There's a new film just out showing at the Apollo in Manchester. *The Italian Job.* William says it's brilliant.'

'Okay.' Karen glanced in the mirror and put the car into gear. 'Sorry, I was just going to come in,' she said. 'I hope they didn't think me rude not doing.'

'I don't think they even noticed.'

'Any news on your sister?'

'Nope.' Richard put his arm along the back of her seat and studied her. She was gorgeous. He pushed the worry and the guilt to the back of his mind. 'Let's go.'

Chapter 17: Linda Booth

Ashford, evening: Saturday, September 20th

'It's usual to stay in for ten days after you've given birth.' Linda helped Harriet Worth into the armchair by the side of the bed. 'You only had the baby last Tuesday. You'll have to tell your husband you won't be going out yet.' She looked at the clock on the wall, almost quarter to seven. 'He'll be here soon.' If he didn't push his way in before visiting time. 'Tell him then.'

'He gets a bit ... you know ... impatient.' The woman winced as she settled in the chair.

That wasn't how Linda would describe the man. But she kept her mouth closed and shook the pillow into the case with more vigour than she would normally have done before sliding it behind Harriet's back.

'He just wants me home.' Harriet settled back with a faint sigh, her arm resting on the small cot next to her, her fingers stroking the baby's hand.

So he can control you, Linda thought. She straightened up. 'You need to stay in until we're sure you're going to be well enough to manage. It's hard work to cope with a young baby but—'

'But worse when you're an older mum?' Harriet Worth smiled, wryly.

'I was going to say, when you're not on top form.' Linda ran her hand over the sheet before lifting up the corners of the mattress to fold it in. 'You had a hard birth with this little one.' She unfolded a white open-textured blanket onto the bed. 'Give yourself a chance to rest. It'll be all go once you're home.'

'I've got my daughter to help me. She's seventeen and a sensible girl.'

'Well, that's good; you'll need all the help you can get. But, like I said, I'm sure your husband can manage for a few more days—'

'And what would you know about that?'

Linda's stomach heaved. She didn't understand why this man had such an effect on her; in her job she'd come across some rough types before. But there was something about him that made her skin crawl. Actually made her afraid, she admitted to herself. She forced herself to carry on making up the bed, not even looking at George Worth when he came to stand close behind her.

'I said what do you know about it?'

She moved sideways to get away from him, pretending to smooth the folded down sheet. 'I was only saying—'

'I heard.'

Linda forced herself to look at him. His grey eyes were bloodshot but it was the way he'd narrowed them that made her swallow hard before saying, 'Your wife needs all the rest she can get.'

'Well, missy, I suggest you keep your neb out of our business.' He stroked the side of his nose with his forefinger.

There was movement behind him and a young girl appeared. She glanced apologetically at Linda before leaning towards Harriet and kissing the top of her head. 'Mum,' she murmured, 'how are you feeling?'

'Karen.' Harriet reached up to touch her cheek. 'I'm fine, dear.' But she kept her eyes on her husband. 'George? Don't. Please. The nurse was only trying to help. It's her job.'

'It's her job to know her place and stop pokin' her soddin' nose in where it's not wanted.' He kept his eyes on Linda. 'Trying to tell me what to soddin' do.'

'I wasn't.' Linda kept her voice level even though she knew her hands were trembling. She clasped them behind her back. 'If you'll let me pass?'

He stayed in her way. 'I'm not stopping you!' But still he didn't move.

She had to shuffle past him; the skin on her arm where it touched his seemed to tighten. Angry with herself, she closed the door with a firm click and stood next to it, breathing deeply. She wouldn't cry, she told herself, she wouldn't, aware of her heartbeat thudding in her ears. Her nails dug into the palms of her hands. The coolness of the wall eventually steadied her.

'Nurse?' The ward sister called to her from the nurses' station. 'Everything all right?'

'Yes, Sister.' What could she say? Instinctively she knew it would be Mrs Worth who'd bear the brunt of any fuss Linda made about her husband's brutish behaviour. Yet she almost succumbed to tears at the concern in Sister Daniels' voice. Linda pushed herself upright and crossed the main ward, now filled with the babble of visitors. All ten beds had two visitors each, cooing over the babies and chatting excitedly to the mothers, all tucked tightly under taut covers. Looking over the top of the Sister's head and blinking, Linda said, brightly, 'I'll go for my break now, if you don't mind?'

Sister Lawson checked her watch. 'Yes, all right. Don't be late back. The meds will need to be sorted and as soon as visiting is over, I want the babies put in the nursery.' She bent her head over some papers on the desk. 'I want the ward settled down for the night earlier tonight. It was chaos until after ten last night.'

'Yes, Sister.' Glad to be able to escape, a few words were all Linda could manage. 'Thank you, Sister.'

The rest-room was empty. She poured herself a strong cup of tea from the large teapot and used the remains of the milk from a bottle in cold water in the sink. The tea was stewed but still quite warm. She sank into the sagging armchair by the window, rested her head against the back and gazed through the glass. It was windy; the sky had that luminous grey quality of a chilly evening and the branches of the beech trees swung away from the shelter of the hospital.

A bluebottle hit one of the panes, crawled around the frame, silent and then frantically buzzing again and again. It was like the nightmare. Just when she thought it had stopped it started all over again. She stood and pulled up the sash window and waited until the bluebottle crawled over the sill and disappeared. If only the bad dream would do the same. She held on to the beige curtains cursing the man who somehow had caused the nightmares to return. She'd dealt with bullying husbands before in her job. For God's sake, she'd even faced up to Uncle Patrick, when he was in one of his rages that always seemed to come from nowhere. She wasn't soft. So what was it about Harriet Worth's husband that upset her so much?

The door opened. Linda turned with a start. Two junior nurses stopped at the sight of her, their laughing trailing away. 'Sorry, Nurse Booth.'

'No worries, girls, I was just leaving.' Linda smiled at them. She rinsed her cup and hurried back to the ward with only a minute before her official break ended.

In the drug-storage room she kept herself busy by preparing the trolley for the evening round of medication. She knew she was really only waiting for the bell to mark the end of visiting-time.

When it sounded she breathed a sigh of relief. She pushed the door almost closed so that she wasn't visible to the stream of visitors leaving the ward.

But she couldn't mistake the loud voice. Once George Worth had passed the room she opened the door and watched him leave. He had his arm around the girl's waist and was chatting to another man.

Just before they left the ward, Linda heard him say, 'Look at me, walking out of here with such a pretty young lady.'

She saw him look down at his stepdaughter. 'Now, how about I get you some fish and chips?' The girl shook her head as she quickened her pace and, shoulders stooped, pushed past the people in front of her.

As though she couldn't wait to get away from him, Linda thought.

All at once the fear took over. She couldn't feel her body, only the beating of her heart. Her breathing quickened and her legs buckled. She flailed her arm behind her, feeling for a solid surface to hold on to. Not able to find one – she slumped to the floor; her head drooped between her knees.

The years that had piled one on top of the last, hiding the memory, were swept away.

It couldn't be. Could it…?

Chapter 18: Linda Booth & Nelly Shuttleworth

Ashford, morning: Sunday, September 21st

On impulse Linda stayed on the bus until it reached the top of Barnes Street.

Hearing George Worth's words, as he had left the ward, had brought the bitter sourness to her throat. She'd pushed through the flood of people to get to the lavatory, gagging on the vomit, and dropped to her knees over the bowl in the first cubicle, retching.

The horror stayed with her throughout the night shift. *Don't think about it*, she'd thought, changing bloodied sheets for a new mother. *Don't think about it,* giving a night feed to a crying new born. *Don't think about it*, handing out painkillers and filling out reports. But it had been no use. The memories of a wet stinking tunnel, a cold damp stone floor, the smell of a dirty hand over her mouth, a man coughing and wheezing, the rasp of a rusty bolt, wouldn't go away. And then the sour smell of urine. Her urine. And the pain as her head hit the ground. The shock. The panic of seeing only blackness.

She'd tried to empty her thoughts but the terror clung obstinately.

'This is a surprise, pet. I thought you said you were on nights.' Linda heard the cautious worry in Nelly's voice, which changed to a forced jollity. 'Owt to do with that daft cousin of yours, our Victoria?'

'No, Gran. No news on that score.' Linda sat on the small footstool near Nelly. It looked as if the old woman had slept in the chair; she was fully dressed and her clothes were rumpled. 'Have you been here all night?' She picked up Nelly's glasses off the carpet and handed them to her.

Nelly pushed them on, adjusted them onto the bridge of her nose. 'Never mind me. Shouldn't yer be tucked up in bed yerself?' She put a gentle hand on Linda's head.

The touch caused Linda to gulp.

'What's happened?'

'Nothing.' Tears smarted.

'Yer don't usually come 'ere straight after work.'

'I just felt like a visit.' It was something she'd often done as a child when there'd been trouble at home. When her mother had been drinking. There was a lot of comfort in snuggling up on her gran's ample lap, in the familiar fusty smell of her.

'Okay.' Nelly pushed down her anxiety, stroking Linda's hair. She would say before long what was upsetting her. 'Owt interesting going on at the hossie?' It was the only thing she could think to say that was normal, that would quieten the niggle of unease.

Linda was aware she was a lifeline to the outside world for her gran who didn't go much beyond her front door these days. But she also knew Nelly's tactics of going all around the houses to get to whatever the problem was, and was grateful.

'We've been busy these last two nights. Sandra Crabtree's in again…'

'Oh aye?' Nelly raised an eyebrow. 'Off Bridle Terrace? Poor cow.'

'Twins this time. That makes seven she's got now.'

'Poor cow,' Nelly said again, sucking in her cheeks. 'Terry Crabtree's a right waster an' all.'

71

'I know.' Linda paused. 'And we have a woman in who's much older than our usual mums. Nice woman. She had a rotten time, ever such a long labour. Little boy was breech. He had to go in one of the incubators at first.'

Nelly screwed her face up in sympathy. 'Always worse when you're on your own in the ward without your bairn. 'Appened to a woman when I was in with my first. She skriked all the time.'

'Oh no, she's not in the main ward, she's in one of the side wards. She's private.'

'Ah well, pet, some woman get mollycoddled by their fellers.'

'Hmm.' Linda tipped her head back to look at Nelly.

Bending forward, Nelly saw the two lines between Linda's eyebrows deepen slightly in a familiar gesture. This was it; whatever came next became her problem as well as her granddaughter's. It was a familiar pattern between them. One that she knew Linda relied on. Her heart gave a quick double thump. 'What is it, love?'

'You know … usually the husbands are lovely…full of excitement and proud of their wives. And they treat the nurses with respect, Gran.' Linda wrapped her arms around her body. Keep calm, she told herself.

'So they should.' Nelly nodded.

'But the first time this woman's husband came on the ward it wasn't visiting time and he wouldn't take no for an answer … just shoved me to one side when I tried to tell him he wasn't allowed in.'

Nelly made a fist. If the bloke had been standing in front of her now, she'd give him what for. 'You weren't frightened, weren't you, pet?'

'I was, to be honest … which isn't like me. I freaked a bit. He was horrible.'

'Bastard.' Nelly's hand was motionless on Linda's head.

Linda hugged herself harder. 'And then last night he came in again. I was telling his wife she needed a few days more rest. She's had an awful time, Gran.' Linda looked up at her. 'She's exhausted. And to be honest, I don't think he cares about anything else but how he's being put out with her being in hospital. He was so nasty.' Her scalp tightened. 'Normally, I can handle anything. But this was different. There was something about him. It was as though I knew him from somewhere.' Linda twisted round to face Nelly, her hand on her gran's knee. 'As though I knew I should be scared of him. Instinctively like. You know what I mean?'

'Right…' Nelly drew the word out. 'Was 'e a big bloke?'

'No, he was same size as me but thickset.'

'Did you report 'im?'

'No, I was just glad to get away from him.'

'You should tell your William. 'E'd sort 'im out.'

'I don't want him involved. To be honest, Gran, the man looks like one of the Kray twins – slick hair, flash … as though he has to prove he has money… One of those astrakhan coats slung around his shoulders. Loads of gold chains round his neck, his wrists. Great big square ring on his little finger. And he looks as if he'd been in loads of fights; he has a sort of half-moon shaped scar on his face. Here.' Linda touched her cheek. 'And a nose that looks as if it's had a bad break. He frightens me.'

Nelly's stomach lurched. She put her hand to her throat but couldn't stop the small groan. She took her glasses off, pressed her fingers over her eyes.

'Gran? What is it?'

Nelly opened then closed her mouth. The tremor started deep inside her until she was shaking violently.

Linda got to her knees, wrapped her arms around the old woman.

'Gran? What's wrong?'

Nelly's shoulders shuddered. 'I can't…'

Goosebumps rose on Linda's arms. She held her breath for a few seconds, waited. When she finally spoke, her voice sounded strange even to herself. 'You know him, don't you Gran? You know who the man is.'

When Nelly next spoke it was in a whisper. 'Not my place to say, pet. You need to go home. You need to talk to your Dad.'

Chapter 19: Linda Booth

Ashford, morning: Sunday, September 21st

Linda sat on the bench, staring unseeingly at her hands clasped together on her lap. The autumn sun was quite warm on the top of her head but inside she felt icy cold. Why was Gran so upset? Who was this man? Instinctively she felt she knew who he was, but how? Where from?

The lake was crammed with families in pedal-boats and canoes, enjoying their Sunday. Shouts and screams of laughter wafted across the water. Dogs barked, children cried. Somewhere an ice-cream van played a tinny tune. *Greensleeves*? But the noises in the park sounded miles away. Occasionally she'd been conscious of someone sitting on the seat next to her, attempting to chat, but she ignored them and eventually they'd moved away. One, a young woman, had a child with her: a small girl who'd touched Linda's hand and smiled. Linda could only stare blindly into the child's brown eyes.

There was a high-pitched yell and a loud splash. Linda jumped; her scalp tingled with the sudden disturbance. One of the men in charge of the boats was hooking a canoe towards him as a girl clung to the side, her paddle drifting away on the water. They were laughing.

Linda stood. There was only one way to find out who that man really was … George Worth. She needed to get home.

Later, she wondered why she hadn't put two and two together when she was talking to her gran.

There was no one in the kitchen when she walked in through the back door but she could hear voices and she went into the hall. Her dad was cleaning the outside of the living-room windows. Bert Robinson, a neighbour from the end of the street, leant against the house wall talking to him, the pipe between his lips waggling from side to side as he spoke.

'Hello, Linda, love,' Bert said, taking the pipe from his mouth and pointing the stem at her when she looked out from the front door. 'You look in a lather … been running, like?'

'Linda.' Ted turned, dropping the wash-leather into the bucket at his feet. 'You're late home, lass…'

'Can we talk, Dad?' She didn't acknowledge the question in his voice and went back into the kitchen.

She heard her father say, 'See you, Bert.' before following her. He put the bucket by the sink. 'What is it?' He dried his hands, bunching the towel up and tossing it onto the draining-board.

Now she was here she didn't know where to start. She leant against the table, clutching the edges of the surface. 'Something happened at work. A man. The husband of one of my mothers…' She saw Ted's mouth tighten, the slight frown. Gran was right; her dad must know something. But his next words threw her.

'Someone been pestering you?'

'Not like that.' Impatience made her voice strident. 'Gran said I should ask you about him. She said you'd know…' Her knees were giving way.

'Know what?' Ted put his hands on her arms and gently sat her down on one of the chairs. He pulled up another chair and dragged it closer to her. 'What is it, love? What's happened?'

'Gran said you'd know who he is.' Linda gulped, the words hard in her throat. 'Who this man is. There's something about him. He's nasty, aggressive for no reason. He bullies his wife.' Linda held up her hand as Ted opened his mouth to speak. 'It's not that … it's something else.' She wasn't explaining properly. Her words

75

tumbled out. 'I keep getting the feeling I know him from somewhere but I can't... I don't...'

'Take it easy, lass. Tell me what he looks like?'

She frowned, picturing the man. 'Like he used to have ginger hair ... more grey now. Not tall. He has a half-moon shaped scar on his cheek. And a nose that looks as if it's been broken. Bent, like. Gran said I had to ask you. She was really upset. *Really* upset,' she stressed. 'He scares me, Dad. It's as though I know – knew him once. I remember...' her words trailed away. She watched Ted. His face seemed to crumble and then harden. But his features weren't the same as before; he looked like a different man. When he spoke his voice was harsh.

'What's he called?'

All at once Linda was frightened – more frightened than she could ever remember. 'Dad?'

'I said, what's he called?' Linda saw her father brace himself. Then his shoulders drooped. 'Sorry, Linda. Just tell me his name, love.'

'Worth. His name's George Worth.' She watched him sway on the chair as though to fall, and put her hand out to him. He grabbed her fingers, squeezed them until it hurt. 'Dad?'

'It can't be ...'

Linda twisted around in the chair to see Ellen holding on to the door as though it was the only thing keeping her upright. Had she been drinking again? The thought flashed through Linda's mind, but her mother's voice wasn't slurred when she repeated, 'It can't be. Ted?'

'Hush, Ellen. Let me think.'

'Dad?' Linda felt the weakening of her bladder, feeling she would wet herself any moment. 'You know him?'

The silence flickered around the room.

'We need to talk, love.' Ted glanced at his wife. 'Ellen, come and sit down.' She shook her head. His voice was sharp. 'I said come and sit down. Here. We need to talk. It's time. Linda needs to know. Now. Come and sit down.'

'Time for what?' Linda whispered. 'Just tell me. What do I need to know?'

Ellen sat opposite them. Her face, cupped between her palms, was grey; her eyes were fixed on Ted.

He kept hold of Linda's hands. 'Now ... you say his wife's just had a baby?' He glanced at Ellen, shaking his head slightly. 'So how old is he?'

'He's about Mum's age, I think. But what—'

'How old's his wife?' Ellen interrupted, leaning across the table.

'Same, round about. But what's that got to do with it?' Linda stared at her. 'There's an older girl as well.' Why did she feel it was important to add that?

'What's he look like?' Ellen again.

Ted answered. 'Short, stocky bloke? Ginger hair, you said?'

'Yes.' Linda nodded slowly. 'Mostly grey but it looks as though it was ginger. And frizzy.' A memory hovered. A man standing over her; the sun, low in the sky, highlighting red greasy curls. There was a sour taste in her mouth. 'And he's called Worth. George Worth?'

Ted glanced over to Ellen, his top lip held between his teeth. 'It has to be him. He's just changed his name a bit.'

Changed his name? An unwelcome slow understanding wavered on the outskirts of Linda's mind. A realisation she refused to acknowledge.

'No!' Ellen's voice was smothered by her hands.

'It's him, isn't it? It's that man.' Linda pulled her hands away from her father's.

'You remember?' The shock slackened her father's face again.

'Oh God...' Her mother had her eyes closed.

'I remember,' Linda whispered. 'The nightmares – I've been having them again lately.'

She looked from one to the other. It was as though a part of her was separate from what was happening: as though she was an onlooker, watching two people fall apart. 'Who is he?' She choked

77

out the words, willing what she was thinking not to be the truth: for George Worth not to be who she thought he was. But... 'It's him, isn't it? That man. But why...? Why did he do it? When I was a little girl... Why did he take me?'

Chapter 20: Linda Booth

Ashford, morning: Sunday, September 21st

The silence was so intense that Linda could hear the slow plop of water in the cistern in the bathroom airing-cupboard above them.

Ted cleared his throat. He tried to take hold of Linda's hand again but she flapped her fingers, avoiding his. 'Who is he?' she repeated.

'I... We think it's George Shuttleworth.' He looked at Ellen for confirmation.

Linda turned to her mother, saw the small, frightened upward movement of her head.

'Gran's other son,' Linda said, her tone flat. So it was true; what she'd been thinking minutes earlier was the truth. Harriet Worth's husband was the son no one would speak of.

A long time ago, when she was a little girl, Linda had found a small snapshot of Nelly with two little boys in a kitchen drawer. Her gran had given her the photo and done the same thing she'd done today – told her to go home and ask her mum and dad to tell her what she wanted to know. That was the first time she'd understood why Nelly was her gran. She couldn't remember her mum being there but Dad had pointed one of the boys out and told her that he was her other dad – one she'd never see because he was in heaven. When she asked about the other boy in the picture he'd clammed up, the look on his face telling Linda not to push her luck.

'Yes.' This time Ted managed to catch hold of her hand. 'Gran's other son.'

'I don't understand.' Linda's heart was thumping fast in her chest. 'Why would he do that? Take me to...' she squeezed her eyes tight, trying to shut out the picture her words were going to bring back. 'Keep me in that place ... that old mill? I was only a kid.'

Ted reached up, stroked her hair. 'It's a long story, love.'

Suddenly the jolt that shot through her pushed her away from Ted, made her stand. She gripped the edge of the table. 'If he's Gran's son... He's Frank's brother...' She needed to move. To pace the floor. To think. 'Why would...' she forced the words out 'an uncle do that to a child? To me...'

'I need a drink,' Ellen said.

'You don't.' Ted's tone was sharp. 'Make a brew. Put some sugar in Linda's.'

'I don't like...' Linda watched her mother take mugs from the cupboard, arrange them on the worktop. She saw the tremor in her hands.

'Just this once, love,' her dad said. 'It'll do you good.'

The anger was unexpected. 'He gagged me.' Linda's voice was high-pitched. 'He left me in that awful place ... that cellar. For days.' The rage left as quickly as it came. 'In the dark,' she whispered. 'It was so dark.' The memory of the air in that cellar – thick and damp, nauseating to breathe in, the scratching sounds, the scuffling of soft noises – was too much. Linda felt the scream rising. Then darkness closed over her.

She was lying on the settee in the living room. Ted was cradling her and her mother was holding something to her lips. Whisky. Linda twisted away. 'No.' The word came out as a croak. 'What happened?'

'You fainted, lass.' Ted pulled her closer to him as she tried to sit up. 'It's okay, take your time.' He scowled at Ellen as she drained the glass.

'I needed that,' she said, on the defensive. 'I'll go pour the tea.'

Against the loud rattling of crockery in the kitchen, Linda said, 'Tell me why, Dad. I want you to explain to me why he did it.'

'I will. Let's wait for your mum.'

'No. Now.' Linda pushed back on the cushions, straightened the skirt of her uniform, mechanically registering that it would need washing. 'Now. You know why he did it. I sensed you knew why. And I felt Gran knew as well. I've a right to know.' Her voice rose as he began to shake his head. 'It happened to me. I've every right to be told.'

'And I ... we will.'

'I can't. Ted?' Ellen appeared at the door, the glass in her hand half-full again.

'For goodness' sake, woman.'

She spun on her heel. They heard her stumble into the coat stand.

'It's always the same; whatever happens, it's always the drink.' The frustration made Linda's voice shake.

'She can't help it.' Ted rubbed his hands over his face. 'She's had to live with what she did for a long time.'

'What *did* she do?' The awful sick nervousness took over again.

'I'll tell her.' Ellen came back into the living-room and held out a mug of tea to Linda before perching on the edge of the armchair next to the settee. She pressed her lips together, looked helplessly at Ted.

'I can do it, love,' he said.

'No. It's my mess.'

All at once Linda didn't want to know. She wanted to go back to before Harriet Worth had come to the hospital, be on a different ward so that they'd never met, a different shift so that she'd not ever come across George Worth. George *Shuttle*worth. There was a cold certainty in her that told her life was going to change after this day. But she couldn't speak. She stared at her mother.

What Ellen next said took Linda's breath away.

'Gran's other son, Frank, was courting your Auntie Mary before she met your Uncle Peter. Peter was a POW at the camp. At the Granville—'

'I know all that,' Linda interrupted. 'Auntie Mary's told me how they met hundreds of times. What's all that got to do with me?'

'Give her time, love.' Ted leaned towards Linda. 'Let her tell it her own way.'

She saw the gratitude in her mother's face when she looked at him. 'Okay. Go on, Mum.'

'Things happened.' Ellen waved an explanation away. 'You don't need to know what, it's not important. But I was jealous of them and I had a ... night with him.'

'A night?'

'Yes. It *was* only a night.' Ellen was answering her, but looking at Ted, her voice a monotone. 'But Frank didn't want me; it was Mary he was trying to hurt.'

Ted's face was impassive.

It was strange, Linda thought, how the only one she felt sorry for right at that moment was her dad. She reached out for him, squeezed his arm. 'And I was the result,' she said.

Ellen dipped her head. 'Yes. And I've never regretted that, Linda, not once. I've always loved you, you must know that ... but I've always felt so guilty about what I did...' She reached across, took Ted's other hand. 'There are so many things I've done wrong...'

Ted lifted her hand to his face, held it there. 'Now then, love,' he murmured.

'I'm sorry to tell you this, Linda, but Frank wasn't a nice man. He made Auntie Mary's life a misery for months. Then one day he waited for her under the bridge on Shaw Street. She used to take a short cut home along the canal.' She looked at Linda. 'After a shift at the hospital in the camp, you know?'

Linda nodded.

'He… He raped her.'

The words cut through Linda's brain.

Ellen rushed on. 'Someone saw what he was doing. There was a fight. Frank finished up in the water. He drowned. We didn't know for a long time who he'd fought with.'

Linda couldn't speak.

'It all gets a bit complicated after that, love,' Ted said, taking a quick look at Ellen.

His wife closed her eyes. 'You tell her, then.'

'George Shuttleworth thought it was your mum's brother, Tom, that Frank had the fight with. You might not remember him.'

'I do. I think I do. A tall man?'

'Aye, that's right, he was,' Ted nodded. 'He was my best friend when we were growing up. You couldn't have found a gentler man. He was a Conscientious Objector, you know.'

Linda shook her head. None of this makes any sense, she thought.

'You were about five when he died. The war was over. Peter had come back from Germany and he and your Auntie Mary were together again. Her and Tom had moved to Wales to get away.'

'Get away from what?' Linda's mind whirled; she still didn't understand what any of this had to do with what happened to her.

'From us. From all of us.' Ted eyes filled with tears. He let go of Ellen's hand, pulled a handkerchief from his trouser pocket and blew his nose. 'You see, *we* thought it was Tom as well. We believed he'd killed Frank Shuttleworth.'

His words were stirring up an elusive memory in Linda. She tried to cling on to it. 'I think I remember something. Something I didn't understand.' She stared at Ellen. There were tears sliding down her mother's cheeks. 'We were in Wales for ages … at Auntie Mary's. But it was just you and me. And then Auntie Jean and Jacqueline.'

'Your Uncle Tom's funeral,' Ted said 'He'd been killed in an accident—'

'It wasn't an accident,' Ellen interrupted, her tone sharp. 'He was murdered … run down in the road.' Now she locked eyes with Linda. 'By George Shuttleworth.'

'Oh God…'

'Like I said, George Shuttleworth thought Tom had killed Frank an' all,' Ted said. 'It was revenge. He'd found out that Peter had come back to this country and was with Mary and Tom. He found them.' Ted blew his nose again. 'Mary told us he drove his van straight at Tom. 'The police said it was a … hit and run.' He shook his head. 'There was nothing we could do. They didn't believe Mary when she said the van was driven at Tom on purpose. Months later she came to stay with us. She saw the van again. George Shuttleworth was in it.'

The room was beginning to feel oppressive and Linda realised she was holding her breath. 'Can we open a window?' she said. 'I feel ill again.'

'Yes, love.' Ted moved swiftly, unlocking the catch and pushing at the frame.

The noise of the street rushed in; someone passed the house, calling out a greeting, laughing loudly at a muffled comment. A door banged shut. It's all wrong, Linda thought, everything just carries on as though nothing's happening. She begrudged that. 'Go on,' she said.

'The police didn't believe her. So she went to see Nelly—'

'Gran.'

'Aye. *She* believed Mary all right. Nelly told her she'd given George an alibi for the days he was in Wales, said he was home, cos he'd made her say it. She was scared of him; he was handy with his fists.

'She must have been terrified, but she still kicked George out.' Ted shook his head. 'She's a brave soul. Anyway, Mary found out later your gran had told him not to come back. That she'd tell the police what he'd done.' Ted paused. He was holding his clenched fists together.

'That Christmas, when Auntie Mary was staying with us …
when she told us she'd seen George in the same van that ran Tom
down, your Uncle Patrick was there. He went after George, gave
him a right beating.' He turned to Linda. 'After that, George
disappeared.'

So many questions still churned in Linda. She watched him,
waited.

'Then he took you.'

Ellen moaned. She leaned forward, her head on her knees.

'But why me?'

'We think he must have somehow thought you belonged to
Patrick. That you were his daughter.'

'So, taking me was a mistake,' Linda said, trying to work it out.
'It should have been Jacqueline?' It wasn't fair that she felt that
spark of resentment but she couldn't help it. She was taken by
error, but only because her Uncle Patrick had gone wading in and
fought with George Shuttleworth.

'It shouldn't have been either of you. But yes, he was after
hurting Patrick. That's for sure.'

'He must have hated all of us.' Linda tasted the fear. 'He must
still hate us. If he finds out who I am— '

'Nothing will happen, love. I won't let anything happen to you.
Besides, he'll still be a wanted man for taking you—'

'And for murdering Tom.' Ellen lifted her head. It was the first
time she'd spoken for a while. 'If ever we could prove it.'

'I doubt he'll be caught for that, not now.' Ted kept his gaze
on Linda.

That happened to me because of Patrick, Linda thought, 'If he
hadn't beaten George Shuttleworth, if he'd left him alone, he
wouldn't have gone after me. She'd never call him uncle again.
For a split second she wished him dead. 'And Uncle Tom died
because he tried to save Auntie Mary that day.' She blinked slowly.
It was all too much to take in. 'Because he killed Frank.'

'Tom didn't kill Frank.' Ted's face was impassive.

84

'What?'

'Tom didn't kill Frank.'

'I don't understand.' Linda was confused. 'Who did then?' The question crackled between them.

'Who did then?' she repeated

'Peter.'

Chapter 21: Richard Schormann

Manchester, afternoon: Monday, September 22nd

William was waiting for Richard when he walked from the entrance of the university onto Moorside Road. He swung off his motorbike and put his helmet on the seat.

'Well?' William ruffled his cousin's hair. 'You got in?' There was a steady flow of traffic going past and, aware that too much background noise made hearing difficult for Richard, he turned to face him, so that Richard could see his mouth.

'Not quite. Second interview Friday.' Richard grinned, batting him off and flattening his fringe.

'You'll get it – you're a clever young bugger.'

'Fingers crossed.'

You'll have to give your mum and dad a ring.'

'They let me do it from the foyer in there.' Richard tipped his head towards the hospital behind him. 'They were over the moon.' His mum had actually been less enthusiastic than he'd expected but he shouldn't be disappointed; she was going mad with worry about Vicky. And she kept asking him if he knew where she'd gone. As if he wouldn't tell them. What she'd done was unfair to them both. And she knew worry was bad for Dad. He'd ring again later.

'They said the weather's atrocious at home.' He looked up at the sky, veiled with thin clouds. 'I'm glad I'm not there.' He dropped his gaze to his cousin. 'Anyway, what are you doing here?'

'I thought I'd make it up to you for being late at the station on Friday. I've been feeling bad about it.' William slung his arm over Richard's shoulder and raised his voice. 'That business with those bloody idiots wouldn't have happened if I'd made it on time.'

'It doesn't matter. Honest, Will. You told me you had a last-minute job on.'

William frowned. 'Which needn't have happened if Jack had just topped the petrol up from the can in the recovery truck. It would have got that dozy girl to the nearest petrol station.'

'Hmmm. Well yes, from what you said, however pretty she was, she was also a bit *twp* – not having a clue how to put petrol in, isn't it.' Richard gave a short laugh. 'And Jack was a lame-brain for missing a chance with a good-looking girl.'

'Way out of his league.' William took the spare helmet from inside the seat and held it out to Richard. 'Now, sir, where do you want to go?'

Richard didn't take the helmet. 'Do you mind if I don't? I'm not sure it'll go on over these.' He touched the hearing-aids.

'Up to you.' William replaced the helmet, smoothed back his long hair and put his own helmet on. Buckling the strap under his chin, he said, 'Now, where to?'

'Mossbridge. If that's okay with you, chauffeur?' Richard got on the pillion seat.

'Oh?'

'It's where Karen lives.'

'The girl you met?' William raised his voice, kick-starting the bike. 'Your saviour?'

'That's the one.'

'For such an innocent, my lad, you must have a good line in chat.' William shouted above the revs.

'What?'

'I said you must have a good line in chat.'

'We can't all have the gift.' Richard jabbed him in the back, laughing.

'How many times is this, then?'

'Just seen her a couple of times over the weekend.' Richard shouted. He didn't want his cousin to know he'd fallen for Karen in a big way – that she was like no other girl he'd known. William might joke about it. And it felt so new, so exciting, he was sure it would be spoiled if shared.

'Good for you. Hold on then. Mossbridge it is.'

Richard tapped William on the shoulder. 'It's around here somewhere,' he shouted. 'I said I'd meet her outside a pub. *The Dog and Whistle?* There!' he pointed so William could tell which direction to go in. 'There it is.'

'Not at her house?'

'No, she's got a pig of a stepfather apparently, so she thought it better we meet here.'

William slowed the bike and rolled it towards the footpath. 'Want me to wait just in case she doesn't turn up?'

'No.' Richard didn't wait for William to switch the engine off before jumping from the bike. 'She will.' He looked around, all at once anxious. The blood rushed to his face as William grinned. 'She will turn up,' he repeated, pulling his comb from the top pocket of his suit and running it through his fringe.

William let the engine splutter to a stop and rocked on the bike. 'Will you stay in Ashford until your next interview?'

'Mum said I might as well … save on the train fare,' But he felt he really should go home. 'I don't know what to do.'

'If they say it's okay …'

The pub door opened and three men in white overalls and fluorescent jackets strolled out. One of them, about Richard's age, led the way. He was combing his black hair into a quiff. Swaggering towards them he rolled his sleeves up to show multi-coloured snake tattoos on both arms.

He stopped to admire the Triumph Trophy.

'Nice bike,' he said to William, 'give us a spin?' Lighting a cigarette, he spun the match towards Richard's feet.

'Sorry, mate.' William barely looked at him.

'Stuff you then!' He kicked a stone towards the back wheel.

William put both feet on the ground and stood astride the bike, his jaw jutted.

The two other men, both middle-aged, gave the younger one a push. 'Cause bother in an empty house, you sodding idiot.' He looked towards Richard and William. 'Sorry, lads.'

'No problem.' William lifted his chin in acknowledgment.

The men ambled down the side of the pub towards a patch of land where there was a white van parked.

William and Richard watched them for a moment as they got into the vehicle. The passenger window was wound down and immediately a stream of cigarette smoke wafted out. The van didn't move.

An old double-decker bus trundled by, followed by a long line of cars. William touched Richard's arm and waited until he'd got his attention. 'If your mum and dad say it's okay,' he said, 'why not stop up here?'

'You're right, I suppose,' Richard said, 'daft to waste money. Anyhow,' he glanced up and down the road, not sure which direction Karen would appear from, 'it's cool. You get off now.'

'You don't want me to meet the lovely Karen?'

'No I don't, you randy old git.' Richard grinned. He pulled at the knot of his blue skinny tie and took it off. Rolling it up and putting it in his pocket, he said, 'Haven't you got somewhere you need to be?'

'Yep, I'm off to Susan's.'

'What's all the mystery about this girlfriend of yours?' Richard saw an opportunity to get his own back. 'You've hardly said a word about her all week.' He stopped laughing when he saw William set his mouth and turn away; he'd apparently hit a raw nerve somehow. 'Sorry, mate, didn't mean to stick my nose in. It's just that I haven't heard you talk about her in your house and I thought you were serious about her.'

'I am. But I like to keep things separate. The way Mam is … you know.'

'Yeah, I know. But that's not your fault. Your dad's cool. And Linda—'

'Can you keep a secret?' William turned back and searched Richard's face, as though trying to make up his mind.

'Sure.'

'She's married … separated … but married. And she has a child. A cracking little lad. Timothy.' There was no missing the affection when he said the name.

'Oh.' It was the last thing Richard expected; William had always been a predictable sort. Nothing to do with him, though. He raised his shoulders. 'No worries, Will. I won't say anything.'

'Thanks.' When the road was clear, William turned the bike around and started it up. 'It'll all come out before long anyway. I'm moving in with them.' He revved the bike, looking over his shoulder and waited for a bicycle to pass before he set off. 'I'll see you later, then.' He gave a nod. 'Looks like you were right. You haven't been stood up.'

Richard looked in the direction William was indicating. In the distance Karen was running down the road. He raced towards her, a strange shiver running through him. How had he got so lucky?

When he turned back to shout goodbye to his cousin, he'd gone, the roar of the engine growing ever fainter.

'I got through the interview,' he said, when he reached Karen. He lifted her up and swung her round. 'I'm in with a chance.' She leant back in his arms, her dark hair swinging, and the rows of bells sewn onto the seams of her bell-bottom jeans tinkling. When they stopped, Karen held his face between her hands and kissed him.

The white van passed them. The lad with the quiff was hanging out of the window, his arm raised in a crude gesture. 'Go on, shag 'er,' he shouted, through the cigarette between his lips. Then it dropped from his mouth. 'Fuckin' 'ell, it's Karen,' he yelled. He looked quickly over his shoulder to the driver. 'Look, Bernie, it's old Worth's kid. Fuckin' 'ell, she's for it, now. Just wait,' he bellowed as the van sped off, 'just wait 'til I tell 'im what you've been up to, you dirty little slag.'

Karen gazed after the van, her arms by her sides.

'Karen?' When Richard turned her towards him, he saw her face was drained of colour. 'Karen?'

'They were George's men,' was all she said.

Richard knew then that, somehow, trouble was coming his way for the second time in a week.

Chapter 22: Jacqueline Howarth

Ashford: Monday, September 22nd

'Have you told Richard?' Jackie mouthed an apology to her sergeant at the same time as speaking to her aunt. 'Yes, I'll talk to him. Make sure he's okay. Didn't he have his interview today? Good.' She twirled the cord of the telephone round her finger and turned towards the opaque glass partition in the corner of the charge-room.

Cupping her hand around the receiver, she whispered, 'Auntie Mary, I can't really talk now. Victoria's not been gone a week yet. And she left a note. And she *is* eighteen.' She listened for a moment before saying, 'I'll ring you back later. Let me make some enquiries.' She nodded. 'I know. It must be an awful worry. But if Uncle Peter has already contacted the local police I don't know what else I can do.' Jackie paused. Her aunt was crying. Her eyes smarted in sympathy. 'Okay, I'll try. Leave it with me.'

She tried three times to finish the conversation before she was finally able to put the phone down.

'More trouble in the family, Constable Howarth?' Sergeant Blackwood rocked up and down on his heels in front of the old-fashioned fireplace.

Jackie nodded. 'I'm sorry, Sergeant.' He was one of the old school, due to retire soon, and he stuck rigidly to the rules. She knew he was only too aware of some members of her family and wasn't shy of letting her know, once telling her he was unable to believe she'd been accepted into the police force, given her relatives. But he wasn't a malicious man, she thought: just totally behind the times.

'Well who is it this time, Constable?'

'That was my aunt in Wales.'

'Ah, I remember that one – came in to accuse some bloke of killing her brother who was in an accident as far as I— '

'I know.' Jackie cut him off. 'She called … it was about my cousin, she's missing.'

She saw the look of concern momentarily in his eyes, then he coughed and looked up to the ceiling. 'Have they contacted the local station?'

'Yes, but they thought we could help as well. With our family living in Ashford, I think they believe she might come up here.'

He rested his chin of his chest and then lifted his head to look at her. 'A possibility,' he nodded. 'How old is your cousin?'

When she told him his shoulders relaxed. 'One of those teenagers, eh? Probably turn up when she's had her fun.'

'She's eighteen: still under age, Sergeant. Still a child.' She waited a moment. 'I wondered if I could ring around the stations in Manchester. Put them on alert, like?'

He cleared his throat. 'It's not something I'd usually allow, Constable Howarth. Still, I suppose it wouldn't be a problem, seeing as we're not busy just now.'

The typist opened the door from the telephone exchange and came into the charge-room with a sheaf of papers. Jackie heard the voices of the two women and caught sight of them sitting back from the switchboard and drinking tea.

So had Sergeant Blackwood. He pushed the door open again. 'Nothing to do, ladies?'

They sat up straighter but the oldest protested. 'What do you want us to do, Donald, pretend to take calls?' She sat back patting her perm, which sat like a tight black hat on top of her head. 'Anyway, we're on our break.'

He backed out. Passing Jacqueline he said, 'Find out which is the nearest station to your aunt and make those calls. Give them,' he nodded towards the typists' door, 'something to do.'

'Thanks, Sarge.'

He raised his eyebrows at that, but Jackie noticed the corners of his mouth twitching.

'I'm going for a cuppa myself, Constable. Make sure you've finished with all this personal stuff by the time I get back.'

'I will, Sergeant.'

'He's a surly old sod; always yakking on about something.' The typist barely waited until he'd left the charge-room. She kept her head over the filing cabinet. 'Don't know how you put up with him, Jackie.'

'Trisha … shut up, he'll hear you. Sergeant Blackwood is okay – just old-fashioned in his ways.'

The girl slammed the drawer shut, trapping a leaf of the large spider-plant on top of the cabinet. 'Huh.' She held out her hand, admiring the bright red of her fingernails. 'I'm just glad I'm in there with them two. Even if they do drive me mad with all their nattering.' She wobbled back to her office on her red stilettoes.

When she'd gone, Jackie freed the leaf but the tip of it was damaged. She broke it off and threw it in the bin. Then she walked over to the phone. The sergeant was right; there was always some sort of bother in her family.

Chapter 23: Mary & Peter Schormann

Llamroth, afternoon: Monday, September 22nd

'So, Richard is through the first interview and is happy. And you have spoken to Jacqueline.' Peter knew Mary had hardly slept since Victoria left. It worried him; there were dark shadows under her eyes and her skin sagged with weariness. 'Do you feel better now?'

'Perhaps. I'm not sure.' Mary stood up, the action making her slightly light-headed. Even though it was mid-afternoon she was still not dressed. Her dressing-gown was tied tight around her waist. She clutched the collar of it close to her neck with one hand. 'He did sound happy, didn't he?' He hadn't mentioned Victoria at all. Did he really not know where she'd gone? She dismissed the thought. Richard had always been an honest lad, even when it got him into trouble. She bit her lip. 'Jacqueline said she'd ring later.'

'Did you tell her I have talked to the police in Pont-y-Haven? That they are looking for her here?'

'Yes.' There was desperation in Mary's eyes. 'You heard me … I said that. But I do think Victoria might be making her way to Ashford for some reason. Where else does she know except around here and Ashford, Peter? She's been nowhere else without us, has she? That's why I wanted to speak to Jacqueline.' Mary twisted her fingers together. 'I can't think of anything else to do.'

'What did she say?'

'She wasn't able to talk; I think there was someone there.' Mary moved to be close to him, trying to take strength from his warmth. He folded her in his arms, resting his cheek on her head nestled against him. Mary could hear the ectopic beat of his heart and silently counted in the pauses between the rapid flutterings and the stronger single beats. She increased her grip, aware how much she still needed, depended on him. Loved him. He didn't deserve all this extra worry.

'I didn't know what else to do,' she whispered. 'We've tried everything … everywhere – her college, the friends we know about.'

'We can only hope, *Liebling*.' Peter looked over her shoulder to the window. The sky was a steely grey. 'Would you like to go out for fresh air?'

'In this?' Mary shivered. 'Where's the summer gone all at once?' She'd listened to the unusually strong wind develop overnight and there was still no sign of it subsiding. Across the road the branches of the trees whipped against each other.

'You haven't been outside for almost a week.'

'I need to be here, in case Victoria telephones.'

'A short walk along the sea-front?' Peter said. 'Before the evening surgery? Gelert needs the exercise.'

At the sound of his name the dog came out of his basket.

'See…? He is ready.' Peter went into the porch and took Mary's coat and scarf from the stand. 'Run, get dressed. If you are wrapped up, you will be warm.'

When she came back downstairs he helped her into her coat and waited until she fastened her scarf before taking the lead from the hook on the back door. 'We will be only a little while.'

'Ten minutes?'

'Ten minutes,' he promised.

The tide was in; waves rose high, roaring fast towards the shore, dragging and churning the pebbles, rolling small boulders. Further over, they crashed against the cliffs where seabirds huddled in the crevices and ledges.

'This is ridiculous, Peter.' They were following the curve of the road leaning into the wind. The cold spray stung Mary's face. 'Let's go back.' She worried they might be missing a call from Victoria. 'I can't tell where the sea ends and the sky begins.' They stopped. Mary peered past him to stare towards the horizon.

'It is a stronger wind than I thought it was.' Peter pulled the collar of his raincoat higher and clamped his hand down on his trilby, taking short wheezing gasps of breath that hurt his throat and jaw. 'This was not so good an idea. We should turn back.' He coughed and wiped his hand over his eyes.

In that moment the wind took his hat. Mary snatched at it but it scudded along the wall in a kind of dance before whirling high in the air until, squinting against the torrent of rain, she couldn't see it any more. 'Damn!'

Peter coughed again.

'Peter? Are you all right?' Mary searched his face. He was grey, a thin line of white around his mouth.

It began to rain, long heavy spurts of water.

'Peter?'

Peter staggered, the wind battering him. Then then he bent forward and vomited, falling to his knees, palms flat on the floor.

'Lie down.' Mary supported him as he rolled onto his side. She took off her scarf and pushed it under his head, then loosened his collar. His eyes were closed, he was moaning. 'You'll be all right, love. Look at me.' He didn't. She pulled her coat off, covered him with it. 'Peter?'

'Es ist Zeit?'

'Time for what, sweetheart?' She couldn't make out his next words. *'Bleib ruhig*, Peter,' she said. 'Stay still.' Holding on to him, she looked around; there was no one in sight. She cursed their stupidity in being out in such atrocious weather. Why had she agreed to it?

For the first time in years, she prayed.

Chapter 24: Jacqueline Howarth

Ashford: Tuesday, September 23rd

The windscreen wipers clunked to a halt as Jackie switched off the engine. Rain pelted noisily on the roof of the Austin 1300 and the four occupants peered reluctantly out at the greyness of the afternoon.

'I appreciate this, Sarge ... Sergeant,' Jackie corrected herself when she saw his frown of disapproval. She knew, with the two cadets huddled in the back of the car, he expected formality.

'We need to follow up on missing children enquiries, Constable,' he said, staring through the smeared glass of the side window at the dark ruins of buildings on the other side of the rusty fence. 'Though we could have picked a better day.' He blew out his cheeks in exaggerated resignation. 'Well, better get on. Out, you two,' He jerked his head backwards. The two cadets opened their doors, letting in a flurry of rain.

'Hurry up,' he barked. 'You're getting the seats bloody wet. Dozy buggers.'

Jackie got out and moved round to the front passenger seat and opened the door for him. She had some sympathy with them; she could still remember her early days and the time she was frightened of the sergeant. 'He's all right really,' she mimed.

The male cadet raised his eyebrows in doubt of Jackie's words. The young girl looked close to tears. Rain bounced on the top of their caps and dripped off the peaks.

Jackie shivered, glad of her cape. 'Come on, then.' They splashed their way through puddles to the large gates. They were padlocked. The sergeant looked them up and down. 'How do you suggest we approach this, Constable? How are we supposed to get into the place?'

'Sorry, forgot to tell you.' Jackie grinned and produced a key from under her cape. 'The squatters were given permission to stay by the Council until it's decided what's happening with the place. The chap in the Planning Department said it was providing the Council could inspect whenever they wanted to,' she said. 'Of course, knowing them, that hasn't happened yet.'

The sergeant harrumphed, hiding a smile behind his hand before coughing and saying, 'Well done, Constable. But hurry up – this isn't the weather to be hanging around.'

He wasn't a bad old stick, Jackie thought, struggling with the lock. He could quite easily have refused to let her do this. She peered through the rusted criss-cross rails of the gate at the broken concrete of the short road leading to the old mill. 'The chap who gave me the key asked if we'd let them know if there was any damage.' Opening the gate and letting them through she shrugged. 'Though how we're supposed to know that, heaven only knows, looking at the state of this place.'

The four of them squinted through the slanting rain at the derelict site. Tall weeds fluttered from piles of rubble and stone. Bronzed rusting fencing lay in a haphazard line around a crumpled concrete square. Broken slates everywhere.

'Apparently they're in there, the old camp hospital.' Jackie pointed to her right. The three-storey building looked remarkably solid. There was glass in the windows and even thin curtains at some.

'Come on, then, what are we waiting for?' The sergeant stomped towards a large porch-way. The doors were boarded up. Jackie stepped back to look up at the rows of windows. She caught a glimpse of a figure. 'Well, they're in there all right,' she said, wiping her hand over her wet face and looking around.

The sergeant banged his fist against the wooden boards. 'Open up!'

The door shifted slightly to one side and a tall man with long black hair, thinning at the front, peered round.

'What do you want?'

Sergeant Blackwood yanked the sheet of wood to one side.

'We're coming in. Okay?' He pushed past the man into an entrance hall, followed by Jackie and the cadets.

The man wore a long blue kaftan. He tripped over the hem as he stepped back. 'Hey, you can't just barge in like this!' He had a strong Irish accent.

'We can do what we want.' Sergeant Blackwood pushed his face at him.

'It's okay, River. Let the pigs in.' In contrast to his words the young man standing behind the man in the kaftan smiled. He held out his hand towards the sergeant who, ignoring it, grabbed the front of the man's loose, cheesecloth shirt and twisted it hard so it was tight against his neck. He was lifted up on to his toes.

'Say again,' the sergeant demanded. 'Better still, say sorry to my constables.' He only let go when the word, 'sorry' was choked out. The young man's face was puce.

'That's better.' Sergeant Blackwood let go of the shirt and brushed it down with the back of his hand. 'Now, let's start again. We're looking for a young girl – missing from home.'

'And?' The man tugged his shirt down, pushed his hair behind his ears and adjusted his plaited turquoise headband.

'You in charge around here?'

'Yes, I'm known as the Master.'

'The girl's called Victoria … Victoria Schormann.'

There was no response, no shadow of recognition in either man's face.

'No one of that name here.'

'Five eight, long blonde hair, blue eyes, pretty,' Jackie said. 'Aged eighteen.'

River leered, sucked on his teeth.

The sergeant glowered.

The man backed off.

'We'll be having a look around.' Sergeant Blackwood said. 'It'll be healthier for you if you cooperate.'

'No problem.' The young man shrugged. 'Most of the women are in the sewing-room. But feel free to search wherever you wish, man.'

Both men still stood in their way.

The sergeant jostled past them. 'Shift.' His voice grim. He spoke over his shoulder to the two cadets. 'Stay together, go to the top floor of the building and start there. Every cupboard, every room. Got it?'

They nodded. Leaving a stream of rainwater behind them, they hurried along the corridor to a flight of stairs.

'Hey, wait, I'll get someone to come with you,' River grinned. He followed them and, pushing a door open called out, 'Freedom, Cassidy, Zen. Go with them.'

Three youths, stretching and yawning, followed the cadets.

The young man turned on his heel and strode away.

'Do you think Jackson and Garner will be all right on their own, Sarge?' Jackie muttered.

'I think Garner could take on all three of those twerps,' he murmured.

Jackie raised her voice. 'I'll start here.' She pushed open a pair of double doors.

'Not scared to be on your own, man?' River tilted his head.

'No,' Jackie replied. 'And I'll look around on my own. Okay ... *man*?'

Even so, she was followed by Sergeant Blackwood. 'Two pairs of eyes better than one.' His voice was gruff.

A girl and a youth, both wearing flowing Hindu robes, trailed hand-in-hand behind them.

Sergeant Blackwood frowned at them.

'Don't worry, Sarge,' Jackie muttered, 'they're too spaced out to know what they're doing.'

It was remarkably quiet in the large room. On one side the windows were half boarded up. In between them rows of thin metal u-shaped rails were fastened to the grimy cream wall. On the floor was dirty cracked green linoleum. Obviously one of the old wards, Jackie thought.

There was a strong smell of cannabis. Small groups of men were sitting or lying on large colourful mats and cushions, reading or talking. Most of them wore jeans and loose cotton tops. All of them had long hair that flowed over their shoulders.

They lifted their heads, watched without speaking.

Sergeant Blackwood stood and sniffed. 'Hmm, interesting,' he said. 'There's definitely some cell fodder in here, constable – some little creeps who fancy a night at our station.' He looked around. 'Who's first?' he barked, walking into the group, moving their feet and legs with a lift of his boots. He picked up an ashtray and sniffed again. 'Don't suppose any of you lot going to own up to this being yours?' He held a joint between his forefinger and thumb.

They shuffled out of his way and, standing up, made for the door. To be stopped in their tracks by the sergeant's roar. 'Wait! Young girl…'

'Five-eight, long blonde hair, blue eyes, eighteen,' Jackie said. 'Called Victoria … Vicky? Anyone seen her?'

Without looking at one another the group of men shook their heads.

'Okay. Bugger off,' the sergeant said. As they left he said to Jackie, 'and I bet at least one of them's wanted for something or other.'

At the far end four men were working at benches and attempting to fasten shelves to the crumbling surface of the wall. They kept their heads down, answering with a quick shake to his questions.

In the opposite corner of the room three makeshift low tables held vases of wild flowers and were surrounded by two long battered settees covered in woollen shawls. Swathes of orange and yellow material were nailed to the walls. Jackie wondered if that corner would be where the women congregated but there was no one there at the moment.

100

She and the sergeant looked around. 'There's nowhere to hide in here, anyway,' he said. 'Let's try somewhere else.'

When they closed the doors behind them Jackie heard one deep voice call out, 'Peace, pigs.' Followed by loud guffaws.

Sergeant Blackwood stopped.

Jackie moved closer to him. 'Not worth it, sir.'

He made a slight movement of his head, his mouth a tight line 'Anything?' The Irish man was leaning against the wall, casually smoking a thin cigarette. He pushed himself upright and walked alongside them. 'C'mon, man, we don't know no what d'ya call her. Give us a break, man.'

They ignored him.

'Next floor?' Sergeant Blackwood said.

'Yes.' Jackie led the way along the corridor, carefully avoiding the broken tiles on the floor. Rubble had been pushed back to the skirting boards on either side but all along the walls were covered in artwork. She had to admit, some of them were skilfully done, even beautiful, but she made no comment. Small rooms led off. One looked as though it had been some sort of sluice or washroom during its time as a hospital. Out of curiosity Jackie turned on the tap. Water gushed out. What's betting the Council don't know about that, she thought. Turning the mains off would have been a sure way of moving this lot on as soon as they'd arrived.

River had dropped back to join the couple behind them. All three waited as Jackie and Sergeant Blackwood peered into each room. Most were bare; possibly they could have been offices or rest-rooms, Jackie guessed. All were empty.

The next floor was different from the one they'd just left. Although there was similar linoleum and the walls were the same grimed-over cream colour, this time the room held twelve mattresses, divided by an assortment of curtains and sheets of material hung on the old rails. Each space was furnished in the same way: a mattress, a small table with a drawer, an upright chair.

The only differences were the assortment of old-fashioned clothes-horses, draped with individual clothes: flowery or striped skirts, baggy cotton trousers, paisley or loosely-woven cotton blouses, long coats. No photographs, no pictures. Nothing. The same sweet smell of cannabis pervaded the room but there was no one. And nowhere for anyone to hide.

'Listen.' the sergeant lifted a finger. 'There's someone talking in the next room.'

They walked between the beds and pushed open the door.

There was no furniture at all. A group of twelve women were sitting cross-legged on mats on the floor. All were either knitting, crocheting or sewing by hand. None of them was Victoria. They stopped their chatter as soon as Jackie stepped inside the room. The sergeant stood back, almost stepping on the trio following them.

'I'm looking for a girl called Victoria,' Jackie said, going from face to face, hoping to see a glimmer of recognition at the name. But the women shook their heads and looked down again, studiously working on their crafts. 'No? No one knows anything about a Victoria? We thought she might be here.'

An older woman stood and came towards them. 'We have no one of that name here.' She looked past Jackie to River and inclined her head. Jackie spun round to see what the man was doing but he only gazed blankly at her. 'As you can see, there's only us here.' The woman turned away with a swish of her skirt and bent to pick up a pair of very fat knitting needles. She wrapped thick multi-coloured wool around them. 'I think that's all for now, ladies,' she said. 'It's time to make the meal.'

They filed past Jackie, heads bowed. One or two let their eyes slide sideways, a small smile on their lips, but most of them averted their heads.

The two cadets appeared at the doorway of the long room.

'Nothing, sir,' Garner called, standing aside to let the women pass. 'Just seems to be mainly a floor where the men sleep, with four smaller rooms off at the side.'

'Sure?' the sergeant glared at them. Jackie could almost hear him seething.

'Sure, sir.'

Sergeant Blackwood turned to Jackie. 'Waste of time then, Constable.'

'Is there anywhere else,' she asked River. 'Any other rooms, any place?'

He shook his head. 'No.'

'I'm going to check again.'

'No, you're not, Constable Howarth.' Sergeant Blackwood's voice was clipped, irritated. 'We've wasted enough time.'

'What about a cellar, a basement?'

'You can go down there,' River drawled, 'but you'll only get as far as the first door. It's blocked off, has been since before we got here.' He lifted his shoulders again. 'Most of the walls inside have collapsed. There's no way you can get through. But by all means have a go, I think we've got some shovels somewhere.'

The young couple, still holding hands and swaying in unison, giggled.

'Like I said, Constable, we've been here long enough,' the sergeant said. 'It'll take all afternoon for you to complete the paperwork on this farce. Car-keys!'

Jackie fished around in her jacket pocket and handed them to him.

'Right. Come on, you two useless buggers,' he shouted at the cadets.

They scurried after him.

Jackie followed them to the ground floor. She took a chance. 'The basement?'

River rolled his eyes and tilted his head to the right. 'Through that door. Like I said, that's about as far as you'll get. You won't get in.'

'I'll decide that,' she snapped. She took her cap off and held it in one hand.

103

The first door was swollen but she managed to squeeze through it, leaving it open enough for her to see. The walls were rough under her palm as she felt her way down a couple of gritty stone steps to a broken door. Bricks and dust shifted behind it but it only opened so far, letting out a smell of damp and mould. 'Damn.' The creepy bastard was right; it was blocked. She stooped quickly as a whistling flutter of pigeons swooped past her head.

'What the fuck!' There was scuffling above her in the corridor where River was waiting. Jackie grinned. 'Hope they've shit on you,' she muttered. The thought occurred to her that if the birds had got into the basement there had to be an opening somewhere. But not big enough for anybody to get through, she reasoned.

Back upstairs she brushed the dust and cobwebs off her hair and cape. The birds had gone. There was a line of pigeon shit on the front of River's kaftan.

Jackie grinned. She couldn't resist. 'You'll need to wash that off pretty quick before it stains,' she said, settling her cap on her head.

As she passed River to leave, he leaned towards her, pursing his lips and making kissing sounds. She glanced around. The others had lost interest and disappeared; she was alone with this revolting man. Without a second thought she lifted her regulation shoe and stamped it down on his sandaled foot. The howl of anguish was very satisfying.

Outside the rain was worse. Jackie looked upwards. The sky was a dark shimmering cover of thick cloud. The others were already at the gate. None of them looked back. Over by the station a train screamed past, its whistle, as it went through, a fading echo.

There was a shout. The sergeant was half-in and half-out of the Austin. Even through the sheet of rain she could see his red angry face. She grimaced; her life wouldn't be worth living for the next few days.

Chapter 25: Victoria Schormann

Ashford, morning: Tuesday, September 23rd

'They've gone.' River crouched down and peered inside the large pipe.

'Thank God for that; it stinks in here.' Seth wriggled out of the blanket that he'd shared with Victoria for the last hour.

River scowled. 'One of the bloody bitches stamped on my foot. I'll be keeping a lookout for her on the outside. She'll be sorry.' When he suddenly grinned he showed nicotine-stained teeth.

'Forget it, River,' Seth said. 'We don't want to invite trouble.'

'Anyway, they've gone,' the Irish man said.

'What's that all down your front?' Seth scrambled on his hands and knees out of the pipe.

'Pigeon shit. Flying rats.' River glowered. 'Pig insisted on going down the basement. The bloody things flew out. Should have locked her in there.'

They hauled Victoria upright. 'They took their bloody time,' Seth said, pulling the blanket from her.

River leaned against the wall of the small building that surrounded the pipe. He finished rolling a joint and licked the cigarette paper to seal it, all the while leering at Victoria.

'Mind you, we didn't waste ours. Eh, Summer?' Seth wiped his thumb over her cheek.

As though he could wipe away all the dirt… Victoria bit down on her lip to stop the trembling. She felt dirty inside. Used. At first, when she'd been bundled out of one of the side doors she was bewildered. Being shoved down into the tunnel was degrading. Even after Seth told her he was protecting her, that the police would make her go back home, she was still angry. She might not have chosen to come to this awful old mill of all places but she *had* chosen to leave home – to be free. No one could make her go back to Llamroth. She was eighteen and she made her own choices about her life.

But she'd no control over what Seth had done. The sex wasn't what she'd wanted. It made her sick to think about him pushing against her, ignoring her protests, oblivious to her cries of pain as she tried to steady herself against the rough surface of the pipe.

However he looked at her now, with the usual tenderness and concern, Victoria realised that she didn't know Seth. Or what she meant to him.

'Just get me out of here,' she said, 'I need a wash.'

Seth frowned.

Since her arrival Victoria had become used to flashes of anger crossing his face when he was annoyed and it made her nervous. Being uneasy wasn't something she was used to. Still, to placate him, she waved her arm towards the tunnel. 'Horrible thing,' she said, unaccustomed to the apprehension that flooded through her and unable to stop the tears.

He stood still, distanced from her. 'At least it hid you from the pigs.' He stared. 'What I don't understand is why they're looking for you here.' He glowered. 'You didn't tell your lot where you were going, did you?'

'How could I? *I* didn't know where I was going. And I haven't been outside since I arrived.' Her hands curled and uncurled.

His face cleared. He leaned forward and kissed her, then stepped back. 'Hell, you're right, you stink.' He grinned.

'You're not so sweet yourself.' She forced a smile, desperate to get away from him. 'I'll go and wash.' But she was thankful he wasn't angry with her anymore. She needed the security of being his favourite. When the warning had first gone around that it was her the police were looking for, she sensed the antagonism that swept across everyone's face as she was passed from one to the other and then quickly taken away by Seth. She knew that as far as they were concerned she was a threat to them, to the commune. But with Seth still on her side they wouldn't dare demand she be kicked out. The last thing she wanted was to be forced to return to her old life: to go back to having to compete and be compared with Richard. For a moment she felt bad, she wouldn't have wanted to go through half what her brother had and still insist on going to that uni. Art college had been an easy option for her – she'd been glad to leave school at sixteen.

The thought was fleeting; she needed to worry about herself.

Even as she hurried back into the building she was excusing what Seth had done, rationalising the rough sex. Love-making, she amended the thought. He'd obviously wanted her so badly. After all they hadn't seen much of one another over the last week; he was still so occupied with settling into this place. So he ... they, she corrected herself again, had just made the most of the situation.

And she wouldn't tell him that she'd caught a glimpse of Jackie, from her window. She'd bobbed down when she saw her look up. She certainly wouldn't tell anyone it was her cousin looking for her. Interfering cow. What on earth had made her look for her here?

Still she'd gone now. Victoria hoped her family ... her old family ... would leave her alone now to get on with her new life with Seth. Now she was out of it she didn't even mind having to hide in that old disgusting pipe. It would all be worth it.

Chapter 26: Jacqueline Howarth

Ashford: Wednesday, September 24th

'Jacqueline?'

'Auntie Mary! I rang last night but there was no reply. Is everything okay?' Jackie did a thumbs-up to Nicki who was standing by the fridge and offering a glass and a bottle of lager.

She'd had to concede the search at the old camp yesterday was a waste of time, despite the feeling that the hippies were hiding something there. She didn't blame him, but she was well and truly in Sergeant Blackwood's bad books for dragging him out of his warm office on what was really only a hunch on her part.

And she'd had no luck with any of the local stations; none of them had anything untoward to report and she wasn't surprised. Victoria was probably hiding out at a friend's house, sulking. She certainly wouldn't be on the streets of Manchester, scruffy and unkempt. Her cousin was too full of herself to allow that to happen.

Her aunt's next words shocked her out of her exasperation.

'Your Uncle Peter had a slight heart attack on Monday.'

Oh, no. 'Is he all right?' She loved her uncle; he was a nice man. 'How is he? Is he in hospital? What have they said?'

'They've kept him in but they say it's not serious.' Mary's voice cracked. Jacqueline heard her sniff. 'I'm sorry I didn't let you know, I've only been back to the house to get a change of clothes—'

'Oh, forget that,' Jackie interrupted. 'What happened?'

Nicki came to stand next her, putting an arm over her shoulder. 'What's up?'

Jackie raised a finger and mouthed 'in a minute', struggling to hear Mary.

'We were walking on the front. Stupid because it was such bad weather but Peter insisted it would do me good after... after—'

'I know.' Jackie said quickly, scowling. 'And, I'm sorry, there's been no sighting of her up here.'

Mary didn't acknowledge what Jackie had just said.

'We were lucky. Some friends of ours were passing in their truck. They got him into the cab and we took him to Pont-y-Haven.'

'Is there anything I can do? Shall I come?'

'No.'

The line hummed for a few seconds. Jackie pressed her ear firmer to the receiver. 'Auntie Mary?'

'Sorry. No, love, that's very kind of you. But it's not necessary, there's nothing you could do. Alwyn and Alun, our friends, are looking after Gelert for a few days. That's one worry off my mind.'

'I'll tell Mum and Auntie Ellen—'

'No. No, don't. And don't tell Richard, Jackie. Peter's insisting he doesn't get told until after his next interview. '

'Oh, of course. I understand.' Though what he'll say when he finds out I've kept it from him, heaven only knows, she thought. 'Do you want me to tell Nelly, then? She could ring you?'

'No, she'll only mither; she doesn't need any worry at her age.'

'You need someone, Auntie Mary. You can't be on your own down there.'

'I'm not on my own. I've got Peter.' The line crackled again for some moments. Then Mary said, 'This is all Victoria's fault. He's literally worried sick about her.'

Chapter 27: Victoria Schormann

Ashford: Thursday, September 25th

Victoria was lonely. It was a week since she'd arrived and she hadn't made any friends yet. She knew that most of the women resented her. Probably because she was Seth's favourite, she told herself, pushing away the memory of two days ago.

She hadn't seen him to speak to since then.

She had thought it would be so different being in a commune; that she'd belong, be accepted for herself. Not as Richard's stroppy sister, or her parents' difficult daughter (which she knew was how they thought of her) but as one of the community – as Seth's girlfriend. It wasn't turning out like that, not yet anyway. Two of the girls in the dorm had already complained about the amount of time she spent on herself instead of taking on a share of the work. Well, stuff them, they could get lost. She had no intention of looking as grungy as they did. Any more than she was going to learn how to do the stupid knitting Jasmine had insisted she tried. She reckoned if she kept on dropping stitches Jasmine would give up on her. As for using that makeshift cooking range... Victoria shut out the humiliating scene. That woman, Chrystal, hadn't needed to be so nasty; how was she to know she was supposed to check there was enough wood to keep the fire going underneath? Wasn't that a job for the men? The tears came easily.

She breathed on the window and rubbed a circle in the grime on the glass with her finger. Peering out, she shivered. She hated it here.

She hated the rusted fence, just yards from the building she was in, and beyond it the expanse of wasteland. Hated the ugly skeletons of old buildings, mapped out on the ground by foundation stones covered in pink weeds and coarse grass. Hated the spindly-looking shrubs growing from the collapsed ruins of the old mill. She especially hated the large corroded metal sheets that had replaced part of an old fence, blocking off any view of the road beyond. By twisting her head she could just about see the large gates, padlocked together and leaning lopsidedly against two brick pillars. Like a bloody prison, she thought.

The excitement she'd felt last Wednesday, as they drove away from the boring little village in Wales, had gone. She'd replaced one stifling place for another.

If only she and Seth hadn't walked by the canal that day.

She flopped down on her mattress and looked down the long room that was allocated to the single women in the commune. There was no one else around but they'd left their smells behind. She crinkled her nose against the smell … no, the stench, she thought, the stench of sweat, of unwashed hair. Body odours. She pulled at the thin, horrid sheet of material that divided her mattress from the next. It didn't reach far enough for her; she'd have liked to shut everybody out completely. The so-called curtains separating the twelve narrow mattresses weren't enough to give Victoria the privacy she'd been used to. But they were enough to make her feel cut off from the other girls when they chatted at night.

That was how she knew that Seth held the daily meditations that she hadn't been allowed to go yet. All he'd said on the second day she was in the commune was, 'I'll know when you're ready to join in.'

She listened to their discussions, jealous of their time spent with him, envious whenever one of them had been singled out for group contemplation. Wanting to feel part of what they shared. To learn how to find that spiritual peace she'd been unable to find. That Seth had promised her that day, way back in the summer.

She'd sneaked out to meet him after her parents and Richard had gone with Auntie Jean to see the rest of the family on Henshaw Street. She'd feigned a headache but, from the scathing look her mother had given her, Victoria knew she wasn't believed. She didn't care; they were due to go home the following day and this morning she was supposed to be meeting Seth.

Her skin tingled with excitement when she saw the Volkswagen parked at the far end of Greenacre Street. She wasn't sure he'd keep the promise he'd made when she left him the week before at the festival. But when he got out of the van and picked her up in a huge bear hug she knew he felt the same as her.

'Let's walk,' she'd said. The farther away from Henshaw Street they were, the safer she'd feel. And, from past visits to Ashford, she knew it wasn't that far to the canal. So when they reached one of the sets of steps leading down to the canal she stopped. 'Down here?' There was less chance of being seen if they were on the path.

They walked, arms wrapped around one another, pausing only for him to kiss her – long slow kisses as though he was claiming her. And she was willing to submit to him, she realised. But not yet. And not here. When they stopped to kiss underneath one of the bridges she felt his hand on her breast, his knee nudging between her thighs and pulled back from him.

'Don't rush me, okay?' She searched his face, frightened he'd laugh, mock her, knowing somehow she still hadn't 'done it'. Because she hadn't. Sex was something she'd yet to discover.

There'd been plenty who'd tried it on with her. She wasn't stupid; she knew some of the boys in college really fancied her. But there hadn't been anyone she'd liked enough to go all the way with them.

Until now.

So she was nervous when she spoke. 'Not yet. Huh?'

He shrugged. 'Okay.' He gave her a light kiss on the lips and let her pull him along the path.

The grass along the edge of the canal lay flat, slimy. The surface of the sluggish water was covered in oily, multi-coloured swirls that almost hid the shapes of objects that had been thrown in over time. Victoria screwed up her nose against the faint smell of sewage. It really was a gross place. She wished she'd not suggested they walked here.

She saw him looking at the canal in disgust as well. She touched his cheek, turned his head so he looked at her. 'Tell me about yourself.' When she'd seen him with the other people at the festival she felt there was something about them she'd missed. 'Tell me about your family.'

'The people you saw me with at the fest – they're my family. Most of us have been together for ages. We don't want to be part of all the crap that's thrown at us day after day by idiots who think they're in charge.' He smiled at her, his eyes creased into laughter lines at the corners.

Victoria's stomach flipped over. She loved this man; she believed she'd loved him the first moment she saw him. So when he added, 'We've dropped out from all that,' she instinctively knew that was what she wanted as well.

'You're a commune?'

'Yep,' Seth lifted her arm, kissed the inside of her wrist. She felt the rush of heat between her thighs. He grinned as though he knew but only said, 'Yep, s'pose that's what we are: a commune. We live together, support one another, believe in a consciousness of a higher Self.'

His last words jarred with Victoria. 'I don't know…' she paused. 'I don't believe in any religion really, I stopped going to church when I was fourteen. I know my mother doesn't really either but, for some reason, she goes when my dad wants her to.'

'It's not like the religion that's been pushed down our throats since forever,' Seth said. 'I should know; my father was a vicar. Biggest hypocrite I've ever come across. He left us, ran off with one of the women in the church choir. Mum started to drink.' His eyes narrowed, he looked almost ugly for a second or two. Victoria caught her breath. Then he relaxed and smiled. 'Nothing I could do but get out. I was on the streets at sixteen. Hooked up with some of the others in '60. Best thing I ever did, believe me.

'You know, babe, all religions started as cults; Christianity was a cult centered around the guy Jesus. We're different from that, we're a commune; everyone is equal.' He hugged Victoria. It felt good. She relaxed against him. 'It's real cool, babe, honest,' he said. 'We meditate together every day. Better than a toke, you know?'

She didn't; as far as she knew there weren't any sort of drugs around in Llamroth. And so far she'd been a bit of a loner in college, so she hadn't been involved in anything going on there either. But she nodded, not wanting him to think she was uncool.

'I've read a lot about Transcendental Meditation,' she said. She'd watched the news about the Beatles a couple of years ago, when they'd gone to Bangor to meet that Yogi. She wasn't interested in the Fab Four: not like Richard, who copied everything about them, even the daft haircut. But for a few weeks after it happened it had been in all the Welsh papers; she'd heard some of the other girls in school talking about it and about Transcendental Meditation. They hadn't included her, of course; they never did. Not that she cared. But she'd listened and afterwards she'd gone to the library to find out what it was all about. It had fascinated her ever since. 'I've tried to meditate, as well. But it's difficult.'

'That's because of the negative thoughts, babe. Think about how many negative thoughts go through your mind every day, huh?'

Victoria flushed. It suddenly occurred to her that he was right. That's why she needed to get away from home. But did she dare? Was she brave enough?

As though he read her thoughts he said, 'Think about it, babe. About joining us? Being free from all the crap, eh? Promise I'll teach you how to meditate. Get peace.'

Had she finally found somewhere where she'd be welcomed just for herself? One where she didn't have to compete to be noticed?

'I'll think about it…'

The possibilities of what it would mean churned around in her head. She walked alongside Seth lost in thought.

'What's that place?' Seth stopped. He pointed past a line of shrubbery on top of the banking.

Victoria glanced upwards towards a long roof, green with a covering of moss. 'Looks like one of the buildings belonging to the old cotton mill.' She frowned. 'It's all in ruins now. Was called the Granville.' She hesitated. 'Used to be a POW camp in the war,' she'd said finally.

'Really?' Seth stared along the path towards the next bridge. Victoria followed his gaze. She could see the heads of two people walking past 'Is that a road there?' he asked. 'Going over the bridge?'

'Yes.'

'Leads to that place? The mill?'

'Passes it, yes.' A breeze ruffled the surface of the canal, rippling out the swirls of oily colours, the water swaying the slimy grasses along the edges of the banks. Victoria shivered, rubbed the skin on her upper arms. 'It's getting a bit chilly, Seth.'

'Let's just go and have a look. Eh?'

'Why?' Everything about the old mill gave her the creeps. Years ago Jackie had brought her here, told her it was where Linda had been kept for days by some weirdo. She debated on telling Seth about it. Decided she wouldn't. 'Let's just go, there's nothing to see. Honest.'

He'd pulled a face but followed her back along the path.

Yeah, letting Seth see this place had definitely been a mistake.

'Victoria?' A girl pulled aside the curtain, holding out a cup. She smiled. 'We missed you; you didn't come down for the mid-day meal. So I brought you this. It's soup.'

Victoria took hold of the cup. The handle felt thick and clumsy in her fingers.

'We haven't really spoken since you first arrived. Blossom? My name's Blossom. There are a lot of names to remember so don't worry if you've forgotten.' The girl waited for Victoria to reply. When she didn't she said, 'May I sit on your chair?'

Victoria nodded, not trusting the tone of friendliness from the girl.

'I suppose you're waiting for Seth.' It wasn't a question. 'It's difficult at first. I know.' She tucked her legs up under her chin and arranged her long purple skirt.

'What do you mean, "at first"?' The wrench of fear shook Victoria.

Without answering, Blossom loosened her long brown hair and shook her head, running her fingers through the strands. Peeping through them she asked, 'How did you meet him? Seth?'

Vicky considered not answering but then, off-handedly, 'A pop fest, just outside Manchester, earlier this year.'

'Hmm.' Blossom leaned forward, let her hair flop over her face. 'Thought so.'

This girl is so irritating, Victoria thought, peering at the brown liquid in the cup. There were circles of grease floating on the surface. She put the cup on the floor. 'What do you mean?'

'That's where he usually finds us.' Now Blossom was plaiting her hair. She spoke indifferently.

'Seth loves me.' Victoria made it into a statement.

'Of course he loves you.' The girl looked surprised now. 'He loves us all.'

Victoria clamped her lips together. After a few minutes the girl got off the chair. Before she left she patted Victoria on the shoulder. A touch Victoria shrugged off.

She was so tired. Perhaps if she could sleep at night she wouldn't feel so bad but she wasn't used to sharing a room with anyone, let alone eleven other girls. All the sounds in the night, the mutterings, the snores, the muffled noises of lovemaking kept her awake. Sometimes she swore she heard Seth's voice. But even when she crept out of the dorm with the excuse of going to the toilet, she couldn't make out the outlines of anyone in the darkness.

Victoria rolled onto her stomach and slid her hand under the mattress. She took out the two photographs that she'd had in her skirt-pocket when she arrived at the commune and studied them. The tears were unexpected. She ran a finger over the surface of the picture of Nain Gwyneth and then the one of her on her own. No, not alone. She peered at the hand holding hers; it had to be Richard next to her, but whoever had taken the photograph had misjudged the image and left him out. She wouldn't have believed how much she'd miss her brother but she did; she was so used to being jealous of him. Even though she loved him. She tried to ignore the next thought; just in that instant she missed all her family, her bedroom, with the walls covered in posters, her paintings. Proper curtains. Even the stupid little village. The feeling quickly passed. She'd made the choice to be here. She looked around the large room; at the bare walls, the mattresses covered with blankets the other girls had made and then back to her own mattress with the grey blankets Amber had given her: 'Until you make your own…'. Victoria blew a sigh out. Fat chance of that.

116

Lonely or not, she was here now. And one way or another she'd make it work. Somehow she'd make herself fit in. It was what she wanted.

Chapter 28: Richard Schormann

Manchester: Friday, September 26th

'*Duw*, I'm glad that's over.' Richard hooked his finger into his jacket-loop and slung it over his shoulder. He held out his other hand. 'You cool?'

'Yep.' Karen jumped down from the low wall.

'Did I tell you how fab you look today?' She'd matched her purple mini-dress with zig-zag patterned purple tights. A silver chain belt hung loosely from her hips. Richard raised her arm and twirled her around. 'Absolutely fab … u … lous.'

'Like it?' She giggled, falling against him. 'Thought we might have something to celebrate?'

'No. Not yet.' He kissed her the tip of her nose. 'They said they'd let me know.' He'd been more nervous than the first time, taking care to face each questioner, make sure he could see what they were saying, watching their expressions. He'd always been good at telling what people thought from their eyes. But today he hadn't been able to fathom any of the board out. They'd been impassive.

She lifted her mouth to his. Her breath smelt of peppermints. 'How did it go? Was it the same panel that interviewed you the first time?'

'No.' Richard pressed his lips on hers, savouring the taste. 'Had a good interview, though. Fingers crossed.'

'Everything crossed.' Karen demonstrated this by crossing her eyes.

'Idiot.' He grinned. 'If the wind changes, you'll stay like that. Mum always says that to Vicky when she's sulking.'

'Does your sister sulk a lot then?'

'All the time. She can be a right pain but she's cool mostly. And funny.'

'Then I'll like her.' She ran off, swinging her white shoulder bag and then turned and ran backwards, watching him and giggling.

'Be careful,' he called, 'you'll fall.' He chased after her and she turned again, slowing to a trot.

When he caught up with her, he held her to him. 'I can't believe we only met a week ago,' he said, kissing her neck.

'I know. I feel like I've known you all my life.' She tilted her face, looking at him. 'So, what shall we do this afternoon?'

'Haven't you got college?'

'No. Monday afternoon next.'

'Okay.' Richard loosened his tie and took it off. 'Need to get out of these threads before I do anything else. Then, if it's okay with you, I have to go and see someone for ten minutes. It's her birthday.'

'Her?' Karen huffed and pouted. 'Her?'

'Think she's about eighty.' He grinned. 'Ancient anyway.' He looked up as a bus trundled past. 'That's ours.' He grabbed her hand again. 'Come on.'

'So, spill the beans.' Karen hauled herself up the stairs of the double-decker bus and flopped down on the front seat. 'Whose birthday is it?'

Richard sat alongside her, folding his jacket over his arm. 'Never mind that for a minute.' He twisted in the seat and faced her, studying her face. 'You would tell me if you'd had any trouble from your stepfather because of that lad who saw us, wouldn't you?'

'Yes, 'course I would. Stop worrying, there's nothing George can do to me. To us. He's just a weird old git who thinks he's some sort of tough guy. I told you yesterday I haven't seen him

118

at all this week. I've been in college. I don't want to think about him, Richard,' she wheedled. 'Tell me again about the old lady.'

'It's a bit complicated.' Richard leaned back, linking his fingers behind his head. 'First of all, she's been a friend of Mum's for a long time, and Mum and Dad gave me a present to give to her for her birthday. But...' How to explain? He didn't understand half of what he'd always taken for granted. 'You know Uncle Ted and Auntie Ellen?'

'Where you're staying? The uncle I met?'

'Yeah. Well Linda is their daughter. My cousin...' Richard looked out at the road in front of them, the bus was stuck in a long line of traffic. 'We'd have been faster walking.'

'Don't be daft. Go on.'

'Well, Linda isn't really Uncle Ted's. Her mum had her before they were married.'

'And she kept her? Brave,' Karen murmured. 'She was brave to keep her in those days.'

Richard was embarrassed. 'Perhaps. Yeah, probably. Anyway Mrs Shuttleworth, the lady whose birthday it is, is the mother of the man Auntie Ellen had a fling with. Linda is her granddaughter. That's about it. Like I said, complicated.'

'Not really. Is she nice? Mrs Shuttleworth?'

'As far as I remember. I haven't seen her much. But Linda likes her. And Mum likes her. So she must be all right, I s'pose. Look, I have to call at Uncle Ted's, ring home to let my parents know how the interview went, and pick up the present and get changed. Is that okay? We can go to the pictures later if you like?'

'It's cool with me.' Karen kissed him.

Chapter 29: Linda Booth

Ashford: Friday, September 26th

'Hi, Linda. This is Karen.' Richard was smiling but felt the flush of heat in his face. He couldn't understand why he was self-conscious in front of his cousin but he was. 'Is it okay if she comes with us to Mrs Shuttleworth's? We're going on to the flicks after.'

Linda was reading. 'Hi, Karen. Course it is. Gran loves visitors.' She glanced up and then back to her book. Then she looked again, staring at the girl standing next to her cousin, her smile frozen on her face. George Worth's … *Shuttleworth*'s daughter. She closed her book. 'We've met, haven't we?' She forced the words out. How the hell could this happen? Nothing had, could have, prepared her for this. She put her book on the arm of the chair and shifted forward onto the edge of the seat. 'You're the daughter, aren't you?' she said. 'You're Harriet Worth's daughter?'

'Yes.' Karen response was wary, the smile strained.

There was something in her eyes that Linda couldn't make out. A plea? For what?

As though sensing the tension between the girls Richard touched Karen's hand. She gripped his fingers.

'Hey, what am I missing, here? Linda? Karen?' His stare switched from one to the other.

'Nothing,' Linda said, brightly.

'You two know one another, then?'

Never one to beat around the bush, Linda thought. 'Karen's mother's one of my mums at the moment. She's had a little boy.' How had she made her voice so jolly? 'Actually, a big bouncing boy.'

'Gosh, of course, you work in Maternity, don't you?' He pulled Karen to him. 'Coincidence, eh?'

'Coincidence.' Linda said, hoping her laugh didn't sound as artificial as it felt.

'Auntie and Uncle not around?'

'No. Dad's at the bakery and Mum's gone shopping for new shoes. Tea?' She attempted to get up from the chair but she was trembling. She willed it to stop.

'I'll make it,' Richard said. 'After all, I'm a modern man.'

Both smiled, smiles that faded once he'd left the room. Karen seemed rooted to the spot. She adjusted the strap of her shoulder bag, not quite meeting Linda's eyes.

'Sit down,' Linda said. It wasn't the girl's fault her father was a bastard. What he'd done to her was years before she was even born. And yet, by her being here, in their house ... their home, made Linda feel sick. She gulped. 'I'm sorry, I need to...' She lurched out of the chair, almost fell. Karen caught her by the arm.

'Steady. You all right?'

Linda shook her off; even the touch of her fingers made her skin crawl. 'Get off.'

Karen stepped back. She looked frightened. 'Sorry.'

Linda saw the fear. 'No, I'm sorry.' She pressed her lips together, waiting for the swirling sickness to settle. 'I think I'm okay now.' She counted three deep breaths: in through the nose, out of the mouth. Something she'd learned long ago to stop the panic after the nightmares. She let Karen help her back into the chair. They stared at one another in silence.

In the kitchen Richard was whistling. He suddenly burst out into song: 'Parsley, Sage, Rosemary and Thyme.' There was the sound of cupboard doors opening and closing. 'She'll be a true love of mine.'

'He's happy,' Linda said. She hoped he would stay that way. 'Does Richard know what he's like...' she couldn't say his name. 'Your father?'

'I'm sorry about my stepfather.' Karen flushed. 'You know, at the hospital. The way he—'

They'd both spoken at the same time.

'Your stepfather? He's not your dad then?' Linda was shocked by the relief she felt; she knew how much Richard liked this girl. Her not being his real daughter made it easier somehow.

'No, I'm glad to say.' This time she looked straight at Linda. 'He's horrible. A bully.'

'Well I won't disagree there.' Linda was calmer now. 'How long have your mum and him been married?'

'Dad died when I was ten.' Karen said. 'George worked for him. Then, before I knew, it he was always around the house. They married…' she stopped to think, 'about five years ago. I can't believe how much Mum dotes on him.'

'Or is afraid of him?'

'Yes.'

'Are you frightened of him?' It was like prodding a tooth that ached.' Linda couldn't help it. She watched Karen closely.

'Yes.'

'Does Richard know what he's like?' It was important; somehow she had to warn him, make sure he was on his guard. Understood what the man was capable of. Understood who he was. But was it up to her to do that? Ted – her dad, she corrected herself – and her mother hadn't said she had to keep it secret. But when they'd finished telling her everything it was almost an implicit understanding between them that she would. So all she could do was to find out if Richard realised the man was dangerous. 'Does he?'

'A bit. I've told him some things. But they haven't met. I don't want them to.'

'That'll be difficult.' Linda crossed her arms. 'If you carry on going out together, I mean.'

'Perhaps.' Karen sounded wary and still hadn't sat down, holding her bag in front of her as though for protection.

She's just a kid, Linda thought, she hasn't a clue what that man did. Any more than Richard knew what his father had done. Gooseflesh rose on her arms. Oh hell, it was all such a mess. She wished Ted and her mum were here. No, just her dad; he'd know what to do, what to say. She glanced at the clock; he'd be at the bakery for at least another four hours. She was on her own with this.

'Nearly ready, isn't it,' Richard shouted from the kitchen. 'Couldn't find the sugar.'

'I don't take sugar,' Linda spoke automatically. Unease rested just below her ribs. 'Nor me,' Karen said.

'No, but I do.' There was a tinkle of spoon in cups. He was singing again. 'Silence like a cancer grows...' He appeared balancing three cups and saucers on a tray, a tea towel over his shoulder. 'The singing waiter,' he announced, 'Mamas and Papas: "people hearing without listening..."' He took one cup off the tray and presenting it to Linda in an extravagant manner before straightening up. He looked at them. 'What's wrong?'

'Nothing,' they both said.

'Okay,' he said, drawing the word out.

It was plain to Linda that he didn't believe them, so she gave a small laugh. 'I was just saying you had a dreadful singing voice and Karen was sticking up for you.'

'Oh.' He grinned. 'I'll have you know I'm auditioning to be a member of the Beatles, cousin dearest.' He passed a cup to Karen and winked at her. 'Before we go, Lin, do you think Uncle Ted'd mind if I just ring home?'

'Don't be daft, 'course not.' Linda put her cup on the coffee table. 'Let me just get my shoes first, then you can have some privacy.' She went into the hall. 'We'll have our tea and then we really should be going.'

Reaching up to take her jacket from the stand she stopped, holding on to it. How was she going to tell Gran who Karen was?

Chapter 30: Linda Booth

Ashford: Friday, September 26th

If anybody else felt the awkwardness Linda couldn't tell. And why would they, she asked herself, forcing a smile as she watched Nelly open the present Richard gave her. None of them knew what she knew.

Nelly held up the blue bed-shawl. 'Ee, in't that lovely, pet? Look, Linda, what Mary sent. It's crocheted – in't it?' She dropped the shawl into her lap and waved Richard closer so she could hold his face between her hands, giving him a loud kiss. 'You pass that on to your mam.' She formed exaggerated lips around each word as though not sure he would hear.

Richard coloured. Linda wasn't sure if it was through annoyance or discomfort but was reassured when he smiled at Nelly.

'Now.' Her gran settled herself back in the armchair. 'Karen, I hear you rescued our Richard then? That's how you two got together? Are you local like? Where do you live?'

'Gran!' Both Richard and Linda spoke together.

'You'll frighten her off,' Richard laughed.

Nelly pushed at her teeth with her thumb. 'Sorry.' She made a sucking noise. 'I swear these bloody things are getting looser?' She worked her chin up and down. 'I only asked if she was local.'

'It's okay.' Karen looked a little bemused and flustered but answered with a smile. 'I live over in Mossbridge.'

'Still in school?'

'No, college. I'm training to be a hairdresser.'

I'll have to stop this, Linda thought. She stood. 'Tea, anyone?'

Nelly jumped. 'Hey up, pet, you nearly frightened the life out of me, getting up so quick. Where's the fire? We can have tea and that cake you brought in a minute. Sit down.' She gave a short laugh which finished in a rheumy cough. 'Sorry,' she said again, when she finally stopped.

Richard gave Linda a worried look. She closed her eyes, willing him to understand. Go now, she urged silently. Go now.

She could tell he was puzzled but still he said, 'Actually, we need to leave now.'

'You've not been 'ere five minutes, pet. And you've neither of you 'ad yer cake.'

'I know. I'm sorry. We've arranged to go … to go out, somewhere.' He added hastily: 'I'll call again before I go home. Promise.'

'When's that?'

'When I go home?'

Nelly nodded.

'As soon as I can book a ticket.'

Linda saw him exchange looks with Karen. She looked surprised; evidently he hadn't told her. 'I need to get back. See if there's any news about Vicky.'

'She's a right one an' that's no mistake.' Nelly pushed herself out of her chair. 'Yer mam must be worried out of 'er skin.'

'I'm sure Vicky's fine wherever she is.' Linda was more worried about her aunt. There'd been something not right in her voice when she'd spoken to her last night. And when she'd asked to have a word with Uncle Peter her aunt said he was out on a call, which was odd; since last year his partners had taken on the out-of-hours calls. And earlier Richard had told her his father wasn't there again. Linda didn't believe her uncle would go out, knowing they must be waiting to hear how Richard's interview had gone.

Chapter 31: Nelly Shuttleworth & Linda Booth

Ashford: Friday, September 26th

'Don't fuss, pet, I'm tons better than I was.' Nelly unpegged the last of the washing and dropped a large pair of bloomers into the wash-basket. She pushed the clothes-prop under the line, raising it up out of the way. 'Just a cough.'

Despite her words Linda thought she didn't look at all well. 'I can do a bit of cleaning for you now I'm here,' she offered.

Nelly swatted away her words with a flap of her hand. 'Good God no, pet. You're working tonight, aren't you?'

'No, I've got a couple of days off and then I'm on days.'

'That's nice.' Nelly reached inside her blouse and pulled at her bra strap. 'I'll be glad to get this off tonight. I don't know why I wear it anyway; nowt'll stop these buggers from going south.' Breathing heavily she laboured up the doorstep and into the kitchen and flopped down on a chair at the table. 'Shame our Richard had to go so soon. Still, that's youngsters for you. Always on the go for the next thing.'

Linda smiled, wryly. She clearly wasn't classed as a youngster any-more in her gran's eyes. 'S'pose. Think they said they were going to the pictures in Manchester. They'll be making the most of it while they can – if he's going home.'

'He looked well, don't you think? To say he's been under the knife again…'

Linda winced at the image her gran's words conjured up. 'It was only a small operation, Gran.'

'Stopped him coming up here when he should have.'

'You're right. Still, he's through it now – he just has to wait to see if he's been accepted.'

'Aye. Make that brew, will you, pet?' Nelly cleared her throat. Linda waited. But when her gran spoke it wasn't what she expected. 'And while you're at it you can tell me what you decided to do about Martin.'

Martin wasn't what Linda wanted to talk about. But, there again, nor was she keen to talk about George Worth – Shuttleworth, she corrected herself. Even worse, she needed to tell Nelly who Karen was.

She filled the kettle and turned the switch until the pilot light lit the gas ring with a whoosh. 'I haven't decided, Gran.' Leaning against the sink, Linda fiddled with the buttons on her cardigan. It wasn't worrying about her boyfriend that had caused her to lose sleep. 'I do feel bad about it, Gran, but I don't know what to say to him.' Even as she spoke her thoughts weren't on Martin.

'How about a flat no? He might get the message then.'

'It's difficult.'

'How, pet?' Her gran lifted her bushy grey eyebrows.

Linda shrugged and changed the subject. 'I'm thinking, if Victoria doesn't turn up, I'll go down to Auntie Mary's after next week. I've got some holidays left.' She glanced up and caught sight of herself in the fly-blown mirror above the fireplace. She looked tired.

'I think that's a grand idea, our Linda…'

The kettle boiled and Linda emptied the used teabags out of the metal teapot into the sink.

'Mind you warm t'teapot, pet.'

'I will.' Linda swished hot water round in it.

Nelly nodded, satisfied. 'It'll do you good to have a break and it'll be company for Mary. She must be worried sick, poor lamb.' She watched Linda drop two more teabags in the pot. 'I don't know that I'm as keen on them PG bags as much as Tetley's. They're a bit piss-shacks. Give 'em a good stir.' She watched as Linda did as she was told and then nodded in satisfaction. 'Good. Now, park your bum for a minute while it brews and cut this cake for us.'

They'd been skirting around what both of them needed to talk about for long enough.

'I wish you'd told me, Gran. About what happened… about everything…'

Nelly's face clouded. She took her glasses off. Her face looked naked without them – naked and scared and old. 'I couldn't, pet, it wasn't my place. It was up to your mum and … Ted … your dad. Ellen told me years ago not to open my gob about it to you.'

'Well, I know now.' Linda sucked on her lower lip. She didn't know where to start, how to tell her gran exactly who Karen was. What a bloody mess.

The back door was still open and she heard the first clear notes of a blackbird. She glanced towards the yard; he was perched on top of the prop.

'Beautiful, in't he?' Nelly said. 'Comes every night to cheer me up.' They listened for a few seconds before hearing an answering call. 'That's 'is missus. She'll be down in a minute, just watch. Surprising what little things make you feel better when you're old.' She reached for Linda's hand. 'You've 'ad ants in your pants since you got 'ere. You've got something to tell me, 'aven't you, pet? Besides the other stuff?'

It was a long night. Nelly knew she wouldn't sleep so she built up the fire Linda had lit, shuffled upstairs, dragged the eiderdown off the bed and settled in her chair. The flames cast long shadows around the room. Ashy cinders clattered every now and then into the pan under the grate.

Eventually, groaning with the stiffness of her limbs Nelly made herself stand and stretch before flinging the back door open and breathing in the cold air. The sky was black, clouded over with dark grey rain clouds.

She'd made up her mind what to do if her youngest son thought he could start any bother again. She'd be ready for him.

Chapter 32: Richard Schormann

Ashford: Saturday, September 27th

Richard couldn't sleep. Two o'clock and still wide awake. The whistling in his ears was driving him mad, he'd hoped the last operation would stop it, but it hadn't. He pushed the heels of his hands against them and pressed hard. It didn't make any difference.

It was always the same when he was stressed. He dragged the pillows higher against the headboard and pushed himself up in the bed.

The room was dark, the unfamiliar furniture vague shapes around him. He fumbled around, feeling for his hearing-aids on the table next to the bed. When he'd adjusted them the whistling was muffled under the night sounds around him: a train in the distance, Ted snoring in the next room, a catfight somewhere. He looked across the room to William's bed. He wasn't there. Richard remembered he'd said he was staying over at his girlfriend's house. Crossing to the window he peered through the curtains. More dark shapes: the yard walls, the houses beyond the alleyway, no moon. Black clouds pressed down over the house, threatening rain.

He shivered. Moving cautiously towards the door, he pulled on his dressing gown. His mouth was dry and he wondered if he would wake anybody if he went downstairs to get a drink of water. One of the top treads always gave out a loud creak but he couldn't remember which one.

The cold anxiety stayed with him. Coming face to face with George Worth as they came out of the cinema in Manchester had been a shock.

Richard saw the wide-eyed panic in Karen's face, pasty in the fluorescent lights of the front of the building. People shoved past them, a constant movement that shifted them this way and that. He gripped Karen's arm, drawing her closer to him. He was taller than the angry-looking man blocking their way but the overcoat made George Worth bulkier, more solid in comparison to Richard and the thought flashed through his mind that he was no match for Karen's stepfather. None of them spoke; they were a moment of stillness in the flowing crowd.

Then: 'Who's this?' The curt question caused Karen to straighten but before she spoke Richard held out his hand towards the man. If he could catch him off-guard perhaps they'd be able to get away quicker.

'Richard Schormann. I'm … a friend of Karen's.' The muscles around Richard's mouth, forcing the smile, loosened when he saw the increased hostility. He let his hand drop to his side.

'Who?'

'Richard Schormann. I'm a friend of Karen's. We've just been to the pictures, isn't it,' he added, knowing he was stating the obvious.

What was wrong with the man? His jaw jutted aggressively; he was bunching and flexing his fingers.

'He's my boyfriend.' Karen's tone was low but defiant. Richard saw her glance from side to side as though looking for a way out from the confrontation.

George Worth took a step forward, pushed his face at her. 'Get home. Now.'

The belligerence sickened Richard. Without thinking, he put himself between them. 'Hey, don't talk to her like that—'

'And you,' George Worth moved closer to Richard, prodding him on the chest, 'you really don't want to talk to me like that.' His breath hot and stinking of beer. 'You really don't.'

Karen stepped back. 'Come on, Richard, come away.' She tugged at his arm.

The pavement was clear around them now. At the entrance of the cinema the doorman gave a discreet cough. 'Everything in order, miss?'

'Yes … thanks.' She smiled at the man. 'Richard?'

He walked away from her stepfather. He'd never been so angry. When the man shouted again, 'Get home,' Richard half turned.

'No,' Karen muttered. 'Keep going.'

They'd hardly spoken on the way back to Ashford. Before getting out of the car at the end of Henshaw Street, Richard studied her. She was pale.

'You'll be all right?'

She didn't smile when she reached across to kiss him. 'I'll be fine.'

130

Richard hadn't believed Karen; the man was unmistakably dangerous. And when the loud banging on the front door started he instinctively knew it was her. He took the stairs two at a time, closely followed by Ted.

'What the heck?'

'I think it might be Karen.'

'Why?' Ted snapped the hall light on.

'Ted?' Ellen was peering around the bedroom door, Linda alongside her on the landing.

'Stay there.' Ted reached around Richard to take the bolt off the door.

Karen stood on the doorstep, her face streaked with tears.

Chapter 33: Linda Booth

Ashford: Saturday, September 27th

It took a long time to calm Karen down. She nursed the second cup of strong tea in her hands, huddled close to the gas fire in the front room. Richard sat on the arm of the chair stroking her arm with the back of his hand while Linda made up a makeshift bed on the settee.

'I'll sleep here. You have my bed,' he said to Karen.

'No.'

'He'll be fine.' Linda smiled at Karen. 'I've crashed here loads of times after a shift, as well.' She didn't add she'd also left Ellen there when she'd been too drunk to get upstairs and Ted was at the bakery. Nor did she show the anxiety she felt that George Worth's stepdaughter was now under their roof.

'She can't stay here, Ted.' In the kitchen, Ellen took a last long drag on her cigarette before stubbing it out in the ashtray on the table. 'God only knows what that man will do if he finds out where she is.'

'There's nothing we can do about it tonight, love,' Ted said. 'Let's just leave Richard to keep an eye on her for now and get to bed.'

'I don't like it.'

'I don't either, but we couldn't turn her away and there's clearly been some kind of bother.'

'Not our responsibility.' Ellen brushed ash off her dressing gown.

Joining them Linda knew if it was down to her mother Karen would be out on her ear, if she'd even managed to get through the door. 'Richard says for you to get some sleep.' Linda looked at Ted. 'And he says thanks for letting her stay, Dad…' She understood; the thought of seeing George Worth … George Shuttleworth … again terrified Ellen. *She* daren't even think of what would happen once he found out where Karen was. But for Richard's sake she wouldn't turn her back on the girl. 'Do you think we should tell Richard?' she asked Ted. 'About you know what.'

'We can't.' Ted frowned. 'Not until we talk to Mary. It's not our place to tell him.'

'Not our place?' Ellen lit another cigarette, her hands unsteady. 'Can I remind you it was our daughter he kidnapped?'

'And why, Ellen? This all started with what happened between Mary and that bastard's brother. What he did to her.'

Linda walked over to him and held him. 'It's okay, Dad, don't upset yourself. It'll all be okay.'

Ellen shook her head 'She can't stay,' she said stubbornly.

Linda ignored her. 'I'm going to bed.'

Chapter 34: Richard Schormann & Karen Worth

Ashford: Saturday, September 27th

'Tell me what happened, Karen.' The house was quiet again since everyone had gone upstairs. The only sounds in the room were the soft hiss of the gas fire and the trembling breath of the girl in his arms as they lay together on the settee.

'He was waiting for me.' She tipped her head back to rest it against his chest; her cheeks were taut with dried tears. 'I thought he wasn't in, but he was in the room where he keeps his canaries. Did I tell you he breeds canaries?'

'No…' Richard held back his anxiety, his frustration to know what happened when she got home. 'No, you didn't, *cariad*.'

'I've always thought it strange that a man who can be so horrible is so gentle with the canaries.' She spoke pensively. 'Mum always says she thinks he feels more for them than her.' She paused, tucked her hands up the sleeves of the pink jumper.

She's in shock, Richard told himself; let her take her time. He waited.

His attention was taken by a light going on in the bedroom window of the house opposite. The tall figure of a man was framed in the glass; he scratched his armpits. Richard looked above him to the chimney-pot on the roof silhouetted against gauzy light streaks of the dawn. Almost morning already. What would today bring?

'Karen?' He manoeuvred himself so he could see her face. 'What happened last night?'

When she spoke it was in a rush as though saying the words in such haste would lessen the harshness of them. 'He said I couldn't see you again. That he wouldn't have me going out with the son of a German.'

She faltered. What he'd actually said was that he wouldn't have her going around with a Kraut's son. His spit had sprayed her face.

'You keep away from him, d'you hear? I won't bloody have it.'

'Mum?' Karen held out her hands to her mother who was pacing the floor with the crying baby clutched to her.

'Don't argue, Karen, just do as your father says.' Her mother's voice was weary, there were dark hollows under her eyes.

133

'He's not my father, my dad's dead. He…' she shot a venomous look at George, 'he has no right to tell me what I can and can't do.'

George took three steps towards her and grabbed her arm. His eyes were narrowed and hard. 'He, madam, has a name. I'll thank you to remember that. And while you're under my roof, you'll do as you're told.'

'That's just it; it's not your roof, is it?' Karen jerked away from him and spun round, the settee a barrier between her and her stepfather. 'Mum?'

'Shush, you're frightening Frank.'

Karen opened her eyes wide to stop the threatening tears from spilling over, watching her mother pat the baby's back in a futile effort to stop the crying. Suddenly she felt so alone. And she was sure her mother felt the same, only she was too scared to admit it. When had this distance come between them? After her father died they'd clung to one another through those awful days. Then *he'd* come along. She glared at him.

'Keep looking at me like that, lady, and you'll be sorry.'

Karen swallowed. When she spoke again she kept her voice low. 'It's not your roof,' she repeated. 'It's not your house, not your furniture.' She thumped herself on the chest. 'And I'm not your daughter.' She stopped; the fear swelling in her.

No one moved. Even the baby was hushed. The stillness blanketed the room.

Then George lunged.

'He hit you?'

'No, I moved too fast for him.' He saw her quiet inward collapse to hopelessness. 'But I can't go back, Richard. I won't.'

'No. You won't.' He pulled her closer to him. 'You can stay here with me, isn't it.' He touched her chin with his forefinger, lifting her mouth to his. 'And when I go back to Wales you can come with me.'

Chapter 35: Richard Schormann

Ashford: Saturday, September 27th

Richard yawned and moved his neck from side to side, trying to ease the crick that had formed over the last couple of hours, and adjusted one of his hearing-aids that had become dislodged.

A line of bright light forced itself through the half-drawn curtains he'd hastily pulled together. It shone across Karen as she slept on the settee, clasped hands beneath her face. He was stunned that a girl as beautiful as her could like him so much that she'd stood up to her bigot of a stepfather.

Yet it worried him as well; what would happen now? He'd come to Manchester for a job and he'd be taking a girl, a stranger to his parents, back to Wales. *She's not a stranger to me, though. I'll make them understand*, he told himself, pushing to the back of their mind their worries about his missing sister

A group of people passed the house, their heads and shoulders shadows that moved swiftly across the window. He glanced down at Karen; she hadn't budged. But he needed to, he needed a pee. Badly needed a pee. He shuffled off the settee, inch by inch, watching her all the time.

He could hear that someone was already up; there were voices in the kitchen. But at the door, one hand raised to push it open, he stopped. One voice sounded agitated. He angled his head, listening.

'No, she can't stay here.' It was his aunt.

'Shush.' His uncle's low voice.

'I won't have that girl in the house any longer.'

The blood rushed to Richard's head. They were talking about Karen. Guardedly he moved the door enough for him to see through. Ellen was pacing the kitchen floor, smoking.

'We can't just kick her out.' Ted was sitting on one of the kitchen chairs, his hands clasped in front of him. 'We owe it to Richard to—'

'We owe nothing to Richard.'

'That's harsh, Ellen.'

'I'm sorry, Ted, but he'll be going home.' Ellen leaned on the table facing her husband. 'He'll go home and probably forget the girl. What happens then? Where does she go? Are you suggesting we let her stay here? For pity's sake, Ted, use your head. If that man ever finds out, God only knows what he'd do.'

'You're getting way ahead of yourself, love.' Richard shifted sideways, saw Ted rub his hands over his face. 'It won't come to that—'

'You know for sure, do you?' Ellen passed across Richard's vision again. Her face was flushed. 'Use your head, man. If he's still as bad as she's made out—'

Still? Richard frowned in puzzlement.

'He is.' Linda was in there as well. Richard couldn't see her but he heard the quiver in her voice. 'That's why we must look after her.'

'You're as bad as him – we don't even know her.'

There was a loud scrape of a chair. 'For goodness sake, Ellen, stop it. Not even you can be this selfish.'

'Are you saying we should do nothing?' His aunt's voice was lower now; he strained to hear. 'We'll be the ones threatened by that man. Again.'

Again? What did she mean? Richard touched the door, it opened further. He saw all three of them now. They hadn't noticed him.

'It won't come to that, will it, Dad?' Linda looked terrified.

What was going on?

'No, love, it won't.' Ted was glaring at Ellen. 'But if Richard gets into the university, he'll come back to Ashford, and if he and Karen stay together…' he reached out for her hands. 'We might have to deal with … things … then.'

Richard pushed the door wide. 'What things?'

In the silence, Ted cleared his throat, coughed, looked

136

uncomfortable. Linda crossed to put her arm around Richard's shoulder and turned to face her mother. The colour drained from Ellen's face and then returned a crimson red.

'Your Auntie Ellen's scared Karen's father would be angry we're letting her stay. But …' Ted waved both hands in front of him in a gesture of denial, 'it's nothing for you to worry yourself about, lad.'

Ellen's lips were a thin line. 'No, I'm sorry, Richard, it's best she's gone.' She paused as though thinking what to say. And then, 'From what I hear, her father—'

'Stepfather—'

'Yes, well … stepfather, then … has got a temper on him. We don't want any trouble but—' She was stopped by the warning look on Ted's face.

'The way you were talking,' Richard looked first at Linda and then at his aunt and uncle, 'it sounded as though you already knew him.'

'No.' Linda and Ted spoke together.

'It's just what Karen said last night,' Linda said.

Richard thought Linda's answer came too quickly.

His temper, usually slow to rise, took hold of him. 'Don't worry, Auntie, we'll both be gone soon.'

'Hey up, lad, she doesn't mean for us to kick you out.'

'Sorry, Uncle, but if Karen goes, I go.'

Linda squeezed him. 'No…'

'It's okay, Lin. Honest. I'll take her home with me.'

'No!' This time it was Ellen. 'No, you can't—'

'Why?' As Richard stared at her, Karen appeared behind him. 'What's wrong?' She gazed from one to the other of them.

No one spoke.

The doorbell rang, shrill in the silence.

Chapter 36: Jackie Howarth

Ashford: Saturday, September 27th

'Sorry it's so early, I'm just on my way home from night shift and I thought I'd call. Can I come in?'

'Bit formal, the front door, Jacqueline?' Ted held the door wider. 'Course you can come in.'

'I nearly came in the back but when I was in the yard I could hear raised voices so I thought I'd better come round to the front.' In the hall she lowered her voice. 'What's up, Uncle Ted?'

'There's been a bit of a to-do, like.' He whispered, holding on to the catch and quietly closing the door. 'Our Richard's girlfriend turned up in the night. Had a row with her dad.'

Jackie gave an inward groan; she wasn't going to help matters much. 'I heard Auntie Ellen; she sounded really upset.'

'Aye.' Ted pinched his nostrils between his thumb and forefinger. 'She is…' He hesitated.

Jackie could tell he didn't want to say anything more. No doubt she'd find out sooner or later. She gave a mental shrug. 'Actually it's Richard I want to see, Uncle. In private.' She looked meaningfully at the living-room door.

'Oh.' He followed her gaze. 'Oh, yes, of course. Go on in there, I'll tell him you're here. And I'll keep your auntie in the kitchen; make sure she doesn't come with him.'

'Thanks.' She smiled, reflecting on how much she liked this quiet man. And wondered, for what felt like the millionth time, how he put up with Ellen. And marvelled, yet again, when he opened the kitchen door and she heard Ellen's irritable questioning, followed by his appeasing tone.

'It's Jacqueline. She just wants a word with Richard.'

Jackie didn't hear what else was said; Ted closed the kitchen door. She wandered over to the window and stared out onto the street, then back around the room, so familiar from her childhood days. Most of the time she'd spent in this house with Linda, they'd had to go to her cousin's bedroom to play but sometimes, in the winter, if Ellen was out, her uncle had carried a shovelful of burning coals from the kitchen fire and laid them in the grate in the living-room. She and Linda had huddled around the fire and read books. Mostly happy memories.

'Jackie? You wanted to see me?' Richard appeared next to her. 'What's up?' He jerked his head towards the dividing wall. 'I can't stop long; Karen's in there, she's a bit upset.'

'Uncle Ted told me there was some bother.' Jackie ran her fingers through her short curly hair and straightened the collar of her shirt. She could sense the tension in him and regretted she was going to add to it. 'Close the door a minute. Let's sit down.'

He did as she suggested, watching her warily.

'How did the interviews go?'

'Okay. I'm just waiting to hear now.'

'You'll sail through.'

'Hope so.' Richard looked down at the carpet, chafed the back of his hand with the palm of the other in an old gesture Jackie recognised. She did the same thing when she was nervous.

She touched his arm, made sure he was facing her before she spoke. This would have been a lot better if they'd been strangers and she was just doing her job. She sighed; she'd try to make this as easy as possible for Richard but it would be difficult.

'I talked to your mum on the phone on Wednesday. It's your dad.' She lifted her hand to calm Richard as he took a shuddering breath. 'It's all right, he'll be all right.'

'What…?'

'He's had another small heart attack.'

'When?'

'Monday sometime.' Jackie said. 'And, like I said, according to your mum, he'll be fine.'

'Why did no-one tell me?' His voice lost the carefully modulated pitch he'd learned to use and now, thick with distress, was a flat monotone. He wiped his mouth with the back of his hand, swallowed against the tears.

'Nobody else knew except me. Your mum didn't want you to know until after your interviews. And to be honest she didn't want Auntie Ellen or Auntie Jean to go flogging down there. She said there was nothing either of them could do.'

'He'll be okay?'

'Yes. Well, they're apparently letting him out of hospital so he must be doing all right. Auntie Mary said to telephone her tonight after visiting time.'

'I tried last night. I wondered why they weren't in.' His voice rose. 'They never go out normally.'

'She must have been at the hospital.'

'I need to go home.' He stood up, suddenly decisive. 'I'll have to get a train ticket.'

'Yes. I'm sure Uncle Ted will help you to sort that out for you.' Relieved that he was calming down, she added, 'I'll come into the kitchen with you and let them know what's happened.'

In the hall, he turned back to her. 'This is all the fault of my stupid cow of a sister.'

'Hi, you must be Karen?' Jackie smiled at her.

'Yes.' The girl answered but her smile was strained.

Ted squeezed his palms together. He looked flustered. 'Let's all sit down, shall we?'

'Never mind that, what's the problem?' Ellen pushed past Karen and Linda. 'Is it Mary?' She moved to steady herself against Ted, clutching hold of him. 'Ted?'

He patted her hand. 'Shush now. I'm sure Jacqueline would have said if it was your Mary.'

'It's not Mary,' Jackie said. 'It's Uncle Peter; he's had a slight heart attack.'

'No.'

Hearing Linda's gasp, Jackie said hastily, 'He'll be all right.

140

They're letting him home so he must be getting better already,' she said, for the second time in ten minutes. 'But Richard should go home.'

'Yes, of course he must,' Linda said.

Karen moved to his side, put her arm around him.

'How did you find out?' Ellen said.

'Auntie Mary told me.'

'Why didn't she ring me? I am her sister, after all,' Ellen said. 'You'd think she would have told me.'

Linda made a small, exasperated noise.

'I'll go to her. Now.' Ellen moved towards the door. 'I'll pack.'

'No.' Richard barely glanced at her. 'No.'

Ted put his hand out to hold onto Ellen. 'He's right, love, you shouldn't go. Not yet.'

'Why not?' She shook him off.

'It's not the right time,' Ted said, firmly. He nodded to Richard. 'We'll go to the station and see if we can get you on a train today.'

'Thanks, Uncle.'

'I'd like to go too, if that's all right with you, Richard?' Linda said. 'I'd like to help.'

'Okay, Lin.'

'Well, then, I should come with you,' Ellen complained.

'No, love,' Ted said, 'our Linda's a nurse, she'll be more use than any of us can be. Let her go.'

'Karen's going to come with me,' Richard said.

'Perhaps better not.' Linda said.

'Why?'

She was flustered. 'Well, with your dad…' The words trailed away.

Jackie watched. There was evidently something going on she didn't know about. Linda was upset. And she was right. With all the worries about Vicky and their uncle's heart attack, Auntie Mary had enough to put up, never mind a stranger landed in her midst. Now Linda was looking straight at her and the familiar silent conversation, which had stood them in good stead since childhood, kicked in.

'How about staying with me until things get sorted?' she said to Karen. 'No problem.'

Chapter 37: Linda Booth

Ashford: Saturday, September 27th

'I don't see why we had to meet here.' Martin scuffed at the gravel on the path, picked up a stone and skimmed it along the surface of the lake. His lower lip jutted out. 'Or this early.'

'It's ten o'clock. And I'm getting a train down to Wales tomorrow, my uncle's ill and there's some family stuff that needs sorting.' Linda waited to get his full attention, wishing she was anywhere but here and with anyone but him. She was going to hurt him and she was sorry about that, but better now than years down the line. Years in which she was sure they would both be miserable.

He ignored what she'd said. 'I was nearly here before the park keeper.' He pushed at one of the canoes with his foot, sending the whole row bobbing one by one.

Linda battled to keep her patience. She sat on the bench pulling her blue maxi-coat over her knees and clutched her shoulder-bag on her lap. Patting the seat of the bench, she said, 'Come and sit down, Martin, there's something I want to tell you.'

'I'm all right here, thanks.' He stood looking down on her, his arms folded.

She met his glare. 'It's not easy and I'm sorry—'

'You want to pack me in, don't you?'

'I wouldn't be being fair if I let things go on.'

'How noble.' His lips moved into a sneer. 'How bloody noble of you.'

She understood his anger. 'Martin—'

He didn't give her a chance. 'I knew it. I've known since the other day ... since you stood me up at the last minute.' He fumbled in the pocket of his sports jacket. When he held his hand out it was to show her a small box. 'Know what this is?' he demanded. 'Cost me a bloody fortune, this ring did!'

Linda winced; it always came down to money with him. But still she said, 'I'm sorry.'

He raised his eyes. 'Stop bloody saying sorry. Just tell me why!'

She couldn't, not really. 'I don't want to get married and that's what you want.'

'You could have told me that before I went chucking my cash around.' He shoved the box back into his pocket, turned his head to one side and spat. The globule just missed her foot. When he looked back at her there was a challenge in his eyes.

Like a spoiled little boy, Linda thought, even as she understood his anger. Had she led him on? She wasn't sure but then admitted she'd let him think they would eventually get married. Why? She'd known for a long time it wasn't what she wanted. And it wasn't just that she needed a career. No, if she were truthful ... even if it was only to herself ... she'd been bored with him for a long time. With his penny-pinching ways, his counting the cost of every time they went to the pictures, went on a bus, a train, shopping together. Last month he'd even chastised her for spending her own money on a new pair of shoes, she remembered.

The sudden spark of irritation pushed the guilt to one side. 'I didn't ask you to. You just took it for granted we'd get married.'

'Round about the same time you let me in your knickers.' He sneered. 'Or do you do that for all the lads? From prick-tease to slut in one easy week.'

That's it; enough is enough, Linda thought, standing up. She pulled the strap of her bag onto her shoulder, watching a girl approach, carrying a transistor blasting out the Rolling Stones' 'Honky Tonk Women'. Linda waited until she was sure Martin

143

would hear her next words. 'I think we've said everything that needs to be said.'

Martin picked up some stones and turned to skim one across the lake without speaking. She watched. The water mirrored the sky: gloomy clouds skating across the surface, now rippled by the bouncing stone until it sunk.

He chucked in the last of the stones with a flick of his wrist. One rattled into the first canoe. 'Don't bother getting in touch again. Cow.' He walked away from her before spinning on his heel and almost tripping over a dog. The owner mumbled something at him; Linda couldn't hear what it was but she heard Martin's reply. 'Sod off.'

Then he pointed at her. 'Oh, and by the way, I'll have that bracelet back I bought you for your birthday. I should be able to sell it. Get my money back – salvage something from the fiasco I thought was a relationship.'

Linda didn't answer. He'd get the bracelet back; she'd make sure of that. She blinked hard against the burn in her eyes. What did she expect?

She watched him walk past two girls, walking arm in arm and giggling, looking at him surreptitiously. He cocked his head at them, gave a wolf-whistle. 'Okay, girls?' she heard him shout, walking backwards and whistling again.

Linda looked back at the lake. She wouldn't give him the satisfaction of knowing she'd seen.

The lake was black; there was no reflection of the sky any more. The first heavy drops of rain splattered on the path.

Chapter 38: Victoria Schormann

The Granville: Saturday, September 27th

Yesterday she'd been allowed to join a group meditation. Candles in each corner of the room cast a golden glow on the images of spider in their webs and different birds – owls, falcons, even sparrows – which covered the walls. One wall was curtained over, a ceiling-to-floor length of purple material. The air was filled with a strange, almost unpleasant, scent.

When she first filed in behind the women Seth was sitting on a chair at the front of the room, his head bowed, his hands folded on his lap. He wore a long white kaftan. Tall cream candles were placed on top of wooden boxes on each side of him. A small table was behind him. On it was a small bowl and a short stump of something that looked like dried grasses.

The meditation had been nothing like the Transcendental Meditation Victoria had tried to learn. Nothing like it at all.

Besides Seth and two of the older men he called the Elders, there were twenty others in the room. After they sat cross-legged on the floor in front of him, he held out his arms as though encompassing them all. It was as if Victoria had never seen Seth before; she couldn't keep her eyes off him. He seemed unapproachable, powerful in some way. Her scalp prickled. Although she didn't dare to look around she guessed all the others were mesmerised as well.

At first he spoke in a calm voice. As Victoria concentrated on her breathing she listened to his words.

'Dear Higher Self, we are here to release past fears and pain. That which no longer helps with our cleansing and purification we discard. Help us to see everything in an enlightened perspective and move forward with wisdom, strength and, above all love.'

Two figures stepped from behind the curtain. Victoria saw they were the girls who'd also been at the Manchester festival and were brought into the commune by Seth and River the week after her. She'd nicknamed them Cow Parsley and Dandelion. She hadn't liked them from the moment they'd arrived, with their simpering stupid faces and creepy-crawly ways of trying to get in with all the other women. Always offering to cook or clean the dorm, sitting with the girls who made the rag rugs, giggling when they had to be shown – yet again – how to thread the material through. She scowled; she'd no time for them.

Now here they were. Jealousy flooded through Victoria; why were they part of this morning's session when this was the first time she'd even been allowed to attend?

One of them picked up the small bowl and taking a cloth from it squeezed out water. The other struck a match and held it to the stick of dried grasses until it smouldered. Holding a plate underneath to catch ashes she wafted the smoke over Seth and into the corners of the room before walking around the group doing the same.

Victoria forced a loud cough. Taking in a breath the smoke caught her throat and she swallowed hard to try to stop the irritation. Worse, through the tears streaming down her cheeks she saw the one she called Cow Parsley take Seth's sandals off, wipe his feet with the cloth before putting them back on. Victoria couldn't prevent the gasp and began to cough again. This time she couldn't stop. She heard the disapproving noises from the people around her. Someone behind patted her hard on the back. At first she was grateful, but the action started to get a fraction too hard and she shrugged the hand away.

When she finally stopped choking she looked towards Seth; he'd stood up. She saw the subtle change in his face, the rise of colour in his cheeks the tightening of his lips. When he spoke he fixed his stare on her. She met his eyes; goose bumps raised the hairs on her arms but she wouldn't let him see how resentful she was.

146

'We have cleared all negative energy from the room. Rain…'

Not Dandelion then, Victoria thought. She forced down the nervous laugh.

'… will open the windows, release old energy and allow fresh air to flow through.'

Seth paced the floor in front of the small crowd, his kaftan softly swishing with each turn, his sandals lightly creaking as he walked. His voice grew louder, melodic. At either side of her the people were swaying in time with his words. She had no option but to move with them.

'Let us leave behind what no longer serves us and cross over onto a new and illuminated path.' He stopped in front of Victoria. 'Leave behind material things, the evil of worldly wealth, those who damage us with their presence.' He lowered his hand to touch the top of her head. 'Stand, Summer.'

She felt she had no option. But he kept his hand on her head so she had no choice but to lower it so that her chin was on her chest.

'We expect complete, exclusive devotion – not merely a partial, lukewarm, half-hearted following. We expect reverence.'

Who is he talking about? Who's 'We?' Victoria thought, conscious of the heat of his hand on her scalp, his fingertips pressing in.

'We expect devotion. It is our right. We are worthy of nothing less.'

Victoria listened in disbelief, unable to keep the shock hidden when he lifted her chin for her to look at him.

He smiled.

Uncomfortable, she rubbed at her upper arms and glanced down towards the girl next to her. She was staring back. For a few seconds Victoria thought to leave. To walk out. She must have made some movement because there was a slight tug on the back of her skirt, stopping her. The two Elders stood in front of the door. It was then that Victoria realised the meeting had been held for her. She was trapped. And, for the first time in her life, frightened.

Seth gave a small murmur of satisfaction and moved away to sit back on the chair. All around her people stood up. Others threw themselves forward on the floor in front of him, weeping and crying out to be saved. Saved from what, she'd thought? By who? Seth? She didn't know how long she stood there but it was long enough for her to stop being scared and to become angry. And long enough for her to decide she wouldn't be going to another of Seth's so-called sermons.

In the middle of the night he'd slipped into her narrow bed. Naked. Pulling at her baby-doll pyjamas he'd whispered, 'Come on, then, shove up.'

Victoria moved to the edge without speaking. The anger bubbled in her again.

'Still sulking?' he laughed, softly. 'You should've seen your face.'

When she didn't answer he slid his hand under her top, slowly moved his palm over her nipple. She arched her back, unable to stop the instinctive tightening between her thighs.

'See, you're not really cross with me.' He laughed again.

Cross? Victoria thought, twisting towards him, trying to see his face in the darkness and failing. 'What the hell was all that, this morning?' she said.

Without speaking he eased her out of her pyjamas, ran his fingers along her stomach. She caught her breath.

'You didn't believe all that, did you?' he murmured, his tongue tracing the inside of her ear. 'It's what they wanted.'

'What they wanted? Come off it.' Incredulous, Victoria pushed him away. 'That was just weird.' The tears smarted. 'And you were cruel. You just wanted to make me look stupid.'

'You have to learn to fit in. Some of the others don't think you're pulling your weight. I had to do it.' All the time he was sliding his fingers inside her.' I want you to stay. You're special to me. I need you by my side. I need you with me.'

Victoria's breath was shallow. She knew she was giving in to him. 'I thought we would be together.' She spoke in a small voice.

'And we will be.' He moved even closer, whispering. 'This lot, they chose to call me the Master. I just play the game. You and me – well, we're different, aren't we. We know the score. There are a few of the others…' She stiffened, he must have felt it. 'But not like us, huh? You and me, we're special. Right?'

He slid on top of her, entered her.

After he'd left her bed Victoria hugged herself. She knew he was right. They were special. Sod the rest of them. She was Seth's girlfriend. Woman, she corrected herself. So what if she wasn't accepted into the group? She'd been on the outside all her life. But she'd make sure some of them liked her. She'd play the game as well.

She refused to listen to the small voice that reminded her she'd left home to find somewhere where she truly belonged. And the reality of it was, it wasn't here.

Chapter 39: William Booth

Ashford, evening: Sunday, September 28th

'Think that's the lot, sweetheart.' William swung Tim up into his arms and gathered him into a hug with Susan. 'I'll be back around seven to put this young man to bed and get settled in.'

He stopped, seeing the apprehensive expression on her face and put the little boy down. They watched him climb onto the settee with two of his lead soldiers, tapping them on the cushions in a make-believe march.

'You are sure about this, Susan? I mean, it's not too late to go back to how we were.'

'No, it's absolutely fine.'

He tipped his head to one side. 'Fine?' he questioned, grinning.

'Okay, wonderful then. I've written to Charlie at his mother's and told him it's over for good. I've been telling him for the last twelve months, he just wouldn't listen. At least he's not been near the house this leave, not even to see…' she motioned her head towards her son. 'So perhaps he's finally got the message after—'

'He got handy with his fists. I remember.' William clenched his own at the memory. 'You should have sent for me. Let me come round. I mean, he'd have got the message quicker then.'

'I don't want him, you, either of you, hurt. You know I don't like violence around Tim.'

'Yes, of course. Sorry, sweetheart. It just makes me mad.'

'I know. Now,' Susan gave him a wide smile and picked up her son, 'you'd better go home and break the news to your mum and dad.'

'You mean go to Henshaw Street and tell them.' William grinned again. 'This is my home now, isn't it, young man?' He tickled Tim. The little boy squealed and leant away from his mother to give William a tight hug around his neck.

'Good grief, that's a squeeze and a half you've got there, little un,' William laughed. His face grew serious as he turned to Susan. 'I'll be back in an hour.'

'Good luck.'

'I don't need luck. I'm my own man, haven't you learned that yet?' He put his thumb up to Tim. 'See you soon.'

'Soon.' The little boy put both thumbs up.

Outside William sat astride his bike and looked at the small terrace where his future lay. He wouldn't let any harm come to the woman and child who lived there. His jaw tensed at the memory of the battering she'd taken. The only time he felt he'd let them down.

Chapter 40: Nelly Shuttleworth

Ashford, afternoon: Sunday, September 28th

'Why are you 'ere?' Nelly settled back in the armchair and took a bite of the bacon butty she'd just made. A blob of tomato sauce, squashed out from between the two slices of bread, dropped onto her thumb and finger. She sucked at it. She was on her own territory and had no need to feel less than the woman sitting at the table in front of her. That's not to say it hadn't been a shock, five minutes earlier, to see Ellen Booth standing on her doorstep. And she could tell from the way the woman looked – as if she had a bad smell under her nose – that she was judging her and her house. As if she had any right.

'Linda's taken a week's holiday and caught a train to Wales with Richard.'

'She said she might.'

'I thought Martin might go with her but when I asked if he was she didn't answer. Something's happened between them, I think.' She stopped as though Nelly might enlighten her but after a moment added, 'I don't know what's happened about Martin …'

Nelly clamped her mouth closed, wiggling her teeth with her tongue to get a bit of bacon from under them. She'd only just managed to put them in when the doorbell rang and they were rubbing her gums. But she was damned if she'd take them out in front of this snooty bitch.

'Something has.' Ellen paused.

'Has what?' Nelly was careful how she spoke, for some reason she'd always tried to speak proper in front of this woman. She'd long since stopped hating her. Now she just disliked her intensely and hoped she wouldn't have to see her too often.

'Happened between Linda and Martin.'

Nelly jerked her shoulders. 'Is that why you're here? I know nowt … nothing about that.' What she did know, she sure as hell wasn't going to tell Linda's mother; a confidence was a confidence. She nodded, agreeing with herself.

'No, of course not. Why should you?' Ellen unbuttoned her turquoise jacket and shook the lapels open to show a pristine white blouse. She looked rattled; Nelly pressed her lips together to stop the grin, yet dreading what Ellen was going to say. 'No, I'm here because of…'

The hiatus between them lengthened, only the low tick of the clock on the mantelpiece and Nelly's rasping breathing broke into the silence.

'You know, I suppose?' Ellen blurted the words out.

'Know what?'

'Oh, for God's sake. About your son?'

'Oh, that.' Nelly wouldn't let her know how that word made her heart race. 'I know. Yes.'

'Linda said last night she'd told you about—'

'George? Yes, she did.' Even saying his name made Nelly nauseous; years ago she could have handled this but now…

'It was a shock when Ted told me, I can tell you that.' Ellen pulled at the cuffs of her jacket, wafted her hair back from her face with a toss of her head. 'Until this last week I didn't even know Linda'd been having trouble at work.'

No, you wouldn't. Nelly thought, studying her, ignoring the fact that Linda had only told her just before telling her mother.

Ellen was pronouncing her words so precisely Nelly wondered if she'd already been drinking, even though it was only early afternoon. 'And about this girl Richard's met?'

'Yes?' Nelly wasn't going to help.

'She's his stepdaughter, I believe.' Ellen shivered. 'I felt sick when we found out who she was. We don't know what to do except hope Richard forgets her once he's home.'

'I think that's a lost hope. He'll be coming back to Ashford, or at least, Manchester, if he gets that job at the hospital.'

'What can we do?'

What did she mean, *we*? 'Nowt. Nothing we can do.' Nelly felt a wave of worry. 'Has anybody told Mary?' She sucked on her teeth. How was poor Mary going to deal with all this?

'Well, no. We can't at the moment. Obviously.'

'What d'you mean ... obviously? Why can't she be told?' She saw from the almost triumphant look on the woman's face that Ellen knew something she didn't.

'With Peter having his heart attack last week.'

Oh, Lord. Nelly's skin tingled with shock. 'I didn't know,' she said, slowly.

'I wanted to go to see her but Ted and Linda thought I shouldn't. Not yet anyway.'

Quite right, Nelly thought – selfish mare. The last thing Mary needs is this one blubbering all over the place and making it all about her.

'And anyway, I thought it better that I come to see what you intended to do.'

'I don't intend to *do* anything.' Nelly's thoughts were still on Mary. She wondered how she could get hold of her, speak to her. She'd never held with having one of them telephones in the house but now she regretted it.

The back gate opened and closed with the familiar squeaking of the hinges and then a tap on the back door, which was slightly open.

'Mrs Shuttleworth? It's Jackie. Are you there?'

'Come in, pet.'

Jackie was clearly surprised by Ellen's presence. The young woman who followed her in had her hand on Jackie's shoulder. Must be her friend, Nelly thought: the one Linda had told her about. 'Nicki, is it, pet?' She was enjoying Ellen's discomfort; she could tell Linda's mam didn't know what to make of the girl in her big boots and dungarees.

'Yes.' The girl smiled, holding out her hand to Nelly. Her grasp was warm and firm. 'I've heard a lot about you, Mrs Shuttleworth.'

'All bad, I 'ope.' Nelly chuckled.

'We popped in to say we just called at your house, Auntie Ellen, to make sure Linda and Richard had got off all right.' Jackie glanced from one to the other of the two women. 'Uncle Ted told me you were here, Auntie. I was a bit surprised.'

Ellen looked discomfitted.

''Ow's Peter?' Nelly asked.

'Uncle Ted said you might let slip about Uncle Peter's heart attack.' Jackie glanced at Ellen.

Let slip my backside, Nelly thought; the woman gloried in telling me.

Ellen bristled. 'How was I to know it was supposed to be a secret?'

'Anyway he's fine, Mrs Shuttleworth. Uncle Ted's spoken to Auntie Mary and she said he was recovering brilliantly.' She looked at Nelly. 'She says she'll write and let you know but, if Richard gets the placement at the hospital, they'll be coming here anyway and she'll see you then. She said she'll ring you, Auntie Ellen.'

Ellen moved her head acknowledging Jackie, but didn't take her eyes off Nicki.

'Well, that's all really. We're just on our way out.' Jackie gave Nelly a hug. 'Linda asked me to keep an eye on you while she's away, Mrs Shuttleworth. She says you have to behave yourself and take your tablets. So I'll… We'll call in tomorrow.'

Nelly had seen Jackie noticing Ellen's gawping. She grinned as Jackie took hold of Nicki's hand as they left.

'Well,' Ellen said, 'Well. How extraordinary. What an odd way for a young woman to dress. And that hair. She might as well have been a bloke, it's that short.' She stood, fastening the buttons on her jacket and smoothing down her pencil skirt. Taking a long breath she stared down at Nelly who couldn't stop the grin.

'You'll let me know if anything… If he turns up?' Ellen's lip was quivering.

The worry was instantly back. Nelly frowned. For once she felt sorry for the woman. 'I'll let you know, Mrs. Booth. But I wouldn't fret. I doubt he'll come here. I doubt you'll get any hassle off him. From the sound of things…from what your Linda said, he's got a new life now, as well as a new name. He won't want to be found any more than we want anything to do with him.'

Ellen lowered her head. 'I hope you're right!' Her mouth almost moved into a smile.

When the gate closed, Nelly blew out her lips in a long sigh. She pulled at her top set of teeth and put them on the table. She hoped she was right as well.

Chapter 41: Ellen & Ted Booth

Ashford, evening: Sunday, September 28th

'Our William's moved out…' Ted was hosing down the yard and sweeping the water out into the alleyway when Ellen arrived home.

'What?' She barely took in what he'd said. Calling on Nelly Shuttleworth was a big mistake; it was as if the woman had been judging her for some reason. And the old bat definitely knew more than she let on. Ellen bit the skin at the side of her thumbnail. She'd learned nothing and, from the look of things, Nelly Shuttleworth wouldn't do anything either. Hell's bells, George Shuttleworth – Worth, whatever he was calling himself these days – was her son, after all. It was up to her to tell him that it wasn't their fault their nephew was seeing his stepdaughter. They hadn't encouraged him.

If anything happened to Linda again she didn't know what she would do. It didn't matter what Ted said about Shuttleworth not wanting to raise his head above the parapet, not wanting to get noticed by the police, he was a nasty piece of work. If he intended to harm them in some way, he would. No police threat would put him off. She was scared.

Ted straightened up, leaned on the brush. He was staring at her, as though waiting for a response.

She noticed her husband fingering the faint scar on his cheek, the constant token of his time as a prisoner of war. And an uncomfortable reminder that she'd learned to love him once – was still quite fond of him sometimes, before too many memories crowded in. Her throat constricted with wretchedness, despising him for his weakness: despising herself because she knew she needed him, would never leave this bloody place.

She frowned, taking off her jacket and folding it over her arm. 'What did you say?'

'William's moved out. He's left home.'

'What do you mean, he's left home?' Her voice shrilled. She knew she'd lost Linda years ago because of the drinking, but her son had never judged her. Now he had gone? 'Why?'

Ted sighed. She had that hard look on her face, her mouth tight into a line, her eyebrows drawn together in a peevish frown. For the first time he saw how bitter she looked. 'He's gone to live with that girlfriend of his. The one he's been seeing for the last year.' And good luck to him, Ted thought, he's better off out of here.

'The one we've never seen, you mean.' Ellen stood rigid in the doorway, poised to attack.

'Aye, well, perhaps there's a reason for that.' Ted was weary. Too much was happening lately. On top of trying to keep Ellen off the booze all the time, this business with George Shuttleworth was tiring him out. The last thing he was wanting was a row.

'Which is?'

'She's married.'

'Oh, my God.' She'd turned away to go into the kitchen but stopped when he spoke again. The tension in her chest only allowed short abrupt intakes of breath,

'And with a kiddie.' Ted watched her warily. 'Separated, he says, though.'

She didn't move. Still with her back to him she said in a taut voice 'And has he told you where he's gone? Like his address?'

'No, I didn't think to ask. He said he'd come round in a couple of days and have a chat with you.'

Air rushed into Ellen's lungs with a huge inhalation. 'So he could have gone to Timbuctoo for all you know. For God's sake, Ted, you're useless.' She threw her hands into the air. 'How much more can I take from this family?'

She crashed the door closed behind her.

Ted shut the yard gate and carried on sweeping what was left of the dirty water into the grid in the middle of the yard. She'd come round; she always did. But no doubt he'd be on the sharp end of her tongue for a few days. And no doubt she'd be down to the offy to get some booze and he'd be eating the corn beef and potato hash he'd gone to all that trouble to make, on his own. Ted folded his hands on the brush and rested his chin on top. Good job Linda's away to Mary's, he thought. He wondered if she and Richard had got to Llamroth yet. And how soon she'd tell Mary about George Shuttleworth.

Chapter 42: Linda Booth & Mary Schormann

Llamroth: Sunday, September 28th

'It's so lovely to see you again, Linda.' Mary hugged her niece as she stepped from the train. 'Richard, sweetheart.' She faced him, touching his cheek. 'You all right?'

'Long day. The train went all over Wales to get here,' he said.

'We're lucky this station stayed open,' Mary said. 'A lot didn't.'

'I know,' Richard said. 'You might have had to come to Cardiff to get us, isn't it. Anyway, more important, how's Dad?'

'It was just a minor scare in the end. He's friendly with the heart specialist at Pont-y-Haven and he pulled some strings. They let him home, providing he rests.' Mary gave a short wry laugh. 'But he's a fidgety patient, to say the least; I've nearly had to tie him down. Anyway, he's much better.'

'Used to being on the other side of the desk,' Richard said.

'You're right. But seeing you two will be the best tonic for him.' She included each of them in a smile but her voice faltered. 'If only your sister would let us know where she is.'

'So no news?'

'No.' Mary's eyes filled; she brushed the tears away. 'Nothing. We can't think where else to look, who else to ask.'

Linda fiddled with the strap on her suitcase, an unwilling onlooker to her aunt's distress. If Vicky was standing in front of her right now she'd give her a good shake. Her cousin's selfishness made what she had to tell Auntie Mary more difficult.

'She'll be fine; you do know that, don't you?' Richard said. 'She's perfectly capable of looking after herself.'

'I hope you're right.'

'I am.' Richard hoisted his rucksack onto his shoulder.

Mary touched it. 'That new?'

'Yeah. I'll tell you about it sometime.'

The porter slammed shut the last of the doors and blew on his whistle. With a squeal of wheels the train stuttered away from the platform and out of the station.

'You must both be worn out after that journey.' Mary linked arms with both of them.

'Exhausted.' Linda picked up her suitcase with her free hand. 'Thought we'd never arrive.'

'Let's get you home, then. I parked the car on the road outside the station.'

Twenty minutes later they were at the cottage.

'It's great to be here. Just look at that sunset.' Linda watched the colours flickering through the trees on the opposite side of the road as the sun dropped below the horizon in a blaze of fiery orange and scarlet, lighting the sea into a ruby redness. High above, creamy yellows and pinks rippled through the layers of clouds. 'Beautiful,' she breathed, 'just beautiful.'

They stood for a moment by the gate, savouring the peace. Then: 'Come on; let's get your bags out of the car and into the house.' Mary shooed Linda in front of her. 'Your Uncle Peter's in the back garden. At least, he was when I left to pick you up. He'll want to hear all about how you got on in Manchester, Richard.'

'I'll park the Hillman round the side of the house and then I'll bring everything in,' Richard said. 'You two go on.'

'Thanks, love. Be careful with it, you know it's your dad's pride and joy.' Mary waited until the dark green Hillman Minx was safely driven off the road before she led the way around the back of the house. She laughed. 'Your Uncle Peter would never forgive me if I got so much as a scratch on that car,' she said. 'Now, young lady, you can have a good rest while you're here.' She'd been shocked by the pallid thinness of her niece. 'We'll have a nice cup of tea and you can fill me in with all your news.' She'd already had a phone-call from Ellen demanding she find out from Linda what was wrong between her and her boyfriend, but she wasn't going to pry. If Linda wanted to tell her anything at all, it was up to her.

'Peter,' she called, 'look who's here.'

'I think we should go in.' Mary swatted at the midges that hovered around their heads as she and Linda sat on the low wall in the back garden. 'I can't stand these things. And it's dark, anyway.'

Linda stood up. 'The house seems so big since you extended it, since you made the two cottages into one.' She gazed along the length of it. 'I keep looking to where Gwyneth's back door used to be.' She glanced at Mary. 'Must seem strange to you too, Auntie Mary.'

159

'Hmm? Yes.' A sadness shadowed Mary's eyes. 'I really miss her. If it wasn't for her ... and her son ... we wouldn't be here. It was a refuge for Tom and me for a long time. And your grandmother. She had a hard life before she came here. She loved Wales.' She smiled, a wistfulness hovering around her mouth. 'You won't remember her, but I think you'd have liked her.'

'Yes, I think I probably would. And, from what I remember, Uncle Tom.'

Mary nodded. 'He and Iori should have had more time together. But...' She folded her arms and held them tightly to her. 'It wasn't to be.' She flapped her hands again at the insects. 'Horrid things. Come on, let's get inside.'

In the kitchen Mary took out two mugs from the cupboard. 'I'm glad your Uncle Peter had an early night, he was tired out. Coffee?'

'Please. Yes, he did look absolutely shattered.'

'Like I said, he's a fidgety patient. Very fidgety.'

Linda peered around the door. Into the living room. It was empty. 'Where's Richard?'

'On the telephone in the hall. He's been on there for ages talking to the girl he met when he was up with you.' Mary opened another cupboard and brought out a tin of Nescafé.

She spooned the coffee into the mugs. 'I spoke to your mother earlier.' She tried to speak casually. 'She sounded a bit ... agitated. Is she—?'

'Drinking again? Yes, she is.' Linda's mouth twisted. 'I don't know what would stop her falling into a bottle whenever anything goes wrong.'

'What is it this time?' Mary held up the spoon. 'CoffeeMate okay? I forgot to re-order the milk.'

'It's fine.' Linda smiled and then pulled her face. 'And I don't know what's up with Mum.' This wasn't the right time to talk to Mary about Karen. 'She gets in a flap about anything.'

Mary stirred the coffee and then spooned in the milk substitute, a thoughtful expression on her face.

Linda realised she hadn't fooled her aunt; she'd always been able to tell when she was holding something back, just like Nelly could. They were so much alike, Auntie Mary and Gran. No wonder they were such good friends. And she knew she couldn't avoid the subject of George Shuttleworth much longer.

Chapter 43: Mary Schormann and Linda Booth

Llamroth, midday: Monday, September 29th

Linda breathed in the sea air, surprised how much more settled she felt in Wales rather than Ashford. It had been her home from home since childhood. She loved the sound of the drag of pebbles under the waves and the raucous calls of the seagulls, the shapes and patterns in the cliffs. And there was no underlying tension between her aunt and uncle. Unlike at home.

She half twisted round and smiled at her aunt who appeared at the front door and sat on the step next to her.

'That's the baking done,' Mary said. 'One Victoria sponge, two apple-and-blackberry pies and some jam tarts with the left-over pastry. Phew! That kitchen's like an oven.' She leaned forward, clasping her hands in front of her. 'Peter and me often sit here watching the world go by. Not that much does … pass by, I mean. It's so quiet here, lovely and peaceful.' She tilted her head toward Linda. 'I know they said it was a slight attack, but it's still a worry. How does he look to you?' she asked. 'Putting your nurse's head on?'

'Better than I expected, I'm glad to say. Where is he now?'

'Gone up for a nap. He gets tired easily. He was so pleased you came back with Richard; I don't think he slept much over the last two nights. But I'm glad you think he looks okay.' Mary smiled. 'I did wonder if I was too close, that I just wanted him to be better than he actually was.'

'No, he looks fine. Must have been a shock when it happened?'

'It was. Worse than the first scare we had, actually. At least then he was in the surgery with the other doctors. Even though the old skills kicked in, it was more frightening because we were out on our own.'

'You should have told me about it, Auntie. I would have been down here like a shot.'

'I know.' Mary gave her a quick kiss on the cheek. 'You're a love.' But there was a quizzical look in her eyes. 'You okay?'

Linda wanted to pour out her own worries. But that would be too selfish; her aunt and uncle had so much on their plate already. And, soon, when she told them about Richard and Karen, she'd be adding to them anyway. So she smiled and avoided the question. 'It's so peaceful. When I'm home I think about Llamroth a lot.'

The dog came and pushed his head between them. Mary rubbed his ears. 'You're glad to be home, Gelert, aren't you, boy?' His tail thumped on the door. 'And we'd love to have Linda here, wouldn't we?' She glanced at her niece. 'You *could* always move down here, you know that. You'd easily get a job at the hospital in Pont-y-Haven, I'm sure.' She sighed. 'Peter and I will miss Richard if … when he goes. He seems quite optimistic about his interviews. Did you think so?'

'Yes.' Linda's spirits lifted. She supposed the constant feeling of sickness was nerves after everything that had happened, but Mary's words were a godsend. If only she could move – it would be the answer to everything.

The dog settled down between them with a long sigh, his head on Mary's lap. She stroked him. 'And with Victoria goodness knows where.' There was a break in her voice.

Linda chided herself for her selfishness. She covered her aunt's fingers with her own. 'I'm sure Vicky's fine, wherever she is. She's stronger than you think, you know.' She grinned. 'She'll be back driving you mad before you know it.'

'I hope so. I miss her so much.' Linda was relieved to see Mary's small smile. 'I even miss that darned wailing music she insists on playing.'

'Bob Dylan still her favourite?'

'She's gone on to Joan somebody or other over the last few months.'

'Joan Baez.'

'Hmm, yes.' Mary nodded. 'I'd just be happy ... well, satisfied, at least, to know where she is. I've always been aware that we over-protected the twins but—'

'But it was understandable.' Linda watched a green single-decker bus drone past; it looked as if there were only two people besides the driver on it. The image of the crowds in Manchester was an instant contrast. Yes, she *could* live here quite happily.

'Perhaps. Peter and I took quite a bit of flak from some people when we first came here. More so when we visited Ashford. I suppose that was because of the camp being there. People have long memories.'

'Some people are just stupid.'

'No, I suppose it was too soon after the war for people to understand. To forgive.' Linda felt the sigh Mary gave. 'I used to worry about what happened to the children when they weren't with us – when they were in school. But they managed. At least, Richard did; Victoria was always railing about somebody or other.' Her voice grew vague. 'Something or other.'

Linda let the quiet moment stretch out. She was aware that she was procrastinating: putting off the moment when she would spoil this visit. Because she was sure that's what would happen. The first mention of George Worth ... Shuttleworth ... and all the peace would be shattered. And she wasn't sure her aunt would be able to cope with it. Let alone Uncle Peter.

But the decision was taken from her. Mary leaned against Linda, giving her a quick nudge. 'Now, then, tell me about this girl Richard's met? He's going around grinning like the Cheshire cat ever since he got home. He was barely up there a fortnight but she's certainly made an impression on him. Whoever she is I'd like to meet her and give her a hug; he's happier than I've seen him for a long time.'

'He does seem to be.' Linda rested her head against the doorframe, watching the high clouds merging and reforming, being driven by a wind that had not yet descended to scatter the seagulls floating over the sea.

'I know it's daft,' Mary said, 'but I still worry about how people treat him.' She touched her ear. 'You know, with his deafness.'

'Oh?'

'I suppose it started when he first went to school. The teachers treated him as though he was slow; they didn't realise how clever he was for years. We always seemed to be going in to school for one thing or another.' Mary frowned. 'And he had so much time off with the operations. It never seemed to bother him, though, he always had good friends.'

'Because he's a nice lad, Auntie,' Linda said. 'And anyway, didn't you tell me it was his last one – he won't need any more?'

'I did. It was. There's nothing else they can do to improve things. His hearing is as good as it'll be, now.'

'I doubt he'll let it hold him back, he's a determined lad. And it's different these days.' She twisted her Saint Christopher necklace around her finger. 'Well, some things are, anyway.'

She smoothed her thumb over the pendant. Now or never, she told herself. 'Auntie Mary, I have to talk to you about something…' she glanced over her shoulder into the porch. 'While we're on our own.'

'Okay.' Puzzled, Mary looked at her.

'You know what happened to me when I was little? The time I was taken and Uncle Peter rescued me from that cellar in the old mill?'

Mary looked shaken. But all she said was 'Of course, love.'

'I still have nightmares about it, you know. Has Mum ever told you?'

'No. No, she hasn't.' Mary slipped her arm around Linda. 'And you've never mentioned it before. I'm sorry you're still troubled by it.'

'It wasn't your fault.'

'No, I know.'

Yet the inflexion in her tone told Linda her aunt was as nervous as she was.

'But I haven't forgotten. How could I?' Linda clenched her fingers together. 'And there's something I have to tell you.'

'Go on.'

'It concerns Richard as well.'

'Richard?' Mary blanched. 'What about Richard?'

On the journey to Llamroth, Linda had thought of all the different ways she might tell her aunt about Karen but none were right. Not one could lessen the awful facts.

'The girl Richard's met is lovely. I'm sure you would like her…'

'What's that got to do with—?'

'I just need you to know that I know you would like her. Before I go on.' This was coming out all wrong; her aunt was looking more and more concerned.

'What do you mean … would? Of course we'll meet her if he wants us to. But what—?'

'I'm sorry, Auntie Mary, I'm not explaining myself very well.'

'Just take your time, love.' Mary put her hand over Linda's clenched fingers.

'This girl. Karen. Richard's completely smitten with her. And, as far as I can see, she is with him. They've been inseparable since they met the first night he was in Ashford.' Linda knew not to divulge how they'd met. If ever Richard wanted his parents to know that he was almost beaten up, it was up to him to tell them. 'But there's a problem. A big problem.'

'Go on,' Mary said, her voice all at once calm.

'Karen's mother was on my ward. She'd had a baby.' Linda swallowed.

'How old is Karen, then? Is she under age?' Mary looked instantly alarmed.

'No, nothing like that, the baby was the result of the mother's second marriage. Karen's about seventeen, eighteen. She has a car. She drives anyway…'

'So, what's the problem?'

'It's her stepfather.' Linda rushed the words, in the vain hope that, if they escaped quickly their impact wouldn't be so devastating. 'He's a horrible man.'

'He found out Richard was half-German?' The relief was palpable in Mary's voice even as her face clouded with anger.

'No. Well, yes, he did find out—'

'Still it goes on.' Mary's jaw set. 'But we've dealt with all this before. If necessary I'll go up north and talk to the man. If this girl is the one to make Richard happy, I won't let anybody spoil it.' She pushed her dark hair back from her forehead. 'I'll have to find a way not to let Peter know, though. It would only upset him and he's not fit enough to deal with all that again.'

'Wait, Auntie Mary. It's not as easy as that.'

'If Richard gets this post in Manchester we'll be taking him up there. I could see the man then … surely his daughter's—'

'Stepdaughter…'

'Stepdaughter's happiness is more important. It isn't fair, not in this day and age, not so long after the war.' Mary insisted.

'No, it wouldn't be fair … or right. But it's not just that, Auntie Mary.' Linda forced the words out. 'It's who this man is.'

Mary looked bewildered. 'Who…?'

'George Shuttleworth. George Shuttleworth is Karen's stepfather.'

Chapter 44: Victoria Schormann

Ashford, afternoon: Monday, September 29th

'I haven't seen you for two days.' Victoria had been going mad with worry and frustration. She'd expected to have been moved into Seth's room on the ground floor by now, to be seen by the commune as his girlfriend. 'You said I was special to you. You needed me by your side.'

'You are. I do.' Seth stroked the back of her hand with his forefinger, then lifted it and kissed her palm.

He spoke so evenly she knew he was holding back.

'Crap.' She snatched her hand away and let her hair swing forward so he couldn't see her face. She was cross to feel the hot tears at the back of her eyes. 'What *you* said at the fest — and what you said that day on the canal…' God, she wished she'd not suggested that walk; she wouldn't be stuck in this shit-hole now. 'And after that … that *meditation* …' She didn't dare say what she really felt about the sessions he held. She sat up, glared at him. 'Bloody hell, Seth, you persuaded me to join this … this…' She swung her arm around the dorm, where each partitioned-off section was identical, and then at her single mattress, her clothes hanging on the rail. 'I gave you my whole savings. Five hundred pounds. You said it would be for things in my room. *My* room,' she emphasised, barely able to keep the sarcasm out of her voice. 'I didn't mind that because I thought it would be *our* room.'

'You don't like your space?'

She heard the irritation.

What's to like, she thought. But she'd need to be careful. She tried hard to soften her voice, to capitulate. Not something she was used to doing. She wanted to stay, but on her terms. She just had to make him see that she was different from the other girls, to make him admit that she was entitled to be treated better than she had been so far. The last thing she was to be kicked out. To be controlled by her family again. That business with Jackie coming to look for her had given her a fright.

'I want to be with you, in your room. Like you promised.'

He stared at her. For a moment she thought she saw a hesitation in his eyes. That he was going to give in, to admit to being wrong. But when he spoke his voice was cold.

'You need to chill, babe. When the time's right, I'll send for you. Unless—' He lifted his shoulders, glanced out of the window. Victoria followed his gaze. A mist covered the West Country moors in the distance. 'Rain's coming in; it'll be chucking it down before dark…' A flock of birds swung past in a V-shape, heading for the hills. 'Looks like they're going back to their nests, to settle for the night.' He turned to her. 'Unless you want to leave? You can if you want, you know.'

Victoria felt a sense of alarm. 'I don't want to go back to my family—'

'Your past life,' Seth corrected. 'You mean you don't want to go back to your past life. So *this* is what you want? *This life?* With your family here?'

'Yes. But with *you*. I mean *really* with you. Not here with all the other girls.' Oh, what the hell; this time she let him see the easy tears of frustration. 'All your letters — that time you came all the way to Cardiff on the train to be with me. You said I was the one you wanted. Only ever me,' she said. 'What happened?'

She waited for him to answer. That day in Cardiff had been one of the best days of her life.

When the train squealed to a halt and the doors flung open Victoria was relieved to see Seth was alone, threading his way through people on the platform. During the hour she'd been waiting she'd worried that he would turn up with a gang of his mates.

She touched the folded paper in her jean's pocket; his last letter to her.

'… you'll live the life you deserve, babe. We're all keen for you to join us in our new place. You'll be free from all the petty crap you're stuck with now. To paint whenever you want, do what you want, meditate with me – into your soul – be with us. Be free!!!! We're waiting for you.'

They were waiting for her. If only she had the courage.

Despite the torrential rain on the glass canopies above the station Seth was dressed in a loose cotton shirt and trousers and sandals. He raised a hand, grinning at her, and she ran to him, glad she'd changed into her flared jeans, flowered waistcoat, smock top and platform boots in the station toilets.

They kissed, oblivious to the crowds that nudged and pushed at them.

'My God, I can tell I'm in Wales,' Seth said. 'Nothing but hills and sheep and rain all the way here.'

'Don't exaggerate,' Victoria said, coming up for air from the kiss that had weakened her knees. She leant against him and he hugged her close as they walked together down the steps.

'What's in the bag?' Seth said.

'Nothing.' Victoria swung her straw shoulder-bag that held the boring jeans and jumper she'd left home in that morning over her shoulder. 'C'mon, let's get a coffee.' Victoria took off her waistcoat so he could hold it over their heads to keep off the rain.

They splashed through the rain along St Mary's Street and down side streets before they found a small café in an arcade. When, laughing, they crashed through the door Victoria marvelled how the drab little place seemed to come alive just having Seth in it.

He pulled one of the plastic chairs from a table and slumped onto it, pushing his wet hair back from his forehead. 'God, Vicky, what a hole Cardiff is.' He didn't bother to lower his voice below the sounds of the orchestra playing some sort of classical music from the radio behind the counter. Victoria glanced at the plump middle-aged woman who stood, arms folded, waiting for them to order, her face impassive. 'Bummer. Nothing like Manchester,' he added, leaning the chair back on two legs and rocking.

'You're not seeing it as its best on a day like this.' Victoria was disappointed that he didn't like the city. She was always excited when she was allowed to go Cardiff on her own; she loved the shops. It might not be as "swinging" as Manchester, she conceded, but it was a lovely city with lots happening. She went to the counter. The woman served her without a word and without eye-contact. The coffee splattered over the rim of the large cups into the saucers when she banged them down in front of Victoria and held out her hand for the money.

'So,' Victoria said, putting the coffee on the table in front of Seth and dropping her bag on the spare chair next to her, 'What shall we do?' His shirt, where it was wet on his shoulders and arms revealed the hard muscles. God, he was fabulous.

Seth let the chair bang down on all four legs and leaned forward to grab her hand. 'We'll talk about when you're going to come and live with me in the commune,' he said. 'I want you with me, babe.'

Victoria savoured the touch, felt the flip-flop of her stomach. When she spoke her voice was a high squeak. She coughed, took a deep breath and lowered the tone. 'No. I mean, what shall we do today?' Pleased with herself, she thought she sounded sexy.

It worked.

'This.' Seth leant forward, holding her face between his hands and kissing her. She felt the tip of his tongue probing between her lips and, conscious of the woman watching them, pulled back blushing.

He laughed quietly and slumped back in his chair. 'Hang loose, babe. Who cares what we do.'

'I know. It's just —'

'Just that you need to get away from all the tight-arsed stuff. Relax. Chill. When are you going to make up your mind?'

'I will—'

'When?'

'Soon.'

They'd had a good day. The rain had cleared, they'd found a small park and sat watching some ducks on a pond. But mostly they kissed. And mostly Seth talked. Cajoling. Persuading. Until, at last, Victoria conceded. She would leave home in a fortnight, on the day Richard was going for his interview in Manchester.

She toyed for a moment with the idea of going with Richard and losing him as soon as she could to meet Seth somewhere there. But then thought better of it. Much as her brother got on her nerves, she couldn't do that. Knowing him, he'd try to find her and probably miss the interview. One more thing that'd be her fault … even if she wasn't there to get the blame. Anyway, she reasoned, her parents would know then where she'd gone. No, better to fall in with what Seth said, what he insisted on; let him pick her up from Llamroth.

She didn't know why she worried about it anyway; her parents would be too busy seeing their precious son going off into the big wide world for them to notice what she was doing.

The excitement churned her stomach all the way home. She couldn't believe she was going to do it. Every now and then, when the carriage was empty, she wrapped her arms around her stomach and laughed aloud. Seth wanted her. Like she'd never been wanted before, by anyone.

On the station at Pont-y-Haven she changed back into the clothes she'd left home in that morning.

'So what's happened?' Victoria repeated. 'What's stopping us being together?'

'Nothing.' He licked his fingers and separating a Rizla paper from the packet, sprinkled the mix of tobacco and marijuana over it. 'Except it seems to me it's *you* having second thoughts.'

171

'I'm not.' Yet, if she'd known where 'the new place' that he'd mentioned in his letters was, would she have been so keen to join them? She'd thought about a lot that since she got here. The answer was yes; she'd always felt on the outside of everything, as though she was the one watching life, not joining in. She'd hoped Seth and the beliefs of the commune might fill the emptiness in her. But being here, in this building, part of the old camp, meant she was still connected in a way with her past … with her old life. 'I'm not,' she repeated, hoping the uncertainty in her wasn't heard.

'Okay.' He shrugged, offhanded. Licking along one edge he rolled it into a tube and lit it. 'Smoke?' He held the cigarette between finger and thumb and passed it to her. 'Here.'

She shook her head.

'Here,' he said again, his voice hard. 'It'll chill you out.'

Victoria took it from him and took a long inhalation. She still wasn't used to the effect the drug had on her and right away she felt the whole of her body relax yet, at the same time her heart begin to race. She repressed a cough. 'I'm sorry, Seth.'

'Master—' he spoke as he sucked at the cigarette.

She pretended she hadn't heard him. 'I'm sorry. It's just that I thought I'd be making my own rules, living my life the way I wanted to and not how – my parents – thought it should be. And yet here I am, following somebody else's rules.'

'I told you when you got here,' Seth said. 'They're not rules; they're ways to be fair to everybody. And someone has to be the one to guide. I was chosen.' His lips were a thin line.

Who by? Who chose you? Victoria just managed to stop the words from spilling from her lips. 'Well, I'm sorry but I do think some of the *ways* are stupid—' There it was again, that flash of anger. 'I mean—'

'Such as?' He took a long drag.

'Being shown how to clean this place by Chrystal. I know how to make a bed, to wash up, to sweep a floor, to mop.' She'd seen her mother do these things a hundred times. True, she'd never actually done them herself but she knew how.

A long pause. Seth studied her. 'She's also teaching you about our beliefs and values—'

'Which you said you'd do.' Victoria couldn't stop now. 'Besides I don't understand what you do believe in.' Shut up, shut up, she thought but still the words tumbled out. 'I didn't like what you did, the other day.'

'I needed to let the others know you were willing to be part of us. It was for your own good. I told you that.' He grinned. 'Besides it turned you on for the sex after, didn't it?'

In a way it had but Victoria wouldn't admit it. 'Is that all it was, Seth? Sex?' Not making love like before? She kept that thought to herself.

'Master.' He corrected her.

Oh, for God's sake… She stifled her exasperation.

'Our beliefs take in all religions … from Buddhism to Christianity.'

'It wasn't … isn't right.'

Seth stood up. His face tight with rage. 'You need to decide what you want to do, Summer.' He spoke louder. 'I think a day's quiet meditation will help.'

'I'm not in the mood,' Victoria said.

Amber and Jasmine appeared in the doorway.

'We're going to the quiet room,' Jasmine said. 'Come with us. It will chill you out.'

'No.' Victoria turned back to Seth. 'I told you, I'm not in the mood.'

He smiled. 'It will help you.'

Smiling, each of the girls put their arms firmly around her waist. Other than physically pushing them off her, Victoria knew she had no choice but to go with them.

Chapter 45: Mary Schormann

Llamroth, morning: Tuesday, September 30th

Mary clipped the hedge in the back garden, breathing in the sharp lemony smell of cut privet. In the last two weeks everything had been neglected: weeds had taken over the vegetable patch, the sparrows had decimated the beetroot and the greenhouse badly needed clearing out for the winter. Tom would be furious if he could see the state I've let everything get into, she thought. Yet, even as the easy tears came, she knew she was wrong. Her brother would have understood; he was one of the calmest men she'd ever known.

She let the shears dangle at her side, gazing across the fields towards the churchyard wreathed in the early morning autumn mist, where Tom had lain for such a long time in a grave next to those of Iori and Gwyneth. And near to their own mother. Four people gone from her life. And now Victoria. Her shoulders shook with the effort of stopping herself wailing out loud. She forced deep mouthfuls of air into her lungs and lifted the front of her cardigan to wipe her eyes with. Pull yourself together, she told herself. Don't fall apart again; she'd done enough of that in the first days of Victoria running away. Peter had been strong for her then; she'd be strong for him now. Another convulsion ran through her; what if she'd lost him as well? What if, on that morning last week he'd – she couldn't even think of that word – if he'd … gone, lying on the road by the sea?

She turned her back on the fields and surveyed the cottage, her eyes lingering on the curtained window of the bedroom where Peter lay, hopefully still asleep this early in the day. What would he say when she told him about Linda's revelation? The thought was so fleeting it was dismissed before it was even acknowledged; she wouldn't tell him. This was something she would deal with on her own. Well, almost. Out of an age-old habit her silent questions were directed to her brother and she wondered what he would have advised her to do about the present situation; Richard bumping into George Shuttleworth's stepdaughter, falling in love with her. It took only seconds for Mary to know. A great believer in being true to himself, Tom would tell her to face up to what had to be done.

She thought back to yesterday. She'd been so shocked by what Linda had said she'd let silence be her answer when her niece had asked her if she was all right. The news that Shuttleworth was once more in their lives was too much. Fear had taken over, but she'd waved away Linda's concern. Now Mary felt ashamed of her reaction; her niece had confided her own fears, her own nightmares and hadn't been comforted. Instead Mary had avoided being alone with Linda for the rest of the day.

A movement through the kitchen window caught her attention. Linda was up. They waved to one another. Evidently there was no resentment, and Mary let the relief settle her troubled mind. At one point in the night she'd had a sudden thought; if she knew that George Shuttleworth was a danger, how much more did Linda know? Had Ted and Ellen told her the whole story, the whole truth of what happened twenty-five years ago? Mary needed to find out.

Linda came to the back door. 'Tea?' She lifted a mug.

Mary nodded. 'Please.' She kept her voice low; she didn't want to wake Peter. And it was better that Richard didn't hear what she and Linda had to talk about.

She put the shears inside the door of the small garden shed, throwing down her gloves next to them.

When her niece finally walked along the path towards the bench on the small patch of lawn, Mary had formed the questions in her mind. She shielded her eyes against the low sun and smiled as she took the tea and leaned back. 'Sorry about yesterday, love,' she said.

'Don't worry about it, Auntie, I could tell it was a shock. And I know how I felt when I found out.'

'You know then?'

'About who he is? Yes. I think I almost knew it the first time I saw him at the hospital. Well, I realised he scared me for some reason and eventually I worked out why.'

'No, I mean do you know *all* of it?' Mary held the mug near her chin, breathing in the steam, watching tea-leaves floating on the surface. Her attention was pulled back by Linda's quiet words.

'Mum and Dad told me. I don't know if it was everything, but enough to know there could be trouble.' Linda took a tentative sip of the hot tea and grimaced as it burnt her lips. She balanced the mug on the arm of the bench. 'Not just for Richard and Karen, for all of us. She's staying with Jackie by the way … Karen I mean. She's left home.'

'Oh good grief, it gets worse.' Mary couldn't stop the words. 'Okay.' She looked towards the house. Still no sign of anyone stirring. 'You tell me what you know … and I'll fill in the rest.' Now she'd decided what to do, maybe she could think of her next step. For now, her anxiety about Victoria's whereabouts would have to be pushed to the back of her mind. For now, it was Richard she needed to protect.

By the time Linda had finished there was little that Mary needed to add. What she did say involved Linda's gran. 'What did Nelly say when you first told her about seeing George at the hospital?'

'Nothing. But I saw a change in her,' Linda said. 'I'd told her that one of the husbands was horrible and he scared me.' She gave a quiet chuckle. 'You know what Gran's like, I think she was ready to go in guns blazing. But when I described him … when I said what he looked like, she got upset. And then she wouldn't tell me why. She said I had to ask Mum and Dad.'

'I don't want you to ever blame your gran for not telling you.'

'I don't.' Linda said. 'She told me a long time ago that Mum didn't want her talking about her family…'

'She did.' Mary chewed on the inside of her cheek, waiting, feeling the change in the air as the sun broke through the mist.

'I didn't understand … then … but Gran seemed okay with it, so I let it go.' Linda looked down, picked at her thumbnail. 'I understand now…' she glanced up at Mary. 'For her own son to do that … she must have always felt so bad.' Linda closed her eyes. 'Poor Gran.'

'You're a good girl, Linda.' Mary hugged her. 'You've always understood how other people feel.' Unlike Victoria, lost in her world of grievances. 'So you know … that it shouldn't have been you … that he kidnapped … that he took you by mistake …?'

'That it should have been Jackie, you mean?' Linda said. 'Yes, they told me that as well.'

Mary sighed. 'It's a bad business all round.' She leaned back against the bench, leaving her arm across Linda's shoulder. Somewhere in the village a dog barked, followed by a volley of answering barks from other dogs.

'Yes…' Linda's voice trailed away.

She must know what Frank did, Mary thought. I should say something. But what if she doesn't? What if I tell her and she didn't know? 'What is it, Linda?'

Linda put her hands in her lap, twisted her fingers. 'I've always known who my real father was, Auntie Mary. Mum and Dad have always been honest about that.' She sighed. 'I mean, I knew he was called Frank and he was Gran's eldest son.' She glanced up and smiled at Mary. 'I don't know how she would have explained Gran to me otherwise.'

Mary returned the smile but she felt sick; she knew what was coming. The open door of the greenhouses swung gently, every now and then the glass catching the glint of the sun. 'I'll just close—' she'd taken her arm off Linda's shoulders and almost pushed herself up from the bench when Linda's words stopped her.

'I didn't know what he'd done to you, Auntie.' Linda's face had taken on an odd colour. She looked queasy.

I wonder if I look as bad as she does. The thought ran through

Mary's mind as her legs gave way. 'Oh.' It was all she could say. She closed her eyes, sat down on the bench. Clasping Linda's hands in hers, she whispered, 'It was a lifetime ago, love. I don't think about it much any more.' She fought against the panic. Everything about her life that she'd carefully built up since that day was threatening to crumble in the effort of protecting Linda. Would they ever escape from the evil of the Shuttleworth brothers?

A seagull startled her as it landed with a screech and flurry on the path and strutted around, its yellow eyes watching them.

A thought made Mary shiver; she didn't want the relationship between Nelly and Linda to be ruined. 'It was never your gran's fault. Nothing either of her sons did was her fault. She thinks the world of you, you know.'

'I know, Auntie Mary.'

Mary sighed. 'And I also know she feels she needs to make it up to both of us for what they did. Frank to me and George to you,' she added. 'She'll never forgive herself for giving George an alibi. She must feel even worse now. If she'd given him up to the police there's no way we be in this situation. Richard would probably never have met Karen.'

'But, in a way, that would be a shame, Auntie Mary.'

'I suppose.' Or would it? They'd only known each other a couple of weeks. Plenty of time for mending broken hearts. There was little remorse in Mary at the thought; to have George Shuttleworth back in their lives was dragging up horrendous memories she'd believed they'd left behind forever.

They didn't hear the sound of Richard's footsteps.

'That was quite a story, Lin.' The words might have been addressed to her, but Richard's eyes, cold and resentful, were fixed on his mother. 'When were you going to tell me?'

The directness of his question took Mary aback. He couldn't possibly have heard.

He answered her unspoken question. 'Finally came in useful

being deaf. I was watching you from my window.' He tapped his mouth. 'I can lip-read – remember?'

Chapter 46: Jacqueline Howarth

Manchester: Wednesday, October 1st

'I won't come in, thank you very much, Jacqueline.' Jean's clipped tones echoed in the communal hallway outside Jackie's flat.

'Why not?'

'There's no need for me to come in.'

'Don't be daft.' Jackie stepped back and opened the door wider.

'I've only come to give you a message from your father. From your father and me,' Jean corrected herself.

'Well, I'm not standing here while you do.' It was clear her mother had come to pick a fight and Jackie had a fair idea what it was about. 'Either you come in or …' She let the rest of the sentence hang in the air.

Jean's face reddened, the lines around her pursed mouth deepened. She took one step inside and moved so Jackie could close the door. Her eyes slid to one side, taking in Nicki but not acknowledging her.

'Hello, Mrs. Howarth.'

Jean ignored her. When she began talking it was evident she'd prepared her speech. 'You're not to come to the house. Your father… We don't want to see you again until you give up this disgusting notion about her.' She tilted her head in Nicki's direction but still didn't look at her.

Jackie felt her girlfriend's closeness before her arm came around her waist. She saw the repulsion that flickered over her mother's face. It hurt and angered her. She raised her eyebrows, challenging her mother to speak.

'As I said to your father, this has nothing to do with my side of the family.' Flecks of spittle escaped with the words. 'Nothing. This … this grossness has to be something to do with the Howarths, something wrong, something inherited from his side. Something that showed up first in his brother, Tom—'

'My God, Mother, you're unbelievable.'

Jean continued her tirade without a pause. '*He* had an unnatural relationship with another man. There was something wrong with him and it's the same with you. It was revolting then and it's equally disgusting now, with you and her. Disgusting.'

'I think you should leave, Mrs Howarth.' Nicki's voice was even but Jackie knew the resentment equalled hers. She leaned against her.

Jean stiffened and half-turned her back to Nicki. 'I've had my say; you know now how I … we feel about all this.' She said to Jackie, fluttering a dismissive hand, 'It's easily solved, Jacqueline. So what are you going to do?'

'I'm going to tell you to piss off, Mother. Now. Before I slap you.'

Nicki pressed her mouth close to Jackie's ear. 'Don't lower yourself, sweetheart.'

Jean's lips curled. 'You both need to see a doctor.'

'Get out!' Jackie flung the door open. 'Now.'

Jean turned but then stopped. 'Good grief, there are three of you.'

Jackie glanced behind her. Karen was by the spare-bedroom door, her hand to her mouth.

The urge to hit her mother was almost overwhelming; Jackie shifted forwards but Nicki's grip on her arm intensified as she spoke. 'Your job?' The two small words instantly calmed Jackie; it wasn't worth losing the career she loved.

'Who's that?' Jean peered over the top of her glasses at Karen. 'Another one?'

A sudden thought made Jackie take in a long pull of air into her lungs. Knowing who Karen was would devastate her mother.

George Shuttleworth was as much an enemy of her parents as the rest of the family. More so for her father.

And it wasn't something her mother would keep to herself; the first thing her mother would do when she got home would be, without any doubt, to tell him. And a whole new can of worms would be instantly opened once her father knew about it. She felt the old chill of apprehension; the last thing she wanted was him storming round to the flat.

So she smiled and said, 'What do you think?' Put that in your pipe and smoke it, Jackie thought, as she once heard Auntie Mary say.

Jean's face drained of colour.

'I can tell you're shocked, Mrs Howarth,' Nicki said, barely hiding a smile. 'If you'd like to sit down, I'll make a cup of tea and Jackie can explain.'

Jean had quickly recovered. For the first time she looked in the direction of Jackie's girlfriend, her eyes travelled from the tall woman's head to her feet and back again. Her tone was cold. 'You know nothing about me, madam. Nothing. And no, I won't sit down.' She faced Jackie. 'I won't spend another minute in this place.'

'So?' Jackie indicated the door with her head. She crossed her arms to hide the shaking; she wouldn't give her mother the satisfaction of knowing how upset she was.

'I won't come here again. Understand?'

Jackie let the silence answer for her.

'And *you* won't come to our house.'

This time Jackie spoke through the surge of anger and distress. 'No, I won't. And you can tell my father you've successfully passed on his message. After all these years he still controls you, Mother. My God, I feel sorry for you.'

She didn't miss the hurt that flashed across Jean's face and felt wretched as she watched her mother leave. But long afterwards, Jean's last words resounded in Jackie's head.

'From now on, until you stop this revolting association with that woman, you're dead to us.'

Chapter 47: Mary Schormann

Llamroth, morning: Thursday, October 2nd

Mary lined the basin with the suet pastry and scooped in the mixture of steak and kidney and gravy. She felt rather than saw Richard's presence. When she glanced up he was standing by the door, his hands tucked into his jeans pockets.

'You all right, love?' Mary kept her voice casual, though the pulse in her neck throbbed. He'd barely spoken to her since Tuesday. Waiting for his response, she pretended to concentrate on rolling out the rest of the pastry and laying it on top of the meat, trimming the remainder with a small knife.

He didn't answer.

Mary sighed. 'Richard, I know it must have been an awful, horrible shock for you. And I am so sorry you had to find out like that. But I was going to tell you—'

'When?'

'Before you went back up north, honestly; I wouldn't have let you go without you knowing everything. I suppose I thought we could have a talk—'

'A talk?' There was quick anger in his voice. He stared at her. 'I can't believe you've just said that.'

'When it was the right time.' She ended lamely, accepting his resentment. She looked towards the back door. The transistor radio was still playing music in the greenhouse. Please, Peter, don't come in yet, she prayed.

'Don't you think the right time should have been years ago?'

'No. That time, when all that happened, it's nothing to do with us as a family.'

He closed his eyes, shaking his head, taking long steady breaths through his nose. Mary could tell he was trying to calm himself.

'It had everything to do with Linda and even she wasn't told.' His voice was even.

'We thought … we hoped, she'd forgotten.'

'Being kidnapped?' his voice rose again. 'Come off it, Mum.'

Mary put the basin down and rested the flat of her hands on the table. She was tempted to retort, to say that if he hadn't met Karen, the past would have stayed in the past. But she couldn't; that would be totally unfair. And untrue. Linda would still have come across George Shuttleworth in the hospital and it hadn't taken long for her to put two and two together by all accounts. So all she said was, 'I'm sorry, love.'

'Does Dad know? About Karen, I mean. Not all the … other stuff.'

'Of course he knows what happened then. But no.' She spoke sharper than she meant to. Softening her tone she said, 'No, he doesn't know about Karen. And I don't want him to. Not yet anyway.'

'So you're keeping secrets from him as well, then?' he glowered at her.

'With good reason. Your father's not well.' Mary pleated a circle of greaseproof paper over the top and around of the basin and tied it quickly with string. 'Please try to understand, Richard. Like I said, I thought all that, everything that happened then, was behind us.' She lowered the basin in water in a saucepan by the loop of string, switched the electric ring on and turned to face him. What she was going to say would make him uncomfortable but she couldn't see a way around it. 'At least, it was left behind as far as not having to talk about it.' Her voice wobbled and she drew in air to calm herself. 'But in my head it never goes away, it's something I've lived with for years. You heard … saw what Linda said.' He hadn't mentioned Peter's part on that day; how

Frank Shuttleworth had died. But she knew it was inevitable she needed to explain – to make sure Peter kept Richard's respect. She felt sick. 'I need to talk to you about your dad. Why he had to do what—'

'There's one bit I don't understand, the only part of the whole thing I missed.' Richard interrupted, his face scarlet. He pushed himself away from the door-jamb and went to the window. 'When the two of you were talking, Linda moved. I wasn't able to make out what she was saying.' He looked out at the garden. 'When he spoke again his voice was gruff. 'When you were being attacked … when you were … you know … the fight.' He spun around to face her. 'I don't know who it was who killed Karen's stepdad's brother. So I don't understand.' He stretched out his hands, palms upwards. 'I don't understand.'

Mary's knees gave way and she sat down at the table. 'Look, love, sit down.'

'No. Just tell me. Who pushed the man into the canal?'

'He fell.' The words were out before she could help it. 'It was an accident. The Coroner ruled it as accidental death.' That bit was true, anyway, she told herself.

'But who was it? Who was the man? The man who saved you?'

'A stranger. We never found out.' May God forgive me, she thought. 'There were a few people who heard my cries, who came. We didn't find out who came to my rescue.'

'So why did George Worth … Shuttleworth … run down your brother? Uncle Tom? And why did he wait until years after…' His face reddened even more. 'Years after what happened to you?'

Mary raised her shoulders, hiding her anxiety. 'He was desperate, set against us because his brother died. He must have kept hold of that anger. We moved here to get away from everything. He found out where we were. That your father was with me. I don't know, Richard – he was, is – a vindictive man. Perhaps because he lost someone he loved he thought we should as well, however many years went by.'

'I don't think he's the kind of man to care about anyone else but himself.'

'Revenge, then.'

'And what he did to Linda? Why take her that time?' He waited for her to speak.

The music from the radio outside stopped. Peter must be coming in. Mary quelled the panic. She hadn't planned for everything to come out like this; she'd mapped out what she would say but his questions were throwing her. She battled with her feelings.

'Okay.' She had to speak coherently – sort out how, and, how much, to tell her son. But there wasn't much time. She heard the crunch of Peter's footsteps on the path. But then the high-pitched squeak of the side gate told her he was going around the front of the cottage.

The reprieve made her head spin. 'Shuttleworth was angry about the Coroner's decision. He thought he needed to get at us, one way or another. Poor Linda was in the wrong place at the wrong time. It could have been any of us he hurt. Especially me.'

'But she was a child.'

'Exactly. Which shows what kind of a man he is.' Mary clenched her fingers together so tightly they throbbed. 'I've always wished it could have been me instead of her, believe me.'

'He was a sicko.'

'Yes.'

'And still is…'

'Yes.'

Richard's shoulders slumped.

The reprieve that surged through in Mary made her feel faint. She laid her head on the table.

'You okay, Mum?

'Yes.' She spoke without moving, her voice muted. 'And I am so sorry, Richard. So sorry.' She sensed his movement. Then his hand was touching her arm.

185

Neither of them spoke. There was a flurry of wings outside; sparrows fighting over the breadcrumbs she'd put out earlier. They must have been hanging on for Peter to leave the garden, Mary supposed. She waited for the uneven beat of her heart and the sick feeling to settle.

When she lifted her head, Richard held out a sheet of paper. 'This came in the post.'

Without taking it from him she quickly read it. 'You got in. Oh, love, I'm so pleased.' She half-stood to hug him but he stepped back and sat in the chair next to her.

'There's another problem, isn't it, Mum. What are you going to do about Karen? Will you tell her? Tell her about all that stuff?'

'What do you want me to do, Richard?' This time he let her touch him. She turned his hand so his palm lay in hers.

'Nothing.' He looked at her, pleading. 'I think it will finish us. I really like her and this will finish us.'

'Not necessarily. You said she doesn't like Shuttleworth.'

'She hates him. But that's not the point.'

'We could tell her together if you like.'

'No.'

'All right. But perhaps you should tell her, Richard.'

'But then what, Mum?'

Mary covered their clasped hands with her other one. 'Then we hope she understands.'

'I still don't, you know. I don't understand why he wasn't arrested. Why the police didn't do anything.'

'Because there was no proof. I tried to tell them about what he did to Tom.' The image was there immediately; it was always on the edge of her consciousness: the fading sounds of the van that had run her brother down, the dark spreading of his blood on the road in the fading light. 'I tried to get justice for him.'

The water in the large saucepan began to boil and splutter. They both looked towards the cooker.

'It's your favourite,' Mary said, standing to lower the heat of the ring. 'Should be ready for six.'

'Hope you're not trying to get into my good books, by any chance, Mum?'

Was that a glimmer of a smile? Mary allowed herself to relax even though the guilt lingered. She wasn't going to tell Richard the whole truth. She would protect Peter until the end of her days – even from his own son.

Chapter 48: Linda Booth & Mary Schormann

Pont-y-Haven, morning: Friday, October 3rd

The sales assistant licked her pencil before totting up the cost of their purchases on a pad. Linda gazed around the different counters in the small Woolworths. 'Anything else we need from here?'

Mary scanned the list in her hand. 'No, don't think so.' She looked towards the other end of the store where a group of youths were gathered around the record booths near the stairs. 'Unless you want to have a look around at the clothes?'

'No, but I think I'll get a quarter of pic'n'mix on the way out.'

'Make it half a pound and put some chocolate misshapes in, will you, love? They're Peter's favourites. I'll pay you later.'

'Don't be daft, Auntie – my treat.'

Out on the High Street, Mary changed the heavy carrier-bag into her other hand. There were already white indentations on her palm where the string handle had dug in.

'I always think Woolworths has a smell of its own, don't you?' Linda joined her at the double doors.

'Think it's as much the wooden floors as anything,' Mary said. 'That and so much all crammed together. Always good value, though.'

'Yeah. Here, pass that to me, I'll be balanced with one in each hand.' Linda prised the shopping from Mary's fingers.

'It *is* heavy. Thanks, love. Fancy a drink?' Mary pointed across the street to a café, its large window festooned with posters advertising local events. 'Looks a bit grotty from the outside but they serve the best coffee in town, and I know what you're like for your coffee. First place I went to with your uncle, just after he'd come back here.' She stopped; she hated thinking about the way Peter was sometimes treated then. 'Waitress was a right miserable biddy. He wouldn't go in again but I used to make a point of going in just to annoy her.'

They exchanged grins.

'I can just imagine you doing that.' Linda glanced along the street before crossing. 'Come on, then, I'm gasping for a drink.'

It was quiet for a Friday. Only two other women and a couple were sitting at the tables. In a corner behind the counter a tape-recorder played the theme from *A Summer Place*. Linda chose a table near the window and placed her bags under her chair. 'I'll get these, you rest your legs. We've been trailing about all morning.'

'Okay.'

When Linda glanced back at her, Mary had unbuttoned her coat and closed her eyes. She wished there was more she could do to help her aunt with Richard but it was something they needed to sort out for themselves, especially as he would now be going to Manchester.

Nodding her thanks at the girl behind the counter she carried the tray to the table and placed it carefully on the cloth.

Startled, Mary opened her eyes. 'Sorry.'

'No, I'm sorry. You look worn out. We should have gone straight home.'

'Not at all, I'm looking forward to this.'

'It's nice here.' Linda looked around. 'The outside does nothing for it, but it is lovely.' The walls were painted white and covered in original seascapes. Linda peered at the label on the nearest painting. 'Local artist,' she said.

'Yes, some of them are from Victoria's college. She had one of hers in here last year. It sold too.' Mary blinked hard.

Linda knew what she was thinking. She dropped seven pennies into her purse. 'I'm getting weighed down with all this change,' she said, 'but it's not bad that; thruppence for a coffee and tuppence for a tea.' She leaned her elbows on the table holding her cup. 'It's all going to change though,' she said 'What do you think of this business of decimalisation? That chap, Robin Day, was talking about it in an interview on the news.' She was aware she was chattering on to take Mary's mind off all the worry about Richard and Vicky.

Mary dismissed Linda's words. 'It's not happening until nineteen seventy-one. I can't worry about something so far off.'

Linda gave up pretending. 'You are pleased that Richard got into that university in Manchester, aren't you? It's what he wanted.'

'Yes. Yes, of course.'

'When does his term start?'

'In two weeks.' Mary bit her lip. 'Don't get me wrong, I'm pleased for him. But sometimes I wish...?' She didn't finish.

'You wish he'd chosen to stay in Wales? Studied here and gone to Pont-y-Haven?' Linda put her coffee down; suddenly she didn't want it. The café was warm and the aroma of cakes together with her drink made her feel vaguely nauseous.

'Yes. None of this would have happened.'

'Have you talked to Uncle Peter about it?'

'No, and he mustn't know.' Mary looked sharply at Linda. 'Please. Not until he's a lot stronger. I don't want to worry him more than he is already. I caught him reading Victoria's note again last night. All that claptrap about finding herself. I really am angry with her; she said she'd keep in touch and not a peep. She's always been a Daddy's girl so she must know how upset this makes him.'

And couldn't care less, Linda thought. The irritation didn't help the curdling in her stomach. 'She's probably having fun, wherever she is and not thinking about anything else.'

'Not thinking is something our daughter does well.'

Linda slowly stirred the spoon around in the coffee. Mary gazed out of the window. The low bubbling of the tea-urn behind the counter and the murmur of conversation washed over Linda. She debated with herself whether to actually say what was on her mind. 'I feel really bad that it was me that let the cat out of the bag.'

'It wasn't your fault, Linda. Richard's caught us out hundreds of times since he learned to lip-read. Peter and I always had to be so careful when we had anything to discuss that we didn't want the twins to know about.'

'What did he say?'

'Not a lot, really. I think he's is still trying to come to terms with everything.'

'He must know none of what's happened is your fault?'

'Hmm. He's anxious now to get back to Ashford. He's worried about the girl – Karen.'

Linda grimaced. 'I'm not surprised ... with George Shuttleworth for a stepfather. Especially now.'

She was shocked at Mary's next words.

'I've decided I'm going to see him. George Shuttleworth, I mean,' Mary said. 'When we take Richard back to Ashford, I'll find out his address and go there.'

'How will you find out where he lives?'

Mary pondered for a moment before her face cleared. 'I could ask Jacqueline. Karen's living with her for now, you said? Shouldn't be difficult for Jacqueline to find out.'

'And you don't think she'll ask why you want to know?'

'I'll think of something. I just want to make sure he knows to leave Richard alone, whether he's going out with his stepdaughter or not.'

'Look, do you think that's wise, Auntie Mary? From what I've seen he's still as nasty a piece as ever he was.' The apprehension made Linda feel sick. She swallowed hard.

'I think it's the only way. Don't forget, he'd have a lot to lose if he did anything that brought up the past. And,' Mary gave a short laugh, 'if a man's brave enough to walk on the moon, I'm sure I can beard Shuttleworth in his own den.'

'It's no joke, Auntie.'

'I know.'

'I want you to promise you won't go on your own.'

'We'll see.' Mary drained her cup and put it back on the saucer. 'You ready to go? Had enough of your coffee?'

'Yes.' There was no point on insisting; her aunt had always been a strong-willed woman.

And if Linda didn't leave right now, she'd throw up all over the table. The anxiety was playing havoc with her digestion.

Chapter 49: Linda Booth & Mary Schormann

Llamroth, afternoon: Friday, October 3rd

'I know this will sound stupid, Linda, but I'm going to give the house a good clean before we go up north. I haven't had much of a chance this last two weeks and the whole place needs a good bottoming.' Mary looked around the living room. 'I could write my name in the dust.'

'Bit of an exaggeration, but I do understand. You'll need to leave the house clean in case you're burgled,' Linda teased.

'Don't say that.' Mary shuddered yet smiled. 'I just like to see the place tidy and clean before we go.'

'Okay. And I'll help.'

'Thanks. And no time like the present. With Richard off seeing his mates before he leaves and Peter having the day out to some garden place near Cardiff with Alun and Alwyn, it's a good time to start.'

'Upstairs first?'

'Yes, I like to do top to bottom.'

'Right, where should I start?'

'If you don't mind tackling the bathroom, I'll do our bedroom.'

Mary stopped on the landing. She could hear Linda humming behind the swish of water in the bath and the squeak of a cloth on the tiles. She touched the top of the old desk. It was dusty. She undid the tin of polish and wiped the cloth over the surface. It would seem old-fashioned to Linda, but she still liked the smell of her Johnson's Lavender. As she smeared it over the desk she absentmindedly pulled open the drawer. She frowned, everything looked different. Tom's glasses-case was open; the broken lens was on top of an untidy jumble of papers. Putting it safely away again she riffled through the papers, looking for the small envelope of old photos. It wasn't there. Photos spilled from a large paper bag. Perhaps, without thinking, she'd put them all together? She sat on the top tread of the stairs and slid them back in, lingering over each one. When she'd finished she frowned and went through them again. There were definitely snaps missing. She rummaged through the drawer again, with no luck. Closing it with a sigh she buffed the desk to a gleam. She must remember to ask Peter about the photographs sometime.

By the time she'd finished the bedrooms, Linda had swept the stair-carpet and wiped down the wood of the treads on either side.

'Brew before we start down here?' Mary said, making her way into the kitchen.

'Just water for me, please, the smell of that Stardrops made me feel a bit sick.'

'It is a bit strong, but a good cleaner. You should have left it for me to do.' Mary called over the sound of filling the kettle with water. 'Oh, by the way, I just did ours and Richard's rooms. I left yours; I thought you might want to do it yourself.' She'd actually seen an open letter on the bed. One sheet had fallen to the floor and, as she picked it up, she'd seen Martin's signature.

'Cheers, that's okay.' Linda followed her into the kitchen. 'Did you notice the letter?'

'I didn't read it.' Mary was quick to reply.

'No. No, I know, I didn't mean that. I was just saying,' Linda said. 'It was from Martin. We've split up. My choice,' she said hastily. 'He wanted to get married. I don't.'

Even though … especially because, Linda surprised herself by the thought, especially because of what she would have to face in the future.

'You don't have to tell me, love. It's none of my business.'

'Not much to say beyond that, really.' Not yet, Linda thought, reaching for a glass from the wall cupboard and let the cold-water tap run for a few seconds before filling it. 'It's just that he's not giving up so easily. He was really angry about it; I think it's his pride more than anything that's hurt. But he's decided he'll forgive me.' She quoted the last two words, caustically. 'He thinks I'm panicking about being married.'

'Is that true?'

'Not at all. I don't want to be married.' She turned the tap off. 'And I certainly don't want to be married to him. Mug or cup?'

'Mug, please.' Mary put the cosy over the teapot. 'I'll let it brew for a minute.' She leaned against the sink. 'You're sure it's over?'

'Uh huh.'

'Well then, that's all that matters. Just stick to your guns and get on with your life.' She turned around and poured the tea. 'Let's take these through. We can drink as we clean.'

They put the mug and glass on the windowsill in the living room.

'If we move everything to the back of the room and do around the fireplace and then shift everything the other way?' Mary said. 'All right with you?'

'Fine.'

'Okay then, let's start with the settee.' They positioned themselves at the front. 'It's on casters but it's a bit awkward.'

They pushed the settee backwards with their knees until it wouldn't go any further.

'Oh, my goodness, I'm ashamed,' Mary said. 'Look at all the fluff and bits under here.'

Linda kneeled down and peered underneath. 'There's something stuck on one of the casters,' she said. 'Looks like some paper.' She felt around. 'It's an envelope.' Handing it to Mary she waited while her aunt studied it.

'It's addressed to Victoria. And it's postmarked Manchester but I don't recognise the writing.'

'Is it empty?'

'I think so.' Mary poked her finger and thumb inside, opening the envelope wider. 'Oh. No, there's a note.' She read the words out loud: '"your group now, your new family … an exciting new world will be yours". What does it mean? And who is this,' she peered at the note again, 'this Seth? I've no idea. Have you, Linda?'

'Not a clue. To be honest, Auntie Mary, Vicky and me, we don't keep in touch, really. It's usually Richard I write to. And he's never mentioned the name as far as I can remember.'

'Well, reading this, it's clear he has something to do with Victoria going.' Excitement mixed with the worry on Mary's face. She chewed on her lower lip before saying, 'There's only one thing we can do. We'll take Richard up to Ashford sooner than planned and then we'll… have to start looking for her around Manchester.'

Linda hoped that meant that her aunt would forget about going to see George Shuttleworth, but her next words dispelled that.

'And I'll make sure George Shuttleworth knows exactly what will happen if he tries to harm Richard. Or any other member of our family!'

Chapter 50: Jacqueline Howarth,
Mary & Peter Schormann

Manchester: Tuesday, October 7th

'I've made a list of places where Vicky could be, from all the info I've got from the other stations.' Jackie helped Mary to take her coat off and hung it on the coat-stand before taking Peter's off him and doing the same. 'Sit down and get your breath back while I make a coffee.'

Mary raised her voice above the music on the turntable of the record-player.

'We're grateful for this, Jacqueline. Aren't we, Peter?'

He nodded.

She put her hand on his shoulder. 'You okay?'

He touched her fingers and nodded again, leaning back on the orange Ercol settee.

'The lift's out of order.' Mary watched Peter, anxious. 'It's taken us ages to climb all those stairs.'

'Again?' Jackie called from the kitchen. 'Sorry, I didn't know – I haven't been out today. I'd have said we should meet somewhere else if I'd known.'

'It's all right, we took our time.' Mary looked around the flat. She thought the orange shag-pile carpet and orange curtains clashed with the purple-painted walls.

She caught Peter's eye.

'Very – er – modern,' he muttered.

'Shush, she'll hear.' Mary walked over to the window. The restless impatience she'd felt since they arrived threatened to boil over. She suppressed the urge to rush Jacqueline, to grab the list and leave. There was no point; from what she'd seen so far, Manchester had changed almost beyond recognition from when she was last here. She and Peter wouldn't have a clue where to start. 'Nicki not home?'

'Working. She said she'll catch up later.'

'You two all right?' Mary asked.

From four floors up the view of Manchester stretched for miles. She let her eyes wander across the view. Streets crisscrossed like rows of dominos, tower blocks of flats stood alongside terraced houses and church spires. In the distance she could just make out a canal. Movement on the skyline caught her attention; a tiny train crossing a viaduct, etched against the pale grey October sky. She moved closer to the window and looked down. Streams of people were going in and out of the brightly-lit stores or moving in jumbled lines along the pavements, lines of cars and double-decker buses edged along the crowded streets. It seems strange that with this going on there is nothing to hear, she thought, except the low drone of the wind. She was startled by a pigeon alighting on the ledge outside and taking off again just as suddenly.

She swung around, anxious to talk, when Jackie came back into the room with a tray that she put onto a small kidney-shaped coffee table.

'We're great,' her niece said. 'Couldn't be better.' She smiled at Mary. 'Where's Richard, by the way?'

'We dropped him off to catch a bus into Manchester. He was meeting someone… some friend.' Mary glanced at Peter and then at Jackie. Linda had told her she'd passed on the message that he didn't yet know about Karen. And the girl wasn't in the flat. But there was always the danger Jackie would say something about the situation.

She needn't have worried. Jackie reached towards the record cabinet and flicked a switch so the arm came off the record. 'Neither of you have sugar. I'm right aren't I?' Without waiting for an answer she closed the drop-down front and picked up two cups and saucers and handed them over. 'It's hot,' she warned.

'The list?' Mary sat next to Peter.

'Oh, yes.' Jackie opened a drawer in a low sideboard by the kitchen door and pulled out a folded sheet of paper. She knelt on the rug by them and held it out. 'There's eight possibles where Vicky could be. There are more but—'

'But?' Mary took the list from Jackie and scanned it.

'Well…' Jackie pulled a face. 'From what you said about the note you found, I don't think she'll be in any of those. It sounds to me as though she's gone to one of the hippie groups, if anywhere—'

'Why? How would she have met any hippies?'

'College? She could have met someone there. What are her friends like? Has she met any new friends?' Without being conscious of it, Jackie moved into questioning mode. 'Has she been talking about anyone new? Anything she didn't talk about before? For instance, how political is she?'

'Political?' Mary gazed at Jackie then at Peter. 'She's not, not as far as we know.' Mary stopped; how much did they know about Victoria these days?

'I think there is a lot we don't know about our daughter.' Peter's voice was soft. Mary felt his hand on her knee. 'She does not talk with us, these days.'

'We should have made her talk,' Mary said. 'We should have shown more interest in what she did at college.' She met Peter's gaze. 'Have we neglected her? Concentrated on Richard so much that she felt left out.'

'That's rubbish, Auntie Mary, and you know it. From what I've always seen, you've always treated them equally—'

'I don't know.' Mary felt overwhelmed. She fumbled for her handkerchief from her cardigan sleeve.

'Well, I do,' Jackie said, taking the paper back and pointing to the first three addresses. 'These are all empty properties, or should be. There's been a rise in squatters taking some of them over in Manchester—'

'Why should she want to go somewhere like that?' Mary was bewildered. 'Why leave home to go with people she doesn't know—'

'We don't know who she knows, *Leibling*.'

'But going into a squat? I've read in the newspapers about what happens in places like that—'

'I'm not saying she has, Auntie Mary, but there's something called the Family Squatting Movement. They get people to take over empty places and use them to house homeless families from the Council Housing Waiting List. That's why I asked if Victoria had got involved in politics … if she felt strongly about social injustice.'

'Like I said, not that we know.' Which actually meant nothing, Mary realised, because, when she thought about it, the only interaction between her and their daughter over the last few months had been rows and arguments.

'Okay,' Jackie said. She pointed to the first two on the list. 'Let's just try these first. I've put them in a kind of order. We might as well start there as anywhere.'

'You'll come with us, then?'

'Yes, of course. I've got a couple of days leave coming to me. You didn't think I'd let you do this all on your own, did you?'

'Thanks, Jacqueline.' Mary sniffed, blew her nose and sat straighter. Now there was prospect of doing something, the relief and hope inside her was the first she'd felt in a month.

Chapter 51: Victoria Schormann

Ashford: Tuesday, October 7th

'Seth set up the community in 1960. He gave us somewhere to belong, to escape from the path of sin.'

Amber had appointed herself as Victoria's best friend and had barely left her side for the last week. Victoria suspected it was Seth's doing, that he'd decided she needed watching. And she resented it. She tried to block out the whine of the woman's voice by watching the faces of the six other girls and the only man in the group. But then Amber spoke louder and Victoria, startled, looked back at her. Her face was an unattractive scarlet and her eyes were wild. 'I was wicked … evil … once; Seth redeemed me.'

The girl sitting next to Victoria in the circle made a scoffing sound. 'Huh.'

A chill silence settled instantly over the group.

When the girl spoke her voice was harsh. 'You … we … I was taken in by him. It's like we've been hypnotised to follow his …' she gave emphasis to her next words, '*so-called* teachings. We've all given up our lives, rejected our families because of him.'

Victoria's heart gave a few rapid beats. She realised that she hadn't kept her promise to her parents; she hadn't written to them since she'd left. When she looked up, the man opposite and one or two of the girls were watching her. Had she let her thoughts show? She forced the settled expression back onto her face: the wide-open eyes, the slight smile. She saw the man relax and he smiled back before turning his attention to the girl next to her.

'Melody—'

'My name's Christine—'

'Melody,' he interrupted her, 'I think you need to go and lie down. It is obvious you are distraught today … not thinking what you are saying … what you truly believe. You know we have welcomed you with open arms … open hearts.'

'So long as I gave up everything.' She threw the words out. 'I was … persuaded … to sell everything I had. It wasn't a lot but I gave all my money to Seth—'

'So he could share it with the group. We have all shared in the largesse from our former lives.' The man, Om – Victoria had been trying to remember his name ever since he first spoke – wasn't someone who often came to the meetings of the younger members, but he'd joined them today. Now she knew why.

'You need to silence the questions.'

Victoria heard the warning from Amber but it was as though Christine – Melody, Victoria corrected herself – hadn't heard.

'You think the outside world is meaningless. But that's all rubbish. Admit it.' Melody spread her hands out in front of her.

Victoria closed her eyes, focussed on the darkness of her eyelids. She breathed in through her nose. Held the air inside her – a trick she'd picked up from Richard.

'What do you think, Summer?'

Let the breath out slowly through open lips.

'Summer!'

With a start Victoria heard the plea in Melody's voice. Keep me out of it, she thought, please keep me out of this.

'Summer?' Now it was Amber speaking.

Victoria heard the impatience. 'I … I'm not sure what you mean.' She'd learned quickly not to question anything. She was trying to not listen to the quiet voice that challenged Seth. Cut off from the world, with no newspapers or anything, his beliefs, and those of his group, were all she had. She had to believe what he'd said to her: that she was special to him and she had to be patient, wait, before he announced it to the others. There was no going back now. He'd convinced her that her family, her other family in Wales, would have rejected her now, as she'd rejected them. She'd hurt them too much.

'He keeps control of us by giving us the rewards he thinks we should value.' It was as though Melody couldn't stop. 'Like he makes us all strive for and rely on one another's friendship, affection. It's almost like having to depend on everyone else just to survive.'

Now, no one was looking at her. They were exchanging shocked gazes, tight-lipped, narrow-eyed.

'I'm sick of it.' Melody moved as though to stand.

Victoria rested a hand on her, gave a small shake of her head. She felt chilled, frightened for the girl.

'I want out.'

No one spoke.

'Shut up.' Chrystal broke the moment.

'The longer we stay here,' Melody insisted, 'the harder it will be to leave.'

'You can't leave.' Chrystal's voice was calm.

'You're all in on it, the entire lot of you … all taken in by Seth. Or *the Master*, as he likes to be called,' Melody shouted. 'Well, I'm not. And I'm leaving … I'm—'

Before she could finish Chrystal stood, walked over to her and hit her. The woman's face was white, except for two bright red blotches on her cheeks. 'Don't ever speak about our Master in that way.' She hit Melody again as she said her next two words. 'Ever again.'

It all happened so quickly. Victoria was stunned. She'd seen girls fight in school a couple of times but she'd never seen anything like this. She saw one or two of the others look at one another, but most of them kept their heads lowered. She didn't know what to do. But when Melody ran from the room, Victoria started to get up, intending to go after her.

'Stay where you are, Summer.' Chrystal's voice was calm. There was no doubt it was an order.

Even though the anger bubbled inside her, Victoria sank back to the floor. It was minutes before she felt the pain of her fingernails digging into her palm. And saw the tiny crescents of blood on the skin.

Chapter 52: Mary Schormann & Jean Howarth

Ashford: Saturday, October 11th

It's glorious up here.' Mary had to shout against the stiff breeze that whipped up the waters of the reservoir and rocked a line of sailing boats tied up on the far side. 'I love Stonebridge; I'd forgotten how much heather comes out at this time of year.' She squinted upwards at the purple-covered rocky hills and moorland that surrounded them. 'So … so open, so exhilarating.'

'So cold,' Jean grumbled. 'I don't know why you wanted to come up here. It's so cold.'

'You were the one who suggested we got out of the house.'

'I didn't suggest coming here. It's freezing.'

'Oh, don't be a wimp. Look around, we're not the only ones with the same idea.'

'Oh, yes. At least four other people,' Jean said.

'Breathe in all this lovely air.' Mary opened her arms, threw her head back, and took a deep breath. She sobered. 'I needed to get away from everything, just for an hour, Jean. And I want to talk to you.'

'What about?' Jean tied her fur bonnet tighter under her chin and turned her head away.

Mary frowned; her sister-in-law had been unusually quiet from the minute she'd opened the door of the house. 'Richard, mainly. There's something—'

'Oh.' Jean started to walk along the gravelled path that skirted the reservoir, her short, squat body rolling from side to side. 'So when does he start at the university?'

Strange – was that relief in her voice? Mary tried to look at Jean but the fluffy fur edging of her bonnet hid her face. 'Not until the twentieth, but there are a few things to sort out first. Like I said, I want us to talk—'

'Where are you staying?' Jean interrupted. She quickened her pace, starting to pant with the exertion.

'Richard's back at number twenty-seven with Ellen and Ted for the time being. He'll go into the Halls of Residence in a few days. We're staying in a bed-and-breakfast place in Manchester. I've left Peter there to have a rest, he insisted on driving part of the way. It was too much for him.' She was talking to her sister-in-law's back. 'Jean!' What was the matter with her? 'If you don't stand still right now, you'll be making your own way back home.' Mary stopped, determined to make her sister-in-law listen. It didn't make any difference; Jean carried on walking.

'You could have stayed with us, you know.' Jean threw the breathless words over her shoulder.

Becoming more exasperated by the minute, Mary caught up

with her. 'I think we pushed our luck in summer, staying with you then, Jean. I don't think that would have been a good idea so soon again. Patrick isn't a big fan of Peter's.' And her brother had been as odd as her old friend when she'd walked into their house – even more surly than normal.

'He wouldn't say anything.'

'No, probably not.' Mary agreed, if only to keep the peace. 'But it's better for us to be in Manchester. There's a good chance that's where Victoria is.'

'You've only got that one letter to go by, though, haven't you?' Jean tugged her coat collar further up the back of her neck. 'What else makes you think she's in Manchester?'

'Nothing. It's a long shot,' Mary admitted, 'but that's more than we had before. And Jackie's given me a list of the police stations and of some of the squats.'

'Is she…' Jean put her hand to her throat and coughed even as she hurried on. 'Is she allowed to do that? Give a list of where people are squatting?'

'Stop. Stop. This is stupid.' Mary held on to Jean's arm. A man with two sheepdogs ambled past them, gave them a cursory glance before whistling to one of the dogs who'd stopped to sniff at a small rhododendron bush.

'Is she allowed to do that?' Jean's face was red, her mouth open to take in more air. Holding on to her side she bent forward until she lost her balance and stumbled.

'Steady.' Mary caught her and took her weight. 'I've no idea if Jackie is allowed to give us that information, but who's going to tell on her?' She led Jean to the small stone wall at the side of the path. 'Lean against this until you feel better.' She kept her arm around Jean's plump shoulders and stared across the steely grey water towards the skyline, where craggy rocks met the overhang of pearlised clouds. 'This isn't what I came to talk to you about, but it's clear there's something wrong with you and Patrick.' She gave voice to the niggle at the back of her mind. 'He's not up to his old tricks again, is he?'

'What do you mean?' Jean's voice rose an octave.

'You know what I mean.'

'Of course not. He hasn't touched me for years.'

What did that mean? He hadn't hit her? 'Other women, then?'

Jean faced Mary, pulling her chin back until the ties of her bonnet disappeared in the folds of flesh. 'No. No. He's kept his hands to himself and, as far as I know, or care, there's been no other women.' But misery crossed her face.

Mary gave an inward sigh. The business about George Shuttleworth was going to have to be put to one side for a while. 'Okay,' she said, 'What's the problem?'

'It's Jacqueline.' Jean pushed at the bridge of her glasses, refusing to look at Mary. 'She's … she's a lesbian.' She pursed her lips.

'Yes, I know. There's nothing you can do about that. She's still your daughter and—'

'A lesbian. She does horrible things with the girl she lives with,' Jean shouted. A small boy, running past, holding the end tip of a kite above his head, stopped and stared, his eyes wide. Then he turned and ran back into the arms of a woman.

'You frightened that child, shouting like that,' Mary hissed. She smiled apologetically at the mother. 'Sorry.' She mouthed the word. 'Jean, hush.'

'With that Nicki woman.' She didn't lower her voice and the woman, arms around her son, hurried past.

'I know.'

'What? How do you know?'

'Jacqueline told me how she felt a long time ago. I thought the whole family knew.'

'Patrick and I didn't.'

'Then you're the only ones.'

There was a low growl of thunder. Mary realised the breeze had dropped. She looked around. The heather, higher up on the hills, no longer swayed in one long continuous line of colour; the water was still, reflecting the dark cover of clouds. 'It looks as though it's going to pelt down,' she said. 'We should get back to the car.' She turned and walked away, then stopped as Jean shouted after her.

'Patrick and I didn't know. And we've disowned her. She's no longer our daughter.'

'I don't believe you.' Mary turned the key and let the engine die before twisting in the seat to stare at Jean. They hadn't spoken in the whole twenty minutes since they'd left the reservoir. The storm pounding on the roof of the Hillman, the rapid clunk of the windscreen wipers working uselessly against the torrent of rain distorting the road, would have made it impossible to talk even if Mary hadn't been struggling to stop the rage bursting out in recriminations.

Now she slapped the flat of her hand on the dashboard. 'I can't believe what you said. What you've done.'

The windows were misting over. The silence from Jean, her back huddled away from Mary was an old one, familiar from the long years of their friendship; she was sulking. Infuriated, Mary clenched her teeth. She turned the handle on her door, winding the window down a fraction, and lifted her face to the damp coolness. The rain was stopping. She looked up to the sky; the light, pale as water, was fading. Glancing at the house she saw Patrick, watching them from the lounge window, his shirt open at the neck, his old-fashioned braces dangling from his waist.

When she spoke Mary kept her voice deliberately low. 'Our daughter is missing, heaven knows where. We're out of our minds with worry. Your daughter is a lovely young woman and has been, and still is, helping us to find her. And you two have disowned her because you don't like how she lives.'

'She has sex with girls.' Jean spun around in her seat to glare at Mary. The tiny veins on her cheeks and her nose where her glasses pressed on the bone were flushed red. 'Sex with girls. Disgusting.'

'One girl.' Mary was so angry she felt she was fighting for air. All the benefit she'd had from being at Stonebridge dissipated. 'The person she loves. What does it matter whether it's a man or a woman?'

205

Jean took her hat off. Her short curls were flattened; there was a thin line of grey along her parting that contrasted with the dark brown of the rest of her hair. The furrows on her forehead and at the corners of her eyes deepened.

She's old, Mary thought, then corrected herself; they were the same age, but her friend, her sister-in-law, looked so old. The surge of compassion was familiar to her; it was an underlying emotion that had been there right from the start of their friendship. Jean couldn't help what she was; her mother had been one of the most bigoted women Mary had ever had the misfortune to know. She knew exactly how Mrs Winterbottom would have reacted to her granddaughter's choice of lifestyle. She would be encouraging Jean to have nothing to do with Jacqueline.

'Don't shut Jacqueline out of your life,' she said. 'I don't care about Patrick. My brother has done exactly what he wanted to do all his life, whether it's right or wrong. And he doesn't give tuppence for anyone else, never has.' She held her hand up to stop Jean's protests. 'And I don't know why you're even trying to defend him – you know that's true as well as me. What I'm saying is that you and Jacqueline have always got along okay. Don't spoil it.'

'Patrick says he won't have her in the house.'

'Then meet her somewhere else. But go to her, Jean, say you're sorry. Make things right.' A sob rose in Mary's throat and her voice cracked. 'Just don't lose her.'

Patrick had left the window and was standing at the front door flicking the ash from his cigarette into the damp air. When he dropped it, half-smoked, the sparks as it flew through the air were extinguished as soon as it hit the path. The impatience on his face told Mary he would be striding to the car any moment to find out why Jean wasn't getting out.

There was nothing else for it. 'Jean, I didn't want to tell you like this. Before, when I said I wanted to talk about Richard, there was a reason … something you need to know—' Jean opened her mouth to speak. 'Just let me explain before you ask any questions. When he was up here for the interviews he met a girl. Her name is Karen. She's staying with Jacqueline at the moment.'

'I saw another girl there. I thought she was one of them.'

'Stop it.' Mary pressed her fingers over her eyes, cupping the sides of her face. 'Just stop it, Jean.'

'I'm just saying—'

'Well, don't. She's staying with Jacqueline and Nicki for a reason. She had to leave home. When her stepfather discovered she was going out with Richard he got violent. She was scared and ran away. You lovely daughter took her in without question.'

Jean gave a dismissive little shrug. 'So what's that got to do with me?'

'Jean,' Mary took hold of her hands. 'Karen's stepfather is George Shuttleworth.'

Chapter 53: Victoria Schormann

Ashford: Saturday, October 11th

Victoria was nervous. She stopped pulling at the roots of the stubborn dandelion in the ground in front of her but kept her head down, afraid to look up in case one of the others were watching her. The atmosphere over the past four days had been tense; everyone was waiting to see what decision Melody would make, what the reaction of the Elders, of the Master, would be.

Without lifting her head she let her eyes slide over the figures surrounding her. There were five of them, including her. They'd been struggling for the past two hours to make the large plot of land into something that would grow vegetables. It was hopeless; the more they dug, hoed and weeded the more evident it was that there was no real soil there, only rubble from the foundations of some old building.

It was a stupid time of the year to be doing this, anyway, Victoria thought, sure that her father would have laughed at them if he could see what they were trying to do. for a minute, she pictured the garden in Llamroth … at home.

She settled back on her haunches and wiped her forehead with her arm.

'Are you here because you couldn't recite the mantra, like me?' One of the girls sidled closer to her.

'No,' Victoria was surprised. 'I thought they'd just allocated the jobs as usual.' She moved forward on her knees to tackle another patch of weeds.

'No. Ask the others; we're all here because of stuff we've done wrong. I forgot the mantra – third time this week. When the Elder came this morning it went straight out of my head, even though I'd tried so hard in the night to memorise it. So here I am.'

The Elders giving them mantras to learn was one of the things Victoria resented but, after three weeks in the commune, she was learning to pick her fights. Or was she? she thought. Was she doing this – she looked around at the other three, silently and hopelessly slogging away at the ground – because of something she'd done? And Seth was letting it happen?

She'd quickly come to see that the stupid mantra-thing had a purpose: it was to stop the girls talking between themselves at night, having any time to question anything that had happened during the day. It stopped them thinking. Or it was supposed to. Victoria had her own way of getting around that: she wrote the words down after the Elder had gone and memorised the long repetitive refrains in the morning as she washed and dressed. She often wondered how many of the others did as she did: how many were like her.

Something had taken her by surprise; she was homesick. She'd mocked herself when she'd first admitted it to herself. She spent the nights wondering what her parents were doing, if Richard had got the job at the hospital in Manchester. If Gelert missed her. She often thought back to the early morning walks she took with the large Alsatian before she went to college, remembering the way he barked and chased the waves.

Remembering the freedom. Now she froze, her hand resting on the soil next to a clump of dandelions. She'd had freedom in Llamroth.

'Summer?' The girl touched Victoria's arm.

'Oh, sorry,' She jumped. 'I don't know what I'm supposed to have done. I can't think…' And then it hit her; they thought she was sympathising with Melody: that she was better kept away from her. She knew she was being watched, as they all were, but she thought she'd kept her increasing resentment of the control Seth and his followers had over her to herself. Obviously not.

For the first time in her life, Victoria saw how understanding her parents were of her. How often they'd given in to her.

She missed them. As the days passed she'd become more and more homesick. Once she came to, with a start, and realised she'd been dreaming of her mother's apple pie, made of the fruit from the tree in the garden – the one planted by her mum's brother, the unknown Uncle Tom, when they first went to live in Llamroth.

And, with another moment of awareness, she realised she didn't even know why her parents had gone to Wales to live in the first place. There was so much not spoken of in the family. Or that she hadn't listened to – that was probably more like it, she thought. In the past she'd presumed all the talk of the past was about her father and the war, and she'd thought all that old stuff boring.

'So could you remind me?' The girl was talking to her, her face anxious.

'Sorry, what?'

'I said, could you remind me of the mantra? Please. The others won't talk to me; they think we're being watched.' She looked anxiously back towards the main building

'We probably are.' Victoria lifted her shoulders. 'But I'm sick of it.'

The girl gave an inward gasp. 'Oh, don't—'

209

'Do you want to know or not?' Victoria snapped.

'Sorry. Yes. He, the Elder, said he'd be back to ask me again later. I'm so scared—'

'Well, don't be – that's daft. What on earth do you think they can do to you?'

'What they're doing to Melody – make everyone ignore her. I couldn't stand that.' The girl chopped uselessly at the ground with her hoe. 'Or worse, they could make me leave and I've nowhere to go. So, please.'

'It's: "Cultivate the habit of being grateful. There is always something to be thankful for. If these key points are not understood, you will neglect clear visualisation and hold on to self-pride,"' Victoria chanted. 'So there you go. Just remember the mantra is always worded to make sure you know which side your bread's buttered.' Without even thinking about it she'd just repeated one of her mother's stock phrases. The groundswell of homesickness made her hands shake as she reached out for another dandelion. 'Just remember you're in their control.'

And, with that thought, the trepidation that had followed her around since Tuesday was swept away by a torrent of resentment.

Chapter 54: Linda Booth

Ashford: Saturday, October 11th

'You need to listen to them, Mum.'

Harriet Worth was on the seat of the large bay window changing the baby's nappy. She didn't look up. 'No, I don't. Coming in here telling me my husband's some sort of gangster. It's ridiculous.' She wrung a cloth out from a small bowl and wiped it over the little boy's skin. 'You've always hated your ... George from the minute he came into the house. So, no, I don't need to listen to this rubbish.'

'It's not rubbish. And this proves I was right to hate him,' Karen said. 'Tell her, Linda.'

'I don't want to hear it.' Her mother spoke through two large nappy-pins held between her lips while drying the baby and lathering cream on him. She took a long time to wrap the towelling nappy around him, before fastening it. Eventually, she sat back, her hands resting on her thighs.

'It's true, Harriet,' Linda said.

'Mrs Worth to you, missy. You're not in charge here, this isn't the hospital.'

'Sorry. Mrs Worth. And I'm sorry, but it's true.' Linda exchanged glances with Richard, sharing the woman's distress. 'It did happen.'

'Okay, then.' Harriet pulled a white cellular blanket off the back of the settee and wrapped the baby in it before picking him up. 'Tell me again. I'm not going to believe it the second time around, but I can see you're not going to leave until you do.' She gazed out of the window at the garden as though disinterested in anything they had to say, but Linda saw how she shook as she held the baby to her shoulder.

'You tell her this time, Linda. It's your story after all,' Karen said.

'And that's what it is, a cock-and-bull story.' Harriet gave them a sideways look. 'Oh, for goodness sake sit down, you look like judge and jury standing there.'

They perched on the edge of the settee. Linda wished she was anywhere but in the house that was contaminated by George Shuttleworth. She couldn't think of him now as anything but Shuttleworth.

'Well, go on.' Harriet swung round, glaring at Linda but there was a tremor of apprehension in her voice.

Linda clasped her hands between her knees and spoke slowly. 'I was about seven,' she said. 'From what I can remember of before …of before it happened, I'd gone off on my own. It was Whit Sunday. The band contest was on so it must have been after six o'clock.'

211

Harriet made an impatient noise. She rocked the little boy, looking back out of the window.

'I think I'd fallen out with my cousin. I suppose I was sulking about something because I ran off.' She stopped, all at once there in that moment: feeling the warm cone of chips in her hand, the noise of the crowded pub, seeing her cousin skipping with two other girls, remembering how cross she'd been that Jacqueline had so quickly forgotten her.

She shivered: images of the deserted prison camp clear in her mind – the old mill with its black and empty windows, the big gates. 'There was new barbed wire all around the fence,' she said. 'I'd forgotten that.'

'What?' Harriet swung round. 'Where?'

Linda hadn't realised she'd spoken out loud. She didn't answer. 'Anyway, I must have fallen asleep. When I woke up he was there; it was as though he'd been watching me.' She couldn't help the shudder.

Richard squeezed her arm. 'You're doing great, Lin.'

Karen held Linda's other hand. 'Go on. Please.'

Linda looked squarely at Harriet. 'He said Mum was looking for me and I should go with him.' It felt as though the words were stuck in her throat and she'd have to push them out. The sun, pouring light across the room in a wide line, divided it into light and shadow.

Swallowing, forcing herself to carry on she said, 'He didn't take me to my mother ... he took me into the old mill. I kicked and screamed but he hit me. Hard. Here.' She touched the back of her head. 'Until then I don't think anyone had ever hit me. He kept me there for days. I was shut away. It was so dark.' She ran her tongue around her mouth but it didn't help the dryness. 'I found out later it was some sort of a boiler-room in the basement of what used to be a hospital. Part of the camp.' For a moment Linda was back there listening to the scuffles of rats.

Harriet frowned. 'I thought you said it was an old mill.'

212

'It was the one in Ashford; the one turned into a POW camp in the war.'

Harriet didn't acknowledge Linda's explanation.

'He tied me up. Part of the time he put something over my mouth because I couldn't stop screaming.' She heard the sharp intake of breath from the woman sitting opposite her, holding the baby close and rocking faster. 'I don't remember much more. I knew I tried to escape, I remember that much. The next thing I knew my uncle, Uncle Peter, Richard's father,' she nodded towards him, 'was holding me in his arms and shouting. I remember the words. He was shouting "She is here."'

'I promise you, the man who took me, who kidnapped me, was your husband. His real name is George Shuttleworth, not Worth.'

She waited, the three of them waited, watching Harriet struggling to keep control.

'But why? Why would he do that? You were just a child.'

Linda felt something give inside her: a release of the tension that had held her rigid from the moment she'd walked into that house. 'He hated my family. There is so much history between them. Too much to explain right now.'

'I have a right to know,' Harriet whispered. 'You're accusing my husband of this dreadful thing. You say he hated your family but you don't tell me why.' Now she was still, tears trickling down her cheeks.

'Richard's told Karen. Let her tell you.' Linda let go of their hands and stood; she needed to leave, to get away. 'But you do believe me, don't you?'

'No. I don't know. I have to think. George will be back any moment. You need to go.'

'I'll come back on Monday, Mum,' Karen said.

'You're not staying?' Harriet clutched the baby tighter. He began to cry.

Karen stroked his cheek. 'No. I'll be back on Monday, when *he's* gone to work. I'll ring first.'

Harriet didn't answer her. 'You should go,' she said again to Linda.

'Yes,' Linda said. She held her hand out to Harriet. It was ignored. But the horror in the woman's eyes told Linda she believed what she was saying.

Chapter 55: William Booth

Ashford: Sunday, October 12th

'Well, well, what have we 'ere, then?' The man in uniform filled the doorway. He slung his backpack on the kitchen floor. 'So this is the fancy man, eh?'

William swung round, the tea-towel and the plate he was drying still in his hands. At the sink Susan slowly lifted her hands from the soapy water. 'Charlie.' Her voice shook.

'Proper cosy little scene, eh?' The man swaggered in. 'In *my* house.' He stood close to William. The sourness of his breath, the tiny blur of red veins in the corners of his eyes was testament to a session of heavy drinking. 'Nice. I'm off to Northern Ireland, not knowing if I'll be coming back in one piece, if at all. And you, you bastard, are here having it away with *my* wife. Playing daddy to *my* son.'

'I'm not. But there again, neither are you.' William put the plate and towel on the worktop. The two men were the same height and William met the other's challenge with a still and steady gaze.

'This has nothing to do with William.' Susan moved next to him, drying her hands. He could feel her trembling.

'This has everything to do with him. I've caught you out at last.' The man's eyes slid sideways to Susan. His top lip curled into a sneer. 'This is who you chucked me out for?'

'I didn't. We were finished long before I met William,' Susan said.

William noticed her upward glance at the ceiling; she was worried about Tim.

214

'William, is it?' He drawled the name out. Will-i-am.' He pushed his chest out at William with each syllable.

'Pearson.' William stood his ground, his arms loose at his side, his eyes still fixed on the man. Inside he was beginning to seethe, his gut tightening, getting ready to strike first if necessary. But he was careful not to let it show.

'I don't want any trouble, Charlie. Not with Tim in the house. Not again.' Susan moved to close the door to the living room.

'Upstairs, is he? Not here? Not here, sharing this cosy little scene?' Charlie slouched against the wall. 'My son. The one you won't let me see.'

'I've told you; you can see him anytime. I've offered to bring him round to your mum's.'

'Just not here though, eh?' Charlie picked at his teeth with his nail.

'Only if your mum came with you. I told you, I can't have you here on your own.'

'Such a big bad wolf, aren't I?' His tongue made a popping noise as he dry-spat some bits from between his lips.

A figure darkened the back doorway.

'Will? What the hell are you doing here?' Jack peered over Charlie's shoulder. He jostled Charlie to one side and repeated, 'What the hell are you doing here? With Charlie's missus?'

Charlie jerked round, his heavy chin jutted out. 'You know this geezer?'

'He's my cousin.'

'Fuckin' 'ell.' For a moment Charlie looked flummoxed. Then he suddenly laughed. It was a high malicious giggle. 'No? Really? The one you can't stand? The bastard who thinks he's God?'

William gently moved Susan behind him and crossed his arms.

'Oh, very heroic.' Charlie jeered. 'You think it's her I'm gunning for, huh? Well you've made a mistake there.' He crouched low, reaching behind him. When he brought his hand forward he held a knife.

215

Susan screamed. William pushed the table so it was between them and Susan.

'Don't be stupid, man.' Jack grabbed Charlie's wrist even as he was circling William.

The man shook him off. 'Keep out of it. The bugger has to pay for breaking up my marriage, for taking my bird.'

'He didn't, Charlie, it was over between us, you know that,' Susan pleaded, holding the edge of the table. 'I told you, we were over long before I started seeing William.'

'Seeing? Is that what you call it? Fucking, more like, you dirty bitch.'

She whimpered.

'Watch your mouth.' William mirrored the man's movements, bunching his fists, the muscles in his arms clenched. They moved in slow motion, never taking their eyes off one another. He knew there would be no reasoning with Susan's husband. He sensed his shoulders hunching around his neck and flexed them, stretching his fingers, ready for any sudden jabbing of the hand that held the flick knife.

'Drop the knife, Chas. Don't be so bleeding stupid.' Jack clutched the back of the man's jacket and attempted to pull him back.

'Bugger off.' Charlie shrugged his shoulder forward, knocking Jack off balance so he fell against the kitchen unit, rattling all the crockery inside.

There was a cry from upstairs. Charlie dithered, glanced upwards as Jack rebounded from the unit onto him. William dived towards them.

William wasn't sure how it happened but the hard thump told him enough. He staggered back, holding his shoulder. Blood seeped through his fingers. He tried to find the wall to hold him up. He kept his eyes on Jack, but his cousin's face wavered and blurred as he buckled and slumped awkwardly to sit on the floor, his head between raised knees.

'Oh, hell,' Jack cried out. 'Get something! Towels or something!' he shouted at Susan.

She pulled so hard at one of the drawers it came off the runners, and towels cascaded to the floor. Grabbing one she shoved the table out of the way. 'Bastard!' She spat the word at her husband and dropped to kneel at the side of William, pressing the cloth on the spread of blood. 'We need to call for an ambulance. Go to the telephone-box at the end of the road.'

Neither of the two men moved.

'It wasn't me, it was him.' Still holding the knife Charlie swung round to Jack. 'You bloody pushed me, you idiot.' There was a sheen of sweat on his top lip. 'And it wouldn't have happened if he,' he shook the knife at William, 'hadn't tried to play the bloody macho man.'

'Get an ambulance,' Susan yelled.

No one moved.

William saw the terror in Jack's eyes. He blinked against the waves of pain that filled his body. He coughed, gritting his teeth to ward off the agony the sharp movement caused. 'No. No ambulance.'

Charlie Pearson collapsed on one on the chairs staring at the knife in his hand. Through the sweat that dripped into his eyes, William saw Jack prise the man's fingers open until the knife dropped. He could hear Susan sobbing, feel her hands holding the towel to his shoulder. Feel the hot rush of blood on his chest.

'Jack,' his voice was a croak. 'Jack.' There was no response from his cousin; his eyes stared blankly at William. 'You need to go and get Linda. D'you hear me?'

'Huh?' Jack's tongue protruded slightly between his teeth. 'What?' He didn't move his gaze.

William's legs were weak, his head swam. He wanted, needed to lie down. To sleep. 'I said, go get Linda. You always wanted a bloody go on my bike,' he whispered, 'now's your chance. Get on the bloody thing and go to Henshaw Street. For Linda. And you'd better bloody pray she's not on a shift.'

217

Chapter 56: Victoria Schormann

Ashford: Sunday, October 12th

Victoria watched Melody being systematically ostracised by the rest of the group. No one spoke to her. They whispered about her and, when she approached or came close to any of them, they turned their backs on her. But, wherever she went, one of them followed her.

Victoria didn't understand why they wouldn't let her just leave.

'She's not allowed to go until the Master says she can,' Amber explained. 'He talks to her at night.'

'At night?'

'All night. He's trying to make her understand how she won't fit in on the outside anymore.'

Seth's brainwashing her, Victoria thought, horrified. He's trying to break her spirit. It made her stomach twist inside her.

Despite all her efforts to avoid any of the groups, all of them had tried to involve Victoria in the exclusion.

'You can't sit on the sidelines, Summer, it's too dangerous,' Amber said, while they were sitting around the table at suppertime.

'What do you mean?'

'She means we are a family, Summer.' Chrystal stood behind them. 'We all rely on each other; for our food, our clothing and,' she spread out her arms and looked around the dining room, 'our shelter.'

'It doesn't seem fair, Chrystal. When you take our meditation sessions, you *preach* good vibes.' Victoria deliberately said the word. She thought back to the last time the woman had gathered them together: yeah, *preach* was definitely the right way to put it.

Still, she made her face impassive when she saw Chrystal bristle.

Victoria looked across at Melody. Sitting on her own at a table that she'd been led to the day after her outburst, she was upright, arms folded. The meagre amount of food on the plate in front of her was ignored.

'She is backsliding into temptation. There is nothing *we* can do for her now, Summer. It is up to the Master.' Chrystal put her hand on Victoria's shoulder. She clenched her stomach muscles, tried to shut out the drone of Chrystal's voice. 'If she goes she will leave without his blessing. She is rebellious, disobedient. A castaway…' Now she was leading Victoria towards the door and it was as though there was nothing for it but to go. 'We have been watching your struggle over the past few days. We see your compassion for Melody. But it is misplaced.' She leaned towards Victoria, her voice soft. 'You need to decide where you loyalties are. With her, or with us, with our Master. He needs to know, Summer.'

Victoria glanced over to the top table where Seth sat alone. He was watching her.

Chapter 57: Linda Booth

Ashford: Sunday, October 12th

'Linda. Is Linda in?'

Jack pushed past Ted, shouting for her.

'What is it? What's wrong?' Linda ran down the stairs, pulling on her cardigan over her uniform. 'I thought you were going back tonight.' It looked as though he was; Jack was in full uniform even if he wasn't as smart as usual.

'You have to come.' There were tears ready to spill over. He passed his hand over his short hair, agitated.

'What's wrong? I'm due in work in an hour.'

'It's William, he needs you.'

'William?' In the lounge, Ellen twisted around on the settee. 'Our William! Why? What's happened?' She stood up.

'There's been an accident.' Jack was tugging at Linda's arm.

'Whoa, steady on, lad.' Ted put his palm on Jack's chest. 'What's going on?'

'William got in a fight.'

'Never.'

'It wasn't his fault.' Jack wiped his mouth with the back of his hand. 'It just happened.'

'Where is he?' Ted went into the hall and took his jacket from the stand.

'At his girlfriend's.'

'Which is where?' Looking up at Jack, Ted shoved his foot into his shoe.

'I told you to find out where he'd gone!' Ellen jumped up, screaming at Ted. 'I told you!'

'Be quiet, Ellen. And turn that bloody thing off. I don't know why you're watching it.'

'I like *Stars on Sunday*.' Ellen muttered, crossing to the television where Jess Yates' face filled the screen.

'You're arguing about a TV programme at a time like this?' Linda stared at them; she'd never heard her father speak to her mum like that. She turned to Jack. 'How is William hurt?' she asked. 'I'll need to know what to bring.'

Jack looked from one to the other. He gulped, swallowing. 'He's been stabbed.'

'What?' Ted straightened up.

'Oh, my God!' Ellen slumped onto the settee.

'How bad?'

'I don't know.' Jack touched his shoulder. 'Here. He's bleeding.' Ellen gave a loud wail.

'Okay,' Linda said, 'I'll get some things.' She opened a cupboard in the sideboard and took out a box. 'This is only a first aid kit, though. We'll need to get him to the hospital.'

'No! No hospital!' Jack shouted. 'William said we hadn't to call for an ambulance. No hospital.'

'Why?' Linda was hurrying to the door. When she looked at him he bowed his head, shamefaced. 'It's you he had the fight with,' she said, thinking she understood.

'No.'

She turned from him. 'Get the van, Dad.'

'I've got his bike,' Jack said, 'William said for you to get there on his bike. It's faster.'

Linda was astride the bike and holding on to Jack as Ted slammed the front door of the house.

'What's the address?' Ted asked.

'Two Bridge Street, Bradlow. Same street as the new supermarket, Payless,' Jack yelled, opening the throttle. The bike lurched and wobbled before he regained some control of it and rode cautiously away.

'I'll follow in the van,' Ted shouted after them, watching which way they turned onto Shaw Street.

'I'll come.' Ellen had flung open the door and was on the step shoving her arms into her coat.

'No, Ellen, you stay here. And ring Patrick and Jean. Jack was supposed to be reporting back to his regiment tonight. They'll need to know he hasn't got there. Though what they'll tell the Army I wouldn't know.' He stopped to put his arms around her. 'I'm sorry I shouted at you, love.' He gave her a quick kiss on the mouth.

'Bring him home safe, Ted. Bring our son back to me.'

Chapter 58: Linda Booth

Bradlow: Sunday, October 12th

'A flesh wound. Messy but not as bad as I thought it was at first. Think it's mostly shock you're in.'

'Still bloody painful, though.' William screwed his face up as he sat back against a leg of the table.

'I'm sure.' Linda sat back on her haunches. 'It's stopped bleeding, but it looks as if you've lost a fair amount. Keep that dressing on. You really should go to the hospital and get checked out though. It looks like you need a couple of stitches.'

'No,' William said, 'I'll be okay.'

'I am sorry, mate,' Jack sat at the table, head in his hands.

'It wasn't your fault,' William said.

'Well, it wasn't mine.' Charlie cast a nervous glance at William and then glared at Jack. 'If that stupid bugger hadn't pushed me…'

Jack moaned.

'If you hadn't had a knife in the first place…' Linda stood up, her hands on her hips. 'Anything to do with me, I'd call the police.'

'No police.' William shook his head. Looking up at her he said, 'Help me onto the chair, Lin, and if you could just ask Susan for a clean shirt. She's upstairs with Tim. I don't want him seeing me like this.'

'Because you care so much for my son,' Charlie sneered. '*My* son.'

'Well, one of us has to, because you don't.' William ground his teeth together as he hoisted himself up, with Linda's arms around him. He waited until she left to go upstairs before saying, 'I won't report this if you just sod off now and don't come back. You heard Susan earlier, she'll tell you when and how you can see Tim. Owt to do with me and you'd be out of his life for good. You're just a nasty bugger with a bad temper. And I'll tell you this just once; come anywhere near Susan when I'm not around and you'll be out of the Army quicker than you can spit. Get it?'

Charlie shrugged. 'Hey, soft arse,' he gave Jack a nudge with his boot, 'we should be getting off before we're reported AWOL.'

'We can't just leave.' Jack let his hands drop from holding his head. 'Will's my cousin—'

'Shame you didn't think that years ago.' Despite the hot pain

222

that was making William's head spin he felt a vague pity for Jack; he must be terrified I'll get him kicked out of the Army as well, he thought. He wouldn't know what else to do with his life. And, to be honest his mother had enough to put up with living with Patrick. And for some incredible reason she adored Jack, a son who was foisted on her, if family folklore was anything to go by. 'Just go, Jack, I'll say nothing.'

Jack came over to him. He held out his hand. 'I'm sorry, Will, I really am.' He faltered. 'Thanks, mate.'

William took hold of the proffered hand with his own left one. He gave Jack a crooked grin. 'Go on, you heard Lin, it's not as bad as it looks. Just be careful over there. From what it says on the news you'll have a rough time of it in Belfast as it is. Just keep in touch with your mother. Okay?'

'Okay.' Jack nodded. He picked up his backpack and gave William a last uplift with his chin. 'See you.'

'See you.'

Charlie waited until Jack had gone before slinging his backpack onto his back. He looked at William for a long time. William returned the stare. Neither spoke. Then Susan's husband walked through the door, slamming it behind him.

Chapter 59: Ted Booth

Bradlow: Sunday, October 12th

'I'm William's dad. How is he?' Ted said, stepping into the small porch of the terraced house and holding out his hand to the small woman who opened the door to him. He could tell she'd been crying and still looked shaken.

He screwed his cap into folds and shoved it into his tweed jacket pocket, wishing for a moment he'd brought Ellen; in the right circumstances she was better at the 'niceties' than him. But then these weren't what you'd call the right circumstances, he thought, and Ellen would probably have gone for the girl; she had a right tongue on her when she was upset. No, better he was here on his own.

'Susan,' she said, taking his hand, looking as uncomfortable as he felt. 'And Linda says he'll be fine.'

'I'm sorry we haven't met before. No, you first,' he said as Susan held the door open for him to go through to the living-room. He followed her. 'And I'm that sorry we have to meet like this now.'

'I'm sorry, too. This is all my fault. William's this way.'

'We knew he had a girlfriend,' Ted said as she opened another door. 'But we didn't know you were married before this last week.' When she looked over her shoulder to him he saw the colour rise from her throat to her face. He heard the cry of a child. Looking up to the ceiling he said, 'And with a bairn.'

She let him pass her into the kitchen. 'If you'll excuse me…?'

'You go, see to…' Ted rubbed his hand over his mouth, embarrassed. He was relieved when he saw William, looking ashen but sitting on a chair at a table opposite Linda, They were drinking tea. 'Son.' He nodded at them. 'Our Linda.'

'Don't judge, Dad.'

'I'm not, lad.' Ted fingered the scar on his cheek. It wouldn't be him that judged; Ellen's face flashed through his mind. 'How're you feeling?'

'I'm okay.' William touched his shoulder under the clean white shirt. 'Lin patched me up.'

'Where did you get to, Dad? We didn't go that fast. I think Jack was more nervous than me on Will's bike.'

William gave a chuckle.

'I thought you were right behind us?' Linda said, standing up. 'Tea?'

'Please.' Ted said. 'I took a wrong turning and couldn't get out of the one-way system. Stupid. I were that frantic.' He saw the bloodied shirt in the sink. 'Bloody hell, Linda, shouldn't he be in hospital?'

'I *am* here, you know, Dad,' William said, 'and no, there's no need for me to go to hospital.'

'I've told him.' Linda said. 'He won't go. But I think he'll be fine, so long as he rests for a few days.'

'I can see Patrick liking *that*.' William shifted on the chair and flinched.

'It's his son that caused this,' Linda said. 'So he can like it or lump it.'

'Aye, she's right.' Ted took the cup of tea from Linda. 'Thanks, love. Jack went then? Didn't wait to face the music?'

'There's nothing for him to face, Dad. I'll not be grassing him up to the coppers.'

Linda pulled a face.

'Your choice, lad.'

The crying stopped. A minute or two later Susan came back into the kitchen.

'How is he?' William looked up at her.

'He's fine. Bad dream, that's all.'

'Sure?'

'Sure.' She smiled at him and then looked at Ted. 'Won't you sit down, Mr Booth?'

'Ted, please. And no, lass, I'd better be off. Let his mother know our William's okay.' Ted drained the last of his tea. 'She wanted me to bring you home,' he said to William.

'No, Dad, I'm fine here.'

'What if he ... Susan's husband comes back?'

'He won't.' William set his jaw.

'He'll be well on his way to barracks by now,' Susan added. 'And he knows he'll never be welcome here again.'

'I'd better be off, then.'

'I'll come with you,' Linda said. 'I'll be even later for my shift if I don't get a move on.' She hugged Susan, knowing already she was going to like William's girlfriend. 'I'll call around after work tomorrow.'

'You sure?'

'Yeah. Need to keep an eye on my little brother. One of the nurses lives around here somewhere. I'll cadge a lift with her.'

'Dad?' William caught hold of Ted's sleeve. 'I'll be right. Honest. Everything will be all right. Tell Mum, won't you, I don't want her mithering. And then getting herself in a state again. You know what I mean?'

'Aye, lad, I know what you mean.' They exchanged looks.

'I'll keep an eye on her.' Linda picked up her coat. Helping her dad to look after her mother would help to take her mind off her own problems.

Ted stopped by the door. 'And perhaps you'll bring your young lady home – to our house sometime? With the little 'un, of course.'

'Thank you Mr Booth … Ted.' Susan hesitated and then gave him a peck on the cheek.

'You look after him,' Ted said, blushing. 'He'll eat you out of house and home, mind.'

They all laughed. It released the tension.

'Well then,' Ted unfolded his cap and jammed it on his head, 'I'll be off. And I hope we'll be seeing a lot more of you in future, Susan.'

'You will.' William grinned. 'Thanks, Dad.'

Ted nodded. 'You be careful.'

When Linda had settled into the passenger seat of the van, Ted stopped and looked back at the closed door of the house. It looked like they were all going to have to be careful in the future. One way or another. Seems they couldn't help getting into trouble, not one of them.

Chapter 60: Richard Schormann

Ashford, morning: Monday, October 13th

'How did it go?' Richard pushed the hood of his parka off and sat up in the passenger seat of the Mini where he'd been waiting for the last two hours, outside the Worths' house. He was frozen. At first he'd tried to read the medical textbook he'd brought with him, but the words wouldn't go in. His mind kept going back to what his mother had told him last week and the realisation of how dangerous Karen's stepfather might be.

Fear had made him anxious; he hadn't thought it would take Karen so long to talk to her mother. He'd constantly turned to try to look through the misted-up back window, uneasily watching in case her stepfather's Jaguar appeared off the main road.

He'd tried hard over the last week to shut out the images his mother had conjured up when she'd told him everything that had happened, even though he could tell she'd spared him much of how she'd felt at that time. He'd searched his memories for some inkling, some clue, that could have told him that something so horrendous had happened to her, to his family. There was nothing: nothing that hinted that they were anything but an ordinary family. Even on the rare occasions his father had spoken of the war, of being prisoner, it had seemed utterly remote: a time so long before he was born that it hardly registered. Everyone seemed so normal.

But now that had all changed; he saw his family in a different light – a group of people who shared secrets. And his nights consisted of broken sleep and nightmares: of him and Karen being chased down dark lanes, of drowning in black still water, of seeing his mother's face silently screaming. And last night, a faceless man, lashing out with knives and blood, so much blood splattered on walls. William lying on the floor. At least he knew why he'd dreamt that; both his uncle and aunt were upset about what happened to his cousin.

He shook his head to get rid of the thoughts and turned to look straight at Karen as she threw a bag onto the back seat and slid in behind the steering wheel. She'd been crying.

'Sorry I was such a long time.' She gave him a wan smile.

'S'all right.' Richard hoped she couldn't see his nervousness. All he wanted to do was get as far away from her mother's house as quickly as he could. 'Just as long as you're okay, isn't it.' He glanced at his watch. 'It's nearly twelve, I was getting worried he might come back for his lunch.'

'No, Mum said he's out for the day. That's why I was in there so long. And I packed the rest of my stuff.' She tipped her head towards the bags. 'I told her I wouldn't be back until she kicked him out.'

Richard had done a lot of thinking since Saturday; he knew that by telling Karen's mother about Shuttleworth's past they'd open up a hornet's nest, as his mother would say. If Karen's mother was ever brave enough to face the truth, to tell her husband to leave, would he go…? Richard doubted it. George Shuttleworth wouldn't leave the life he'd got used to. When he'd married he'd gained a lot, from what Karen had said: a good business, money, a large house, different from the one he'd grown up in. And then there was the baby; surely he'd put up a fight for his son. And if he threatened to take Frank, Karen's mother would certainly back down. No, George Shuttleworth wouldn't leave the life he'd grown used to.

And then he'd be out for revenge. What would happen then? Shuttleworth would know it was because of Richard and his family. Who would he go for first? There was no doubt in Richard's mind. Because of Karen, it would be him.

'Do you think she will? Kick him out, I mean?'

'Who knows?' Karen was near to tears again but still smiled at him as he took hold of her fingers. 'She hasn't said anything to him yet. I think she's scared stiff of him.'

'Has he ever done anything … like hit her?'

'Not that I know.' Karen deliberated a moment. 'No, she would have told me, I'm sure. No, he's just nasty, controlling.' She sighed. 'Like I said, he's a pig.'

'You told her everything?'

The more he thought about it the more he was convinced they'd done the wrong thing.

'Everything you've told me, yeah.'

He'd believed he was right when he'd asked Linda to go with them to warn Karen's mother. He'd really thought that if Shuttleworth was made to leave he'd be out of their lives for good. What an idiot he'd been.

Karen was talking again. 'But this is so far outside of her world, Richard. Dad always looked after her. She's always been such a home-bird. She's not come across anything like this before.'

'He's fooled her then.'

What a mess. Even if Karen's mum didn't believe what she'd been told, it was possible she'd still tell Shuttleworth. Richard knew he'd have to tell his mum what they'd done. Warn her so she could tell the rest of the family that they needed to be watching out for trouble. Or should he tell Jackie? One way or another, this wasn't something he should keep to himself.

Karen let go of Richard's hands, pulled on a pair of gloves, and turned the key to start the car. 'Oh, George has kept his life outside the house as much a secret as his past. So I'm still not sure she totally believes he's not really called Worth.' The engine ticked over as she fastened her seat belt. 'Let's get away from here.' She bit her lower lip as she checked the rear view mirror.

She was clearly as worried about her stepfather coming home as he was. Richard stretched back and wiped as much of the rear window as he could, so they could see the main road. No car yet. He breathed a sigh of relief.

'We knew nothing about him before he came to work for Dad,'

Karen scowled as she manoeuvred the car across the lane. 'Mum told me once he used to say he thought George was a rough diamond but a good worker.'

'Hmm. Do you want me to get out to check the wall while you reverse?'

'No, you're okay.' She spun the steering wheel and the car bumped backwards over the uneven ground. Her voice was strained. 'He was a quick worker after Dad died, I know that. Anyway, it's up to her, I suppose.' She put the car into first gear and straightened it. Before they set off she looked at Richard. 'I just wonder if she's really too frightened of being on her own, especially since she had Fra— the baby.'

Couldn't she even say the baby's name, now she knew about Shuttleworth's brother? Richard thought. Poor kid, to be named after such a sicko.

'Is there no one in your family that can help her?' he said.

'No, neither Mum nor Dad had any brothers or sisters. I think there's a cousin of Dad's somewhere but we haven't seen him since George came on the scene.'

The main road was busy. Richard watched through his window. 'You're right this way,' he said, when there was a clear space in the traffic. He turned back to her. 'How does she feel about you leaving home?'

'Thanks.' Karen pulled out onto the road. 'I've wanted to leave for a long time and she knows that. She's not happy about it. But, like I told her, I can't ... won't ... stay there.'

They turned onto the road towards Ashford.

'You sure Jackie doesn't mind me staying with them a bit longer?' she said.

'No, I'm sure she's cool with it.' *Could* Jackie help, with her being in the police? Would it be any different from when Mum had tried to get them to believe her about George Shuttleworth? Should he try to persuade Linda not to tell his mum what they'd done? Or should he own up?

What a bloody mess. A week ago Richard had thought his life was perfect. Now who knew what was going to happen?

Chapter 61: Mary Schormann & Ellen Booth

Ashford: Tuesday 14th October

'You could stay here, now our William's gone.' Ellen gave her nose a long blow and shoved her handkerchief in her cardigan pocket. She flopped onto the chair. 'Where's Peter?'

'Out at the car, tidying it up.' Keeping out of the way more like, Mary thought.

Ellen had been pegging Ted's white overalls on to the line when they'd opened the gate of the yard. She'd dropped them into the wash-basket and burst into tears.

Peter had retreated.

Now Ellen adopted a pained expression. 'I've hardly seen our Linda since she came back from your house. Ted works all hours. I get so lonely, Mary. And with all this business about Shuttleworth…'

Mary looked round, worried that Peter might still be within hearing distance and was relieved to see that he'd gone.

Ellen began pleating the hem of her black cardigan, nervously plucking at it. 'You could stay here.'

Mary had known what was coming and had words ready. 'No thanks, love, we're better to actually be in Manchester; gives us more time to get around the places Jackie's listed for us.' She put her hand over Ellen's to stop the frantic movement of her sister's fingers, recognising the old signals that meant she'd been drinking heavily again. 'How is he? William? We couldn't believe what had happened when Ted rang the B&B.'

'He'll be fine. We called round at his girlfriend's house after Ted came back from the shop last night. That's when he phoned you.'

'Right. Well... Good. It could have been nasty. What's she like, his girlfriend? What's she called?'

Ellen pushed her lower lip out. 'Susan. Ordinary. Married. With a kid – a lad.'

'Now, Ellen, you should be the last to judge her on that.'

Ellen lowered her head so Mary couldn't see her eyes. 'I didn't mean it that way. I just don't see why William had to keep it all so secret.'

Mary could: her sister was obsessed with her son, had been since the day he was born. And he knew it. And he knew how she'd react to Susan. Quite clearly, Ellen had had her nose pushed out of joint.

'As long as he's safe, and happy with her, that's all that matters,' Mary said. 'What's going to happen about the husband?'

'He'll get away with it, I suppose.' Ellen hunched her shoulders. 'Ted says they're sure he's off the scene for good. That he'll just be so relieved he got away with it he won't dare come back. Apparently, if he can't have her he's not interested in the boy.'

'Nice, I must say. Still it'll be easier for them.' Mary looked up at Peter, who was hovering at the door. 'Look, we only called in to make sure you're still all right to have Richard stay here. I could ask Jean—'

'Don't you dare. I don't want that woman lording it over me again. Stuck up cow.'

Mary let that one go; Ellen and Jean had never got on and she wasn't going to be drawn into old arguments. 'Okay. Well, thanks for looking after him. Where is he, by the way?'

'Out. He was out all day yesterday as well. With that girl. Sooner or later there'll be trouble about that, Mary—'

'It'll be okay,' Mary interrupted. 'But yes, I know what you mean. He has some studying to do before next week. I'll have a word when I ring him tonight.' Worried that Ellen was going to start talking about George Shuttleworth in front of Peter, Mary stood up. 'We'd better go.'

'Sure you won't stop here?'

Mary saw Peter's look of alarm. 'No, thanks. Like I said, better we're in the city; we have more places to check.'

'No news on Victoria, then?'

'No. Not yet.'

'You could stop for a brew?'

'No.' Mary felt guilty that they were leaving her sister when she was so distressed. No doubt she'd hit the bottle as soon as they left but there was nothing she could do about that; they had to make the most of their time here. She nodded at Peter.

He fetched his wallet from the inside pocket of his tweed jacket and took out two ten-pound notes.

'There's a tenner for Richard and ten pound for you, for his keep this week.'

'You don't need to do that. You've just had Linda staying with you,' Ellen protested.

'Richard eats like a horse,' Mary said. 'And Linda ate like a sparrow. I think this business with Martin's upset her more than she's saying.'

'*She* finished with him, so she says.' Ellen followed them to the door, keeping hold of Mary's sleeve, as though trying to stop their leaving. 'It was her choice.'

Peter was already at the back gate. He was pushed backwards when it was abruptly opened.

'Jean!' Could it get any worse? Mary frowned at her old friend, hoping she wouldn't start on about George Shuttleworth. She needn't have worried.

'Is William going to report Jack?' Jean crossed her arms and glared at Ellen. 'I've worried about it since Jack telephoned from the barracks last night and told us what had happened. It wasn't his fault – you do know that, don't you? It was that lunatic friend of his.' She sniffed, her mouth like a tight red rosebud. 'The husband of that girl your William's got himself involved with—'

'Jean—' Ellen let go of Mary's sleeve.

'Yes or no will do. After all, we've done you enough favours in the past. Just yes or no.'

'How have you done us any favours?' Ellen looked at Jean challengingly. 'When, exactly?'

'Now, you two… Stop it.' Mary said.

Jean played her trump card. 'I'm only thinking of Jacqueline. It could affect her career.'

'The daughter you've stopped speaking to, you mean?' Mary couldn't stop the quick anger.

'Yes well… I'm still concerned—'

'For that bastard that your husband lumbered you with years ago?' Ellen snapped.

'Pot calling kettle!' Jean raised her eyebrows in triumph. 'Pot calling kettle!'

Mary brushed past her. She wasn't stopping to witness yet another vicious row between the two women. 'Come on, Peter, let's get out of here before I lose my temper. I'll leave you two to sort yourselves out. Tell Richard I'll telephone,' she said to Ellen. 'Jean.' Mary nodded towards Jean who didn't meet her gaze.

Chapter 62: Linda Booth & Nelly Shuttleworth

Ashford, evening: Wednesday, October 15th

Linda heard the soft laughter, the quiet chatter coming from the back of the house when she opened the front door of Nelly's house. She stopped, putting the carrier bag of groceries on the floor and listened. The last thing she needed right at this moment was having to make polite conversation. What a mess everything was. Her encounter with Martin earlier had left her with a sense of determination that she would cope with what was happening to her. A feeling that had almost disappeared by the time she was back in Ashford. But now she was here she had to go through with it. The last person to judge her would be Gran.

She dropped Nelly's door keys into her purse, picked up the carrier-bag and straightened her shoulders. Fixing a smile she walked through to the kitchen. Her gran was sitting in her chair with two of her neighbours, each on low stools by her side. They were so engrossed in their conversation they didn't notice her standing in the doorway at first.

When they did, the two Asian women rose with a flurry of their brightly-coloured saris and birdlike greetings as they edged their way towards the back door. Linda returned their bows of the head with one of her own, joining in with her gran's calls of goodbye,

She waited until they'd closed the door before bending down to Nelly and giving her a quick kiss. 'Sorry, Gran, I didn't realise you'd have company.'

'S'okay, pet. Sakhi and Fazeela often call in for a chat an' to see if I need owt from their shop.' She smiled. 'They're good neighbours.' She leaned back in her chair, studying Linda. 'You're a bit pale, lass.'

Linda dumped the bags on the table and took off her coat. 'I've brought sausages for tea. I thought I'd stop for a bit.'

'That's nice, pet.' Nelly leaned forward and, picking up the tongs from the hearth, took a lump of coal from the scuttle and threw it on the fire. She wheezed with the effort and took a second or two to get her breath back before continuing. 'But I know summat's up. So spit it owt.'

Linda stared at the patterns that the new flames made on the tiles of the large hearth. 'Now it comes to it, Gran, I don't quite know where to start.'

'The beginning?' Nelly steepled her fingers over her stomach and settled back in her armchair. 'Allus the best place, an' you know you can tell me anything, pet.'

'I think I'll peel these potatoes and get them going for the mash before I sit down.' Linda picked up the bag and moved towards the sink but Nelly caught hold of her arm.

'Never mind that. Just sit down and tell me what's wrong.'

Linda flopped down on the armchair opposite her gran. The brittle shell she'd kept around her over the last nine weeks to hide the secret from all the family was cracking. 'I'm pregnant,' she said. The liberation of those words made her feel quite giddy. 'And I've just come back from telling Martin. He doesn't want to know.'

It had been a short visit. Once Martin knew, he couldn't wait to get her out of his parent's house.

Although it was only mid-afternoon the daylight was already fading fast; dark shadows filled the spaces between each of the hedged gardens, and the air felt heavy and still along the quiet avenue. The small semi-detached house where Martin lived with his parents was in darkness when she rang the doorbell.

Linda tapped on the glass panel. A faint light lit up the hall and she heard the thump of feet on stairs. When Martin opened the door she thought he wasn't going to let her in but then, without a word, he turned and led the way into the kitchen.

'Your mum and dad not in?' Linda asked. They were a quiet old-fashioned couple who'd taken her into their hearts almost as soon as she'd started going out with Martin, and it upset her to know she'd probably hurt them. She'd been hoping she could explain how she felt, at least to his mother.

'No.' Martin folded his arms and adopted a stiff stance. He clearly wasn't going to make this easy for her. 'Why?'

'No reason.' Linda's legs were beginning to tremble. 'Mind if I sit down?'

'Please yourself.'

She pulled one of the high stools away from the breakfast counter and sat on it. When she couldn't stand the uneasy atmosphere between them any longer she said, 'We need to talk, Martin.'

He cleared his throat. There was almost a smile spreading across his lips. 'Things would have to change,' he said. Linda was taken by surprise. She'd expected that he'd fling angry words at her across the space of the kitchen.

'Sorry?'

'If I was to take you back…' His head bobbed up and down. 'There's a lot that'd have to change.' Before she could answer he carried on. 'All this nonsense about a career … it's a job you've got, not a career. I'm the one who has the career; I'm going places in the insurance world and I'd expect you to support me with that. Of course, at first, until I'm on better money and we can afford a mortgage, we'd live here, but you get on with my parents and—'

'I'm pregnant.' Linda stopped his flow of smug words. 'I don't want us to get back together, Martin, and I certainly don't want to marry you. But you have every right to know I'm going to have your baby.'

His arms dropped by his side and, for a moment, the way his face contorted, she thought he was going to cry. He blinked rapidly, his mouth opening and shutting, a string of spit between his lips. Then his eyes narrowed. 'You're blaming me?' he said. 'You're saying it's my baby?'

That shocked her; it was the last thing she'd expected from him, a denial of his part in the tiny life inside her. She pushed herself from the stool so quickly he stepped back as though afraid she would lunge at him.

'Of course it's yours,' she said.

'Well how do I know?' he blustered. 'How do I know what you were getting up to behind my back? You chucked me in. God knows who else you'd been seeing.' He paced the floor, not looking at her, wringing his hands.

He's scared. He's scared of the responsibility. Perhaps even frightened what his parents would say. 'I'm not trying to trap you, Martin,' she said. 'Like I've said, I've no intention of getting back with you, let alone marrying you.' She might one day regret her next words, but she pushed the thought away and said, 'And I want nothing from you.'

'Really?'

His eagerness was insulting. What the hell had she ever seen in him?

'Really.' She paused, waiting for him to speak but he didn't. 'Not even money. But if you wanted to see the baby, I wouldn't stop you. You should be part of our child's life.' Saying those words made it all at once a definite; she was going to have this child in her life forever.

She watched his hesitation as he continued to pace. When he slid down onto the floor and held his arms over his head she was shocked. The loud gasps and blubs almost frightened her. She stood, waiting for the paroxysm of tears to end. After a while he looked up. His face was covered in tears and snot. He wiped away the wetness with his sleeve and all she could think was that he was like a child himself

'I'll be in touch,' she managed to say.

Watching him crumble was humiliating for both of them; Linda couldn't get out of the house fast enough.

'So that's that, Gran. I don't know what to do. I know what I would like to do…' She stopped.

'What, pet? What would you like to do?'

'I'd like to get right away from here.' Linda clasped her hands tightly. 'As far away from Ashford as I can.' She was sorry as soon as she'd spoken. She hadn't thought what it would mean.

If her gran was upset by it she didn't show it. She seemed to be thinking. Then her face cleared. 'You could go to Mary's. Your aunt would love to have you with her in Wales.'

'It would mean I'd be leaving you, Gran.'

'Away with you. You can't make your plans around me. I'll be fine.'

'I would like to stay with Auntie Mary, at least until the baby's born.'

'So…?' Nelly said.

'With everything they have to deal with at the moment, I couldn't.'

'You could ... you can. If Mary knew how you feel, she wouldn't hesitate. So tell her.' Nelly heaved herself to her feet. 'Now, you start on the potatoes, I'll get the plates out of the kitchenette and set the table.'

Chapter 63: Jacqueline Howarth

Manchester: Thursday, October 16th

The rusted corrugated-iron sheet was dragged back over the doorway of the derelict house with a shriek of metal on stone.

'That's it, then.' Jackie stared for a moment at the large black 'Ban the Bomb' signs daubed over the front of the large Victorian house. She turned on the top step to look at the terrace of three-storey houses on the opposite side of the road. All were in the same state of disrepair, all covered in graffiti and boarded up. 'That's the last place around here.' She crumpled the piece of paper in her hand and stuffed it into her pocket. 'Just that church on Ancoats Road left.'

Hunched into their coats against the chilly wind, her aunt and uncle looked desolate. 'I'm sorry,' Jackie said.

'It is not your fault.' Peter hugged Mary.

'You've done your best, love,' Mary's smile looked forced but still she repeated her husband's words. 'It's not your fault.'

They hadn't been allowed into the last two buildings, both houses on the same street. 'I suppose you can't blame the people in there. They must be scared of being thrown out. They looked in a bad way.'

They looked stoned, Jackie thought. And filthy. 'I can't see Vicky in either place, to be honest, Auntie, can you?' She glanced back at the house. Her cousin wouldn't be seen within a mile of anywhere they'd looked at so far, she thought. Too fond of her home comforts to slum it this much. What was left of the guttering sprouted weeds and grasses, there were missing tiles off the roof and, except for one window on the top level, all the others were boarded up. The man who had pulled the corrugated sheet open a few inches and sworn at her minutes earlier now watched them from that window. Without warning, it was opened and two bottles were thrown out.

'Watch out!' Jackie seized hold of her aunt and uncle and pulled them to the middle of the street just as the glass hit the pavement and splintered in all directions. 'Let's get out of here.'

They didn't stop until they were a few streets away. She could tell they were badly shaken. 'Look,' she said, 'How about waiting until I can come with you to the last place, that church? Have a couple of days off? I really need to get back home now; my shift starts in an hour and I don't want you going anywhere on your own.' Jackie looked at each of them, she was worried. Her uncle looked particularly tired.

'I think Jacqueline is right, Mary?' Peter said.

'Yes, I think so.' Her aunt's smile was sad.

'So that's settled? I'm free on Saturday,' Jackie said. 'I'll come to that old church with you then.'

'And then we stop looking?' Mary sounded firm.

'And then we stop.' Peter agreed.

'Okay.' Jackie was relieved; if she knew anything about her cousin, she'd go running home as soon as wherever she was now didn't suit. And her aunt and Uncle had gone through all this searching for nothing.

Chapter 64: Mary & Peter Schormann

Manchester: Friday, 17th October

'Jacqueline will be cross when she finds out we didn't wait until tomorrow,' Mary said. 'You could have had another day's rest.'

'I am fine.' Peter cautiously pushed opened the heavy door of the old Tabernacle church. Shouts and giggles greeted them. They could see children running around. 'I do not want to wait until tomorrow.'

'Can I help you?' A young man, dressed in flared jeans and a red-beaded loose smock, blocked their way. His face was difficult to read but Mary didn't feel threatened.

Peter held out Victoria's photograph. 'We are looking for our daughter?'

Instantly the man smiled and turned away from them 'Karl? Someone here you might like to talk to.' He opened the door wider. 'Come in. I'm Col.'

Did this mean they knew Victoria? Mary wondered. She felt as though her heart was thumping so loud Peter would hear it as he held her hand and led her inside. 'This Karl,' she whispered, 'do you think he knows where Victoria is?'

'Let us wait to see,' Peter said.

A youth appeared, smiling and tucking his long blond hair behind his ears in a self-conscious gesture.

Col gave him a friendly shove on his shoulder and said, 'One of your lot to chat to, I think. Same accent anyway.'

The youth tilted his head in question. '*Ja?* Yes?'

Mary saw the way Peter's face lit up.

'*Hallo. Ich hoffe daß Sie mir helfen können?*' he said.

Apart from his friend in Ashford, Heinz, a man who used to be a barber, it was a while since Peter had spoken to anyone in his own language and it was strange to hear him now, Mary thought. In a way it separated him from her. Even though she had long ago learned to speak some German with him it wasn't the same as him talking with someone so easily.

'Wie kann ich Ihnen helfen?' Karl grinned, seemingly as delighted as Peter. But he frowned and shook his head as he scanned the photograph. *'Nein.'* There was regret in his voice. He looked up at Peter. *'Wo ist Ihre Heimatstadt in Deutschland?'*

'Sachsen. Saxony,' Peter said, glancing at Mary.

She smiled, concealing her disappointment that the youth hadn't seen Victoria. 'You stay here for a minute. Have a chat,' she said to Peter.

'Danke. Thank you.' He squeezed her hand.

Col grinned at Mary. 'Right, let's ask the others if they've seen your daughter. What's she called?'

'Victoria,' she said, following him.

Inside, the church was beautiful. High arched ceilings were ornate with sculptured cornices. Rugs were scattered over black-tiled floors. Now devoid of pews, the room held an assortment of tables and chairs, covered with knitted blankets. And though some of the small panes of glass were missing in the windows and had been boarded up, those that were left cast multi-coloured light over the walls.

'Okay. If she's been around this way, someone will know. We've come from all parts of the north here.' He swung his arm around to indicate the clusters of people. 'Drink? Sal here…' one of the girls, barefoot, wearing a bright blue kaftan and bouncing a baby on her hip, smiled at Mary. 'Sal makes a brilliant nettle tea.'

Mary looked back at Peter, who was engrossed in conversation with Karl.

'I think we should leave those two to chill out,' Col said. 'Nobody here speaks German so Karl will be in his element, having your husband to himself. Come on, then, let's see what we can find out about Victoria.'

A line of laughing, children, each clutching the one in front, were following a tall red-headed man who sang tunelessly to the conga song: '*Dah dah dah dah dah da da, dah dah dah dah dah da da, la la la lah.*' They waved at Mary as they passed her, kicking out their legs. She felt the ready burn at the back of her eyes; when had she been so easily moved to tears? Even as she thought it, she knew; she felt she was on the edge all the time.

If Col noticed he didn't say anything. As they crossed the large room he introduced her to each person and showed them the photograph of Victoria. There were too many names for Mary to remember but she thanked them all, comforted by their warmth and genuine sympathy.

They stopped at a table where a woman was weaving on a frame loom. She looked up and smiled at them, quickly threading green woollen thread through the warp yarn. A tiny sleeping baby was in a sling on her back. She scrutinised the photograph of Victoria but shook her head, her eyes compassionate as she looked up at Mary. 'Sorry, no.'

'Thanks anyway, Nina,' Col said.

Carrying the nettle tea, which, to her surprise, Mary found delicious, they went from table to table with no success. By the time Peter and Karl joined them she was having a second cup and sitting on a bench alongside Col and Sal.

'No luck,' Col said. 'But we'll keep a look out for her.'

'Excuse me?' It was the woman, Nina, who Mary had watched weaving. 'I wonder if I could have another look at the photograph. I've just remembered something.'

Mary's fingers trembled as she handed it to her. Is this it? She thought. Is this when we find out where our daughter is? She glanced at Peter, but his expression was unfathomable.

'Hmm. I think I have seen her. Perhaps. Once.' She looked puzzled. 'I think it might have been at that festival on the other side of town, in summer; the one we took the kids to because they wanted to see Herman and the Hermits. Remember?'

Col nodded.

'Well, I think she was there.' The baby on Nina's back woke with a squeal. She unhitched the sling and, opening the front of her tie-dye shirt, put the baby to her breast.

'No, she couldn't have been.' Mary smiled as the baby latched on and, snuffling, began to feed. 'We live in Wales and we've only been here once this year.'

'It was in the summer,' Peter reminded her. 'When we came with Richard.'

'But she was with us all the time.'

'Except for the one day,' he said. 'The day we took Richard to see the hospital.'

'The day when she wanted to go to the shops in Manchester.' Mary spoke slowly. 'And we let her. And she was late home. There were grass-stains on her dress and legs. She said she'd fallen in the park in her hurry to get back to the house.' She searched Nina's face. 'Are you sure it was her?'

'Not really. But I noticed her because she looked out of place. She had a red mini-dress on and all the others with her wore jeans, or were in maxis, shawls, gear like that. I don't know. If it was her, though, she was with a guy.' She paused while she changed the baby to the other breast before adding, 'I remember because the guy was sitting near us at first. Then he went away and when he came back with her he sat further away. I think the kids annoyed him. It didn't take them long to get it pretty full on, if you know what I mean.'

Mary heard Peter's sharp intake of breath. 'A man? All the others?' she whispered. 'What others? Peter?' The apprehension curdled inside her. She held her hand out to him. 'Who would they be?'

'She has no friends here,' Peter said, holding Mary's fingers between his. 'You must be mistaken.'

Nina shrugged. 'I'm probably wrong, then.' She pondered for a moment. 'Yes, I'm probably wrong and I'm sorry if I've upset you.' Still holding the baby to her breast, she wandered away.

Mary pulled out the note and showed it to Col. It was creased and grubby from the number of times it had been handled in the squats they'd been in. 'Does this mean anything to you? Do you know anyone called Seth?'

He frowned. 'No, but I could ask around,' he suggested.

'Please.' She watched Col going around the room, seeing the shaking of heads. Disappointment quenched the sudden revival of hope.

'Sorry, nobody here knows anyone of that name,' he said when he came back to them.

'No,' Peter said, 'it is good that you asked. Thank you.'

Mary stood. She had to get out, to leave before she began crying. She shook hands with Col. 'Thanks, anyway. And thank you for the tea, Sal, it was delicious.'

'We will see you again?' Karl asked Peter.

'That is possible,' he agreed. 'But now we must go.' He could see how distressed Mary was. He took her arm and, amid many cries of goodbyes and giggles from the children, they made their way outside.

The door was shut firmly behind them.

'That's it, then,' Mary said. 'That's the last.' She fingered the folded list of addresses Jackie had given them and shoved it into her coat pocket.

'We can do no more, *Liebling*. Now we must wait—'

'And hope nothing has happened to her.'

Peter curled his little finger around hers in the old familiar gesture. 'Nothing bad has happened to our daughter, Mary. She left home because she wanted to explore the world beyond Llamroth. We must now wait for her to return. We must try to understand.'

'I know.' Mary looked back into the depths of the church. 'I can't believe anyone would want to evict those people. Col said this place was empty when they found it and now it's immaculate. Lovely people. They couldn't have been more welcoming.'

'Once they knew who we were and what we wanted,' Peter said. His smile was wry.

'Well, I suppose they've had a lot of opposition to them being in there.' Mary rested against him. 'I couldn't believe how clean and well-organised it all is. They must feel it's their home now, and they want to protect themselves. Especially the children.'

'*Ja.* Yes.'

Mary studied the notices in the porch. There was a rota of chores and child-minding duties pinned to the old board. 'We should have known Victoria wasn't here,' she said. 'She wouldn't have liked all these rules one bit.'

They laughed. It was good to be able to. They linked arms and walked down the stone steps.

Chapter 65: Victoria Schormann

Ashford: Friday, 17th October

It had all gone wrong. Seth had no intention of keeping his promise; he'd become more and more distant each day. In fact, Victoria admitted, she knew he was avoiding her. Except for the other night. She'd hated that. Now she didn't want to be part of the commune; it wasn't anything like she'd thought it would be. But how to get away without all the unpleasantness Melody – Christine, she corrected herself – was going through?

She stood by the window at the side of her bed, twisting a length of her hair around her finger until it was knotted. Untangling it, close to her face, she saw how bitten down her nails were. The skin on the sides of her thumbnails was raw.

It seemed like months since she'd arrived, yet it was only about four weeks.

She peeped through the plain grey curtain at her window. Christine was walking stiffly behind one of the men towards the large gates. She was dressed in flared denim jeans and a white tee-shirt, unlike the long flowing dresses Victoria had seen her in before. She carried nothing: no bags, no clothes.

'They're sending her out with nothing,' Victoria murmured, looking hastily around to see if there was anyone else in the dormitory. But all the other girls were in morning prayers, being talked at by the Master.

It was strange, she thought, how easily she'd slipped into calling Seth that, even in her head: how easily she'd managed to stop herself being so mesmerised by him. Two nights ago, when he'd summoned her to his room she'd gone, not knowing what to expect. She'd thought by explaining to him how she felt, that she didn't fit in and had to leave, he might understand because her time with the commune had been so short. And she'd been determined to tell him that she wasn't going to be treated the same as Christine; she just wanted out.

But she hadn't had the chance; he'd wanted sex and he gave her no chance to refuse. It had been horrible; he had used her as if she was somebody he didn't know, let alone loved. Like a prostitute, she told herself; no kisses, only his thrusts inside her until he'd collapsed, rolled over and gone to sleep. She'd crept away to sit shivering in one of the baths, pouring cold water over her body time and time again.

Now she shuddered, grasping the curtain tighter and trying to get rid of the images.

She saw Christine waiting by the gate, her head held high. Victoria could see that the man was talking, his face contorted with the venom he was spitting out at her. At last he opened the gates just far enough for Christine to squeeze through. Victoria saw him deliberately tread on her heel, taking her shoe off with the toe of his sandal. For a moment the girl faltered. But then she bent down, picked up the shoe and walked away, limping.

Victoria wasn't aware she was weeping until the scalding tears fell onto her hand gripping the curtain.

When the man turned round she froze; it was River, the older Irish man who, over the past week, had shadowed her, touching her whenever he had the chance, whispering foul words. He wanted sex with her, she had no doubt about that, and she was running out of ways to avoid him.

'I need to leave as well,' she muttered. If only she'd had the courage to go with Christine, she thought. Now she'd missed her chance.

'Summer?'

Victoria spun round.

Jasmine stood by the door of the dormitory. 'If you don't hurry you'll miss the meeting with the Elders. The Master sent me to look for you.' She crossed the dorm and stared out of the window. She gave a short laugh. 'Ah, it was River you were so engrossed in.' She raised her hand and waved to him. 'Think he's looking for you, too, Summer,' she murmured. 'You two going to get it together?'

'No.' Victoria caught her breath; she'd spoken too harshly. She gave the girl a smile and shrugged.

Jasmine laughed again. 'Well, you'll have all the time in the world to decide. The Master has given him permission to talk to you.' She sat by Victoria and rested her head on her shoulder. Victoria forced herself not to recoil. She took small shallow breaths to prevent any movement. 'And he's told me to tell you, you can have two days off from your chores.' She whispered in Victoria's ear. 'He's allocated you the purple room for three nights next week.'

The purple room? Victoria's heart thumped. The purple room was only given to those couples who had made a commitment to one another. Sour bile rose in her throat as she pictured the festoons of flowers and ribbons laced over the makeshift four-poster bed, the mirrors on the ceiling. The false artful glances of the other girls.

'No!'

Jasmine moved away. She scowled. 'You should appreciate how privileged you've been. You've been the Master's special one for longer than most of us were…'

Longer than most of us? Victoria thought. Less than a month? What an idiot she'd been.

Jasmine was still speaking. 'It's about time you learned you're no different or better than the rest of us. Don't think we didn't see how you sucked up to Melody.'

Victoria wished she had been brave enough to comfort the girl. What should she do. Say? Play for time, she thought, making herself smile. 'Let me brush my hair and I'll come down in a minute.'

'No time for all that.' Jasmine's grip on Victoria's arm was like a vice. 'We're late already. We'll be lucky if we don't have sanctions placed on us.' She pulled Victoria close, her eyes narrow slits. 'And if we do, I'll make sure *you* do the extra chores they give *me*.'

Chapter 66: Mary & Peter Schormann

Manchester, evening: Friday, October 17th

Peter took off his old trilby, rested his head against the red plastic seat – and stifled a yawn. He looked around the Berni Inn, a place they had got to know quite well; it was the sixth time they'd eaten here in the week they'd been searching Manchester. He was exhausted and over the last day or so he'd had an ache in his shoulders. He rolled his head from side to side. He knew Mary was aware of his every move and was grateful she didn't say anything about him being so tired.

Knowing how Peter disliked fuss, Mary carried on reading down the list Jacqueline had given them. Her lips moved silently as she read the notes she'd put alongside each address. It made depressing reading, she thought. Some places so squalid, with the people living there so aggressive she'd been afraid and they'd left before they'd even managed to find a way into the buildings. Some, mostly young kids, gathered together and made their living conditions in disused stores and churches almost attractive, believing they were making a better society for themselves.

But nowhere did anyone know anything about Victoria. Or so they said.

'You look tired, Mary.' Peter put his trilby on the seat next to him and unfastened the buttons on his black overcoat.

'I am, love. Exhausted, if truth were known.' She made a rueful face that hid the despair she felt. 'Like I said before, that's the lot, there's nowhere else on Jacqueline's list. We've been to them all.'

All around them families were laughing and chatting as they ate. The all-pervading smell of steak and chips mingled with cigarette-smoke and the sweet aroma of sherry.

'And Victoria has not been in one of them,' Peter said.

'No. I think we both knew it was hopeless, really.'

'But what else to do? And we have shown her photograph at all the police stations.'

Mary studied him; he was sallow. 'I think we have to presume she doesn't want to be found.'

A waiter came towards them. 'What can I get you?' He brushed back his pageboy haircut, fingered his drooping moustache. He smelled heavily of Brut aftershave.

All at once Peter felt cold. 'I am not so hungry now, Mary.' His voice was a whisper.

She looked at him again. There was a line of sweat along his hairline.

'No, nor me, love.' She looked apologetically at the young man. 'I'm sorry; we've decided not to eat.'

With a long drawn-out sigh, the waiter closed his order-pad and stomped towards the bar.

Peter settled his trilby on his head and stood up. He felt shaky. Mary tucked her arm through his.

Outside, although the air was filled with the smell of exhaust fumes it was still better than inside the restaurant, where the smell of food and smoke nauseated him. With the evening had come heavy clouds and it was almost dark. Shops threw oblong light across the pavements, neon lights above advertisement-boards flickered. The headlights of cars left short bursts of gloom as they passed.

They stepped away from the doorway into the stream of people, arms still linked. 'Let's go back to the B&B,' Mary said. 'You can have a rest over the weekend and then we'll take Richard to the university and get him settled.'

And then they could go home. All at once Mary felt homesick for Llamroth, for the peace of their home and for the sound of the sea.

She didn't know what else they could do to find Victoria. For the first time she allowed herself to concede that even if they did find her, they wouldn't be able to make her go home with them.

Chapter 67: Linda Booth

Manchester, evening: Friday, October 17th

'Auntie Mary?' Linda had seen them from the other side and, dodging through the traffic, crossed the road. 'Any luck?'

When they turned back to look at her the answer was in their faces. In between shifts, she'd met up with them a few times since they all arrived back in Ashford; they'd looked increasingly worn out. She grimaced. 'I'm sorry.' She linked arms with them, one on either side of her.

'No,' Peter pressed her hand to his side, 'it is fine. We have decided we can do no more. Time to go home.'

His voice was hoarse. Linda frowned, trying to study his face but in the artificial shop lights it was difficult. 'You okay, Uncle Peter?'

He smiled down at her. 'Your aunt and I are both tired, that is all. And—'

'Once we've settled Richard in at the university, we are definitely going home.' Mary finished the sentence for him.

Compared to her uncle, her aunt looked angry, Linda thought. *And I don't blame her; Vicky has led them a merry dance these last few weeks.* 'I'll walk with you. It's not much out of the way and I've got at least another hour before my train home.'

'You sure?' Mary said.

'I'm sure,' Linda said. She'd ask her aunt about moving down to Wales, but now wasn't the right time. She'd leave it for now.

They walked on, still in a line of three, each with their own thoughts, oblivious to the people who moved to let them pass.

When they arrived at the front door of the tall Edwardian house where Mary and Peter were staying, she kissed them both on the cheek. 'You two look done in,' she said. 'Get a good night's sleep. Look after one another. I'll probably see you tomorrow.'

She waited until they'd pushed open the door and gone along the hallway to the stairs before she moved away.

Chapter 68: Richard Schormann

Ashford: Sunday, October 19th

'*Duw, cariad,* it's been a cool week.' Richard folded the last of his clothes into his suitcase and closed the lid.

'Yeah,' Karen smiled. 'And cool meeting more of your family … even William.'

Richard grinned. 'I couldn't believe it when Will said you were the girl who'd run out of petrol.' He did up the top button of his shirt, folded the collar over his and fastened the knot of his new green skinny tie. 'Okay?' he asked.

'Yeah. Looks good against the white of your shirt,' Karen said. 'And I couldn't believe it when he said he was your cousin.' Karen returned the grin. 'Looks like I'm never going to get away from being, er, what was it you called me? A bit *twp*?'

They laughed.

But it wasn't all good. And Richard knew that sooner or later there would be trouble with George Shuttleworth. He pushed his feet into his black Beatle ankle-boots.

'I like the Cuban heels on those,' Karen said.

'Hmm, feel a bit odd, though.' Richard looked down at them. It felt wrong to be fussing about how he looked with all the crap going on with Shuttleworth. 'I still wish you'd been able to see your mum again though,' he said. 'Make sure she's okay.' The ringing in his ears started up again, a sure sign for him that he was getting stressed. He put the flat of his hands against the hearing aids and pressed on them.

Deep down, he knew Karen's stepfather wouldn't let things lie. Not with her leaving home. Not knowing she was seeing him. Something would happen – Shuttleworth would come out of the woodwork some time. Then there'd be trouble.

'Don't you think you should go and see her?' Richard shrugged on his waistcoat and fastened the buttons. He checked the fit of it in the wardrobe mirror before taking the grey suit-jacket off the hanger and turning to look at Karen. He wanted to look right for today, but he was more worried about her.

'And chance seeing *him*?' Her voice was defiant even as he saw his fear reflected in the deep blueness of her eyes. 'No way. But I've spoken to her on the 'phone a couple of times.'

'What has she said? About him?'

'She wouldn't talk about it. She was angry. And then she cried.' Karen faltered. 'I felt rotten.'

Richard threw his jacket on the bed and sat next to Karen. He hugged her and looked into her face. 'Must be awful for her.'

'It is. And there's nothing we can do.'

They'd already done too much, Richard thought.

'Do you think he knows where're you're staying?'

'No. I didn't let her know I was at Jackie's. So hopefully there's no way he'll find out where I am.' She looked at Richard. 'We shouldn't be so frightened of him, Richard, I know that. But I am. Knowing what he's done in the past, I am.'

'Yeah.'

'We should be able to tell the police.'

'And say what? There's no evidence he's done anything wrong. Mum tried hard at the time. It's no use. And we can't say he's threatened us in any way.'

'He did, though – outside the cinema that time.'

'Nothing the police would be interested in,' Richard said. 'Wonder if he knows I'm back.'

'If Mum has talked to him about it, she'll have had to tell him you're in Ashford.'

'Well, we'll just have to hope he leaves us alone.' Starting at the university meant there'd be times when he would be unable to look out for Karen. Richard already had it in mind to ask William to keep an eye out for trouble.

'S'pose. I'm worried he'll come to college. I wouldn't put it past him to try to start a row there. He threatened to do that when I said I wanted to leave home before.'

'Why? What did it matter to him if you left home or not?'

'I don't know. He gives me the creeps. But I'm out of there now and I'm staying out.'

'Can you afford to get your own place?'

'Yeah – Dad left money for me. I have an allowance. And our solicitor would release enough for me to find somewhere, I'm sure.'

Richard leaned towards her. Her mouth was soft, trembling beneath his lips. He put his hand around the curve of her slender neck. Karen stayed still, so still, he didn't know what she was thinking. The kiss was gentle at first but then he felt the urgency stir in him and he moved back. There was plenty of time – all the time in the world to get to really know one another. He wasn't sure if Karen was the one true love of his life but right now, right at this minute, he believed she might be. 'Whatever happens,' he murmured, 'whatever he does, you and me, we'll be okay. You do believe me?'

'Yes,' she said. She was quivering. Richard could tell she'd wanted him to make love to her, that it had been as difficult for her to hold back. 'Yes,' she said again.

She held his head between her hands. The hearing-aids pressed against his ears and, self-consciously, he tried to move away so she wasn't touching them.

'It's all right,' she whispered, raising her face to his. 'They don't matter. Nothing matters, only us.'

It was the first time she'd acknowledged his deafness.

Chapter 69: Linda Booth

Ashford: Sunday, October 19th

Linda pulled the key from the lock and closed the front door. Switching on the hall light, she checked herself in the mirror. Her eyelids were still red and swollen but there was nothing she could do about that. Taking off her coat and scarf she repeated the words her gran had told her to say, the ones she'd practised in her mind all the way home on the bus.

'You can't go on like this, pet.' Nelly hugged Linda goodbye on the front doorstep. 'Come right out with it. Tell your mam and dad you're pregnant, that it's Martin's, but you won't marry 'im. They'll stand by yer ... and so will your Auntie Mary when you need her. Just remember, you're not the first to get into a pickle like this ... and you won't be the last.' She waved to her next-door neighbour, Sakhi, who was standing by her garden gate watching her two boys riding their bicycles. 'But you 'ave some decisions to make for yourself. You know that, and I know you; you'll do the right thing ... for you and the bairn.' Holding on to the door-frame she heaved herself off the doorstep and shuffled after Linda. 'It'll be fine. You'll see. Just remember wot I said.'

Linda kissed Nelly. 'Thanks, Gran.' She let her face rest against the wrinkled skin of the old woman's cheek, breathing in the comforting faint smell of soap and mustiness that had belonged to her gran for as long as Linda could remember. 'I will.'

Keeping a firm smile on her face, she nodded at the small Asian woman as she passed her.

Just before turning onto Manchester Road she turned around and waved. The two women were chatting by her gran's gate. But her gran's eyes were on Linda and she returned the wave.

Waiting at the bus stop, the apprehension returned in waves of cold sickness in the pit of her stomach.

Linda stared into the mirror. 'I'm pregnant. It's Martin's,' she murmured. 'I'm not marrying him. We're finished.' She nodded; it was enough. She'd leave the ranting to her mother.

A ripple of light laughter came from upstairs, followed by another, lower, laugh. Richard and Karen. Linda envied them; whatever troubles faced them they had each other. The sob in her throat was unexpected. 'Pull yourself together,' she muttered to her reflection. It wasn't that she even wanted Martin, the memory of him crouched on the floor disgusted her. But still the fear of what was happening panicked her in the nights. She was going to be an unmarried mother. It was what she was choosing to be. But she'd have no husband, no job, no money. Soon she'd be starting to show; at thirteen weeks her uniform was already straining across her bust and waist and the local gossips would have a field day. Well, not at my expense, she thought. One way or another she'd get away from Ashford. And right now Auntie Mary was her only hope. 'What a mess,' she breathed, dumping her coat on the end of the banister at the bottom of the stairs.

'Linda?' Ted opened the door at the end of the hall. 'I thought it must be you. We heard the front door. You've been ages out here. Are you okay, love?'

'Is it our Linda, Ted?'

Did she sound drunk? 'Course it is, Mum. Who else were you expecting?' Linda followed her father into the front room.

Her mother seemed sober enough. She was flicking through the *Radio Times*. She sighed, flinging the magazine onto the seat next to her. She curled her legs up under her on the settee. 'There's not a thing on the telly tonight,' she complained. A shout and then giggling came from upstairs. 'And I'm not happy with them being up there on their own.'

'Richard's a sensible lad.'

'Our Mary will go mad if he brings trouble to their door on top of everything else he's managed to do.'

'It's not his fault Karen's got George Shuttleworth for a stepfather.' Ted spoke mildly but Linda heard the worry underneath the words.

'Yes, well…' Ellen stood up. 'Either of you two want a drink? A brew,' she said, defensive against her husband's steady stare. 'A brew, that's all.'

Linda waited until her mother closed the door behind her. 'Is there anything in the house, Dad?'

'Sherry. But I've hidden it in the pantry.'

'She'll sniff it out.' Linda's stomach was knotted. Her news was going to tip her mother over the edge again, there was no doubt about that. She felt sorry for her dad. He bore the brunt of all that went wrong in her mother's life.

'Nowt I can do about it if she does, love. You know that.'

'I know.' Perhaps it would be better if she told him now, while they were on their own. Linda cleared her throat. When she looked at Ted, he was waiting for her to speak.

'What is it, love?'

She should have known; he could always read her like a book. She folded her hands over her waist. 'There's something I need to tell you,' she said.

Chapter 70: George Worth/Shuttleworth

Ashford: Sunday, October 19th

'If you think I'll go you're bloody mistaken, woman.' George glared at Harriet; what the hell had got into the stupid bitch now?

'This is my house, George.' Her voice quavered, but she met his eyes.

His tongue moved rapidly against the inside of his cheek. He'd known something was wrong the moment he came home. She'd taken the baby into his room and put him in his cot. Closing the door, she'd said, 'I want you to leave.'

'If you think I'm leaving you to bring up Frank,' he repeated stabbing his finger towards her face, 'you're bloody mistaken, you soddin' idiot. You'd turn him into a right mardarse!' He took off his overcoat and threw it over the back of the chair before sitting down and unfolding the newspaper he'd carried in with him. He turned to the sports pages and feigned reading but was aware she stood in front of him, refusing to budge.

'Karen came home the other day,' Harriet said, twisting the top button of her cardigan. 'She had Richard with her.' She hesitated, then, with a rush, continued. 'They had his sister with them as well. Linda. Linda Booth.'

George didn't move. The headline on the back page wavered: *United: 1—1 against Nottingham Forest. George Best not on top form.*

He snapped the pages together, pretended to turn them, pretended to read.

Harriet didn't move. 'She told me you'd kidnapped her when she was a little girl—'

'Load of crap.' He kept his eyes on the newspaper.

'Is it true?'

'Course it's soddin' not.'

'I don't really know you, do I, George?' He heard her take in a long shaky breath. 'Your name's not even really Worth, is it? It's Shuttleworth. George Shuttleworth.'

'Fuckin' hell. Give me some bleedin' peace, you stupid bitch.' He stood up and, crumpling the paper, threw it at her.

Harriet gasped and fell back against the settee.

Satisfied, he grabbed his coat and strode to the door. He needed to clear his head. One thing was sure; he wasn't going to leave this cushy number. Or Frank. His son was the one good thing to come out of being married to the stupid cow. That and the money, of course. He wasn't going to give it all up just because of those bastard Howarths.

He'd sort it one way or the other; he'd sort them out once and for all.

Chapter 71: Mary Schormann

Manchester, morning: Monday, October 20th

'Well, this is it.' Mary stepped forward to give her son a hug and then stopped, glancing up at the rows of windows along the front of the large building. She gave a short laugh that she hoped hid the sudden pangs of anxiety. 'I won't kiss you, Richard. Who knows who's watching? I wouldn't want to damage your image before you start here.'

'Don't be daft, Mam.' He enfolded her in a bear hug. 'Who cares?'

But when she leaned back to study his face he looked apprehensive.

'Look after yourself, son.' Mary touched his cheek so he was watching her mouth. She spoke softly so Peter wouldn't hear. 'And don't worry about anything. Karen will be all right. George Shuttleworth won't bother you. He'll keep his distance, I'm sure of that.' She raised her voice so Peter would hear. 'Keep in touch. Ring us at the weekend; let us know how you're going on.'

He nodded. 'Will do.'

Peter shook hands with Richard and then gave him a quick hug. 'Work hard, son.'

'Look after yourself, Dad.' His gaze took them both in. 'Look after one another.'

'We will,' they chorused.

Mary gave Richard's arm one last squeeze before getting into the car. 'You look so smart,' she said.

They didn't speak as Peter manoeuvred the car into the traffic. There was a huge lump in Mary's throat and she knew if she started to cry she wouldn't stop for a long time. All she could think of was that both her children were now living lives that she had no place in. Letting herself glance at Peter, she saw his set profile and knew that similar thoughts would be going through his mind.

They slowly followed a double-decker bus towards a set of traffic-lights. Mary gazed unseeingly out of the side window, the image of Richard waving to them before turning away and walking through the double doors of the hospital still in her mind. Peter manoeuvred the car into the next lane, alongside the bus. There was a large banner advertisement for Outspan oranges and grapefruit between the lower and upper deck. Above one of the little stick figures between the fruit a young girl stared down at Mary.

'Victoria.' Mary clutched Peter's leg. 'Look, it's Victoria.'

Peter ducked his head lower to peer through the passenger-side window. 'No, *Liebling*. No, it is not our daughter.'

'I could have sworn... I thought she'd done her hair differently'

'No.'

The cars in front of them moved forward and left the bus at a standstill.

'Sorry, love,' Mary said. She took her handkerchief from her handbag, wiped away the quick tears and blew her nose.

Peter patted her knee.

The lights changed again and Peter eased up on the accelerator and let the Hillman Minx drift forward. The line of traffic filtered to turn left hadn't moved. Peter pulled on the handbrake.

Pushing her handkerchief back into her bag, Mary glanced sideways at the car they'd drawn up alongside. 'That's posh,' she said, still sniffing.

Peter studied the long black bonnet. 'A Jaguar,' he said. 'It is very nice but too expensive to run.'

As both lanes moved forward again Mary peeped at the driver. In a heartbeat she felt cold fear. Even after all these years, even with the heavy jowls, there was no mistaking the profile. She shifted in the seat, turning her back to the window.

'Mary?'

She heard the concern in Peter's voice. 'I'll miss Richard so much.' Her voice was a croak. She cleared her throat. 'I hope he'll be all right.'

'I am sure he will.' Peter smiled and patted her knee again. 'Now,' he said, as the traffic moved again. 'Today? Back to Llamroth?'

As casually as she could, Mary said, 'Can we stay on another couple of days? I know you're as anxious as me to get home but you look tired. And, if you don't mind, I think we'll go to Henshaw Street. Ellen keeps asking if we'd stay with them for a day or two and I really do need to talk to her. Linda says she's right off the rails again with the drinking.' She didn't miss the grimace on his face. 'I know … but it's for Linda.'

Just the mention of Linda made him move his head in agreement. 'Yes.'

'You could spend some time with Ted?' Mary said. 'And

261

perhaps see Heinz? You haven't seen him since he retired. You never know, he might give you a free haircut.' She ran her hand over the back of his neck. 'You'll be looking like a hippie yourself before long.'

He gave a quiet chuckle. 'We will stay, if that is what you want, *Liebling*. But, please, for only two days?'

'Okay. Thanks, love.'

Seeing George Shuttleworth in that Jag, feeling the fear, had decided her. She wasn't going to wait to see what he intended to do. She'd go and face up to him.

Chapter 72: Mary Schormann & Ellen Booth

Ashford: Monday, October 20th

Ellen lay on the settee. She raised one hand languidly towards Mary. 'Sis.' She was pale, dark shadows circled her eyes. She didn't bother to wipe away the easy tears. 'Linda's pregnant. On top of everything else, she's gone and got herself pregnant.'

So that was what was wrong. Mary had known there was something but she'd put it down to the trouble with Ellen's drinking. 'Don't let that be an excuse for you to go off the rails again, Ellen. She'll need your help.'

Ellen lifted her head off the cushion, looking aggrieved. 'Why do you always have to get at me?'

Mary wasn't in the mood to pander to her sister. 'It's not the end of the world. She'll be all right.'

'That's what I said.' Ted looked gratefully at Mary.

'She'll be a single mother. Them two next door will have field day.' Ellen sank back onto the cushions

'Since when did you care what people thought?' Mary said, sharply.

Ellen had the grace to look sheepish.

Mary put the flowers and chocolates on the coffee-table. 'A little thank-you for having Richard stay with you,' she said, determined to change the subject. She wasn't going to discuss Linda without her being there.

'It was no trouble,' Ted said, cottoning on to what she was doing. 'He's a nice lad—'

'Except for the company he keeps.' Ellen set her mouth.

'What does that mean?' Peter spoke for the first time since he and Mary came into the house.

Mary shot a look at Ted. She'd told him on the telephone she didn't want Peter knowing who Karen was. At least for now.

His nod was imperceptible. 'Nothing.' He glared at Ellen who rolled her eyes.

Mary felt the tension inside her lessen. Her brother-in-law would keep her secret. 'What you need, my lady,' she said to Ellen, 'is some fresh air. Come on. Let's go for a walk.' She took hold of her sister's hands. 'Up!' She dragged Ellen into the hall, snatched their coats from the stand and flung open the front door. 'See, it's a lovely afternoon.'

'Bit cold. We could call in at the Crown.' Ellen fastened the buttons of her coat and looped her headscarf around her neck.

'Rubbish. And no.' Mary was adamant she wasn't going to let Ellen get drunk. 'Anyway, they're closed. We'll have a walk in the park.' She banged the door shut and set off at a brisk pace down Henshaw Street with Ellen trailing behind.

'I'm bored with Skirm.' Ellen dug her hands into her pockets.

'Okay, then. Along the canal?' Even as she said it she didn't know why she'd suggested that. She hadn't been on the canal path for years – since that day.

As though she understood, Ellen said, 'We could walk Mossbridge way instead of … the other. It's a nice walk, so Linda tells me. Her and Martin used to walk that way a lot … before.' Her voice wobbled. 'I thought she had more sense, our Mary. Being a nurse and with the pill … you know.'

'These things happen, love. She'll be okay. She's strong.'

'Not like me, eh? I couldn't manage on my own.'

'Things were different, Ellen. She's got you and Ted behind her. He's nothing like our dad was.'

'Thank God...'

They linked arms. 'You wouldn't have married Ted if he was even a bit like Dad.'

'I married him for all the wrong reasons though; you always knew that, didn't you?'

'Mmm. But you're okay now,' Mary said. 'Aren't you?' Was this the right moment to talk to Ellen about her drinking?

Ellen didn't answer.

They reached the steps of the canal without talking. When Mary moved off the last step she winced, refusing to glance towards the bridge nearby. She wouldn't look; didn't want to see where it had happened. Didn't want to think about Frank Shuttleworth – alive or dead.

'This way.' Ellen tugged at her arm. 'I'm worried about Linda. I have no idea why she's finished with Martin. Especially now. A baby needs a dad.'

Apparently the subject of her drinking was off-limits. Later, then, Mary thought, determined not to let Ellen ignore it. 'And he or she will have one in Martin.' Mary kept quiet about his lack of interest but there was no fooling Ellen.

'I'm not sure he'll be bothered. Linda said he was so angry that she finished with him, you know. And what about her job? She's always said she wants to get on in the hospital. Now what?' Ellen demanded. 'What happens to her career now?'

'It's not like when I had the twins,' Mary said. 'They take married women and mothers back now. Things will work out. You'll see.'

They strolled on. The path was rutted; a pattern of holes gouged out by footsteps and filled with shallow rainwater, the reflection in them like scraps of sky where shadows of cloud drifted across the surface.

'I still miss you, you know, our Mary. I do wish you'd come home.'

It was a refrain that had echoed down the years.

Chapter 73: Peter Schormann & Ted Booth

Ashford: Monday, October 20th

'Good evening, I'm Brian Baines and that was the weather for the next twenty-four hours. It's six o'clock. And now, "Look North", giving you the latest news from the Manchester area. Here are the Headlines.'

'Turn it off,' Ellen grumbled. 'I hate this programme – it's boring.'

'Come on, then, let's see if that stew's ready,' Mary said. 'I haven't had tripe and onions since we were last here. I liked that new UCP shop in Bradlow – lovely and clean.' She peered out of the window at the rain before she drew the curtains. 'Looks set in for the night.'

Ellen shivered. 'Turn the fire up, Ted.'

They closed the door behind them, leaving the men in comfortable silence.

Ted settled back on the settee, watching the flames of the gas-fire turn from blue to red and yellow with satisfaction. 'Much easier than a real fire – no messing with coal and what-have-you.'

'Mary, she likes a real fire. But I can see it is good.' Peter stretched his arms over his head and yawned.

'The Museum of Science and Technology at Grosvenor Street was opened to the general public today...'

'Tired?' Ted looked across at him.

'A little.'

'You're still not on top form?'

'I will be fine.' Peter smiled. 'I am well enough to go for a beer tonight...'

'Sounds good.'

'Eric Bainbridge, former Labour M.P. for Littleton, died today aged eighty-nine…'

'How is business?'

'So-so.' Ted joined his fingers behind his neck and stretched his arms back. 'I'm struggling to compete with the big commercial companies.'

'Oh? That is hard.' Peter nodded.

'Yeah. Got harder o'er the years – ever since '61 when they invented the new-fangled method of making bread so it doesn't go stale so quick. You know, the white sliced stuff?'

'Ugh. I know. Tastes as cotton wool.'

'Yeah, and filled with chemicals and bigger amounts of yeast, which I don't like. But it's cheaper and quicker to make, so it's cheaper to buy which seems to be what folk want these days. Can't compete with it, and it's got harder and harder to make any profit. I know of three other bakeries in the area that have gone bust.'

'Will you?'

'Not if I can 'elp it. We're making more cakes these days, which seem to go down well with the customers.'

The silence between them drifted on.

'This news of Linda's has upset Ellen.'

'Yes. But it happens, Ted. Has Linda decided what she will do?'

'She'll keep the baby, of course. She'll manage. We'll make sure of that.'

'Good. It is good when a baby is wanted.'

They shifted their attention back to the television

'The Headlines again.'

Ted sat forward. 'Think we've heard it all.'

The announcer shuffled his papers and looked into the camera. *'In yet another raid, police have raided a disused corn-mill in the Longsight area of Manchester and evicted squatters who have occupied the building for the last six days.'*

Peter held out his arm to prevent Ted from reaching towards

the television set. 'Would you leave it on for another moment?'

'What is it?'

'Listen.' Peter pointed at the screen.

'It took just five minutes for the police to storm the four-storey building. The first cordon of about 50 police officers had to break through a large boarded-up door to get in. As they attempted entry, they were bombarded by water-filled plastic balls, roof-slates and pieces of wood thrown through windows on the upper floors.'

Ted stared at the television. Peter twisted his head around to watch his brother-in-law's response to the announcer's words.

'The operation involved over 100 policemen and there was little resistance once the police were inside.

'A spokesman for the Commune, calling himself "Father Paul", said the squatters were attempting to establish a home for many of Manchester's homeless people. This is the third mill in the Manchester area to be taken over in the last six months.

'Negotiations have been going on to allow the Commune to leave peacefully, but the squatters ignored a High Court Order issued a week ago ordering them to get out, and the police were brought in to evict them by force from the old mill.'

'A mill, Ted.' Peter breathed. 'They say about a mill.'

'What about it?'

'Where do we know where there is a mill?'

They stared at each other.

'You and Mary were so sure that Victoria would be in Manchester…' Ted slowly fingered the faint scar on his cheek. He shook his head. 'No, it's too close to here. She wouldn't…'

'Still, we should look. *Ja?*' Peter's voice shook. 'We must go there.'

Chapter 74: Victoria Schormann

Ashford: Tuesday, October 21st

'What's the big deal?' River leant against the kitchen door-frame. He took a long drag from his spliff, holding it between his thumb and forefinger. 'It's only a shag.' His voice was strained as he held onto the smoke before letting it trickle out of his nostrils. 'Or two.'

He threw the tab-end onto the flags, ground it beneath his sandal and took a couple of steps into the room, pulling the door behind him and wedging a chair under the handle.

Victoria dropped the tie-dyed skirt she'd been washing into the sudsy water in the tin washtub, and whirled around to face him, wiping her hands on her purple chiffon kaftan . 'Take one step towards me and you'll be sorry,' she said. She cursed inwardly in disbelief; she'd spent the last few days making sure she was never alone. Ignoring the snide whispers behind her back that she'd been 'let go' by Seth, she made herself stay with the other girls, whatever they were doing. But this morning she'd made the mistake of assuming River would still be in his bed.

His face was impassive as he watched her glancing around for something she could protect herself with. The only thing that looked any good was the thick rounders bat that someone had once found and brought to the commune to be used to pummel the washing in the large metal tubs.

He moved closer. She could smell his odour; the mix of sweat and bad breath made her want to heave. She inched sideways, feeling with her hand along the draining-board whilst still keeping her eyes on his. The sunlight from the window behind her lit up his greasy hair and the grime in his lined features.

He moved again, this time so close he was almost touching; Victoria turned her head away from him but could still see him from the corner of her eye. He was a tall skinny man but deceptively strong, she guessed; there would be no way she could fight him. She had to get hold of the bat. Her fingers scrabbled for it.

Then his hand came down on hers. 'No you don't, missy.' His voice was gruff, his breath hot on her ear.

Putting both hands on his chest Victoria shoved him, grabbed the bat and, with a shout, brought it down on him. It missed his head and landed on his shoulder. She thought she heard a crack beneath his shout of rage and pain. She lifted her weapon again, enjoying the surge of anger in her.

This time he caught hold of her hair and dragged her head back, wrenching the rounders bat from her and flinging it across the room.

Flailing out at him, Victoria was forced to her knees. 'Let me go!' The anger dissipated just as quickly as it had come. She heard the tremor of fear in her voice. Not this, she thought, not this.

Somewhere there was chattering and laughter, somewhere a guitar played, somewhere outside birds sang.

She should have hit him harder. Even as she thought it, Victoria knew it was hopeless; he was too strong. She tried to stand but he forced her back down, crushing the bones in her wrist with his grip. He tugged at the back of her woollen waistcoat, her kaftan. She wrenched her neck from side to side, held on to the front of her clothes with her free hand, trying to stop him pulling them over her head.

He let go of her wrist and gave a last pull until the sleeves of the waistcoat and kaftan were bunched over her arms pinning them together in front of her. Victoria was naked except for her knickers. Panting, she kicked out at him, twisting and turning, aiming for his crotch but he avoided her feet, dropping to his knees at the side of her and forcing her arms upwards until, wrapping her clothes around the iron legs of the sink, he tied them in tight knots.

Victoria didn't scream; she knew there was no point. It hadn't taken her long to see that the girls were scared of River, that they were glad he wanted her and not them. Nobody would come to help her.

He got hold of her legs and dragged her onto her back. The grit on the stone flags burned her skin. She put her feet flat on the floor and tried to push herself back into a sitting position but he knelt astride her hips, holding her down with his legs and, at the same time, whipping his grubby kaftan over his head. He wore nothing underneath and he was ready for her.

When he forced her legs apart Victoria closed her eyes and let her body go limp. His weight held her down as he pushed himself into her. She tried not to hear the grunts of each thrust, the regular scrape of the toe of his sandals on the floor. The tears slid sideways off her face as she stared at the dirty floor, the mouse-droppings, the pile of clothes and worn blankets waiting to be washed.

After the final groan River was silent except for the quick drawing-in and letting-go of his breath. Victoria felt him loosen the knot that tied her to the sink, heard the rustle of clothes, the scuffle of his feet, the squeak of the chair being pulled from the door, the click of the handle.

When she was sure he'd left, she opened her eyes and scrambled to her feet. Then she stepped into the washtub and squatted down into the cold water.

Chapter 75: Jacqueline Howarth

Bradlow: Tuesday, October 21st

'No, Uncle Peter.' Jackie rested her arms on top of the police station counter, winding a pen around her fingers.

'But why?' Peter held out his hands. 'She could be there! And it was not on the list that you gave us. Why was that?' In his agitation, his accent became more pronounced.

Jackie closed the door to the telephone exchange where the two telephonists were listening in silent curiosity. 'Because I've already checked the Granville out myself.' She watched him carefully. Hesitated. 'I went with two colleagues and my sergeant the week Vicky disappeared,' she said. 'We'd been before, when they first arrived. The sergeant was all for getting an Order to move them on, but they did a deal of some sort with the Council and they're being allowed to stay. For the time being.' She put her hand on his arm, stilled him, hating to see the pain in his eyes. 'The place will eventually be demolished.'

'That is good.' Peter groped in his pocket for his handkerchief and dabbed at the sweat on his brow.

'The Council have been talking about putting houses on the site.' Jackie spoke softly, watching for a reaction, knowing she wouldn't want a house there. Not in a place where there'd been so much misery.

But Peter only nodded to show he'd heard her and stuffed his handkerchief back into his pocket.

'The people there ... it's some sort of commune ... they seem pretty harmless.' Jackie glanced at the closed door. The low murmur of voices and clicks of the metal covers on the switchboard told her the telephonists weren't listening any more. She relaxed. 'Anyway, they let us look all around the buildings; we took ages. Believe me, Victoria's not there.' She went to one of the four-drawer metal cabinets and pulled out a file. 'I'm not supposed to show you this, but the sergeant's giving evidence in court this morning and I'm on my own, so I will.' She ran her finger down the page until she got to the paragraph she wanted. 'See?' She turned the file round so he could read the words with her.

'"Conclusion: A thorough search was carried out. There is no evidence that the missing person, Victoria Schormann, is, or has been, present in the above-named premises," That's the Granville, Uncle Peter. And look at the date ... "Tuesday the 23rd of

September 1969." That's the day after Auntie Mary telephoned me.'

'She didn't tell me that you had searched there.'

'She doesn't know.' Jackie closed the file and put it back in the cabinet. 'It was the day of your heart attack—'

'Small scare, that is all.'

'Yes, well, she had enough to deal with. What was the point of upsetting you both?'

'I think still I should go. Victoria may have gone there afterwards.'

Jackie shook her head in exasperation. 'I doubt it. And it will only distress you; you have bad memories of that place.'

'I already have been to look. There is a lock on the gates. So I want you to come with me,' Peter insisted.

'No. There's no need. You'll only upset yourself.'

'I know how I will feel. It was a bad time in my life. But I need to do this. I insist, Jacqueline.'

She blew out a long breath and leaned against the counter, aware she wasn't going to win the argument. 'Okay. But it will have to be before my shift tomorrow.'

'I want you to go in your uniform – show that you are official?' His voice was strong, determined now that she'd agreed.

Jackie pressed her lips together; she knew she would get into trouble if caught. 'I suppose I could do that, if it was right before my shift. But it wouldn't be official, Uncle Peter. I couldn't tell my sergeant; he'd want to know if there was any new evidence that she's there. And there isn't.' It would be a complete waste of time. Jackie inwardly cursed her cousin. But she'd do this for her uncle. He didn't deserve all the worry his daughter had selfishly put him through.

'And I do not want your aunt to know this,' Peter said. 'She will only worry.'

Chapter 76: Mary Schormann

Ashford, morning: Tuesday, October 21st

Mary rested her hand on the lichen-covered pillar at the end of the drive and stared towards the large grey stone house, a whole range of conflicting emotions rippling through her: fear, anger, apprehension. She took in a long quivering breath. It looked like an old rectory with the large bay windows. Three long steps led up to a porch and double doors. Ironic that such an evil man was now living there.

A car passed behind her on the lane and she jumped, glancing over her shoulder, half-expecting to see the black Jaguar again. Putting her hand to her throat she steadied her breathing, looking down at the ground. There were curved marks in the gravel as though the large gates were often closed, but today they were pushed back against the low walls that separated the lawns from the drive. George Shuttleworth could be out. What if his wife answered the door? Mary hadn't prepared for that. Stupid, she berated herself; what would she say?

She looked back at the house, studying each window. There was no sign that anyone was at home but the thick white net curtains could have hidden anyone behind them.

The gravel crunched under her feet, echoed in her head as she marched to the front door. If he was inside, if he was watching her, if he even recognised her after all this time, she was determined to show no fear.

She needn't have bothered; the slack-jawed shock on his face told her she was the last person he expected to see standing in front of him. His expression tensed, his eyes narrowed.

'What the fuck do you want?'

Mary had practised what she was going to say from the second she knew this moment would come. She'd gone over and over it as she drove from Henshaw Street, parked the Hillman Minx further down the lane and pulled on the handbrake. Each time she stopped to read the names of the large houses she recited her speech.

But now, faced with the man she'd hated for so long she couldn't get the words out.

'Well? What do you want?'

'I've met your step-daughter, Karen,' Mary said, her voice husky.

She saw him half turn to look behind him, 'Where is she?' His voice was abrasive, coarse 'Where's she hiding?'

'She's perfectly safe.' Mary swallowed; that wasn't how she'd intended to start. 'I hoped I'd never see you again,' she continued, 'but it was inevitable you'd crawl out from under your stone sometime.'

The skin of his face blotched; his top lip drew back over an uneven row of teeth.

Mary forced herself to speak again. 'My son and Karen are seeing one another.'

'Over my dead body.' The knuckles on his fisted hands whitened.

Mary raised one shoulder, ignoring the threat. 'It was as much as a shock for me and Peter to find out who she was—'

'Where is the Kraut then?' George Shuttleworth cut in, peering over her head, balancing on his toes and moving from side to side in an exaggerated fashion. 'Oh, I see, nowhere,' he jeered. 'Too much of a coward to come with you?'

'He doesn't know I'm here.' As soon as she spoke Mary realised her mistake. He took a step towards her, locked his bloodshot eyes on hers. She didn't move, even though she could feel the panic tighten her scalp. 'Think yourself lucky he's not with me,' she managed to say.

He smiled, casually leant against the wall of the porch, his thumbs jammed into his trouser-pockets. 'I'm scared!' He pretended to shiver. 'So fuckin' scared.'

'I've come to tell you...' Mary lifted her chin. 'You hurt one hair on Richard's head and I will make sure you go to prison. I will tell the police how you killed Tom. How I saw you run him down in cold blood.'

'And how you were the only witness … hmm? Of this so-called killing?' He looked into the hall of the house behind him and lowered his voice. 'How long ago? Nearly twenty years? And no proof?' he mocked. 'I don't think they'd be interested, somehow.'

He straightened up and, with the flat of his hand, pushed Mary, following her as she stumbled backwards down the steps. The heel of her shoe turned on the gravel, twisting her ankle. Despite the sudden pain she kept her face impassive, instinct telling her he would do no more than this – not in front of his own house.

'Your fuckin' brother died because he murdered Frank.'

'Tom didn't kill Frank.' She'd said it without thinking, a subconscious denial. As soon as she'd spoken his eyes became slits. For a moment everything became still and quiet. 'I mean…'

'Yeah, what do you mean? Huh?'

She couldn't think. Her voice seemed to come from a long way off. 'I didn't…' she couldn't breathe for the fear filling up in her.

'So?' He stroked his forefinger along the side of his nose. 'Tom didn't kill Frank.' It was a statement, an awareness of the truth. 'But, looking at you, you know who did.'

'No, I…' Mary stepped back as he closed in.

With a slight movement of his shoulders, he said, 'Don't matter to me – must have been one of you by my reckoning. Getting rid of one bastard Howarth is one less anyway.'

He caught her arm as she swung her hand towards his face, his grip viciously pinching her skin.

'What is it they say? "An eye for an eye"? Well, maybe killing one of you isn't enough. Maybe I'll want more. Something different, after all your lot did to me.' Still holding her arm, he was so close his face was almost touching hers. 'Your niece has grown up to be a looker. Bit different from that skinny kid I last saw. Looks like she could be some fun now. Hmm?'

Mary tried to steady herself by filling her lungs with air. Jerking her arm away, she forced herself to stay so close to him. She gritted her teeth. 'Don't even think about it.'

It was as though she hadn't spoken. 'And didn't I hear somewhere you had a girl as well? How old will she be? Seventeen? Eighteen? Oh – now, didn't I hear you had twins? So same age as that bastard son of yours. Good age to start learning the facts of life.'

'Leave my family alone.'

'Well, you see, I can't do that. Now your son has taken my stepdaughter off me, it's reminded me of everything else I've lost.'

'Then be prepared to lose more.' Mary's breath came in shallow gasps, her head swam. 'I'm not the only one who knows what you did,' she said. 'Your mother has nothing to lose by telling the truth. She knows you killed Tom. You told her. Remember?'

'The old cow still alive then?' He looked shocked, but gave a low laugh. 'Don't go near that crummy side of town any more so wouldn't know one way or the other.' He pulled his mouth into a sneer. 'Still, I'm bloody amazed.'

'She is, and, believe me, she's not afraid of you.' As soon as she'd said that Mary knew it was a mistake. She listened in dismay to his next words

'Well, she should be. You tell her that.'

Mary straightened up, lifted her chin and met his eyes. 'I promise you this,' she said. 'Touch my son, harm anyone in my family, any of my friends, including your mother … and I will kill you.'

The silence between them was dense with hatred.

Then George Shuttleworth laughed. He patted her cheek. 'You can fuck off now,' he said. 'Go on, on your way. You've had your say.'

Despite the pain in her ankle Mary walked firmly to the end of the drive. She went cold when, as she turned on to the road, he called out, almost casually. 'But watch your back. That goes for the rest of your bloody family, too.'

Chapter 77: Mary & Peter Schormann

Ashford, afternoon: Tuesday, October 21st

'You should not have gone on your own.' Peter was agitated; he sat on the bed, then got up and paced the room. Up and down. Up and down. Rubbing the palms of his hands over his head when standing and over his thighs when he sat.

'Well, I did.' Mary knotted her fingers together. The enormity of what she'd done frightened her, but she was stubborn enough not to admit her fear. Still, the thoughts played over and over in her mind. In her arrogance she'd believed she could put a stop to anything George Shuttleworth planned. Now she'd fired him up until heaven knows what he would do. She'd put her family in more danger, told him Tom hadn't killed Frank, and let him know that Nelly would be prepared to tell the police what she knew about the day her son had murdered Tom.

But worse than anything else, she'd lied to Peter: she hadn't told him about Karen's relationship to the man, that the whole family knew George Shuttleworth was back in their lives. She'd kept it secret that she was going to see him, to tell him to stay away from their son.

And she still hadn't told him that Linda knew the truth about Peter's part in Frank Shuttleworth's death. That Peter was the one who'd killed Frank.

And it was that which would hurt him the most. She pressed her knuckles to her mouth. Peter idolised Linda. From the day he'd rescued her from that dreadful place in the old camp, he'd had a special place in his heart for their eldest niece. For her now to see him as someone who'd killed in anger would hurt him bitterly.

And was it even fair to expect Linda to keep a secret that really only belonged to their generation? What if she couldn't? What would Richard and Victoria think of their father?'

'You should have told me what you were doing.'

Mary hadn't even been aware that he was standing in front of her. 'You would have stopped me.'

'Yes. Or gone alone to talk to him.'

'Fat lot of good that would have done, Peter.' She spoke wearily, the throb of a headache increasing. 'The man's dangerous.'

He gave her an impatient look. 'And you have not made him more so?'

'I'm sorry.' She closed her eyes, waited until she was sure her voice was even. 'There's something else.'

'*Ja*? What is it?'

'I told him Tom didn't kill Frank.'

She watched him from under her lids, unwilling to meet his eyes.

He sighed. 'So…'

That was it. That was all he said.

The minutes passed.

Tentatively Mary moved her hand from her lap, held it out to him. When he took it her relief was intense. 'I'm sorry,' she said again.

'So, tell me again what it was he said.' Peter sat at the side of her. 'So that I know what we must do.'

She leaned against him. 'He said for us to watch our backs.' She whispered. 'In other words, Peter, he was threatening us. All of us.'

Chapter 78: Linda Booth & Jacqueline Howarth

Bradlow, evening: Tuesday, October 21st

From the moment she'd walked into their flat Linda knew her cousin and her partner were, in Gran's words, "tiptoeing around her", exchanging anxious glances. She waited for them to speak while she studied the plaques and cases of medals hung on the wall.

'You managed to find room for them all then?' She smiled at Nicki.

The tall woman rolled her eyes. 'Just about. From the minute she moved in here she mithered me until I nailed the last hook in.' She had her arm slung affectionately over Jackie's shoulder as they sat together on the settee.

They made an odd couple, Linda thought; her cousin, plump with black curly hair, and her girlfriend, almost skeletally thin, with a mass of ginger hair and the most amazing green eyes. Chalk and cheese they might be, she corrected herself, but their love for one another was evident.

She wondered how her uncle and aunt were dealing with the news that these two were a couple. All she'd heard, and that was from her dad, was that there'd been a commotion after Jack had told Patrick in the pub last week. Linda gave an inward smile at the picture her thoughts had conjured up, of Ted scratching his head and saying he was flummoxed that they didn't already know.

There was a clump of footsteps on the stairs outside the flat, the low murmur of voices as people passed.

Nicki lit two cigarettes, passing one over to Jackie. The exchanges of looks, the silent mouthing of words were enough for Linda. She took another sip of the lager they'd poured for her. 'Right,' she said, 'I know there's something going on. There's something you're dying to tell me so spit it out, one of you at least.'

Jackie extricated herself from Nicki's arm and moved to sit on the buffet next to Linda.

'It's about Vicky.'

'Oh?' Well, that was unexpected; Linda felt the tension ease in her jaw. 'Has she been found?' A moment of anxiety. 'Is she okay?'

'No, and yes as far as anyone knows,' Jackie said. 'It's not that.' She picked imaginary bits of fluff off her jeans. 'Uncle Peter's got it into his head that she's here in Ashford.' She cleared her throat. 'In particular, in the old mill. In the Granville. And he wants me to go with him to look for her in the morning.'

The muscles clenched in Linda's throat. She put her drink carefully down on the glass-topped table in front of her. 'Why there?' She cursed the quiver in her voice, hating the evident sign of her fear.

'Some hippie types moved in a few months ago,' Jackie said. 'With all the news being full of the hassle between police forces and squatters, he thinks there's a chance she's there. Although I've told him we've already looked all over the Granville.'

'Does Auntie Mary think the same?'

'She doesn't know about it. She wasn't in when he saw some news programme on it. And then when Uncle Ted told him about the commune at the Granville…'

'Uncle Peter put two and two together?'

'Yep. And made five.' Jackie moved her shoulders again in a dismissive action. 'I think he's clutching at straws.'

Nicki ground her cigarette out in the ashtray on her lap. 'But let's face it, in the last few days they've been all over Manchester looking for her and putting up those notices with no luck. I suppose he thinks it worth a try.'

They both spoke with such nonchalance but Linda wasn't fooled. They were watching for her reaction. She sat as still as she could, even though the pulse in her temple was pounding and her heart was keeping time with the short breaths she took in through her nose. She closed her eyes, opened them instantly as the memory of darkness closed in on her.

'I need some fresh air.' She bolted for the balcony doors and pulled at them. They were locked. She scrabbled at the key.

'Here, let me.' Nicki's calm voice broke through Linda's anxiety.

'Thanks.' Linda let the woman reach past her to turn the Yale. Once outside she grabbed the iron rail surrounding the small balcony, comforted by the sturdiness of the metal beneath her hands and breathing in the coolness of the evening.

'I'm sorry, Lin.' Jackie stood alongside her. 'I thought you should know.' She clasped Linda's hand, nodding towards some fields just visible over the tops of the houses opposite. A bank of thin cloud blurred the misty lines of the pink and lemon sunset. 'Remember the hours we spent up there?'

Linda managed a tremulous smile. 'You mean the hours you spent running round them?' She nudged Jackie. 'And insisting I time you on my watch.'

'Which you never did, because you always had your head in a book.'

Their shared low laughter faded.

'It'll all be all right, you know,' Jackie said.

'Perhaps.' Linda couldn't check the ripple of fear that puckered the skin on her arms again. Neither could she block out the knowledge that there was so much that her cousin didn't know. 'But I'll be coming with you.' She held her hand up as Jackie opened her mouth to protest. 'No argument.'

Chapter 79: Peter Schormann, Jacqueline Howarth & Linda Booth

Ashford, early morning: Wednesday, October 22nd

Peter knew this might be his last day of freedom. And he was content; this way, when the whole truth came out, George

Shuttleworth would have no hold over his family. He would not be able to harm them.

And, perhaps, even after all these years, there would be a chance for Tom's death to be reinvestigated. Shuttleworth might yet be found guilty of his murder.

Except for the soft monotonous call of ring-collar doves there was little sound so early in the morning. Beyond the sycamores the allotments were empty; water dripped silently from the guttering of the greenhouses into barrels. Glass glinted in the glow of the sun, slowly rising over the north country moors in the distance. Inside the nearest greenhouse Peter saw pots of orange and gold chrysanthemums, Mary's favourite flower.

His heart thudded. In the long sleepless night he'd prepared himself for this moment. There would be no such reasoned planning for his wife. She'd wake up to find him gone. Gone for good from the life they'd shared for almost twenty years. Would she hate him for that? Or would she understand it had to be the one last secret he'd kept from her?

Because he needed the truth to be told about Frank Shuttleworth's death. It would be a release; he'd lived with the guilt for many years. He'd tried so hard to be accepted by the people of Llamroth, relying on his reputation as a good GP, but underneath, always, he felt a fraud. However many lives he'd saved with his knowledge as a doctor, he had still taken a life in anger.

And soon his son would know his secret. Whatever Richard said, he would not feel the same about his father, would not respect him for not speaking out before now – for not living within the moral code he'd taught his children. Peter hated the thought that Richard might think him also a coward. But that was how he thought of himself.

Standing outside the padlocked gates he dragged his gaze towards what was standing of the ruined mill, his old prison. In the steely light the broken windows that were left were jagged flashes of reflection. His eyes were drawn to the second level, remembering his old friend Pensch who'd slept in the top of the shared bunk. Wolfgang Pensch! Peter hadn't thought of him for years. He'd heard that the man had died of stomach cancer – the reason for his early release from the Granville.

Nausea rose up in his throat and he suppressed it. There had been many times when he'd thought *he* would never leave the place alive.

So far the two young women at his side had been silent, their closeness comforting him as he hunched under his coat, but now Jackie spoke. 'Are you all right? You can change your mind, you know, Uncle Peter. I can go in on my own.'

'No.' For a moment he thought he was going to pass out. He steadied himself. 'No, it is not that. It is—'

'Don't worry, Uncle Petey,' Linda interrupted, squeezing his arm, her voice unsteady.

Peter's face softened into a semblance of a smile at the childish nickname.

'You okay as well, Linda?' Jackie was smiling but only with her mouth; her eyes were sharp with worry. 'I don't know why you want to put yourself through this, either. This place holds bad memories for you too.'

'You don't need to tell me that.'

Peter heard the fear under Linda's words. 'She is right, *Liebling*. Neither of us should have to go in there. But especially you—'

'But I ... we will.' Linda linked him, staring towards the old hospital. 'Lay old ghosts and all that,' she said, borrowing one of her gran's expressions.

No one knew better than Peter what she meant. He switched his gaze. The compound was crammed with shadowy grey figures moving restlessly in aimless circles.

He ran his tongue over his lips and swallowed. 'There is something I have to tell you, Jacqueline. I asked for us to come here … not only because there is a chance that Victoria is amongst these people … but because it is the right place for me to tell you something. Tell you, because you are a policewoman.'

'No.' Linda shook his arm. It was as though she knew what he was going to say. 'No, Uncle Peter.' No childish nickname now. His niece was pleading with him. 'There is no need—'

It suddenly struck him. 'You know don't you?'

'Yes.' The understanding passed between them.

Peter was grateful in a way. Whenever she had learned the truth about what he had done, it hadn't altered her fondness for him. 'Then you know there is every need, *Liebling*. Every need.'

'Know what?' Jackie demanded.

Peter smiled at her as she looked from one to the other. He was right; it felt correct for him to tell the truth here, at this godforsaken place. Even though it meant waiting to find out if his daughter was in there. If she was, he would be able to reunite her with her mother before he was taken from her. Again. As he had been taken from her so many years ago back to Germany. If not – well, if not, he would trust Mary's family to help her to carry on looking for Victoria.

'What do you mean, Uncle?' Jackie moved to stand in front of him, arms folded.

Peter forced out the words that had been hidden for so many years. 'Once I killed a man.'

'No!' Jackie's voice betrayed her disbelief and then her tone changed. 'You mean in the war?' Her arms dropped to her sides. 'No one blames you for that, Uncle Peter. It's all in the past. Men – and women – did things they wished they hadn't had to do. People were killed. It was horrible, but please don't get het up about it now. Not here. You've not been well.'

'No, you don't understand. I don't mean in the war. The man I killed was not the enemy. Not of this country I mean. He was my enemy. The enemy of myself and Mary.'

The sudden tears were hot on his face. He fished into his coat pocket for his handkerchief. 'It is necessary that I hand myself in to the police ... to you. It is time.'

Jackie studied him for a moment, her forehead crinkled. 'Whatever it is you think you've done, Uncle Peter, please don't get upset. Let's just find Vicky – if she's in there. We can talk about this after.'

He lowered his head. Nodded. Satisfied. Whatever was going to happen would now happen. He took his eyes off Jackie and looked up. Ten feet above him in the sentry-box his old enemy leaned over the parapet, slowly waving the Bren gun from side to side. Grinning.

'Shuttleworth,' he murmured.

'Uncle?'

'It is nothing, Linda. I am fine.'

She drew in an uneven breath.

If Jackie noticed she didn't show it. She spoke briskly as though already she had dismissed his confession. 'I should have thought someone would have seen us by now.' She studied the rows of windows on the building opposite the old mill. 'But, like I said, I've been here before when this lot first squatted here. They took ages to come out then. I think they hope we'll go away. They're in there,' she nodded towards the building. 'Unbelievable how quickly they took it over, got it all set up. Wasn't it the camp hospital?'

'*Ja.*' Slipping back in time, the language easiest for him... 'Yes,' he corrected himself. The image of him and Mary standing outside the main doors, a careful few feet away from each other even while speaking words of love, was strong.

Linda was leaning against him. He could feel her shaking. 'Courage, *Liebling.*'

'I wish I'd got the keys.' Jackie rattled the bars of the gates. 'But my sergeant would have found out if I'd gone to the Council for them.' She rattled the gate again. 'Hey. Anybody about?' After she shouted a second time, a man, dressed in jeans and a paisley shirt, appeared. 'What's the problem?'

'Open the gates.' She kept a steady gaze on him.

'I'll have to go for the keys,' he drawled.

'Then get them. And be quick about it.' She showed her identity card.

The man looked over her shoulder at Peter and Linda. 'They're not police.'

'No. But I am.'

He scowled. 'Like I said, I'll have to get the keys.'

'Like *I* said, get them and be quick about it.' Jackie gave him a calm smile.

Peter watched the man saunter away, his hands in his pockets like one of the guards slouched against the sentry-box. His eyes flooded suddenly, remembering the note he'd given to another prisoner, Kurt Trept, to smuggle to Mary. He'd passed it to the man, right under the stare of a British soldier, before being taken back to Germany. He'd believed he and Mary would never be together again. In his mind he was sitting inside the back of the lorry, as they left the camp. Through the flaps of the canvas he saw the gates close as he held the cold dry fingers of his friend, Pensch, already skeletal.

He took short breaths, struggling against the memories crowding in.

Jackie noticed. Misunderstanding, she said, 'It's only an off-chance Vicky will be there, you do understand, Uncle Peter? She wasn't here last time.'

'I know.' Peter fought against an overwhelming sense of unease.

Mary was crossing the yard towards the compound. Looking apprehensively over her shoulder towards the hospital, she stopped at the fence behind the sentry-box. Someone was there, a shadow. She reached out towards them. Peter saw the two hands clasp, felt the warmth of her skin.

He blinked. The man in the paisley shirt strolled towards them. There were faces at some of the windows of the hospital. Mary was at one of them. She was holding her arms out to him.

The pain started first in his chest and then his neck, his breath hurting in his throat.

He saw a door open, felt a cold blast of air coming into the cottage. Mary was clinging to the door-frame. Tom was smiling. She was in his arms. Finally. After five long years.

He became aware of a sensation of tightness travelling from his chest to his arms, of feeling sick, of a loud pulsation in his head.

He dropped to his knees; the rusty wire of the gates ripped into his cheek as he slid down it but he felt nothing, only heard the gurgling breaths from someone nearby.

He didn't hear the rattle of the key in the lock of the gate. Nor the screams of the girls. He didn't see his daughter running towards him.

Then he was sitting on the small wall that separated the road from the beach in Llamroth. The tide was in; the waves swirled closer, dragged at the pebbles as they fell back, bubbling and foaming. He turned to peer back towards the cottage. And then along towards the village. There was no one in sight. He was alone. It was dark.

Chapter 80: Linda Booth, Jacqueline Howarth, Victoria Schormann

Bradlow, late afternoon: Wednesday, October 22nd

It felt wrong to be leaving him. Without speaking, they got into the car. At first Jackie couldn't find the headlight button and they sat in silence while she tried. Eventually she put the car into first gear and they drove slowly away from the bright entrance of Bradlow Hospital.

Word had quickly spread to Linda's ward and Sister Lawson had appeared at the door to the side ward in the Accident and

Emergency department just after the doctors declared Peter dead on arrival.

'You've had a shock, my dear,' she'd said to Linda. 'Just let me know when you're ready to return to work. You need to be with your family for now.' She'd even given Linda a quick pat on the arm, which made her cry even more.

Jackie blinked through each pool of light from the street lamps. Concentrating on driving the Hillman Minx kept her calm, but she could feel the iciness of the grief in her stomach. Driving along Huddersfield Road she tried to double-de-clutch into third gear but failed, so they chugged slowly along in second. Most of the houses had the curtains drawn, but every now and then the brightness of downstairs rooms was revealed and drew her eyes. It seemed impossible that people should be doing ordinary things – laughing, chatting, sitting, eating around tables, listening to the radio – when such a devastating thing had happened to her family.

Finally drawing the car carefully alongside the kerb outside number twenty-seven, she pulled on the handbrake. 'You ready?' It was the first thing spoken in the last half hour.

Linda turned a blotched and tearful face towards her. 'No.' She screwed the wet handkerchief tighter in her fist. 'What do we say?'

'What can we say?' Jackie bit her lip. 'That the hospital said he died instantly – that he felt no pain.'

'How do they know that?' Linda sobbed. 'You saw him. You heard the horrible noises he made.' It wasn't the first death she'd witnessed, but it was the first time she'd lost someone she'd loved so much.

There was a loud wail from the back seat. Both girls twisted around to stare at the figure slumped in the back. Victoria had her face in her hands.

Linda and Jackie watched her in silence and then looked at one another. Jackie's face was grim. Tears flooded again down Linda's face.

After a couple of minutes Victoria looked up at them. 'What?' she said. 'What?'

The slow, hidden rage that had been forced down inside Jackie for the last few hours burst out in a flood of recrimination. 'We're not going to tell your mother anything, Victoria. You are.' She jabbed her finger at the girl. 'You were there. We were there because of you—'

'That's not fair—'

'It's not fair that Uncle Peter has gone. It's not fair for Auntie Mary. What you did – what you've done to them, these past few weeks – hasn't been fair. You're bloody selfish … always have been. Nobody's ever mattered – only you.' Jackie was weeping as she shouted. 'You … you…' she took in great gulps of air, struggling to get more words out.

'Jackie. Hush.' Linda rested her head against Jackie's arm. Reached out to hold her. 'Hush, love.'

Victoria sat up. 'It's been hard for me too—'

'Shut up.' Linda lifted her head and glared at her. 'Bloody shut up.' She felt in her jeans pocket for another handkerchief but didn't have one. Instead she picked up the cloth from the dashboard that Peter used to use to wipe the windows and gently dabbed at Jackie's face. 'Come on, love,' she murmured, 'be brave?' She felt Jackie nod against her.

'Now,' Linda turned the driver's mirror so she could see Victoria again. 'I'll tell you what's going to happen. We're going into the house and you're going to do as Jackie said.' She widened her eyes in warning as Victoria started to protest. 'You'll do as Jackie says, because you owe it to your mother. And because it's the right thing to do. Your father went to the one place he feared, the place he hated most in his life, just to look for you. Because he'd convinced himself that was where you were. He was a good man, a brave man. You were lucky to have him as a father. He loved you and he took care of you all your life. Now it's your turn to repay that. You can't do anything for *him* now, but you can do something for your mother.'

She gave Jackie a small shake. 'You okay, love? You ready?'

'Yes.' Jackie took a juddering breath. Without looking at Victoria she opened the car door, hesitated and then stood.

'Right?' Linda looked at Victoria. The girl didn't move. 'Right?'

With a tiny move of her head Victoria pulled on the handle of the car door. 'I'll do it,' she said. Her grief was mixed with the fear of facing her mother, of telling her what Victoria knew was the worst thing she would ever have to hear.

'Too right you will,' Linda said, in a determined voice.

The door to the house next door was flung open. The two Crowley sisters stepped out onto the pavement.

'Linda, what on earth is going on in your house?' Ethel shook her head. The dewdrop on the end of her nose threatened to fall but stayed put. 'Such a commotion, such comings and goings! We haven't had a minute's peace, have we, Agnes?' Without waiting for confirmation she hurried on. 'Your mother and father are here.' She pointed at Jackie who stood staring at her.

'Not now, Miss Crowley.' Holding on to Victoria's elbow, Linda tried to side step the two old women.

Ethel blocked her. 'They tried to park in front of our window but I told them I'd call the police.' She sniffed, looking Jackie up and down, taking in her uniform. 'Your father is a very rude man.' She wagged her finger at Jackie. 'Luckily for him your mother persuaded him to park further down the road.' She flapped her hand in the direction of Shaw Street. 'And—'

'Piss off.' Jackie pushed past her. Linda ushered Victoria in front of her.

'Well!' the woman's voice was piercing. 'I'll report you. You're a disgrace to your—'

Linda slammed the door.

Chapter 81: Mary Schormann

Mary heard the front door bang. She flung the kitchen door open. 'Where have you been?' she cried. 'We've all been worried about you.' She felt for the light-switch but something stopped her, her hand over it. 'Peter?' When there was no answer she clicked it on.

For a moment it was too bright and she shielded her eyes with the flat of her hands. When she saw Victoria she thought her heart had stopped. Then, with a sudden leap, it was thundering in her chest.

'Victoria! Where have you been?' The relief tumbled quickly over into anger. 'Where have you been? We've all been worried out of our minds. Your father and I have been looking all over Manchester. We searched for you everywhere.' She flung her arm out. 'At home, around here. Your father—' She looked over the girls' shoulders at the closed door. 'Is he outside? Is he with you? Have you seen him? He's been gone all day.' She stopped, all at once really seeing them for the first time, seeing their faces, their swollen eyes. 'What is it? What's wrong? Where's Peter?'

She saw Linda nudge Victoria. Push her forward.

'Mum.' Her daughter faltered. She walked towards Mary, leaving the other two girls watching, apprehension on their faces.

'Linda?'

'Let Vicky tell you, Auntie Mary.' Linda spoke softly.

'Tell me?' Mary was bewildered. 'Tell me what?' She grabbed Victoria's shoulders. Shook her. 'Your father? Where is he?'

'I'm sorry, Mum.' Victoria had her fists clenched to her chest.

Dreadful understanding flooded through Mary. 'He's had another heart attack, hasn't he? Which hospital? I'll get my coat.' She turned towards the kitchen. The door was crowded with figures: Ted had his hand on Ellen's shoulder, Patrick stared at Mary over Jean's head. 'My coat!'

She spun back towards the girls, noticing for the first time the dishevelled state her daughter was in: her blouse torn at the shoulder, the long rip in her skirt. No shoes.

Mary looked from Victoria's bare feet to her face. Saw the anguish.

Terror blinded her. She began to shake. 'No!' Her legs gave way, folded at the knees. 'No!'

Chapter 82: Mary Schormann

Ashford: Thursday, October 23rd

The room was light. Too light. But it didn't seem to matter.

Mary lay on her back, savouring the moment between sleep and waking, her forearm draped across her forehead. She let her hand drop back onto the pillow next to her, waiting for Peter to take hold of her fingers, his thumb caressing the palm of her hand, in the way he always did. He always woke before her. She couldn't remember a time when he'd slept longer than her.

'Peter,' she murmured. Her hand moved over the pillow. It was cold, flat.

Her eyes snapped open and she sat bolt upright. The realisation of everything that had happened swept away any remnants of sleep.

A movement in the corner of the room made her fling the covers back. She knelt up, pushing her hair from her face

'Auntie? It's me. Linda.' She was standing there, a look of concern on her face. 'How are you feeling?'

'I don't know. What time is it? I've slept. I shouldn't have slept.'

'The doctor gave you something.'

'Why?' Mary stared down at the unrumpled side of the bed. 'Peter. I should go to him.'

There was a choked sob. Linda came to kneel by the bedside. 'Later, Auntie Mary, there's no rush.'

The words thrust Mary into a reluctant acknowledgement. Her husband was dead. 'No!' She flung herself backward on the bed.

Linda crawled alongside her, held her tightly, crooning, as the grief racked Mary's body. Eventually she quietened, but still the tears slid from under her lids and her body shook so hard her teeth chattered. It was as though, in some primitive way, she knew she needed to get the crying over and done with. Otherwise she wouldn't be able to confront what needed to be faced in the coming days.

'You're cold,' Linda whispered, trying to move to bring the covers further up the bed, over Mary.

'No. Don't let go.' Mary felt hollowed out, empty. She thought she would float away if Linda didn't hold her down, keep her safe. She wrapped her arms around Linda's neck.

'It's all right. It'll be all right.'

It wouldn't. Mary didn't like to contradict her niece, but it would never be all right again. 'I must get up.' But she didn't move. She was too frightened to move. Still she clung to Linda.

'Let me go and get you a cup of tea.' Mary felt Linda unwinding her arms from around her neck.

'No.'

The door opened. For a moment Mary didn't recognise the wan face. Then: 'Victoria?' And the memory of the past few weeks rushed back into her consciousness. 'Get out.' She said it calmly. Then she was screaming. 'Get out! Get out! Get out!'

Somewhere at the back of her mind she registered the fear on her daughter's face before the door was quickly closed. But she didn't care.

When it opened again she was ready to yell. But it was Ellen. There was something different about her: a quiet assurance.

'I'll take over now,' Ellen said to Linda. 'You've been up all night.' She lay on the other side of Mary and pulled her to her. 'Go and get some sleep. She'll be fine with me. Tell your dad to make a brew. Plenty of sugar.'

They were talking as though she wasn't there. The independence in Mary flared for a moment, then faded. It was too much effort, she felt too sluggish. Let them do what they wanted, it didn't matter to her. Nothing mattered.

The two sisters lay in silence. After a while Ted came into the bedroom, carrying a tray of mugs. He placed the tray on top of the chest of drawers and picking up the chair from beneath the window put it next to the bed. 'There's tea there, for when you want it,' he said, before sitting down and resting his hand on Ellen's thigh as though he needed to connect in some way with what was happening in the room.

'Thanks, love.' Ellen rhythmically stroked Mary's hair.

Ted cleared his throat. 'I have to tell you something, Mary. It won't make any difference to what's happened, but I couldn't live with myself if I didn't tell you.'

Mary stared unseeing at the bedroom wall. The pattern blurred. What now? What could be worse than what had happened?

It was almost a relief when Ted said, 'Peter got it into his head on Monday that Victoria could be at the Granville.'

Because she already knew that. Now. But as she repeated her brother-in-law's words in her head, her breath caught in her throat. 'On Monday?' She sat up, throwing Ellen off her. 'On Monday? You knew then?'

'Yes. But not when he was going.'

Mary saw Ellen's mouth drop open. So her sister didn't know either. 'We were worried about him all day yesterday,' she said.

'But I was in the shop. Nobody told me.' Ted scratched his thumb against the scar on his cheek. 'He said he wanted to go and look for 'imself, even though Jackie had looked there just after Victoria left home. Honestly, I didn't know 'e was going. I'd made him promise he'd tell me when he wanted to go, and I'd go with him.' Ted stood.

'It wouldn't have made any difference, Mary. And Linda and Jacqueline were with him when … when it happened.' Ellen touched Mary's back.

She was right, of course. The long intake of breath was held in Mary's chest before she let it go. 'You're right.' Without looking, she reached out to Ted. 'You weren't to know,' she said.

He squeezed her fingers. 'Thanks.'

There was a sound of a car braking, followed by two bangs of doors. 'That'll be Patrick and Jean,' Ted said. 'I asked them to bring William when they came back this morning.'

'Jacqueline?' She must thank her for being with Peter when … she cut short the thought.

'She stayed all night,' Ellen said.

'Richard?'

'You didn't want us to get him last night, Mary. You said to leave him until today.'

'I want him here.'

'I'll ask Patrick.' Ted stopped, his fingers on the door-handle. 'I'm sorry, Mary. Peter was a good man and a good friend. I…' She saw his throat working to keep the tears from spilling over. 'I loved him like a brother.' He swung the door open and ran down the stairs.

'He means it, love.' Ellen stroked Mary's back again.

'I know.' It didn't help the emptiness inside but she said again, 'I know.' Mary swung her legs over the side of the bed. 'I'd better get dressed.'

'Mum?' Victoria was dressed in a pair of Linda's jeans and a polo-necked jumper. She sat very still at the kitchen table, her hands holding the edge. Her eyes were still puffy and reddened but Mary hardened herself.

'I don't want to see you, Victoria. Go back to where you came from yesterday.' She couldn't bring herself to name the place.

'She can't.' It was Linda. 'She ran out. They tried to stop her.'

'I've wanted to leave for days,' Victoria whispered. 'I didn't know it was going to be like it was. I knew it was a mistake almost from the start.'

'But still you didn't come home.'

'When I saw Dad I was so glad.' Victoria pleaded. 'I knew he'd rescue me—'

'Rescue you?' Mary shouted. 'Rescue you? You went there by choice, you stupid thoughtless girl.' Right at this moment she hated her daughter.

There was a collective sudden hush in the room. The family waited, moved closer to one another. Except for Patrick; he was on the back step, staring out at the yard. Keeping out of it as usual. The thought was automatic. Mary's eyes wandered over the group. Jacqueline stood next to Nicki, hand in hand. Had she been here all night as well? William was between Ted and Ellen, his arms on their shoulders. Linda was next to them.

'Mum?' Victoria pushed herself away from the table, knocked the chair over, reached out towards Mary.

Mary knocked her hand away. 'Get off! Don't you dare touch me!'

Victoria cried out. It was the cry of a young child.

Mary told herself she felt nothing. 'We all have choices. You made yours. Now live with the consequences.'

'You don't mean that, Mary.' Jean spoke for the first time. She pushed her glasses further onto her nose. 'Remember what you told me? You said not to shut Jacqueline out of my life. And you were right.' She moved to put her arm around Jackie's waist. '*Whatever* anybody else says.'

Patrick looked slowly over his shoulder at her, working his cigarette in the corner of his mouth. He took a final drag on it and then flicked it into the back yard. Closing the door he pushed the tip of his tongue out, picking at a flake of tobacco with his finger and thumb. 'Whatever anyone says?'

Jean nodded.

He walked to the hall door. Passing Jackie, he touched her arm. She looked up at him and smiled. He glanced at Mary. 'I'll go and get Richard.'

'No. I've changed my mind. I want you to drive me to pick up Richard. And then we're going to see Peter.'

296

'Mum?'

Mary turned back to her daughter. 'No. Not you.' She heard the sharp sigh from Jean. She looked at her. There hadn't been many times in Mary's life when she'd taken Jean's advice. She wavered. Perhaps this time was one of the few occasions she should. Maybe she and her children needed to face this together. 'Come on, then,' she said.

Chapter 83: Richard Schormann

Ashford: Saturday, October 25th

Richard didn't want Karen to touch him. If she did he'd begin crying again.

So she'd wrapped her arms around her knees, her feet up on the seat of the bench, waiting for the harsh, painful gulps to end. And he was grateful for that.

The park was empty. The canoes, their paint faded and flaking, lay sideways on the grass. Under the surface of the grey water of the lake he could see a random pattern of trailing weeds.

He blew his nose, embarrassed that she'd been a witness to his breakdown. 'I'm sorry.' He dropped his head, looked sideways at her.

'Don't be daft.'

'I've tried so hard not to cry in front of Mum. After that first time, you know? She's being so strong.'

Karen nodded, her chin on her knees.

Her silent understanding was comforting.

'I watched her face when we went to see Dad. It was like…' He stopped, thinking about the moment when they'd stood next to the trolley his father lay on. 'It was like something in her had died as well. There was no movement in her face, in her eyes. She was so still.' The tears came again. He drew in air. 'And then she just went down – she collapsed. So quickly we couldn't catch her.'

He held his palms over his face. 'She wasn't hurt, but it was ages before she came round properly. I think she just didn't want to. I heard her tell Auntie Ellen last night that it was like if she didn't open her eyes it would all go away.'

Karen shuffled across the bench to him and rested her hand on his leg.

'It's the thought of them having to do a post-mortem that's getting to me.'

She winced.

'Sorry,' he said again.

He was so glad she was with him. He hadn't told her about the guilt he'd carried around. Settling down at the university, finding his way around the myriad of seminar and classrooms and sorting out his lectures, timetable, room had taken up so much of his time over the last week. And when he did stop his mind had been so full of worry about George Shuttleworth that not once had he wondered how his parents were. As always he'd taken them for granted, even knowing about his father's ill-health.

He put his arm around her. 'We're going back to Wales as soon as it's done and we can take him home. I've been given a fortnight's compassionate leave from the university. I want you to come with me...' He felt her nod. 'I don't want you here, on your own,' he said. 'I don't want you here with Shuttleworth around.'

'I don't think he'll come near.'

'I'd rather not take the chance.'

A black-and-white terrier ran past them. They watched it disappear into some bushes, yelping loudly, and then back out, crouched down on its front legs. Seconds later, a cat shot out and ran straight up a nearby tree. The dog danced around at the base of the tree, barking.

A large man ran towards them, red-faced and panting. 'Bloody stupid mutt,' he gasped, fastening its lead and dragging it to the bench so he could sit down. Richard saw his face change when he looked at him. 'Sorry, mate,' the man said, 'am I in the way?'

298

Richard managed a smile, 'It's okay. We have to be going anyway.'

'Let me guess,' The man grinned, 'Welsh? And summat else?' He stopped, as though noticing for the first time the hearing aids and looked uncomfortable. 'Sorry,' he said again.

It was a reaction Richard was used to and, right now, didn't need. It was a reminder of the hurdle he would need to get over each time he met someone new – that he'd always be seen as someone to be pitied. He clenched his jaw; he would never quite fill his father's shoes. Stupid, he knew, but he'd lived with the thought for so long it was automatic. And now his dad wasn't here anymore to reassure him, to brush his worries away. To say, 'We stand in our own shoes, son. Life, it is what we make of it.' As he had said so many times in the past.

Richard fought down a sob. 'Have to go,' he said.

Walking back to Henshaw Street, he linked fingers with Karen.

She swung around, walking backwards in front of him. 'I'll go in and ask at college tomorrow, *cariad,*' she said.

The Welsh endearment brought a small smile to his lips. He pulled her to him. Ignoring the people who passed by, they kissed.

'Mmm,' Richards gave her a hug and a quick last kiss on the nose and leaned back, gazing into her eyes. She smiled but he saw the apprehension in her eyes. 'What is it?' he said quietly.

'What will you do?'

'What about?'

'University?'

'I don't know. Perhaps I should apply to one of the Welsh universities and an affiliation to Pont-y-Haven hospital. It's what Dad wanted.'

'Your dad accepted you going to Manchester.'

'I know. But now…' He lifted his shoulders. 'With Mum. She's only got me.'

'And your sister,' Karen reminded him.

'Yeah, well. Who knows what Vicky's going to do, isn't it?'

'I think, when it's all over,' she smoothed his hair back from his face and gave him another kiss, 'you need to talk to your mum. From the few times I've seen her, I think she'll want you to do what you want.'

Chapter 84: Nelly Shuttleworth

Ashford: Monday, November 3rd

'I wondered when you'd finally show your face again.' Nelly wrapped her fingers over her ample stomach and tried to quell the panic that lurked inside her. 'Walking in without a by-your-leave.'

George's squat frame blocked out the light from the back yard. She couldn't see his face, and the stillness of him unnerved her. Yet still she waited for him to speak, determined not to show her fear. Deliberately she steadied her breathing, taking in long slow breaths that crackled in her chest.

The fire that Linda had lit earlier had subsided into glowing coals that warmed the left side of Nelly's body but did nothing to light up the room. The back of the kitchen was in shadow. And now, with the back door open and letting in the coolness of the evening air, she was rapidly becoming chilled.

'In or out,' she said, 'but either way put the wood in th'ole.'

He didn't close the door but pushed at it with his foot and moved further into the kitchen.

A click of his lighter as he put the flame to the cigarette in his mouth revealed the face of the son she hadn't seen for the last twenty-odd years. A face she'd hoped never to see again. Even in those few seconds, she was able to study him. Underneath the fleshy jowls, the heady-lidded eyes, the purple criss-cross of veins on his cheeks and across his nose she still recognised the son she'd pushed out of the house that day long ago, and then she saw the half-moon scar, white now, almost faded, the slightly crooked top lip.

The cigarette-end flared as he took a long drag on it. When he spoke it was through a trail of smoke.

'So, Mother, even after all these years you still haven't had the decency to croak.'

His words chilled Nelly. She realised how vulnerable she was. And she had no illusions about him; he'd as likely kill her as look at her, of that she was sure. 'What do you want?' She held tightly to the arms of the chair, moved her feet so that they were flat on the floor. If necessary she would launch herself at him. The thought vanished as quickly as it came. There was no way she could move that quickly.

'Thought you might have cocked your toes up by now, like that bastard Kraut.'

Nelly waited.

'Thought I'd call in the Crown on my way 'ere; heard the good news there. Must say the place's gone downhill since I were in there last. Stan Green must be turning in his grave. Heard the soddin' Jerry just keeled over ... heart attack was it?' He clutched his chest, staggered on the spot, grinning. 'Good fuckin' riddance. I thought *you* would've had the decency to drop off your perch. I thought you wouldn't be able to stick your neb into my business anymore.'

He dropped the cigarette onto the kitchen carpet and ground it out with the heel of his boot. If he expected a response from her she wasn't about to give him the satisfaction. 'Looks like I was wrong.' He moved his forefinger along the side of his nose.

She didn't flinch when he came nearer, stood over her. But her heart was jumping in her chest.

'I think you know why I'm here, Mother.' He circled her chair until he was behind her. 'You know too much, and a little bird tells me you're about to spill the beans.' He leaned on the back of her chair until his mouth was close to her ear. When he turned his head and took another drag on his cigarette and blew smoke out, it enveloped her.

She choked and coughed, her chest tightening. The panic made her shake. She grabbed the arms of the chair and tried to stand.

He pressed his hands on her shoulders, held her down.

'Get off, you bugger.'

But he didn't let go. 'After all this time, I didn't think you'd be a problem,' he whispered. 'I was wrong. So I realised I'd 'ave to do summat about you after all.'

The cushion was over her face before she realised what was happening. She tried to free herself but he'd folded his arms across it and was forcing her against the back of the chair. His head, bone to bone on hers, hard, hurting.

Her breath was hot on her cheeks and mouth as she strained through the crackle and wheeze of her chest to get air in and out of her lungs, past her top set of teeth which had fallen from her gums. The blood coursed, throbbing, through the innermost parts of her ears: a rhythmic whooshing, like waves breaking on a shore. It was almost comforting. And then there was silence, and the black pressure on her eyelids became a blinding lightness that hurt.

Until it was easier to give up.

Chapter 85: Linda Booth

Ashford: Monday, November 3rd

'It's only me, Gran.' Linda burst through the back door. 'We're going in an hour. Just wanted to make sure you were okay… '

There was a second, Linda told Ted afterwards, when she could have acted differently. A brief moment when she could have run back out into the yard and yelled for one of the neighbours. Over the years more and more Asians had moved into the houses around Nelly, until she was the only white woman on Barnes Street and she'd happily welcomed them. In turn they had adopted her as a grandmother figure to be cherished and admired for her colloquial wisdom. Linda knew that at least half a dozen of them would have come running to help.

Instead, she launched herself at George Shuttleworth and clung onto his back as he twisted one way and another trying to dislodge her, ramming her into the wall, the sideboard, the table. And, all the time, through her gasps and the stabbing hot pains in her back and legs she was aware of the awful sounds of Nelly heaving for breath.

It happened too fast for Linda to question her actions. Her instinct kept her clinging in tandem with him as he lunged around the kitchen. Until he kicked open the cellar door and, with one violent thrust, hurled her into the darkness.

There were six stone steps. Linda knew that, because it was where Nelly kept her tins of food, on a stone slab attached to the wall. She knew that because she'd never been as far as the flags at the bottom. She knew that because, by keeping the door open with her foot, while putting Nelly's shopping on that shelf, she'd placed it in the safe light of day.

But now the cellar door had been slammed shut and she was on the flagged floor. In the darkness. And she hated the dark. And everything seemed to hurt. She felt the ground around her and touched some material, harsh and prickly. A vague fear, an unwanted recollection of something from the past, made her rapidly pull her hand back.

She listened, struggling to control the scream that wanted to burst out of her. She was so frightened her body wouldn't respond, even though she pushed with the flat of her hands against the ground in an effort to stand. Unable to move she tilted her head to one side, holding her breath until it burned in her chest, and listened.

At first there was nothing. And then a gritty scraping of footsteps. She counted. Six heavy slow deliberate footsteps. Her stomach jerked. And the scream burst out, ricocheting around her head.

Then there was no more breath left and the scream died away. She licked her lips, the tears salty on her tongue.

'Well, well.' Suddenly George Shuttleworth was kneeling down next to her. 'Here's a bonus I didn't expect.'

Linda hit out at him, felt the crunch as her hand connected with his nose.

She didn't see his fist coming out of the darkness. The first blow knocked her head sideways. The second back the other way. Her teeth jarred in her mouth. She tasted the blood as she floated into oblivion.

At that moment she remembered the baby. The beginnings of life she had to protect.

With a great heave she pushed at him, rolled away from the stink of him and scuttled backwards. All at once she had a memory of a frightened little girl doing exactly the same thing. The rage in her was welcome and when her shoulder-blades touched the wall she used the momentum to stand. Her outstretched arms knocked something cold and it rocked, making a hollow echo. Fumbling around, her fingers touched what seemed to be a handle, then another.

Straining her eyes into the darkness she thought he was standing now, moving towards her. His breathing was low. He gave a stifled cough.

Linda felt around with both hands. In between the two handles there was a cold ribbed surface. It was Nelly's old rubbing-board in her washtub, the one she'd used years ago when she'd started taking in people's washing.

Now he was so close she could smell the beer and cigarettes on him.

She gripped each handle, swiftly lifted the board from the tub and held it above her head as his hand touched her neck, slid lower to cup her breast.

'So,' he muttered, 'here we are.'

She brought the board down as hard as she could.

He gave a loud grunt and slumped, holding on to her blouse in his effort to stay upright. It ripped, the buttons flying off in all directions, and she fell forwards with his weight until she was kneeling on him. Sobbing, she threw the board to one side and scrambled away into the darkness, crouching down and swinging her arms in front of her, feeling for a wall, anything that was solid. She stumbled over the tub and it rolled away, metal echoing in the emptiness, gasping as her legs touched the coarse bristly material she'd felt before, registering vaguely that, of course, it was the pile of old army blankets that Nelly had squirrelled away years ago.

George Shuttleworth groaned. Linda screamed, dropped to her hands and knees, feverishly feeling for the steps. She heard the rustle of his clothes as he moved, felt his touch on her foot and she screamed again.

Light poured down from the cellar door as it opened.

Afterwards, Nelly couldn't remember what she'd done. She knew she'd seen Linda, battered and bloodied. She knew there was someone holding her granddaughter on the ground. She didn't have any memory of going down the cellar steps; she hadn't been able to go down there for years. Neither did she realise she had the bread-knife in her hand.

For one fleeting moment, she recognised her son.

Chapter 86: Mary Schormann

Ashford: Monday, November 3rd

'Nelly? It's Mary.'

There was no answering shout. Mary peered through the pitted brass letterbox one last time, then straightened up, letting go of the flap. She tried one more time, banging on the knocker before going to the old bay window and cupping her hands around her face to look in.

A group of Asian children had gathered in curiosity around the Hillman Minx. One, an older boy of about thirteen, bounced a ball on the ground, skilfully balancing it on his foot every now and then.

'You okay, missus?' he called. 'Missus Nelly okay?'

Mary barely glanced at him. She didn't answer. 'I'm going round the back,' she said to Ted, who stood by the driver's door. 'Linda's probably just lost track of the time.'

'Want me to come with you?'

'No.' Mary looked at the children, who were surrounding the car, touching the mirrors, rubbing their sleeves along the bonnet. She didn't want one of them damaging Peter's car. 'You stay here, I won't be a minute.' She hid her uneasiness about the silence from inside the house. 'They're probably chatting in the back.'

She needn't have worried about the car, because the children followed her along the back lane at the back of the houses. At the gate of number four she felt over the top for the bolt. It was already slid back.

She crossed the yard. 'Nelly? Linda? It's me, Mary. Linda, we'll have to get a move on if we want to get to Llamroth before dark.' Oh, how she needed to be home. How she equally dreaded being there without Peter.

For a moment the vision of Peter's body being loaded onto a hearse to be driven to Llamroth flashed through her mind. She blocked it out. Don't think. Don't think.

At the back door, Mary hesitated, her skin prickled; there was something wrong, it was too quiet. 'Nelly? Are you there?' She glanced back at the open gate. The children were crowded around, the tallest lad was peering over their heads. For a moment Mary and he had eye-contact and then he looked back along the lane.

'I'll get someone,' he said.

Mary gave a brief nod then stepped inside the kitchen.

'Nelly?'

She listened. Nothing. She crossed to go to the stairs but

something was wrong in the room. She looked around. That was it: the cellar door was open. The prickle on her skin increased. She walked slowly towards it.

It was too dark. At first she couldn't see anything beyond the first three steps. Then her vision cleared and she saw them. The scream stuck in her throat. She grabbed the door-frame. 'Linda? Nelly?' Her voice came out as a croak. There was someone else there, lying half under Nelly, but couldn't make the figure out.

'What's happened?'

The voice behind her made Mary jump. She fell against the wall, turning away from the cellar. Two Asian men stood in the middle of the kitchen. By the back door were three women in saris. One of them was holding back the crowd of children.

'I'm Arun.' The man nearest to Mary spoke. 'I'm a neighbour. Is it Nelly?'

'Yes.' This couldn't be happening. Not now. Not after … Peter's still form imprinted itself on her mind. Mary squeezed her eyes tight, forcing it away.

'She's hurt?' Arun's face was anxious.

'I think she's dead.' Mary heard her voice from far away, her mouth dry, sour.

One of the women screamed, held her hands over her face. Some of the smaller children began to cry.

'My niece … Linda … is there as well. And someone else. They're all so still. I don't know what's happened.'

'I'll call an ambulance,' the other man said. 'But we need to go down there. See if we can help.'

'No, I can't.' Mary stumbled backwards but she couldn't let go of the door-frame.

Gentle hands prised her fingers from the wood. 'Not you,' Arun said. 'We'll go. You need to sit down.'

She was led to Nelly's armchair in front of the old range, a woman at each elbow.

A glass was pushed into her hands. The water spilled over, cold in her lap. She stared blindly at the spreading stain. On her red coat it looked like blood.

Sounds hurt her ears: the grit under the feet of the men going down the cellar steps, the sobs of the woman, the muttering of the children, the soft shifting of coal and ashes in the fireplace.

'Mary?' Ted pushed his way through the increasing crowd in the back yard, followed by the boy with the football. He wasn't carrying the ball any-more. Mary vaguely wondered where he'd dropped it.

'Ted.' She half stood. But he gently pushed her back and knelt at the side of her.

'What's happened?' He looked bewildered, stared around at all the neighbours. 'The boy says Nelly's hurt? In the cellar?'

Linda. She had to tell him about Linda. But even as the thought came to her, Arun and the other man were struggling up the steps supporting Linda between them. They shouldn't have moved her, Mary thought, even as she gasped at the sight of her niece. The vomit rose up in her throat and she clamped her fingers over her mouth. Ted launched himself from the floor to catch hold of his daughter.

Linda's face was so battered it was almost impossible to recognise her. One eye was closed. A long cut on her forehead sliced across her eyebrow. Blood congealed around her nose and cheeks. Blood and saliva bubbled from her swollen lips. She groaned as Ted laid her carefully on the carpet, grabbing the cushion Mary handed to him and putting it under Linda's head.

'Who did this?' He didn't attempt to brush away the tears as he looked around.

'There is a man down there as well. I think he's dead.' Arun had taken off his coat and was carrying it towards the cellar. 'Nelly's still alive though. But she's in a bad way. I'll cover her with this.'

'A man?' Mary stared at Ted. As soon as the confusion cleared on his face she knew he was thinking the same as her.

'George Shuttleworth.'

308

Chapter 87: Nelly Shuttleworth

Bradlow: Thursday, November 6th

Nelly heard the hushed sounds of movement in the room but was too tired to open her eyes.

'Hello, Gran.' A touch of soft lips on her cheek, the light familiar floral scent.

Ah, the beloved sound of Linda's voice. Nelly smiled to herself.

'What did the doctor say?' Another voice, another kiss, a brush of sweet-smelling hair across her face.

Mary. Best friend a body could have. Like a daughter. The woman both her rotten sons had hurt so badly. Nelly felt the habitual anger rumble around inside her.

They were whispering now.

'She'll not last the night.' A stifled sob.

Linda again. *Don't cry, pet.* Nelly fought to speak but it was too much of an effort. She strained to listen.

'Do you think she can hear us?'

Nelly felt one of them put their cool hand on her forehead. Mary, she guessed.

'No, the doctor said it was a massive stroke.'

A warm tear fell on Nelly's arm. She tried to lift her hand but it wouldn't move.

'I hope she's at peace.'

Oh, I am, my pets, I am.

'She will be. And at least where's she's going she won't meet those two blasted sons of hers.'

Not if I've got owt to bleedin' do about it, I won't, Nelly thought, smiling inside.

Chapter 88: Richard Schormann & Linda Booth

Llamroth: Monday, November 10th

'Do you remember him?' Richard faced Linda and pointed to the grave where Mary had placed a spray of bronze chrysanthemums. The small stitches across the cut on Linda's forehead hadn't yet been taken out; one eye was still swollen and the bruises on her face were now a blend of purple, yellow and green.

'Uncle Tom?' She sighed. 'Not really. I remember kind eyes, a gentle smile, gentle hands. I think I remember him picking me up and swinging me around once. Vague memories.'

'Mum idolised him, I know that,' Richard said. 'There's the family story about him getting Mum and Dad together after the war.'

'Yes, I heard that from my mum too. She helped as well, she says.' Linda traced the words on the headstone. 'What's that mean?'

'Hedd perffaith hedd?' Richard read it out. 'Peace perfect peace.' He pointed to the next grave which had single white chrysanthemums threaded into a metal vase. 'Same as there. *"Hedd perffaith hedd".* That's Iori's grave, Tom's friend. Nain Gwyneth's son. Actually they were more than friends, Mum says. They loved one another. He was killed in prison. Both he and Tom were conscientious objectors.'

It was as though all the sad memories had been resurrected over the last few weeks, Linda thought. 'They must have been really brave,' she said. 'It would have been so hard to stand up for what they believed, when the whole country was at war.'

'Yeah. Nain Gwyneth was proud of both of them. She used to say she wouldn't have had the courage. She'd tell us that Dad was brave too: that coming here so soon after the war to find Mum was one of the most courageous things she'd ever known.' He looked around. 'That's Gwyneth's grave,' he pointed to a headstone just behind them. 'And over there, that stone covered in the green lichen, is Grandma Howarth's.' He smiled. 'Mum would never let us clean it off; she said Grandma would like it because she really liked gardening.'

A scuffle of noise made Linda look up. 'Your mum's leaving,' she said.

They watched Mary being led out through the lych-gate by Jean and Ellen. Ted was talking to a large group of villagers just outside the church wall.

'A good turnout,' Richard said. 'I wish Dad had known how popular he was.'

'How could it not be? He was a lovely man.' Linda looked up at the scudding grey clouds that covered the pale yellow smear of winter sun. She blinked back the tears. After a moment she said, 'Should we go too?'

'In a bit.' Richard looked around. Over by the yew-trees Karen was talking to two men. One of them was constantly blowing his nose, the other talking and waving his arms around in an enthusiastic way. 'Karen's talking to Alun and Alwyn. We should go and say hi.'

'Okay.'

'The landlord at the pub's putting food on. Mum won't go, but she says she's grateful to him.'

'Do you want to go?'

'No.'

'Nor me. William and Jack have gone. William said they have some stuff to sort out without Patrick being there. I think he's always been the one to stop them being friends.'

'Hasn't Uncle Patrick gone to the pub, then?'

Linda allowed herself a small chuckle. 'No. Auntie Jean wouldn't let him. She told him to walk Jackie and Nicki back to the cottage while she stayed with your mum.'

Richard grinned. 'Perhaps she'll make him into a nice chap yet.'

'Don't hold your breath.' Linda glanced towards the church. Victoria was sitting alone on the seat by the porch. 'She's quiet.'

311

'Yeah.' There was an edge to his voice.

'She's learned her lesson, Richard.'

'Has she? I wonder.'

'She talked to me last night…' Linda remembered the increasing horror and sympathy she'd felt as she listened. 'The lad who got her involved with that group … she called him Seth, but she said they were supposed to call him Master, he— '

'Call him what?' Richard caught hold of her arm, turned her towards him so he could see what she'd said.

'Master. They had to call him Master.'

'Huh.'

'When he got fed up with her he gave her to an older Irish bloke. The bloke forced himself on her. Like I said, she's learned her lesson.'

'Bastards.' Richard closed his eyes but not before Linda saw the rage in them. 'I've a good mind to—'

'To what? You've never believed in violence, so don't start now. Anyway, they won't be there; Jackie says the Council and the police are moving them this week.'

'Is Vicky going to report them?'

'She says not. She says she just wants to forget it all. But I persuaded her to tell Jackie. She's had a hard time forgiving your sister. She blames Vicky for what happened.' She looked back at Peter's grave beyond which three Council workers waited trying to look inconspicuous.

Richard followed her gaze. 'I know. I do a bit, too,' he said.

'I thought if Jackie knew what Victoria's been through she might not be so hard on her.' Linda sighed. 'Perhaps you should talk to your sister as well, Richard. Time to forgive and forget? If your mum can do it…'

'I suppose you're right, Lin.'

'Good.'

A sharp breeze scuttled leaves around their feet and over the graves. A few caught in the flowers on Tom's grave.

Linda bent down to clear them away. She shook them from her fingers and looked up at him.

'What will you do now, by the way?'

'How?'

'Your place at university?'

He thought for a moment. 'Mum says I should carry on in Manchester.'

'Will you?'

'If she's okay. I don't like the thought of her being down here on her own. We'll see.'

'What about Karen?'

'She wants to be near her mum now Shuttleworth's gone.' Richard looked directly at Linda. 'But she won't go back to that house; she's got a flat in Manchester. We'd be okay if I stay here. I could go to see her sometimes.'

Linda straightened up. The road outside the church was empty now. 'We should go and rescue Karen, she's looking a bit overwhelmed.'

'Alun and Alwyn are smashing chaps, but they can go on,' Richard said. 'Well, Alun anyway.'

'And we should ask Vicky if she's going to come back to the house with us.'

'Yeah.'

They wandered down the path towards Karen and the men.

'Alun, Alwyn.' Richard shook hands with each of them.

The brothers pulled at the cuffs of their black jackets, shiny with age, and straightened matching black ties.

'We've been telling your, er, friend what a fine man your da was, haven't we, Alwyn?' Alwyn nodded, rubbing at his eyes with his knuckles. 'And what a good friend he's been to us. Anything we can do for your mam, we will. We mean that, don't we Alwyn?'

'Aye.'

'Anything at all.' Alun looked earnestly at Richard. 'You'll never have to worry about her when you're not here, *dyn ni'n addo hyn i chi.*'

'Promise,' Alwyn repeated.

'We'd better be going now.' Alun shook hands with the three of them and nodded towards Victoria

'Are you going to the pub?' Richard asked.

'No. We nearly always met with your da for a pint on Fridays. Somehow it don't feel right to be there without him today. We'll miss him.'

'Aye, we'll miss him.'

They watched the two men amble away.

'They've been friends with Dad since he came to Llamroth,' Richard said. 'They will miss him.'

We all will, Linda thought, he's left a big hole in all our lives. 'Come on,' she said, holding out her hand to Victoria, 'Let's go.'

Chapter 89: Linda Booth & Mary Schormann

Llamroth: Monday, November 10th

'It was a lovely service.' Linda took hold of Mary's hand. 'So many people.'

They sat on the low wall overlooking the sea, watching the creamy foam at the edge of the waves, smaller now at low tide.

Gelert ran along the beach, barking and chasing seagulls, which flew effortlessly into the air before he got within yards of him.

'Yes.' The tears dripped off Mary's chin. 'Mr Willingham retired years ago. It was kind of him to agree to take the service. He married Peter and me, you know.' Mary was trying hard to keep control. 'Even though Peter was divorced.'

'Was he? Divorced, I mean,' Linda said. 'I didn't know that.' So much she hadn't known about her family.

'Oh, yes. Before the war he married in Germany.' Mary glanced at Linda with watery eyes. 'It was over almost before it began. She left him for another man while he was a POW. I never questioned him about it. He said he never knew what love was until he met me.'

Linda didn't know what to say.

There was a small ladder in her tights just above her knee. She covered it with her other hand. She would have liked to have taken off the black suit she'd bought for today, but didn't want to upset her aunt. She didn't like black. She would have to wear it again next week, for Gran's funeral. Then she would throw it away. She'd had enough of black to last a lifetime.

'Are you okay with Richard going back to Manchester?'

'Yes it's what he wants … probably what he needs. And, who knows, he might come back to work at Pont-y-Haven one day.'

A gust of wind lifted a line of sand off the beach, swept it across in light, grainy threads.

Mary shivered.

'We should go back to the cottage.' Linda made to stand, calling to the dog.

'No, I can't. I can't face everybody there.' Mary pulled her back to sit on to the wall.

'You're cold.'

'I don't think I'll ever be warm again.'

Linda let go of Mary's hand and wrapped her arm around her, pulling her closer. 'It will be all right.'

'When?' There was almost anger in the older woman's voice. 'When, Linda?'

'I don't know…'

A group of shearwater strutted around the rocks, pecking. Linda watched their busyness.

'Will you—?' Linda stopped.

'What?'

'Are you thinking of going back to Ashford, Auntie Mary?'

'Going back?' Mary looked astonished. 'Why on earth would

I want to go back? Peter's here ... and Tom, my mother, Gwyneth. Iori.' She repeated the question as though she was asking herself. 'Why would I want to go back? *There.*'

'So what will you do?'

'I don't know what you mean.'

Then they both spoke at the same time.

'I don't suppose—'

'I was wondering if—'

'You first,' Linda said.

'No, I interrupted you.'

'I was wondering if...' Linda didn't look at Mary; she kept her eyes on the horizon where the clear divide on sea and sky was a bright silvery light. 'I have to think of my ... our future.' She touched her stomach; the small life inside her was already moulding her own life. 'It's early days, I know, but I need to look forward. I've spent so much time lately looking back into the past. I wondered what you might think about me moving down here, Auntie Mary?'

'I was going to ask if that's what you'd consider doing. Just until the baby ... you know?' Mary scrubbed at her cheeks, wiping away the last of the tears with her handkerchief.

'I was thinking on a more permanent basis... if you didn't mind?'

Linda saw a glimmer of hope in Mary's eyes and closed her own in relief; it was going to be all right.

'With us?' Mary tilted her head towards Victoria, who was walking along the shoreline kicking at the sand.

'Yes.' Linda knew, even if her aunt didn't realise it yet, that Vicky wouldn't stay long in the village. She'd confided in Linda that Llamroth stifled her, and in the post yesterday Linda had seen an envelope with the logo of an art college in London stamped on it.

'I'd love it, Linda.' Mary hugged her. 'And, if we're going to be living in the same house, I think you should start calling me

316

Mary.' She looked along the beach for Gelert. He was racing towards a man walking the shoreline. For one heart-stopping moment she thought it was Peter.

Mary looked beyond him. The weak low sun cast a pale light across the sea, emphasising the swirls and shadows of the underwater currents.

Epilogue: Linda Booth

Linda can hear Gelert softly whining.

'You want to go out, boy?' she whispers, opening the back door. Stepping outside, she closes it behind her to keep the night air from rushing into the house.

She tries to wrap her dressing-gown around her. Nowadays it won't fasten. She places her palms over the mound of her stomach. The baby has been a little quiet for the last few days: not long now. And spring is on the way. She feels a thrill of excitement.

Sometimes she worries what he or she will face without a father on the scene. A wave of protectiveness washes over her. It will be all right. She supposes the apprehension must be similar to what Mary and Peter went through with the twins, so soon after the war. And, just like Richard and Victoria, her baby would be okay. She'd make sure of that.

Looking back, the cottage is in darkness.

Mary is asleep; lately she's been sleeping a little better, crying less in her sleep. But there's no doubt in Linda's mind that Mary will always miss Peter.

She walks along the garden path, looking towards the village; the whole of Llamroth is a muted pattern of shadows in the low light of the crescent moon.

The dog is snuffling and whining around the hedge at the top of the garden. Linda hopes he hasn't found the hedgehog she saw venturing out from the field last evening. She tiptoes towards him, but before she's even passed the greenhouse Gelert trots toward her and sits by her side.

Resting her hand on his head she gazes upwards, trying to identify the constellation of flickering stars against the blackness.

Clouds move across the sky, first leaving only a thin white streak of light around the edges and then covering the moon completely.

The dog pads away to the house.

Linda is alone in the darkness of the night. But she isn't afraid.

More from Honno

Short stories; Classics; Autobiography; Fiction

Founded in 1986 to publish the best of women's writing, Honno publishes a wide range of titles from Welsh women.

We That Are Left *Juliet Greenwood*
August 4th, 1914: It was the day of champagne and raspberries, the day the world changed.
Elin lives a luxurious but lonely life at Hiram Hall. Her husband Hugo loves her but he has never recovered from the Boer War. Now another war threatens to destroy everything she knows.

'Powerful and moving' Trisha Ashley
'It is, quite simply, a riveting read.'
Suzy Ceulan Hughes, www.gwales.com

ISBN: 9781906784997   £8.99

Motherlove *Thorne Moore*
One mother's need is another's nightmare... A gripping psychological thriller from the author of A Time for Silence.
'...a heart-wrenching tale of three mothers and their love for their children... which kept me enthralled until the end.'
Rosie Amber

ISBN: 9781909983205   £8.99

In a Foreign Country *Hilary Shepherd*
Anne is in Ghana for the first time. Her father, Dick, has been working up country for an NGO since his daughter was a small child. They no longer really know each other. Anne is forced to confront her future and her failings in the brutal glare of the African sun.

'Intelligent, subtle and sensitive... a thought-provoking, absorbing and rewarding read' Debbie Young

ISBN: 9781906784621   £8.99

Left and Leaving *Jo Verity*
Gil and Vivien have nothing in common but London and proximity, and responsibilities they don't want, but out of tragedy something unexpected grows.

'Humane and subtle, a keenly observed exploration of the way we live now...I am amazed that Verity's work is still such a secret. A great read'
Stephen May
ISBN: 9781906784980   £8.99

Someone Else's Conflict *Alison Layland*
Jay is haunted by the ghosts of war who threaten his life and his love. A compelling narrative of trust and betrayal, love, duty and honour from a talented debut novelist.

'A real page-turner about the need for love, and the search for redemption... If you like a fast-paced thriller but want more – then buy this book' Martine Bailey, author of An Appetite for Violets

ISBN: 9781909983120   £8.99

My Mother's House, *Lily Tobias*
A poignant story of belonging, nationhood and identity set in Wales, England and Palestine.
The twenty-fourth publication in the Welsh Women's Classics series, an imprint that brings out-of-print books in English by women writers from Wales to a new generation of readers.
ISBN: 9781909983212   £12.99

All Honno titles can be ordered online at
www.honno.co.uk
twitter.com/honno
facebook.com/honnopress

ABOUT HONNO

Honno Welsh Women's Press was set up in 1986 by a group of women who felt strongly that women in Wales needed wider opportunities to see their writing in print and to become involved in the publishing process. Our aim is to develop the writing talents of women in Wales, give them new and exciting opportunities to see their work published and often to give them their first 'break' as a writer.

Honno is registered as a community co-operative. Any profit that Honno makes is invested in the publishing programme. Women from Wales and around the world have expressed their support for Honno. Each supporter has a vote at the Annual General Meeting.

For more information and to buy our publications, please write to Honno at the address below, or visit our website:
www.honno.co.uk

Honno
Unit 14, Creative Units
Aberystwyth Arts Centre
Aberystwyth
Ceredigion
SY23 3GL

Honno Friends

We are very grateful for the support of the Honno Friends: Gwyneth Tyson Roberts, Jenny Sabine, Beryl Thomas. For more information on how you can become a Honno Friend, see: http://www.honno.co.uk/friends.php